DEVIL'S CUT

BY J. R. WARD

THE BOURBON KINGS

The Bourbon Kings

The Angels' Share

Devil's Cut

THE BLACK DAGGER BROTHERHOOD SERIES

Dark Lover

Lover Eternal

Lover Awakened

Lover Revealed

Lover Unbound

Lover Enshrined

The Black Dagger Brotherhood: An Insider's Guide

Lover Avenged

Lover Mine

Lover Unleashed

Lover Reborn

Lover at Last

The King

The Shadows

The Beast

The Chosen

BLACK DAGGER LEGACY

Blood Kiss

Blood Vow

NOVELS OF THE FALLEN ANGELS

Covet

Crave

Envy

Rapture

Possession

Immortal

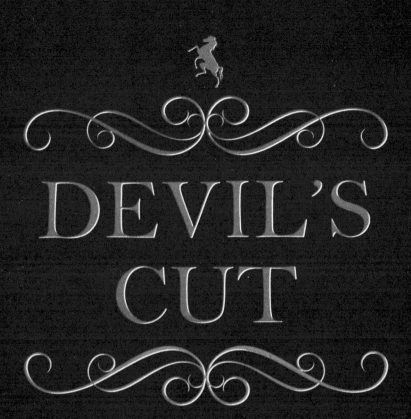

DEVIL'S CUT

A BOURBON KINGS NOVEL

J. R. WARD

BALLANTINE BOOKS

NEW YORK

Published in the United States by Ballantine Books, an imprint of Random House, a division of Penguin Random House LLC, New York.

BALLANTINE and the HOUSE colophon are registered trademarks of Penguin Random House LLC.

Hardback ISBN 978-0-451-47530-5
Ebook ISBN 978-0-698-19305-5

Printed in the United States of America on acid-free paper

randomhousebooks.com

2 4 6 8 9 7 5 3 1

First Edition

Dedicated with love to:

Dominique Boel Freese

and

Mindy Wiseman,

a.k.a. Greta and Lizzie

Note from the Author

It has been such a privilege to write about my adopted home state, its proud history of bourbon making, and these wonderful, complicated, and sometimes broken people who live and work at Easterly. This series was born of my old-school love for the television show *Dynasty*, fueled by my deep reverence for Kentucky, and directed by my fascination for how people and families evolve through stressful times.

As a New Englander who was transplanted from one Commonwealth to another, I had a hard adjustment in the beginning. Now, well over a decade later, I can truly say that I can't imagine living anywhere else but here. The NCAA basketball tournament is happening right now, for example, and I have a huge TV set up in the foyer with six sofas and coffee tables arranged around it. The entire house is dismantled, and yesterday, a big crowd of friends was screaming and yelling at the games (there was also a boxing match in the basement during one halftime that resulted in a busted lip as well as Ping-Pong grudge matches that were nearly as bloody as the boxing). This kind of devotion to a college sport would have been unthinkable before I moved here—and what a joy, and sorrow!, it is to me (my beloved Cardinals did not advance).

The making of bourbon requires time and temperature. After the nascent alcohol is put into the charred barrels, it is stored in uninsulated conditions in the rackhouses and left to interact with the caramelized sugars of the oak over the heat and the cold of the seasons. This dance, and the alchemy that ensues, is what gives bourbon its beautiful color, and is part of how it gets that special taste. I have often thought the process is analogous to the way places, people, and the various eras in our lives affect us, tempering our core characteristics, emphasizing certain traits, bringing forth our strengths—or highlighting our weaknesses.

My two favorite terms of art from what I have learned about bourbon making and its traditions are "the angels' share" and "the devil's cut." Roughly speaking, about fifty-three gallons of "white dog" are put into each barrel, but at the end of the aging process, much less than that actually comes out. This loss can be upward of two percent per year and happens due to evaporation, "the angels' share," but also absorption into the oak of the barrel, "the devil's cut." What this means is that, if you age a bourbon for, say, ten years, you may get around forty-three gallons out the other side, and the longer it stays in there, the less you have on the far side. For example, some of the oldest Pappy van Winkle, which is aged for twenty-three years, yields only fourteen gallons of bourbon at the end of its rackhouse days.

The angels' share is a romantic-sounding term; the devil's cut something more sinister, although that is really because of the *"d"* word. In both cases, they refer to the environment owning a piece of that which is within it. In my situation, when I came down here, I never expected to like Kentucky, and I certainly wasn't interested in being influenced one way or the other by anything about it. Now? If, God forbid, I ever had to return to life in Boston? I would most certainly leave a piece of my soul in the land of the Bluegrass.

And you know, that seems only fair, given all the good that has come to me here, and all the wonderful people I have met and things I have enjoyed.

But, again, I have no intention of going anywhere else, anytime soon, God willing.

I have absolutely loved writing these three books, and I thank you for taking some time from your life to have a stroll in through Easterly's grand front door and a walk around her beautiful, complicated rooms. I'm so grateful I got to do this series!

Oh, and Go, Cards!

—J. R. Ward

Dramatis Personae

Virginia Elizabeth Bradford Baldwine, also known as Little V.E.: Widow of William Baldwine, mother of Edward, Max, Lane, and Gin Baldwine, and a direct descendant of Elijah Bradford, the originator of Bradford bourbon. A recluse with a chemical dependency on prescription pills, there are many reasons for her addiction, some of which threaten the very fabric of the family.

William Wyatt Baldwine: Deceased husband of Little V.E. and father, with her, of Edward, Max, Lane, and Gin Baldwine. Also father of a son by the family's now deceased controller, Rosalinda Freeland. Also the father of an unborn child by his son Lane's soon-to-be ex-wife, Chantal. Chief executive officer of the Bradford Bourbon Company when he was alive. A man of low moral standards, great aspirations, and few scruples, whose body was recently found on the far side of the Falls of the Ohio.

Edward Westfork Bradford Baldwine: Eldest son of Little V.E. and William Baldwine. Formally the heir apparent to the mantle of the Bradford Bourbon Company. Now a shadow of his previous self, the result of a tragic kidnapping and torture engineered by his own father. Edward has turned his back on his family and retired to the Red & Black Stables.

Maxwell Prentiss Baldwine: Second-eldest son of Little V.E. and William Baldwine. Black sheep of the family, who has been away from Easterly, the historic Bradford estate in Charlemont, Kentucky, for years. Sexy, scandalous, and rebellious, his return to the fold is problematic for a number of people in, and outside of, the family.

Jonathan Tulane Baldwine, known as "Lane": Youngest son of Little V.E. and William Baldwine. Reformed playboy and consummate poker player, he is in the throes of a divorce from his first wife. With the family's fortunes in turmoil, and embezzlement rife at the Bradford Bourbon Company, he has been forced into the role of family leader and must rely now more than ever on his one true love, Lizzie King.

Virginia Elizabeth Baldwine Pford, known as "Gin": Youngest offspring and only daughter of Little V.E. and William Baldwine. Previously a rebellious contrarian who thrived on attention, she has been the bane of her family's existence, especially after having had a child out of wedlock and barely graduating from college. She has just married Richard Pford IV, the heir to a liquor distributing company and fortune.

Amelia Franklin Baldwine: Gin's daughter with Gin's one true love, Samuel T. Lodge—although neither Samuel T. nor Amelia is aware of his parentage. Previously a student at Hotchkiss, she is returning to Charlemont to continue her schooling close to her family.

Lizzie King: Horticulturist who has worked at Easterly for nearly a decade and has kept its gardens nationally renowned showcases of rare specimen plants and flowers. Now engaged to her love, Lane, she is fully committed to him and their relationship—however, she is not into his family's drama.

Samuel Theodore Lodge III: Attorney, sexy Southern gentleman, stylish dresser, and pedigreed, privileged bad boy, he is the only man who has ever gotten through to Gin. He has no idea that Amelia is his daughter.

Sutton Endicott Smythe: Newly elected CEO of the Sutton Distillery Corporation, Bradford Bourbon Company's biggest rival in the marketplace. In love with Edward for years, she has excelled professionally, but stagnated in her personal life—in large measure because no one compares to Edward.

Shelby Landis: Daughter of Jeb, a thoroughbred racing legend who mentored Edward when it came to horses. A hardworking, strong woman, she takes care of Edward—even when he doesn't want her to.

Miss Aurora Toms: Easterly's head chef for decades, capable of serving up soul food or Cordon Bleu cooking with a strong hand and a warm heart. Suffering from terminal cancer. Maternal force in the lives of Lane, Edward, Max, and Gin, and the true moral compass for the children.

Edwin "Mack" MacAllan: Master Distiller of the Bradford Bourbon Company. Cultivating a new strain of yeast, he is racing against time and limited resources to keep the stills running. Has recently met the love of his life, but is worried about the future of the BBC.

Chantal Blair Stowe Baldwine: Lane's soon-to-be ex-wife. Pregnant with William Baldwine's illegitimate child. A beauty queen with all the depth of a saucer, she is threatening to expose the paternity of her unborn baby as a way to get more money from Lane in the divorce proceedings.

Rosalinda Freeland: Former controller for the Bradford Family Estate. Committed suicide in her office in the mansion by taking hemlock. Mother to Randolph Damion Freeland, eighteen, whose father was William Baldwine.

DEVIL'S
CUT

ONE

Easterly, the Bradford Family Estate, Charlemont, Kentucky

here was someone trespassing down in the garden.

In the lazy, hazy Southern night, beneath the flower-tasseled fruit trees, and between the saucer-sized tea roses and the squads of trimmed boxwood hedges, a figure was inside the ivy'd walls, moving over the brick paths, heading for the back of the mansion like a stalker.

Jonathan Tulane Baldwine squinted and leaned closer into his bedroom window. Whoever it was . . . they were in a crouch and sticking to the shadows, and the efficiency with which they chose their way suggested they knew what they were doing and where they were going. Then again, it wasn't that hard to find a twenty-thousand-square-foot white birthday cake of a house in the dark.

Turning away from the wavy old glass, he looked to his bed.

{ 3 }

Lizzie King, the love of his life, was deeply asleep in the pillows, her blond hair gleaming in the moonlight, her tanned shoulder peeking out from the silk sheets.

Funny, these moments of clarity, he thought while he pulled on a pair of boxer shorts. As he considered who it might be, and came up with nothing good, he realized without a doubt that he would kill to protect his woman. Even though she could take care of herself, and he felt like he was relying on her now more than ever . . . if anybody tried to hurt her?

He would put them in a grave faster than his next heartbeat.

With that resolve, he went silently across the Oriental rug to an antique bureau that had been in his family since it had been made in the 1800s. His gun was in the top drawer on the left, under the rolls of finely woven socks he wore with his tuxedos. The nine millimeter was compact, but it had a laser sight, and it was fully loaded.

He disengaged the safety.

Letting himself out into a hall that was long as a city street and appointed with all the grace and formality of the corridors in the White House, he kept the weapon down by his thigh. Easterly had twenty or so family and guest bedroom suites under its prodigious roof, and as he passed by doors, he counted who was inside—or should have been: His younger sister, Gin, although not her new husband, Richard, who was away for business; Amelia, Gin's sixteen-year-old daughter, who had yet to go back to Hotchkiss for finals; Jeff Stern, Lane's old college roommate and newly appointed CEO of the Bradford Bourbon Company. And then of course, Lane and Gin's mother, Little Virginia Elizabeth.

It was possible that any of them could be down there for a two a.m. stroll. Well, except for his mother. In the last three years, Little V.E. hadn't been out of her room for anything other than his father's visitation mere days ago—and even though that occasion had warranted the effort, seeing her dressed and on the first floor had been a shock.

So it was unlikely it was her.

And as for staff? The butler had quit and none of the maids stayed overnight—well, and the maids had all been let go anyway.

No one else should have been on the property.

Halfway down the hall, he walked through the second-story sitting area and paused at the head of the formal staircase.

The security alarm was not going off down below . . . but he hadn't put the system on when he and Lizzie had gotten home from the hospital.

Dumb.

Hell, had he even bothered to lock the thousand or so doors on the lower level? He couldn't remember. It had been nearly midnight and his brain had been a mess, images of Miss Aurora in that ICU bed tangling him in knots. Dear Lord . . . that African-American woman was more his mother than the neo–Daisy Buchanan who had birthed him—and the idea that the cancer was taking Miss Aurora away from him organ by organ was enough to make him violent.

Descending the grand stairs, which were right out of Tara's playbook, he bottomed out on the entry foyer's black and white marble floor. There were no lights on, and he stopped again and listened. As with all old houses, Easterly talked when people moved through its rooms, its beams and boards, hinges and handles, conversing with whoever walked around.

Nothing.

Pity. Kentucky law provided a homesteader defense if you killed a trespasser in your house—so if he was going to shoot somebody tonight, he'd prefer to do it inside rather than out. That way, he wouldn't have to drag the body through some doorway and arrange things so it looked like the sonofabitch had been breaking in.

Continuing on, Lane went through the shadowy rooms in the public part of the house, the antiques and old paintings making him feel like a security guard checking a museum after hours. Windows and French doors were all around, bracketed by great swaths of vintage Fortuny, but with the lights off throughout the first floor, he was as much a ghost as whoever in that garden was.

In the rear of the mansion, he went to one of the doors and stared out across the flagstone terrace, searching through the wrought-iron loungers, chairs, and glass-topped tables, seeking that which did not belong or was in motion. Nothing. Not around the slate skirt of the house, at least.

Somewhere out in the greenery, however, a person was stalking his family.

Turning the brass handle, he gently opened the door halfway and leaned out, the mid-May night embracing him with warm, heavy air that was fragrant as a bouquet. He looked left. Looked right. The gas lanterns that ran down the back of the mansion threw flickering light, but the peachy pools of illumination did not carry far.

Narrowing his eyes, he scanned the darkness as he exited and carefully shut things up behind himself.

As with all homes of its stature, the great Federal manse had extensive formal gardens sprawling around it, the various layouts and planting zones forming landscapes as unique and distinct as different zip codes in a city. The unifying element? Elegance at every turn, whether it was the Roman statuary striking poses in the midst of miniature hedge patterns, or fountains that sprinkled crystal clear water into koi ponds, or the pool house's wisteria-covered arbor.

This was Mother Nature subjected to the will of man, the flora cultivated and nitpicked and maintained with the precision one would use to decorate an interior room. And for the first time in his life, he thought of the cost to keep it all going, the man-hours, the plant material, the constant mowing and weeding and pruning, the worrying over those two-hundred-year-old brick walls and walks, the cleaning of the swimming pool.

Craziness. The kind of expense that only the super rich could afford—and the Bradford family was no longer in that stratosphere.

Thank you, Father, you sonofabitch.

Refocusing on his mission, Lane put his back against the house and became a deer hunter in a stand. He didn't move. Barely breathed. Stayed quiet as he waited for his target to present itself.

Was it Max? he wondered.

His parents' loveless marriage had produced four children— a shock, considering his mother and father had rarely, if ever, been in the same room together even before she had taken to her bed three years ago. But there was Edward, the golden eldest son, who had been hated by their sire; Max, the black sheep; Lane, who had turned being a playboy into an art form—at least until he'd been smart enough to settle down with the right woman; and finally Gin, the promiscuous rule thwarter.

Edward was in jail for the murder of their dreadful father. Gin was in a hate-filled marriage for money. And Max had come home after several years of being unreachable, a bearded, tattooed shadow of the frat boy he had once been, who despised everyone, including his own family—to the point where he was staying in one of the staff cottages down at the back of the property because he refused to be under Easterly's roof.

Maybe Max had come up here to the big house for . . . God only knew what. A cup of sugar. Bottle of bourbon. Perhaps to steal some silverware?

But how could he have gotten into the gardens? How could anybody? Two sides of the acres of flowers and lawn were protected by that brick wall, which was twelve feet high and had barbed wire on the top and two padlocked gates. The third side was even more difficult to get through: His father had converted the old stables into a state-of-the-art business center, from which the Bradford Bourbon Company had been run for the last couple of years. God knew you weren't getting through that facility, not unless you had a pass card or the codes—

From over on the right, a figure darted down the allée of blooming crab apple trees.

Gotcha, Lane thought as his heart kicked into high gear. Shifting his position forward, his bare feet were silent over the flagstones as he rushed across the terrace and took cover behind an urn big enough to take a bath in.

It was definitely a man. Those shoulders were too broad to be a woman's.

And the bastard was coming this way.

Lane leveled his gun at his target, holding the weapon steady with two hands as he straight-armed the autoloader. As he kept himself perfectly motionless, he waited for the trespasser to funnel down that pathway and come up this set of side steps.

He waited . . .

. . . and waited . . .

. . . and thought of his extremely estranged, soon-to-be ex-wife, Chantal. Maybe this was a private detective sent by her, coming to get some dirt on the financial scandal at the BBC, some information on how bad the bankruptcy was, some angle that she could use against him as they ground their non-existent relationship into dust.

Or perhaps Edward had broken out of jail and was coming home.

Doubtful on that one.

The trespasser made a last turn and then was coming right for Lane. But his head was down, a baseball cap pulled low.

Lane kept tight until he was absolutely sure he could hit the chest. Then he squeezed the trigger halfway, the red laser sight slicing through the night and forming a little dancing spot right where the guy's heart was.

Lane spoke up, loud and clear. "I really don't care if I kill you."

The man stopped so quick, his feet skipped on the brick. And those hands popped up like whoever it was had mattress springs in their armpits.

Lane frowned as he finally saw the face. "What are you doing out here?"

TWO

Washington County Jail, Downtown Charlemont

Moonlight entered the jail cell through a barred window, the shaft of creamy light getting sliced into five sections before it tripped on the lip of a stainless-steel sink and fell in a sprawl to the concrete floor. Outside, the night was humid, which accounted for the murky quality of the illumination. Inside the cell, it was no-season-whatsoever, the walls and floor and heavy solid door painted in shades of incarceration gray, the air stale and smelling of metal and disinfectant.

Edward Bradford Baldwine sat all the way back on the bunk, the more mangled of his two legs cocked at the strange angle that provided a modicum of relief, the thin mattress offering little to no padding under the bones of his withered lower body.

This was not the first time he had been held in custody, but at least now it was not against his will. He had volunteered himself for this; he had confessed to the murder of his father and thus placed himself in this lockdown. He was also not the only prisoner, in contrast to his previous experience, the sounds of snoring, coughing, and the occasional moan reaching his ears in spite of that reinforced door.

A muffled thump and corresponding echo made him think of his thoroughbred breeding farm, the Red & Black. All of these men in their single compartments were like his mares in their stalls—restless, churning, even at night. Perhaps especially after dark.

Pushing his palms into the mattress, he relieved the pressure points on his seat for as long as he could. Too soon, he was forced to resettle himself, his upper body no stronger than his lower was, the background chatter of physical discomfort something he had grown well familiar with.

As he glanced around the cell, with its concrete block walls and its polished concrete floor, that stainless-steel sink and toilet, the barred and chicken-wired window, he thought of Easterly's splendor. The basement of his family's mansion was kitted out with greater luxury than these lodgings, especially that wine cellar, which was like an English study that had fallen through the floor above and landed on the bedrock of the hill.

For no particular reason—well, other than the obvious one, which was that he had nothing better to do and no chance of sleeping—he thought of a story he had read years ago, about a young boy who had grown up in a cardboard box. In fact, hadn't there been a TV show about a character who'd been similarly tortured . . .

Wait, what had he been going on about?

His mind, doughy and sluggish, tried to catch the tail of the cognition.

Oh . . . right. The kid in the cardboard box. So the boy had actually been fairly un-traumatized when he'd been rescued. It wasn't until he'd discovered that other kids hadn't been subjected to that kind of abuse that he'd gotten upset.

Moral of the story? When you were being raised in a given environment, and that was all you ever knew, the lack of comparison and contrast meant the oddities of your existence were invisible and unknowable. Life in his family and at Easterly had been utterly normal to him. He'd assumed that everyone lived on an estate with seventy people working on it. That Rolls-Royces were just cars. That presidents and dignitaries and folks on TV and in movies coming to your parents' parties was merely an as-you-do.

The fact that the vast majority of people at Charlemont Country Day and then the University of Virginia had been of similar social and financial stature had not challenged his bias. And after his graduation? His perspective hadn't evolved because he'd been so distracted trying to get up to speed in the family business.

He'd also taken for granted that everybody was hated by their father.

Of course, his two brothers and his sister hadn't been despised as much as he had been, but sufficient animus had been shown toward them as well that his construct and conclusions had remained unchallenged. And the beatings and the cold condemnations had come only behind closed doors. So when he had been out and about and seeing fathers acting in a civil way around their offspring? He'd just assumed that it was for show, a privacy curtain's worth of social subterfuge drawn in place to hide the far darker reality.

As it was in the Bradford household.

The eye opening had finally come after he had progressed up the management levels at the BBC to a position where he discovered his father wasn't just a shitty sire but also a poor businessman. And then he'd made the mistake of confronting William Baldwine.

Two months later, Edward had gone down to South America on

a routine matter and been kidnapped. His father had refused to pay the ransom, and as a result, things had been done to Edward. Partially because his captors had been frustrated, partially because they had been bored.

But mostly because his father had told them to kill him.

That was when he decided that William was in fact an evil man who had done bad things all of his life and hurt many, many people, in many, many different ways in the process.

Fortunately for Edward, an unexpected rescuer had materialized in the jungle, and Edward had been first airlifted to a U.S. Army base and then eventually returned home to U.S. soil, landing here in Charlemont like a battered package that had gotten mauled and delayed while going through customs.

As memories of re-learning how to walk and go up stairs and feed and clean himself threatened to break down the door to Edward's mental castle, he reflected on how much he missed his alcohol.

On a night like tonight, when all he had was insomnia and his cannibalistic brain for company? He would have killed for a blackout.

In the aftermath of his initial, more medically intensive period of recovery, liquor had been the sustainer for him as he was weaned off the opiates. Then, as further days and nights had dragged on, the numbness and the relief he reliably enjoyed thanks to liquor, those little floating vacations on the good ship *Lolli-booze*, became the only respite from his mind and his body. Quitting that cirrhotic hobby had been necessary, though.

As soon as it had become clear that he was headed to prison, he knew he'd needed to detox and the first seventy-two hours had been hell. Actually, things were still hard, and not just because of his psychological crutch being gone. He felt even more weak in his body, and though the trembling in his hands and feet was improving, the shaking was not yet over its torment of his fine motor skills and sense of balance.

Glancing down at his loose orange prison pants, he remembered his old life, his former body, his previous mind. He had been so whole back then, preparing himself to take over the Bradford Bourbon Company after his father retired, making strategic business decisions, blowing off steam playing racquetball and tennis.

Like the kid in the cardboard box, it had never dawned on him that there was another kind of life waiting for him. A different existence. A change coming around the corner that would take him to a new consciousness.

Unlike the boy in the box, however, his life had gotten worse, at least by nearly all objective measurements. And that was even before his actions had put him in here with a toilet that had nothing to offer but a cold rim to take a seat on.

The good news, though, was that everyone he cared about was going to be all right now. His youngest brother, Lane, had taken over the BBC and was going to run the bourbon business appropriately. Their mother, Little V.E., was so addled by age and medication that she would live out her remaining days, perhaps at Easterly, perhaps not, blissfully unaware of the change in the family's social standings. Gin, his sister, was married to a man of great means whom she could manipulate at will to her ends, and his other brother, Max? Well, the black sheep of the family would stay what he had always been, a drifter content to live outside of Charlemont, a ghost haunting a legacy he neither valued nor cared about sustaining.

And as for himself? Perhaps when he was transferred out of this county holding pen to a proper prison, they would have some physical therapy that could help him. He might get another master's. Reconnect with his love of English literature. Learn to make license plates.

It wasn't a life to look forward to, but he was used to hopelessness.

And more importantly, sometimes the only solace one had was to do the right thing. Even if it required great sacrifice, there was peace to be had in knowing that loved ones were finally safe from a nightmare.

Like his father.

In fact, Edward decided, the reality that no one mourned William Baldwine seemed a defense enough to the murder charge. Damn shame that it was not a legally recognized justification—

The footsteps that approached were heavy and purposeful, and for a moment, the present shattered apart, the past rising up like a monster out of the swamp of his consciousness, his brain no longer clear on whether he was in the jungle bound with rough rope, about to be beaten again . . . or if he were in the judicial system of his city of birth—

A loud clanking at his door sent his blood pressure through the roof, his heart pounding, sweat breaking out under his arms and across his face. Frozen by fear, his fingers clawed into the pad beneath him, his broken body trembling so violently, his teeth clapped together.

The sheriff's deputy who opened the door made the confusion worse instead of better.

"Ramsey?" Edward said in a thin voice.

The African-American man in the tan and gold sheriff's uniform was enormous, with shoulders so wide they filled the jambs, and legs planted as if they were bolted into the floor. With a shaved head, and a jaw that strongly suggested argument was a waste of time, Mitchell Ramsey was a force of nature with a badge—and this was the second time he had come to Edward in the night.

In fact, the only reason Edward was alive was because the deputy had gone into the jungle looking for him. As a former Army Ranger, Ramsey had had both the survival skills and the contacts down at the equator to get the job done—he also routinely played the role of "fixer" for issues within wealthy families in Charlemont, so the rescue was in his wheelhouse.

If you needed a bodyguard, an enforcer, a P.I., or someone to interface with law enforcement, Ramsey was on the short list of people to call. Discreet, unflappable, and a trained killer, he dealt with the dicey nicely, as the saying went.

"You got a visitor, my man," the deputy said in his deep Southern voice.

It took some time for the words to process, the fear-scramble in Edward's mind causing him to lose traction on his command of the English language.

"Come on." Ramsey indicated the way out. "We got to go now."

Edward blinked as his emotions threatened to overspill his chest and come out on his face through his tear ducts. But he could not allow himself to drown in PTSD. This was the present. There was no one coming with a bat to break his legs. There were no knives about to dig into his skin. Nobody was going to punch him until he vomited blood down his arm and his head lolled off the top of his spine.

Ramsey came forward and offered his bear claw of a palm. "I'll help you."

Edward looked up into those dark eyes and spoke the exact same words he had two years before: "I don't think I can stand up."

For a moment, Ramsey, too, seemed caught by what they had shared in South America, his lids closing briefly, that great chest expanding and contracting as he appeared to try to steady himself with a deep breath.

Evidently, even former Army Rangers had memories they didn't care to revisit. "I gotchu. C'mon."

Ramsey helped him off the bunk and then waited as Edward's legs took their own damn time to unknot, the hours he'd spent in a sit having turned his deformed, badly healed muscles into stone. When he was finally ready to ambulate, the hobbling was humiliating, especially next to the deputy's incredible strength, but at least as he limped out of his cell and onto the parapet, a clarity came, reality reasserting itself through the morass of his trauma.

As their footsteps clanked across the metal weave to the stairs, Edward looked over the railing at the common area below. Everything was clean, but the steel tables and benches were hard worn, the orange paint jobs faded where games of cards had been played and prisoners had slid on and off. There was no debris anywhere, no magazines or books, no articles of clothing left behind, no wrappers from candy bars or empty soda cans. Then again, anything could be a weapon under the right circumstances, and nothing was expected to be respected.

Edward was halfway down the stairs when he stopped, his higher reasoning finally kicking in. "I don't want to see anyone."

Ramsey just gave him a nudge and shook his head. "Yes, you do."

"No, I—"

"This is not a choice, Edward."

Edward looked away, everything clicking into place. "Do not believe them. This is much ado about nothing—"

"Let's keep walking, my man—"

"I already met with the psychiatrist this afternoon. I told him there was nothing to worry about."

"FYI, you are not the one qualified to make an assessment as to your mental state."

"I know whether or not I'm suicidal."

"Do you?" Ramsey's stare was direct. "You were found with a shank—"

"I told them. I picked the thing up in the mess hall and was going to turn it in—"

Ramsey grabbed Edward's forearm, pulled it out, and yanked up the sleeve of his prison uniform. "You used it here. And that is the problem."

Edward attempted to get his limb back, but the deputy wasn't having any of that until he was good and ready to let go. And in the bright fluorescent lights, the raw wound at his wrist seemed like a scream.

"Look, do us both a favor, my man, and come with me now."

Ramsey shifted his hand to Edward's elbow and gave a nudge that was so insistent, it was clear the deputy was prepared to pull a fireman's hold on the situation if he had to.

"I'm not suicidal," Edward muttered as he re-gripped the rail and resumed his awkward, shuffling descent in his prison-issue slippers. "And whoever it is, I do *not* want to see them. . . ."

Out on Easterly's terrace, Lane immediately lowered the muzzle of his gun, the brilliant red laser sight sweeping free of the man's chest and then disappearing as the trigger was fully released.

"I could have shot you! What the hell?"

Gary McAdams, the head groundsman, removed his cap and held it with both his work-worn hands. "I'm sorry, Mr. Lane."

In the moonlight, the man's wrinkled, perma-tanned face had grooves so deep, they were like tire tracks in mud, and as he smoothed his flyaway hair, his apology was everywhere in the jerky movements.

"Dint mean to disturb nobody's sleep."

Lane went to tuck the gun into the small of his back—and then realized he only had boxers on. "No, you're welcome anywhere on the estate. I just don't want to put a hole in you."

"That there pool filtration system in the pump house been short-ing out. I ordered the part, but then remembered I dint turn the damn thing off. Came here through the back gate and shut it down. When I got out, I noticed that." The man pointed to the back of the house. "Middle gas lantern's out. I was worried it was leakin' and was fixin' to turn off the feed."

Sure enough, there was a black hole in the lineup of those old-fashioned brass fixtures, like a row of teeth with an incisor missing.

Closing his eyes, Lane shook his head. "You're too damn good to us."

With a grunt, Gary shuffled up the stone steps and put his hat back on. "House and grounds like this, she's an old lady. Something's always gonna be wrong. Gotta stay on top of 'er."

Will we even be able to keep this place, Lane thought as he followed along.

For the first time in Easterly's history, the property and house were carrying a mortgage. Fortunately, it was with a family friend, not a bank—but Sutton Smythe was going to want her money and interest. And what about repairs? Gary was right. Something was always needing to be fixed, and if that "thing" was the roof? The electrical systems? The over-two-hundred-year-old foundation?

It was going to be a long, long time before those kinds of things were coverable: Not only had his mother's primary trust been drained, but the Bradford Bourbon Company was running at an over hundred-million-dollar deficit—even after Lane had paid off the fifty million his father had borrowed from Prospect Trust.

Over a hundred million dollars. Plus the depletion of his mother's trust.

It was a staggering deficit, and all thanks to his father's off-balance-sheet financing of a crap ton of businesses that had two things in common: One, they were all in William Baldwine's name; and two, they didn't just under-perform, they either tanked . . . or didn't even exist.

Lane was still working to get to the bottom of it all.

On that note, he decided to pay attention as Gary went up to the lantern, took a screwdriver out of the back pocket of his overalls, and began working around the base of the fixture.

"Do you need some light?" Lane asked.

"Plenty out here."

"You must eat your carrots." Leaning up against Easterly's clapboards, Lane rubbed his face. "It's dark as the inside of a skull."

"I can manage."

As Gary eased the heavy glass and brass casing away from its base, Lane straightened. "You want me to hold that?"

"Nah, you'll probably drop it."

Lane had to laugh. "Is my incompetence so obvious?"

"Ya got other skills."

"That better be true."

With a curse, Lane stared across the flower beds to the darkened expanse of the business center. The conversion of what had originally been the stables had been done back when money had been no object, and as a result, the architecture was so perfectly blended that it was hard to tell where the antique stopped and the modern began. Under that slate roof? Behind that lineup of French doors, each of which had been handmade to match the original ones on the mansion? There were enough offices for the BBC's CEO and senior management team, plus assistants, a full catering kitchen and also formal dining and conference rooms.

The full corporate headquarters were technically downtown, but for the last three years, all decision making had been done right across the garden.

William had maintained the relocation was required so that he could support his wife, who had taken to her bed and was ailing. The truth, however—which hadn't come out until about two weeks ago— was that the man needed privacy for his embezzlement. That self-contained facility, with its limited staff and very extensive security measures, had allowed him the isolation to do what he needed to for the misappropriations to remain under wraps.

It was the perfect ruse to protect himself from prying eyes. And the perfect plan, at least in the short term, for diverting BBC assets into William's own name and control.

Too bad the bastard had been horrible at business: Abandoned mines in South Africa, bad hotels out west, failed communications and technology endeavors. William's money had been a curse, it seemed, on any investment opportunity and Lane was still trying to get clarity on exactly how many failed entities were out there—

"How's Miss Aurora doing?" Gary asked as he shoved his fingers into the arteries of the lantern and then followed up with the screwdriver. "She any better?"

Ah, yes, something else Lane didn't want to think about.

"No, I'm afraid she is not."

"She gonna die?"

For the past few days, whenever anyone asked him that question, he always answered with optimism. Out here in the dark with Gary, he spoke what he believed was the truth. "Yes, I think so."

The head groundsman cleared his throat. Twice. "She's a good woman."

"I'll tell her you said that."

"You do that, boy."

"You could go see her, you know?"

"Nope. Can't."

And that was that. Then again, Gary McAdams came from the old school, before people talked about what was bothering them. He and Miss Aurora had both been working for the Bradford family since they were teenagers, and neither of them had married or had any children of their own. The estate was their home, and the staff and family on the land and in the house was their community.

Not that he would speak of any of that.

Still, the man's sorrow was as tangible as his reserve, and not for the first time, Lane recognized and respected the dignity in that taciturn nature.

"I'm glad you're staying on," Lane heard himself say. Although he might as well have talked about Miss Aurora's funeral arrangements for all this was going to go over well. "And I'll continue to pay your—"

"I think the valve here is clogged. I'ma come back in the morning and work on it. But least now it won't leak so it's not no fire hazard."

As Gary picked the lantern casing up and muscled it back into place, Lane found himself with a lump in his throat. For so many years, the estate had seemed to magically function on its own. Just as he'd never worried about how much it cost to keep the gardens going, he'd never considered the prices of the food or liquor for all the parties, or the insurance on all the cars, antiques, and other assets, or the heat, electrical, and water bills. He had gallivanted through his life, floating on the surface in the golden sunshine of wealth, while below him, people were toiling at minimum wage, squeaking by, just to keep up the standard he enjoyed.

The idea that Gary McAdams was staying put without a thought of whether or not he'd get a check each week made Lane feel about as tall as the sole of a shoe.

"Okay, so that's what we got."

The older man stepped back and returned his screwdriver to whatever pocket it had come out of.

"You, ah . . ." Lane grabbed ahold of his own shoulder and squeezed at the knot there. "You always keep one of those on you?"

"One-a what? M' Phillips head?"

"Yeah."

"Why wouldn't I?"

Well, there was that. "Good point—"

In the corner of Lane's eye, a flash of something moving caught his attention. "Wait, what is that?"

"Nothing," Gary said. "Whatchu think you saw?"

"There was something white over there." Lane pointed with the gun's laser sight across to the terrace that faced the river, the one where cocktails had always been served at sunset. "There was . . . I could have sworn that I saw someone there in a white dress. . . ."

He let his words drift off, aware that he sounded crazy.

"You think you seen a ghost or sumthin'?" Gary asked.

The groundsman didn't seem particularly perturbed. Then again, you could probably drop a car on his foot and he'd just take out his screwdriver and remove the damn thing piece by piece.

Lane walked over and looked around the corner of the house. Nothing was on the terrace that shouldn't have been there, yet he continued all the way to the edge and the drop-off down the mountain. It was a helluva view, he had to admit, the Ohio River off in the distance, easing its way to Charlemont's financial district. Against the dark horizon, the twinkling, unevenly spaced lights of the skyscrapers made him think of bubbles rising in champagne glasses, and the scant, isolated cars and semis on the interlocking highways were a testament to Midwestern bedtimes.

Leaning out over the wall, he checked the old stairway that snaked down the great rock embankment. Easterly had been built upon the crown of the highest hill in the city, and the mansion's footprint had been so large that the plot of land had had to be shored up with backfilled earth held in place by cement and stone. When the leaves were out, as they were now in May, you couldn't appreciate just how precarious the house was on its lofty perch, the thickly leafed branches hiding the truth. In the winter, however, when it was cold and the trees were bare, the dangerous free fall was so clear, it was a rare vertigo that was not triggered.

Nobody was scooting down the steps. And nobody could have gotten through the padlocked gate down at the bottom.

Turning back to the mansion, Lane got worried he was seeing

things. He'd much rather it just be a case of his ancestors returning to haunt their former home than some form of insanity setting in.

And, dear Lord, if that was your data screen? Things really were in the crapper.

"Thanks, Gary," he said as he re-approached the groundsman.

"What fer. Just doing my job." The guy took off his hat and repositioned it in exactly the same place on his head. "You go get yourself some rest, there. You look tired."

"Good advice. Very good advice."

Not that he had much hope of sleeping.

"And ya should keep something in mind."

"What's that?"

"God don't give ya more than you can handle. That ain't mean it's gonna be fun, but I guarantee ya that He knows you better'n you do yourself."

"I hope that's right."

The handyman shrugged and turned away. "Don't matter whether you hope or not. It's true. You'll see."

THREE

The interrogation room Edward was let into was the same one that he'd been in earlier in the day, when he'd met and fired his public defender. And as with the common area and his cell, the furniture was stainless steel and bolted down, the table and four chairs hard and cold and going nowhere.

He picked the seat facing the door, and as he eased his broken body down, he didn't bother holding the groan in. That was one nice thing about being around Ramsey. Mitch had seen him in even worse states so there was no need to hide anything.

"Are you going to tell me who it is?" He prayed it wasn't Lane. His little brother was the last person he wanted to see, even though he loved the guy. "Or are you going to make me guess?"

"Wait here."

"As if I'm going anywhere?"

The deputy backed out and there was a clank as the door was locked. Left to himself, Edward linked his hands loosely and put them on the tabletop. The air-conditioning was more intense here, the cold air falling like snow, silent and chilly, from the vent over his head. The lower temperature did not mean it was fresh, however. The stuff still smelled of institution, that unique bouquet of metal, astringent, and body odor.

Please, not Lane, he thought.

His little brother was his Achilles' heel, and he was concerned that Lane was going to spoil everything. Back when they had been growing up, Edward had always been in control—well, except for when Maxwell acted out, and no one was ever in control of that, not even Max. But Edward had always been the voice of authority and reason, and it had been from out of that venerable tradition that he had instructed Lane to accept the reality that their father's death had come about by Edward's own hand and no one else's.

And that Lane now had to take care of everyone.

After all, their mother was in no condition to deal with anything more stressful than getting her hair set and brushed out before her head returned to its silk-covered pillow. And Gin was going to struggle enough with downgrading from private jets to commercial business class. And Max? Not a chance. That vagabond was more likely to leave town on the back of some stranger's truck than man up and make the hard decisions that were coming soon.

But if this wasn't Lane, who could it be? Not the psychiatrist Edward had blown off earlier in the clinic. Not a priest for last rites, because although he felt like death, he wasn't dying. Certainly not anyone at the Red & Black Stables—Moe Brown could run that place with his eyes closed.

Who—

From the recesses of his mind, the image of a tall brunette woman with classically beautiful features and the elegance of European royalty emerged and took over.

Sutton . . . he thought. Would she come to see him?

Sutton Smythe was both his perfect match—and, when he'd been at the Bradford Bourbon Company, also his biggest business rival as the heir to the Sutton Distillery Corporation. Not only had they grown up together in Charlemont, but after they'd returned to work in their families' businesses, they had seen each other at charity galas, private parties, and as they sat on various boards. They had never been officially together, never dated, never merged their lives in any way—although there had been years of attraction and, most recently, twice when they had made love.

It was right out of Shakespeare, the two of them. Star-crossed lovers following different destinies.

But he loved her. With what little he had to give to anybody.

Just before he had made his confession to the police, he had told Sutton there was no future for them. It had killed him to hurt her as he had, but she must have seen his arrest on the news by now—so maybe this was her, coming to give him hell. After all, Sutton was the sort who would demand to know the why's and the where's and the how's, and she'd be well aware that Ramsey could get her in after hours in order to reduce the risk of the ever-hungry media finding out she was coming to see him—

There was a clank as the door was unlocked, and for a split second, Edward's heart pounded so hard he got dizzy.

With a jerky shift, he covered his wrist with his hand, even though his sleeve was down—and then the heavy panel swung open. As Ramsey came in, there was no seeing around his huge shoulders and chest, and Edward pushed his palms into the table and tried to stand—

"Oh, no," he muttered as he let himself fall back down. *"No."*

Ramsey stepped aside and indicated the way forward—and the young woman who followed his direction was like a pony walking past a Clydesdale. Shelby Landis was barely five feet tall, and between the no-makeup and that blond hair pulled back in a rubber band, she looked barely legal to drive.

"I'll leave you two alone," Ramsey murmured as he started to shut them in together.

"Please do not," Edward said.

"I've turned the monitoring equipment off."

"I want to go back to my cell!" Edward yelled as the door was closed and re-locked.

Shelby stayed where she'd stopped, just inside the room. Her head and eyes were down, and her arms tucked in around her chest, her T-shirt and her blue jeans clean but almost as old as she was. The only expensive thing she had on were her steeled-toed leather barn boots. Other than that, a Target sales rack was a step up from her wardrobe. Then again, when you spent your life working around thoroughbreds, particularly the stallions, you learned that everything you wore was going to need nightly washing, and your feet were among your most vulnerable points thanks to all those shod hooves.

"What." Edward tried to move backward in his chair, but the damn thing offered about as much flexibility and comfort as a cement block. "Well?"

Shelby's voice was as soft as her work-honed body was not. "I just was wantin' to see if you was okay."

"I'm fine. It's like Christmas every day in here. Now, if you will excuse me—"

"Neb cut his face open yesterday. In the middle o' that storm. I couldn't get the hood on him fast enough."

In the silence that followed, Edward thought back to just a week or so before, when Shelby had showed up on the doorstep of the Red & Black's caretaker cottage where he'd been staying. She'd had nothing to her name but an old truck and a directive from her dead father to find a job from one Edward Baldwine. The former had been nothing special, just four tires and a rusted-out shell. The latter had been a debt that Edward had had to honor: Everything he knew about horses, he'd learned from her ornery, brilliant, alcoholic father. And what do you know . . . everything Shelby had learned about ornery, alcoholic men had certainly given her a leg up in dealing with Edward.

"My stallion is an idiot," he muttered. Then again, so was its owner. "Moe and you get the vet out?"

"Fifteen stitches. I'm padding the stall. The whole thing. He always been like this?"

"A hothead with a temper, who alternates between arrogance and panic? Especially when he can injure himself? Yes, and it's gotten worse with age."

On that note, maybe he and his stallion could get adjoining cells in here. He'd certainly appreciate the company, and the perennial spring thunderstorms were harder to hear in the middle of this concrete jail building.

"Them new foals all doin' well," Shelby murmured. "They love the meadows. Moe and I are rotating 'em pasture to pasture."

He thought of his stable manager. Such a good guy, real salt of the earth Kentucky horseman. "How's Moe?"

"Good."

"How's Moe's boy?"

"Good."

As a blush hit her cheeks, Edward was so glad he'd pushed her in the direction of that kid, Joey, and away from himself. Just because you were used to dealing with a problem didn't mean you needed to sleep with it, and for a short while there, Shelby had teetered on falling into him, no doubt because the chaos was familiar.

And in turn, he had tottered on falling into her, because suffering hated solitude.

When they both went quiet, he was tempted to wait out the real reason she had come to see him. However, in spite of the fact that he had nothing to do but time, he couldn't stand the inefficiency.

"You didn't drive all the way down here in the middle of the night to talk about the farm. Why don't you just out with it."

Shelby's eyes lifted to the ceiling, and the fact that she seemed to be praying to God did not fill him with happy anticipation. Maybe this was about money? The breeding farm, which had been started by his great-great-grandfather, had been the last place Edward had expected to end his career, not just a step down but a slip, fall, hit-your-head-and-pass-out from the lofty CEO-ship of the Bradford Bourbon Company. Yet what had been just a rich man's hobby to his ancestors had turned out to be a salvation for him—and he'd thought that he'd left the enterprise in the good books.

"Now hold on," he said, "if this is about cash flow, we were just beginning to show a profit. And there was enough money in the operating account—"

"I'm sorry?"

"Cash. In the operating account. I left fifty thousand in there at least. And we've got no debt, and the sales of the yearlings—"

"What are you talking about?"

As they looked at each other in confusion, he cursed. "So you're not here because the bank account has run dry?"

"No."

That should have been a relief. It wasn't.

Shelby cleared her throat. And then those eyes of hers locked on his. "I want to know why you lied to the police."

*L*ane could have gone back upstairs, but he didn't want to disturb Lizzie, and there was no rest for the weary. His brain was a shack in a tornado, his thoughts getting splintered and becoming flying debris thanks to all the emotions roiling inside of him—and as much as he loved being in bed with his woman, the idea of lying there in the dark, his body frozen in deference to her while this F5 raged within his skull, seemed like hell.

He ended up in the kitchen.

Walking into the dim open space, he didn't bother with any light switches. There was plenty of ambient illumination from the back courtyard, and the restaurant-worthy stretches of stainless-steel counters and professional-grade appliances rebounded the glow, making it seem as if twilight was taking a breather inside until it was called in for duty again the following evening.

The bowling alley–sized space was split into two halves, one for banquet cooking when you had a dozen chefs grinding out hundreds of passed *hors d'oeuvres*, followed by identical plates of some fancy sprigged and sauced delicacy, and finally a small army's worth of miniature *pots de crème* in ramekins. The other side was for Miss Aurora's family cooking, when she was whipping up breakfast for the guests in the house, pulling together lunch, and making dinners for four or six or twelve.

How many people had been fed out of here, he wondered. Conference hotels probably did less business, especially back when his parents had been up and functioning: While he'd been growing up, there had been cocktail parties every Thursday, a formal sit-down dinner every Friday for twenty-four, and then Saturdays had been reserved for three- or four-hundred-person gala events for charities and civic causes and political candidates. And then there had been the holidays. And Derby.

Hell, Derby brunch here this year had served mint juleps

and mimosas to more than seven hundred people before they went to the track.

Now, though, crowds like that were part of Easterly's past. For one, there wasn't the money to afford them. For another, given the fact that only a handful of people had showed for his father's visitation, the bad news about "the Bradford Bankruptcy" had clearly driven away the hordes.

Funny thing, how rich people were so insecure. Scandal was only good if it happened to someone else, and then only at a gossip-distance. Anything closer than chatter and it was like they were afraid they'd catch the insolvent virus.

Lane went over to the center island and pulled out a stool. As he sat down, he looked across at the twelve-burner stove top and re-membered the number of times he'd watched Miss Aurora do her thing with her pots and her pans there. To this day, his idea of com-fort food was her collard greens and fried chicken, and he wondered how he was going to get through life never having either done her way again.

He thought back to when he'd touched down in Charlemont just weeks ago. He'd come because one of Miss Aurora's relatives had called him and told him his momma was dying. It had been the only thing that could possibly have gotten him back here—and he'd had no idea what was in store for him.

For example, he'd had no idea that he'd find the family's control-ler dead from suicide in her office.

Hemlock, for godsakes. Like something out of the Roman court.

Rosalinda Freeland's death had been the start of it all, the tipping domino of bad news that had sent all the others falling, from the money that was missing at the Bradford Bourbon Company to the debt that his father owed the Prospect Trust Company to the empty-ing of his mother's trust to the unacknowledged son Rosalinda had had with Lane's father. Lane had been in a scramble ever since, trying to find the bottom of the losses, restructure the company, save his family's house, and grow into the role that everybody, including himself, had assumed was his older brother Edward's mantle to bear.

And then his father's body had been found floating in the Ohio River.

Everyone, including law enforcement, had assumed that the cause of death had been suicide, particularly after the autopsy and medical records had showed William Baldwine had had metastatic lung cancer from his having smoked all his life. The man had been dying, and that reality, along with all the financial laws he'd broken and funds he'd squandered, had been the kind of thing anybody would kill themselves to get away from.

Oh, and then there was also the little picky detail that the guy had gotten Lane's estranged wife pregnant.

But really, on the list of William's sins, that was practically a footnote.

Suicide had not been the cause, however. And a finger, literally, was what had pointed to the truth.

His Lizzie and her horticultural partner, Greta, had been in front of Easterly, replanting an ivy bed, when they had found a piece of William Baldwine. His ring finger, to be exact. That discovery had brought the Charlemont Metro homicide department to the house, and the subsequent investigation had led the police out of the county, but not out of the family.

To Edward at the Red & Black Stables.

Lane groaned and rubbed his aching eyes as he heard his brother's voice in his head: *I acted alone. They're going to try to say I had help. I didn't.*

You know what Father did to me. You know that he had me kidnapped and tortured. . . .

For all intents and purposes, William had tried to murder his own son. And didn't that provide an intent and a purpose for Edward.

Let this be, Lane. Don't fight this. You know what he was like. He got what he deserved, and I don't regret it in the slightest.

Yes, the revenge motive had been clear.

With a curse, Lane reached across and pulled a copy of the most recent *Charlemont Courier Journal* over. And what do you know, a picture of Edward emerging from the back of a squad car at the big jail downtown was right above the fold.

The article underneath spelled out exactly what Edward had told the police: The night of the killing, he had waited outside of the business center until their father had left his office. Edward's intention had been to confront the man, but William had collapsed before any argument ensued. When it became clear that the man was suffering some kind of stroke, Edward had decided that instead of dialing 911, he would finish what the neurological storm was starting.

A winch had helped him get the two-hundred-pound deadweight onto the back of a Red & Black Stables truck, and then Edward had driven out into the vacant woods at the shore of the river and awkwardly dragged the still-breathing man through the underbrush. Just as he'd been about to push their father into the water, he had paused, gone back for a knife . . . and returned to cut off the finger. After that, he had shoved William into the storm-swollen current and returned to Easterly to bury the gruesome souvenir out in the front ivy bed as a tribute to his long-suffering mother and family.

And that was that.

When the finger had been discovered and the police had gotten involved, Edward had tried to cover things up by erasing the security-camera footage recorded from the back courtyard. He'd been stupid about trying to hide his tracks, however. The detectives had traced the computer sign-in at the time of the deletion to him, and that was when he'd confessed.

Lane shoved the newspaper away.

So that was where they were now. The son everyone loved in jail for the murder of a man no one missed.

As swaps went, it was a grossly unfair one, but sometimes, that was where life landed you. Bad fortune, as with good, was not always driven by virtue or free will, and it was best to remember these things were not personal.

Otherwise, you were liable to lose your damn mind.

FOUR

"What in the hell are you talking about?" Edward demanded.

The acoustics in the interrogation room were like that of a shower stall, the bald walls and general lack of furnishings providing an outstanding echo chamber for his voice to racquetball itself around.

And okay, perhaps his tone was a bit strident.

But this was the thing with Shelby. She was used to dealing with big, unpredictable animals as part of her day job—and that meant that she wasn't scared of much. Certainly not a crippled husk of a man whom she'd already had to deal with drunk too many times for his liking.

"I want to know why you lied to the police," she reiterated.

Edward glared at her. "How did you come down here?"

"I drove."

"Not what I'm asking. How is it that you were able to get into this jail after midnight?"

"Is that important?"

Time to cut the shit. "What did you tell Ramsey?"

She shrugged. "I said I needed to talk to you. That was all. When the police was at the cottage with you that day, he gave me his telephone number and told me if I needed help to find him. I knew you wasn't going to take my calls, and I also knew you wouldn't want anyone seein' me coming or going. The reporters is all over the place in the daytime."

"I didn't lie to the police. Everything I said about how I murdered my father is the truth."

"No, it isn't—"

"Bullshit—"

"Don't you *dare* swear in front of me. You know I hate it." She marched over and sat across from him, like his cuss word had meant she could take her gloves off. "You told them that you hurt your ankle when you was draggin' the body from the truck to the river. You said Dr. Qalbi had to come out to see you because of it."

"Exactly. You were there when he examined me."

"That wasn't how you hurt yourself. You tripped and fell in the stable. I saw when it happened, and well you know it. I helped you back to the cottage."

"I am *very* confident you are mis-remembering how the injury occurred—"

"I am *not.*"

Edward tried the whole sitting-back thing again and got no further than he did with his first recline attempt. "My dear girl, you've seen me naked. You know exactly how . . . shall we say . . . compromised I am. I have fallen many, many times—and may I remind you that just because you were not out in those woods with me and that body does not mean I didn't hurt myself there. What is it that people wonder about trees falling and no one being around to hear the sound? I can assure you, when they crash, they make plenty of noise without the benefit of your monitoring."

"You lied."

He rolled his eyes. "If I did, and I most certainly did not, what does it matter? I turned myself in for murdering my father. I confessed. I told them I did it and how—and guess what? The evidence backs me up. So I can assure you there is not going to be a lot of conversation about my ankle."

"I don't think you did it. And I think you're lying to cover for someone else."

Edward laughed with an edge. "Who died and made you Columbo? FYI, you're going to need a new wardrobe that includes a raincoat and the nub of a cigar."

"I saw how drunk you was the night he were killed. You was passed out. You most certainly wasn't driving yourself anywhere, much less movin' a dead body around."

"I beg to differ. We alcoholics rebound very quickly—"

"None of the trucks was gone. I sleep over Barn B and they was all parked right under my window in a row. I would have heard the engine start—and what's more, that winch you was talking about? It was broken."

"No, it wasn't."

"Yes, it was."

"Then how did I use it to get my father's body on the goddamn trunk bed—"

She banged the table. "Do *not* take the Lord's name in vain—"

"Annnnd we're still on that, are we? Look, I'm a murderer. I have very low standards for conduct and I'll vain all the hell I want."

Shelby leaned in, and as those eyes of hers clashed with his own, he wished he had never hired her. "You are *not* a killer."

He was the one who broke the game of ocular chicken. "It appears as if we are at an impasse. I will deny everything that you are saying and stick with my original story because that is what happened—as your precious God only knows. The question then appears to be, what are you going to do about this?"

When she didn't reply, he nonchalantly glanced back over at her. "Well?"

As she dropped her eyes and twisted her work-rough hands, he took it as a skirmish won. "Don't do this, Edward. Please . . . whoever killed 'im, let them do the time. It ain't right, this whole thing ain't right."

Oh, for godsakes, she was starting to cry. And not in the manner of a hysteric he could write off, but as someone who was in deep pain and feeling helpless to right an injustice.

Christ, it made him wish she would hop around the room and rant and rave. Maybe jump up on the table and scream.

"Shelby."

When she refused to look at him, and instead rubbed her nose with all the elegance of a hunting dog, he felt worse. She was, he had come to believe, a real person. Not one of those fake cutouts he had spent so much time having to socialize with back in his old life. Shelby Landis had no more time for airs and emotions than he did.

So this was legitimate.

And also highly inconvenient.

Edward glanced up at the security camera that was mounted in the far corner. When he had been questioned in this room by that detective, Merrimack, there had been a little red light blinking on its undercarriage. Now there was not.

Good thing, he thought as he sat forward and put his hand on Shelby's forearm.

"It ain't right." She sniffled. "And I spent a lotta time around 'ain't right' with my dad. Kinda done with it, t' be honest."

"Look at me." He squeezed her arm. "Come on, now. If you don't, I'm going to start taking it personally."

When she just mumbled something, he gave her another squeeze. "Shelby? Let me see those eyes."

Finally, she lifted her head, and damn it, he wished he hadn't made her. That sheen of tears punched him in the chest.

"What are you really worried about here?" he asked. "Hmm? Why are you causing this trouble? Moe's going to run the stables just as well as I could have, probably better, and you will always have a job at the Red and Black. You've got that nice young man in your life. Listen to me." He shifted his hold to her hand. "You're safe. You're not going back to having nothing, okay? You're not an orphan anymore."

"Why are you doing this? Why you lyin'?"

Edward released his grip and shifted his mangled legs out from under the table. It took him two tries to stand up before his thigh muscles were willing to do their job and he fucking hated the delay.

"Shelby, I need you to let this lie. I want you to leave this jail, go back to the stables, and forget about me and all this nonsense. This is not your problem. Do not worry about me."

"You already suffered so much—"

He knocked on the metal door and prayed Ramsey was right outside.

Just as the lock was being released, Edward glanced over his shoulder. "If you want to help me, you will walk away. Do you hear me? Just walk away, Shelby—and as long as you do that, you and I are even. When you needed it, I gave you a job and a place to stay, and you owe me for that. So let's be even and both move along."

As the dawn's rays surmounted the roof peaks of the garages behind the mansion, Lane was still sitting on his stool at Miss Aurora's counter. He couldn't feel his butt, and one calf muscle was hurting like he might have thrown a clot. Yet, he stayed where he was and watched the golden glow penetrate the windows and creep across the spotless tile floor.

Thank God day had finally arrived. Some obstacle courses had nothing tangible about them, and yet they were crucibles nonetheless, and grinding his way through those dark hours with nothing but regrets he could do nothing about had been torture.

A quick glance at the clock by the bread box and he shook his head. On any other day, Miss Aurora would already be up and putting homemade cinnamon buns and pecan rolls in the oven and getting out her omelet pans to do eggs for everyone. There would be coffee brewing, right over there, and in the sink, there would be a strainer full of blueberries or strawberries. Cantaloupe would be ready for slicing, and oranges set for juicing, and by the time the household was down in the family dining room, the first meal of the day would be all set in warmers and on the table.

If there were no overnight guests, Miss Aurora served things herself. If there were, she called in reinforcements.

Lane's eyes traveled around, going from the pantry to the cupboards to the stove to the sink . . . then once more around the catering section.

It was pacing. For someone who was too tired to move—

With a frown, he slid off the stool and went around the island. By the burners, there was a stand of knives in a butcher-block holder, their various-sized black handles sticking out, ready to be grabbed by an expert hand. One of them was missing.

"Okay, who was the idiot who put a blade in the dishwasher?"

The idea that somebody had used one of his momma's Wüsthofs and then tossed it into Cascade-land with the mixing bowls and the wire whisks? It was downright sacrilegious. She always washed her knives by hand. Always.

Sharpened them herself, too.

Opening up the machine, he pulled the top rack out and riffled through the utensils, measuring cups . . . spatula . . . small bowl . . . small bowl. Sliding all that back into place, he checked the lower level and didn't find anything knife-ish, either.

Well, at least it hadn't gone through with the rest of the stuff.

Lane closed everything up and leaned over the sink. Nothing in the basin. Nothing in the drying rack.

"Damn it."

With a sense of urgency, he went across to the catering section in the unlikely event the other two dishwashing units had been run. Both were empty. Nothing in any of the sinks over there, either.

Somewhere in his brain, finding that missing knife equated to saving Miss Aurora's life. It made absolutely no logical sense, but try making that argument to his growing sense of panic. With his heart pumping hard, he began yanking at drawers, going through all kinds of pot holders, mixing spoons and ladles, peelers—

"Lose something?"

With a curse, he spun around and grabbed his heart. "Hey. Hi . . . good morning."

Lizzie was standing just inside the kitchen, her sleepy eyes and mussed-up blond hair, her strong body and clean smell, like a sunrise inside of him, bringing him light and warmth.

"What are you looking for?" she said with a smile as she came forward to meet him halfway.

As they embraced, he closed his lids. "Nothing. It's nothing."

Yeah, he thought, just the fact that he was convinced if the phone rang and Miss Aurora had died just now, it was because he couldn't find her knife.

Straightening, he brushed a strand of her hair back. "Let me make you breakfast?"

She shook her head. "I'm not hungry. Maybe I'll try some coffee? Or . . . I don't know. Water."

"You sure?"

"Positive."

She went over and sat on his stool. "Have you been down here long?"

Leaning back against the counter, he shrugged. "A little while."

"Makes sense. This is Miss Aurora's space. If you can't be with her, you might as well be here."

He glanced around for the hundredth time and nodded. "You're too right."

"So are you ready for today?"

With both hands, he rubbed his face until his nose felt chapped. "I mean, yes and no. I want to go visit with her some more. There's no way I'm not going to—but it's so damn hard to see her in that bed with all those machines keeping her alive."

"I was talking about your father's interring?"

Lane frowned and dropped his hands. "Is it—oh, hell. It's today, isn't it." When she nodded, he curled up his fists and wished he could make a big frickin' loud noise. "Guess I've lost track."

What he wanted to say was that the last thing he needed right now was to waste even an hour dealing with his father's ashes. He hadn't respected the man in life. In death? Who the hell cared.

"Are you having a preacher come?" Lizzie asked.

Okay, he had to laugh at that. "I thought about it and decided there was no reason to waste a man of God's time. That sonofabitch is in Hell, where he deserves to be—"

"Huh? And here I thought I was in Kentucky."

At the sound of the male voice, Lane looked over his shoulder. Jeff Stern, his old college roommate, was coming into the kitchen, looking about as fresh as a daisy that had been without a water source for six days. On a windowsill in the sun. After someone had played He Loves Me, He Loves Me Not with all of its petals.

Still, his dark hair was wet from the shower, his big city-chic, rimless eyeglasses were in place, and he was in his uniform of business suit slacks, a button-down with an open collar, and wingtips: Wall Street veteran trying to be casual. The jacket to the suit was draped over his arm and there was no tie to be seen.

"So, boys and girls," Jeff said as he put that jacket down on the counter and checked out the paper. "How we doing—oh, heeeeeey, nice picture of me. That's the one from the bank's annual report. Wonder if they got permission or just stole it."

He unfolded the first section and kept reading with a nod. "Yup, I liked that reporter. I'm going to use her again when I have to lie about what's really going on at Bradford Bourbon."

"How were you untruthful?" Lizzie asked.

"Are you going moral on me?" Jeff smiled and put the paper aside. "This is wartime. Okay, fine, maybe I should have used the word 'spin.'"

Lane shrugged. "He told her that the off-balance-sheet financing my father did was part of an overall strategy of diversification—that just happened not to go well."

"Instead of outright embezzlement." Jeff went over to the refrigerator and grabbed the milk. "Although I declined to name any of the companies, the media will find some of them—and there'll be chatter about how William Baldwine's name is on a lot of assets outside of the BBC. We're not out of the woods on this problem yet."

"Samuel T.'s going to handle everything." Lane took the liberty of heading for the pantry and getting the Raisin Bran. "We're creating a trust for those assets and backdating it. It's going to have all those secondary investments in my mother's name and there will be provisions so the banks can't come looking to the family to satisfy any debts arising from the purchasing of said equity outside of the

BBC. It will make the misappropriation look more legal if the Feds come knocking—especially because the company is privately held and we are the sole shareholders."

"When." Jeff snagged two bowls and two spoons. "That would be 'when' the Feds show up. And I'm a shareholder too now, remember."

"Oh, right. Guess I'll give you a cut of the ten cents my father managed to generate—after the banks are finished fighting over it. I swear, that man could pick 'em."

As the two of them lined up at the counter and traded the box of cereal for the Dean's skim milk, Lane could sense Lizzie staring at them.

"You know," she murmured with a smile, "I can picture you boys in college."

"Yeah," Jeff said, "who knew a guy from Jersey and this overbred piece of white bread would end up together."

"Match made in Heaven."

They clinked spoons and went back to eating.

Thank God for Jeff, Lane thought. The investment banker was sorting out all the cash-flow problems at the company, working with the board, which Lane and Jeff had bought off, and hiring new senior vice presidents.

There was a chance that at least the Bradford Bourbon Company wasn't going to go down on Lane's watch. As long as Jeff Stern was in place, they might just pull it all off.

The guy was a white knight in shining pinstripes.

FIVE

In the various branches of the Bradford family tree, there were a total of seven women called Virginia Elizabeth, a phenomenon that resulted from the Southern practice of naming one's sons and daughters after oneself. Three of these V.E.'s, as they were known on the familiar, were still alive: The oldest one, who was ninety, lived independently in a high-rise in downtown Charlemont and still enjoyed regular bridge games and lunches out at the club. The middle one was faring far less well in her sumptuous quarters at Easterly, although given all the prescription drugs she was on, it was probably fair to say that "Little" V.E. was also "enjoying" herself.

And then there was Gin.

The youngest Virginia Elizabeth envied her mother's medicated existence. To be blissfully unaware of the terrible state of affairs was probably a close second to their family's reversal of fortune never happening in the first place. After all, what was it they said about reality? Perspective was everything.

Thus that which one refused to acknowledge did not exist.

As Gin walked into her bath and dressing room suite, she was fresh out of the shower and draped in a monogrammed silk robe the color of the white Frau Karl Druschki roses that bloomed in the gardens below her window. The decor she had chosen for her personal spaces was the same: white, everywhere. White carpeting, white bedsheets and duvets, white balloon drapes around all the windows.

She always preferred to be the splash of color, the gloss amid the matte, the full moon dwarfing the less bright, tiny stars, whether she was at a party, on a plane, in a room, or in repose.

And hadn't that been so much easier to accomplish when money had been no object.

Taking a seat at her makeup and hairstyling bar, she regarded the display of professional products and tools and thanked God she knew how to use them all. She most certainly did not have the three hundred dollars to pay that woman with the spray tan and the bleached teeth and the poorly disguised aspirational affect to come in here and roll brunette locks around a three-hundred-degree wand. And apply all that Chanel. And tender a vote on the outfits for the day.

What time was it, anyway?

Gin picked up her Piaget watch and cursed. Ten eleven. So she had a mere forty-five minutes until she had to leave.

She preferred an hour and twenty to get ready—

"Where is my engagement ring."

Gin looked up into the three-sided, vertically lit mirror. Richard Pford, her husband of just a matter of days, was standing behind her, his Ichabod Crane body in yet another variation of his uniform: Brooks Brothers dark suit, button-down white shirt, club tie.

She was willing to bet he'd come out of the womb wearing that sartorial snooze.

"Welcome back, darling," she drawled. "How was your business trip."

"You mean welcome home."

Gin made a show of unwrapping the towel from her hair, triggering the curling iron, and palming the dryer. She waited for him to speak again.

"Where is the ring—"

She hit the dryer's *on* switch. And then did that one better by leaning over in the chair and fluffing her damp hair in the blast of hot air.

When Richard yanked the cord out of the wall, she smiled in the midst of her hanging locks.

Flipping herself back up, she gave him a moment to be struck by how beautiful she was: She didn't need the mirror to show her that her shining, thick hair was curling up at the ends, and her skin was glowing, and her eyes were heavy lidded and thickly lashed. And then there was the fact that the robe's slick tie had loosened, the lapels falling open to show her astonishing cleavage and delicate collarbones.

She deliberately crossed her legs, so that the hem was split to reveal her thighs.

Gin had no interest in turning this scarecrow husband of hers on; she put on this show solely to remind him of her hold on him. Richard Pford was a miserly sonofabitch with a bad temper, but after a childhood of being picked last for teams at Charlemont Country Day, his brain was still trained in patterns that supported him believing the truth.

Namely, that he was a loser tolerated by the popular people solely because his family owned the largest liquor distributor in America— and because the cool kids enjoyed picking on him.

Her marriage was a fundraiser for herself and her lifestyle, nothing more. And in return, Richard got her, the ultimate trophy he had sought in high school, his ticket, at least in his own mind, to the status he could not achieve on his own, no matter how much cash he and his family had.

Unfortunately, the arrangement had come with some hidden costs to her.

But it was nothing she couldn't endure—

Couldn't *handle*, she corrected.

"I'm sorry, were you saying something?" she inquired in a pleasant tone.

"You know damn well I was. Where is my ring?"

"Why, right there on your finger where it belongs, dearest." She smiled sweetly and nodded at his hand. "See?"

With a curse, he reached out and grabbed some of her hair. Twisting it in his fist, he forced her head to the side, the pain lighting up down into her neck and opposite shoulder.

Boy, that ugly flush on his hollow cheeks was unattractive.

"Do *not* toy with me, Virginia."

Gin smiled brightly, the very worst part of her reveling in the discord, that appetite for destruction she had fed off of for so long seeking more, more, more of the conflict—until one or both of them snapped.

Even as she had resolved to change, her relationship with Richard was so deliciously familiar and fun.

"May I remind you," she gritted out, "that the last husband who mistreated his wife under this roof ended up with his ring finger cut off and his body on the wrong side of the falls. Perhaps you should recall this before you go grabbing at me?"

Richard hesitated. And she was almost disappointed as he released his hand and stepped back. "Where is it?"

"Why do you want to know?"

"I've been gone for two days. It occurred to me, given your family's financial situation, that you might sell it and pocket the cash to go buy another Birkin bag."

"I already have twenty of them. Including ones in crocodile, alligator, and python."

"If you do not tell me where that ring is, I'm going to pull out the contents of each and every drawer, and all of the closets, in this dressing room until I find it."

For a moment, she got excited at the prospect of watching him trash the place, all red-faced and uncoordinated and furious. But then she remembered that they'd had to let all the help go—and given that she hated things out of place, she knew that she would have to be the one to clean it all up.

There was no way she was going to be his maid. Ever.

"It's in the silver dish between the sinks in my bath." She plugged the dryer back in. "Go see for yourself."

As he turned around, she noted how baggy the jacket was, how loose the pants were. No matter how much the man paid to have his clothes altered, he always ended up looking like he was wearing his father's suits. In a wind tunnel.

She turned the hair dryer on again, but kept her head level. Pushing her foot against the cabinet under the counter, she turned the chair so that she could watch him in the mirror's left flank. Now her heart beat faster.

She'd taken her engagement ring off and put it where she had so that no soap got under the basket of prongs. She had to keep that stone as clean as possible, for occasions just such as this.

Because, yes, she had done exactly what he had said. She had taken out the stone, sold it, and replaced it with a fake—although not for a Birkin bag.

For something so much more important than that.

Richard came back over like a lion tamer. "Put it on."

Or something to that effect. She couldn't hear him over the din. "What?" she said.

As he threw his hand out like he was going to rip the plug free again, she turned off the dryer herself. She wasn't sure where to find a new one if he broke it. Or how much the damn thing cost.

And who in the world ever thought those two things would ever be an issue for her.

"Put. Your. Ring. On."

"I have my wedding band on already." She held up her middle finger. "Oh, sorry."

As she corrected her "mistake," he went for her wrist and yanked her arm out at a bad angle. Forcing the enormous solitaire onto her finger, he managed to draw blood across the top of her knuckle.

"Both of them stay on. Next time I catch you not wearing it—"

"You'll what." She stared up at him with boredom. "Hit me again? Or do worse? Tell me, do you really want to end up a murderer like my brother? I don't imagine Edward is enjoying jail very much. Unless your goal is, in fact, to find yourself in the communal showers with a bunch of men?"

"I own you."

"My father tried that approach. It did not work well for him."

"I am not your father."

"You know, your voice is too high for Darth Vader impressions and that line's wrong anyway. Although you're correct, he never was a father—and neither shall you ever be."

She cued the hair dryer back on and met Richard's eyes steadily in the mirror. When his mouth began to move again, she smiled some more. "What? I can't hear you—"

"What are you doing today?" he shouted. No doubt because he needed to let his temper out as much as he wanted to be heard.

Gin took her sweet time, allowing him to steam. When she was good and ready, she cut the dryer and put it aside.

Fluffing her hair, she shrugged. "Lunch at the club. Manicure. Sunbathing—which is cheaper than a tanning bed and to hell with skin cancer. Surely you will appreciate the cost savings in that."

"You forgot something."

"Not your ring," she said dryly.

Richard closed in on her like a storm, his rough hands dragging her out of the chair and pushing her down to the white carpet. She had been expecting this. It was why she had goaded him.

She didn't care what he did to her body, and he seemed to recognize this.

Thus, enduring him in this fashion was yet another way of remaining one up on him, unreachable even as he put his clawing mitts all over her.

Samuel Theodore Lodge III left the woman he had been with all night in his bed and walked naked into his bathroom, closing the double doors behind himself.

He had no interest in showering with her. He was finished, their energetic escapades during the dark hours certainly appreciated and enjoyed, but that was that. She would drive herself home, and he would put off her inevitable phone calls and invitations for as long as it took her to understand that there was no emotional potential going on here. No trajectory for a relationship. No hope of her ever becoming the grand dame of this gracious old manor house with its eight hundred acres of prime Kentucky farmland.

Turning on the six-headed shower, he looked out the bank of windows over the tub. The sun was well-risen above the verdant rolling hills, the intersecting lines of leafy trees delineating crop plots that he had left uncultivated. Perhaps when he retired from the law, some thirty or forty years hence, he would once more call forth from the good earth rows of corn and clutches of soybeans and fat, squeaky-leafed tobacco plants.

For now, however, he was resolute in his destiny to follow the well-trodden legal path of so many men in his long, proud Southern lineage.

While he drank enough bourbon to pickle his liver.

Which was another fine Kentucky tradition.

As he was not a person to move quickly or without deliberation, at least not while sober—or nearly sober—he took his time under the steaming hot rush. He did not shave until afterward, and when he did, it was at his sinks, using a cake of soap, a horsehair brush, and a straight-edged razor that he sharpened on a strop.

With a clean face and body, he felt far more awake, and he went into his dressing room and pulled on one of his monogrammed white button-downs. On the left, his lineup of hanging suits was a subdued collection of grays, blues, and blacks, but not all was dour. On the other side, he had sport coats and seersuckers in every color under the sun.

Today, he wore black, and not with one of his hundreds of bow ties.

No, today, the tie he wore was also black. As were his polished shoes and his nameplated belt.

Back out in his bedroom, he went over to his very messy bed and smiled at his overnight guest. "Good morning, lovely one."

He used the term of endearment because he couldn't remember whether she was Preston or Peyton. She'd been given her grandfather's surname, he recalled that much, but she hailed from Atlanta, which was not where his people were from—so the particulars of the story hadn't sunk in.

Dark-blond lashes lifted from a smooth cheek and bright blue eyes drifted over. "Good morning yourself, kind sir."

Her accent was smooth as a sweet tea, and just as pleasing as when she had been gasping his name in his ear.

The woman went for a stretch and strategically pulled the sheets back with her manicured toe. Her body was as supple and well bred as any thoroughbred mare's, and he quite imagined she would be a fine match for him in so many ways. He could provide her with the Lodge name as well as sons and daughters to carry on the traditions so important to both their families. She would age appropriately and nip and tuck only when necessary, recognizing that the best plastic surgery was that which was never noticed. She would join the gala committees of Steeplehill Downs, the Charlemont Museum of Art, and Actors Theatre of Charlemont. Later, when their kids were off to U.Va., his alma mater, the two of them would travel the world, winter in Palm Beach, and summer in Roaring Gap.

He would be faithful to her always in Charlemont, and also wherever they had vacation homes, his indiscretions discreet and never spoken of between them. She would be utterly monogamous to him, recognizing that her value was in both the appearance and reality of her virtue. He would respect her, quite sincerely, as the mother of his children, but he would never seek her opinion about anything concerning their money, his business, or plans about their homes, bills, or major purchases. She would resent him over time but resign herself to her role, taking enjoyment in besting groups of women with her status, diamonds, and the performance of her children, all of that one-upmanship occurring in social settings that were photographed by *Vanity Fair* and *Vogue*.

He would die first, either of throat or tongue cancer because of his cigar habit, or at the wheel of his vintage Jag, or perhaps from a cirrhotic liver. She would be relieved and never remarry, her choice to remain a widow one made not out of loyalty to him but rather because she would lose her life estate on the farm and in the other houses as well as the enjoyment of the interest on the stocks and money he would leave in trust to his children. In her later years, she would enjoy her freedom from him and the company of her grand-children, until she died in this very room, some fifty years from now, a private nurse by her side.

Not a bad run for either of them, considering all the other varia-tions on the human condition one could get stuck in by virtue of the genetic lottery. And perhaps he would volunteer for precisely that blueprint, perhaps when the need to procreate finally struck him as a priority—which it absolutely had not up until now.

But until then?

"I'm so sorry"—Peyton/Preston . . . or was it Prescott?—"but I'm leaving for the day. My estate manager and the cleaning people will be here, and I don't think it's appropriate for you to be in this sort of dishabille around them?"

She stretched again, and if her goal was enticement, he was afraid she was falling far short. Having already had all of that, there was nothing left to conquer and little to actually connect with.

And when he didn't respond as she had no doubt hoped—i.e., by throwing himself in between her legs—she pouted. "Where are you off to in all that black? A funeral?"

"Nothing of the sort." He approached her and leaned down, brushing her lips with his. "Come now, let's get ourselves dressed."

"I thought you preferred me naked?" She licked her mouth with the tip of her pink tongue. "That's what you told me last night."

Samuel T. glanced at his watch to avoid telling her that he didn't remember much of the particulars past eleven p.m. Maybe ten-thirty.

"Where is your dress?" he asked.

"Downstairs. On the red sofa."

"I'll go get it. Along with everything else."

"I wasn't wearing panties."

Now, that he did recall . . . from when they'd had sex in the Char-lemont Country Club's shoeshine room at around eight. The party

they had both been at, a gathering to celebrate the impending nuptials of one of his fraternity brothers, had progressed from the grill
room out to the pool. It had been himself, fifty of his brothers, and
then Prescott/Peyton—or had it been Peabody?—and a number of
other Tri-Delts who were sorority sisters of the bride.

Your typical May evening out, the kind of thing that was as lovely
and forgettable as she was.

He'd be lucky if he remembered any feature of either as he drove
away from his farm.

"I'll be right back," he said. "Get yourself up, dearest one. The
day isn't getting any younger and neither are we."

When he returned with her Stella McCartney dress and her
Louboutins, he was relieved to find her out of bed—and he had to
admit, she cut quite a vision standing at the window on one side of
his fireplace, her rather spectacular rear assets on display.

With her hands on her hips and her head tilted to the side, he was
willing to bet she was trying to figure out exactly how much of the
view he owned.

"As far as the eye can see," he said dryly. "In all directions."

She twisted around and smiled. "Quite a spread you have, then."

"My father and mother own the thousand acres to the east." As
her eyes bulged, he simply shrugged. "I just have this smaller parcel."

"I had no idea there was so much land in Kentucky."

What did one say to that? Somehow, he didn't think quoting the
study that suggested intelligence was passed on to children through
the mother's side of things—and that perhaps she might be concerned on that point—was going to help matters much.

"Here." He held out her things. "I really must go."

"Will you call me?" She frowned. "I put my digits in your phone,
remember?"

"Of course I do. And I will absolutely call you." It was a lie that he had used many times, particularly in these situations that required expedited egresses. "I'll be waiting for you downstairs. On the porch."

Turning on his heel, he proceeded out and shut the door softly behind himself. As he bottomed out on the first floor, he went into his study and loaded up his great-uncle's forty-year-old briefcase with files and notes. The packing was just for show, however. Where he was going next, work was going to be the last thing on his mind.

He was in the process of closing the old-fashioned leather satchel when his fingers lost their dexterity and the worn brass buckles became too much for him.

Hanging his head, he closed his eyes. In less than an hour, he was going to see her, and he was not ready. Not prepared.

Neither sober enough nor drunk enough.

Gin Baldwine was the sort of woman who, if he was going to be in her presence, he needed to be either completely aware of himself or totally obliterated. Middle of the road was not his friend.

Indeed, with him and Gin, it had always been extremes all around, great love, great hatred, great joy, great pain.

Theirs wasn't a romance so much as a collision that kept happening over and over again.

With a familiar rush, all kinds of crystal clear memories came back to him, and as the onslaught hit, he reflected that perhaps it wasn't the alcohol that had dimmed his mind to the events of the previous night with that P-named woman. When it came to Gin Baldwine, for example, he could relive countless bacchanals of longer duration and far surpassing intensity with the specificity of a *New York Times* article.

Oh, Gin.

Or, as he at times had thought of her, the Gin Reaper.

The littlest of the Bradford family's Virginia Elizabeths was the thorn in his side, the arrow in the center of his target, the bomb planted under his car. She was the opposite of that lovely woman upstairs: She was not monogamous, she was never easy, and she didn't care if you called her.

Gin was as predictable as an unbroken steed under saddle for the first time.

In the middle of a Civil War reenactment battle.

With a stone in one hoof and a horsefly biting its butt.

Things between the two of them had been an epic competition since they'd first gotten together when they were teenagers. No quarter asked, no quarter given, nothing but a steady stream of tit-for-tat that had left everyone else around them in ruins while they had continued to square off.

They had used so many others mercilessly in their game. Had trampled countless hearts more genuine than their own in the process.

At least until Gin had . . .

Dear Lord, he'd never thought she'd actually marry anyone—except for him, of course.

Gin had walked down the aisle with Richard Pford, however.

Well, presented herself in front of a judge with the other man, at any rate.

So now it was done.

Samuel T. thought back to her begging him to become her husband. She had come to him first—and he had blown it off as merely the newest incarnation of their legacy of chaos. But Gin had been serious—at least about the marriage issue. Who fulfilled that role was evidently unimportant—

No, that wasn't true. The fact that she had picked Pford in the midst of her family's bankruptcy? Talk about unassailable logic. Richard's net worth made Samuel T.'s own fortune seem like lunch money for a kindergartner—and that was even, as they said, before people in the Pford family started to die on the guy.

Yet Gin was paying a high price for all that "security." True, she was never going to have to worry about money again. . . .

But Samuel T. thought about her bruised neck. The hollow pits her eyes had become. The fact that she had gone from being a Roman candle to a barely lit match.

The idea that man was hurting her?

Well, that just made a fellow want to go get a gun, didn't it.

Opening his eyes, he tried to remember what he was doing and where he was. Ah, right. In his study, packing up work he was not going to do, before he left for a funeral that wasn't a funeral for a man that no one mourned.

Just another day in the life.

Proceeding out to the base of the stairs, he checked his watch and called up to the second floor. "Let's go, my love!"

If he had to, he was prepared to carry the woman down on his shoulder and set her out on the curb. Which was not to suggest she was trash. More like a mis-delivered bouquet of flowers that had to move along to its rightful addressee.

"Let us go!" he called out.

As he waited for the woman to come down, he couldn't decide whether he wanted to see Gin—or was desperate to avoid her. Either way, there was no denying that he prayed she would call him for help.

Before something happened with Pford that there was no coming back from.

SIX

As Sutton Smythe gripped the rough railings of the cabin's porch, she took another deep inhale of the forest. The view before her was classic eastern Kentucky, the Cumberland Plateau of the Appalachian Mountains offering a rugged terrain of stoic evergreens and leafy maples, high rocky cliffs and low flowing rivers.

This was God's country, where the air was clean, the sky was as big as the land, and you could leave your city problems behind.

Or at least one felt that surely such issues should fade in the face of the dappling sunlight and the childhood-summer-camp nature of this retreat.

"I made some coffee."

As Dagney Boone spoke up behind her, she closed her eyes briefly.

Yet when she turned around from the view, she had a smile on her face. The man deserved the effort. Even though he'd made it clear he was attracted to her, and wanted to pursue a relationship, he was content to sit things out as a friend for as long as it was required.

Even if that was forever.

God, why couldn't she just open her heart to him? He was handsome and smart, a non-douchebag widower who took care of his three kids, mourned his dead wife, and conducted himself with honor and commitment in his job.

"You are a gentleman."

Dagney held out the heavy mug, his eyes warm and steady. "Just the way you said you liked it. Two sugars, no cream."

To avoid staring at him, Sutton made a show of inhaling the fragrant steam. "Perfect."

The floorboards of the porch creaked as he went over and sat down on the swinging bench at the other end. Easing back, he kicked out with his hunting boot, the chains releasing a sweet chiming sound as he pendulum'd back and forth.

As he looked at her, she refocused on the view, leaning up against a vertical support and crossing one foot over the other.

"You've done a historic thing," he murmured.

"Not really."

"Gifting thirty thousand acres to the state? Saving these four mountaintops from the coal companies? Allowing the families who have been here for seven generations to stay on their land? I'd say that is very historic."

"I would do anything for my father."

As she thought of the man she loved so much, that once tall, majestic force of nature now crippled and wheelchair bound from Parkinson's disease, her sadness overwhelmed her. Then again, depression had not been far of late. In the last couple of days, all she had known was sorrow, and though experience had taught her that whatever moon or star in her This Sucks quadrant would inevitably move on to someone else's life, it was hard to think she was ever going to feel happiness again.

And so, yes, to try to get away from herself, she had taken this trip out here with Dagney, the two of them making the three-hour drive from Charlemont with a packed dinner and breakfast, and all kinds of boundaries, emotional and physical, in place. She had been hoping she could clear her mind on the principle that geographical distance sometimes helped—and it wasn't just the travel time. These hunting cabins, isolated up on their mountain and maintained by one of the rural families she had gotten particularly close to, were as far removed from her life of luxury as you could get: no electricity, barely any running water, and BYO sleeping-bag bunks.

"Don't mourn him before he's gone, Sutton."

It was a shock, but not a surprise, that she thought first of Edward Baldwine.

And as she switched tracks away from him, it was something she was long used to doing. "I know. You're so right. My father is still very much alive. Yet, it is so hard."

"I understand, believe me. But you know, when my wife was . . . coming to the end of her illness, I wasted so much time trying to brace myself for what it would be like when she was gone. I kept trying to anticipate how I was going to feel, what my kids were going to need from me, whether or not I was even going to be able to function at all."

"And it was totally useless, right?" When he didn't say anything, she glanced over and prompted him with, "You can be honest."

"The reality . . . was so much worse than I imagined that I shouldn't even have bothered. The thing is, if you're being forced to jump into ice-cold water, dipping your toe in the stuff and trying to extrapolate that sensation all over your entire body?"

"Silly."

"Yes." Dagney shrugged and smiled into his own mug. "I probably should stop talking about this. Everyone's journey is their own."

Pivoting toward him, she was struck by how attractive he was. And how uncomplicated. How reliable and non-dramatic.

Too bad her heart had chosen another.

"Thank you for last night," she said awkwardly. "You know, for not . . ."

"I didn't come out here for sex." He smiled again. "I know where you stand. But as I told you before, if you want me to be your rebound from Edward Baldwine, I'm more than happy to play that role."

His tone was gentle, his face and body relaxed, his eyes clear.

Maybe I can get there, she thought. Maybe with him, sometime in the future, I'll be able to get there.

"You're such a good man." She didn't even attempt to keep the regret out of her voice. "I really wish—"

With a lithe surge, he got off the swing and came over. Standing in front of her, he met her in the eye. "Don't try to force anything. I'm not going anywhere. I've got my kids to take care of and a big job, and honestly, you're the first woman who's gotten my attention in the four years since my Marilyn died. So you reallllly don't have a lot of competition."

Sutton smiled a little. "You are a prince."

"Not my title and well you know it." He winked. "And I'm uncomfortable with the idea of monarchies. Democracies are the only way to go."

Leaning in, she kissed him on the cheek. And as she looked back out over the view, he said, "Tell me something. Where do you actually wish you were right now?"

"Nowhere."

"Okay, now I have another question. Are you lying to yourself or me?"

Sutton shook her head ruefully.

"Is it so obvious?" She put her hand on his forearm. "And I don't mean any offense."

"None taken. Especially if you tell me the truth."

"Well, there's an event back in Charlemont today that I'm torn about."

"Is it the hearing on developing Cannery Row?"

"Ah, no. It's a private thing, actually."

"We can head back now?"

"It's too late. But thank you—"

The sound of an ATV approaching through the trees brought both their heads around—and a second later, an old man dressed in hunting camo, with a shotgun strapped to his back, motored into the clearing. With a rough sack in his lap and his well-lined face, he was every bit a mountain man, someone who had been born and been living off these hard hills for the six or seven decades he had been alive. In fact, it was difficult to place Mr. Harman's age. He could have been fifty or eighty. What Sutton knew for sure, though, was that he had been married to the same woman since he was sixteen and she had been fourteen, and they had had eleven children, of which eight had survived to adulthood.

By now, he was a great-great-grandfather.

As he got off his machine, Sutton waved. "Mr. Harman, how are you?"

As she went over to the shallow steps off the porch, she saw Dagney glance off to the side and shake his head. Then he joined her.

Mr. Harman narrowed his eyes on the other man like he was wondering how much it would take to taxidermy the guy. "The wife made you breakfast."

"Mr. Harman, this is my friend, Dagney. Dagney, this is William Harman."

Dagney offered his palm. "Sir, pleased to meet you."

"We didn't stay together," Sutton said quickly. "I was in this cabin—he was in the other one, right over there."

"I did make her coffee just now," Dagney explained as he clearly got the gist. "But that is all. I went to my own bunk when it got dark at ten. I swear on my wife's soul, may she rest in peace."

Mr. Harman measured them for a long moment. Then he nodded once as if he approved. "We don't cohabit on our land."

That out of the way, Mr. Harman shook what Dagney was holding out to him, and then he gave the sack to him. With a jab of his gnarled finger, he said, "Biscuits made just now. Venison sausage. Sweet tea."

"Thank you," Sutton said.

Mr. Harman grunted. "You got time to come see the new baby?"

"Actually, we're heading back to Charlemont," Dagney said. "Sutton has something she needs to go to."

"Oh, that's not—"

"I know ya from somewheres." Mr. Harman crossed his arms over his chest and stared at Dagney. "Where'd that be?"

"I'm the governor of our Commonwealth, sir." As Mr. Harman's eyes widened, Dagney mirrored the other's man pose exactly, linking his arms and leaning back into his boot heels. "And you know, I'd really like to come back and meet your family, hear what's on your mind, talk to you about how I can help?"

Mr. Harman whipped off his cap. "I didn't vote fer ya."

"That's okay. A lot of people 'round here didn't."

"It true you're from Daniel Boone's people?"

"Yessir."

"Might have something in common, then."

"How 'bout we find out by talking sometime?"

As Sutton looked back and forth between the two men, she found herself liking Dagney even more. Here he was, one of the richest and most powerful men in the state, and you would never have known it.

"Yup, you can come back," Mr. Harman pronounced. "But only with Miss Sutton. The wife don't like outsiders."

"Aggie likes me," Sutton offered.

"You ain't no outsider." Mr. Harman slapped his cap back on and nodded like that was that. "You know where t' find us. Safe travels."

The man left with the same lack of fuss with which he'd arrived, taking off into the wilderness on his ATV, disappearing down the mountain trail.

Dagney glanced over. "I'm pretty sure he would have shot me if I'd slept in your cabin, whether or not anything happened."

Sutton nodded. "Mr. Harman is very old-fashioned—and also good with a gun."

Dagney lifted the sack. "We'll eat this on the way home."

"Oh, listen, we don't have to leave. It's a long drive—"

"Who said we're driving?" Dagney whistled and the pair of state policemen who were his guard jumped out from behind the cabin. "Boys, we'll be getting Ms. Smythe back to town now. Call ahead and tell them to have the 'copter at Southfork Regional. We'll intercept in thirty minutes."

"Roger that, Governor."

"Thank you, boys."

As Dagney turned back around, Sutton shook her head. "You don't have to do this."

"Hey, if you can't impress a girl with the perks of the office, what good are they? Besides, I've got about fifteen people in Charlemont who have wanted to meet with me for the last two weeks. I'll line up the meetings on the way so this is official business."

"I'm not sure what to say. Other than it's really not necessary."

Dagney tilted in and spoke like he was sharing a secret. "I think you came out here to escape and it didn't work. You keep staring out at those hills like you're trying to convince yourself you did the right thing, and sometimes, it's better and more efficient to just give in and do what you have to do."

"What if it's the wrong thing, though?"

"When was the last time that you steered yourself off course listening to your heart? And don't worry that it will hurt my feelings. I've been through much worse and I'm still standing. Besides, I had a great time driving out here with you last night and the stargazing was phenomenal. How many meteors did we see? Twenty? Twenty-five?"

Damn it, Sutton thought as he waited for her inevitable capitulation. Why could she not be in love with this man?

*B*ack at Easterly, Lizzie left her and Lane's suite and headed for the staff staircase in the rear of the mansion. As she went along, she checked to make sure her black shift dress was in the right place on her shoulders. The Talbots number was nothing she would ordinarily wear or own—when she was on the job as the Bradford family's horticulturist and landscape designer, she was in her uniform of khakis and a polo with the estate's crest on it. Outside of work? Blue jeans, T-shirts, and sneakers were just fine.

You needed a funeral dress, though, or you weren't a grown-up, and she'd gotten this one in a consignment shop in the little town by her farm in Indiana. Heaven only knew how it had found its way onto that rack filled with colorful castoffs, but for twenty bucks, she had plugged a major hole in her wardrobe and was totally willing to overlook that the thing was a little tight on top.

As she went down the hall, she made mental notes about vacuuming, dusting, and—

The wave of nausea tackled her from behind, sneaking up from out of nowhere and sending the world on a wonky-spin that had her throwing out a hand to catch herself.

With a frantic glance over her shoulder, she thought, Nope, not going to make it back to their room.

Rushing forward, she threw open the first door she came to, plowed across a vacant guest room, and beelined right into a peach marble bathroom.

She hit the floor so hard, she bruised her knees, and then she nearly caught her chin as she popped the toilet lid open and gave in to the dry heaves.

Nothing came up. Which made sense because the last time she'd eaten had been at dinner the previous night. Or wait . . . she had felt ill then, too. Had it been lunch? At the hospital?

As she sat back and sagged into the cool wall, she thought, Great. The stomach flu.

Just what she needed right now. She had to leave with Lane for the cemetery in, like, ten minutes, and she wasn't sure how she was going to make it down to the car, much less through whatever ceremony—or non-ceremony—was going to happen relative to his father's ashes.

Taking a deep breath, she lifted her head, looked around—and cursed.

"Oh, come *on* . . ."

Of all the bedroom suites she could have chosen? Really? Chantal's?

Lane's soon-to-be ex-wife's previous crib was the last place she wanted to revisit. And okay, yeah, sure, fine, there were so many no-longer-a-part-of-their-lives in that preamble that she really shouldn't have cared one way or the other. In the wake of that woman's departure from the household, this fancy'd-up repository for plumbing was no different than the other fifteen or twenty loos in the mansion: elegant, well appointed, and—as with most now—vacant.

But Lizzie really didn't like to think of Lane's impending divorce. Or that hateful female.

As she waited to see if her stomach was going to cramp up again, she thought about all the effort she and Lane had put into moving Chantal's things out—while the woman had stood on the sidelines flapping her arms and stamping her feet. Clearly, it had been one of the first consequential learning experiences of a very privileged life.

Cheat on your husband with his father + Get yourself pregnant = Eviction

The math was quite simple.

Putting her knees up, Lizzie balanced her arms on them and let her fingers dangle. Breathing slowly and evenly, she tried to reason with what was going on underneath her diaphragm. And what do you know, memories of all of Chantal's bullcrap were soooooo helpful.

That elegant blond woman with her Virginia pedigree and her wedding-ring entitlement was both the reason Lane and Lizzie had broken up two years ago—and why they'd ended up back together.

Well, actually, it had been two breakups and two reconnections, Lizzie supposed—but certainly most, if not all, of the ugliness between them had been because of Chantal. Which was what ensued when a wife falsely accused a husband who wasn't in love with her of domestic violence. While pregnant with his own half brother or sister.

It was something out of an old episode of *Dynasty*. Except they were actually living it.

And yet Lizzie couldn't hate the woman. She knew what had happened behind closed doors between Chantal and William Baldwine. She'd seen the shattered makeup table in here, the blood on the vanity, the aftermath of the real violence that had gone down—and thus proved that wealth and social standing didn't guarantee you safety and security.

Or love.

All things considered, it had only been a matter of time before someone killed Lane's father. It was just too bad that Edward had had to be the hero, once again.

"So what's it going to be?" she said as she stared down at her midsection. "Are we done here?"

She gave things another couple of minutes to percolate; then she got to her feet and washed her face off with cold water. Cleaned her mouth out. Waited a little longer.

As she looked at herself in the mirror, the reflection that stared back at her was a washed-out version of her normal appearance, her skin sallow, dark bags under her eyes, a faint green line around her mouth.

Rearranging the top of the dress again, she thought about Chantal's wardrobe. The woman would never have gone the consignment route—or put anything from Talbot's on her perfectly proportioned body. She had been Gucci, Prada, Louis Vuitton, Chanel, all the way.

And only the current seasons, of course.

On Lizzie's side? Jeez, before she had worked here, she couldn't have named those designers, much less recognized their work. And even now, after a decade of rubbing shoulders with the likes of the Bradfords' kind of money—or what they'd used to have, at least? She really didn't care.

Rich people had a way of inventing stress for themselves, and what was considered fashionable or not was exactly the kind of self-engineered, arbitrary obsolescence that gave them a bad name.

Now, ask Lizzie about the different sorts of flowering plants in the *Aquifoliaceae* family? The perfect time to plant new trees? What kind of sun hydrangea needed? On it. Then again, that's what you focused on when you'd gotten your master's in landscape architecture at Cornell. As opposed to your Mrs. from some rich guy.

Chantal and she were polar opposites. And although Lizzie didn't like to be arrogant, she could totally understand why Lane had made the choice he had.

Turning away, she walked through the suite, taking note that it, too, needed a vacuum job and a dusting. She would take care of that later, along with the rest of this wing. With all the staff let go, except for her and Greta in house, and Gary McAdams and Timbo on the grounds crew, Easterly was definitely a roll-up-your-sleeves-and-get-'er-done situation.

Plus, she was stressed with everything Lane was dealing with and there was no better remedy for that than making tidy little Dyson tracks in rugs.

Unless you were mowing a lawn, of course. And Gary was getting used to letting her do that, too.

Back out in the corridor, she was almost at the back stairs, when Lane came up them.

"There you are." His worried eyes went over her as if he were looking for signs of an internal injury or a worrisome rash. "Are you okay?"

"Just fine." She smiled and wished there was time to brush her teeth. "I'm ready to—oh, shoot, my purse. Hang on—"

"I've got it." He held the simple clutch up. "And I've brought the car around in front. Gin and Amelia are coming with us. Max is on his own—if he goes at all."

"Great."

As she came up to him and got her purse, she took a moment to enjoy the view. Lane was a classically handsome man, with thick, old-school Hugh Grant hair that cowlicked on one side, a jaw that was strong but not hard, and eyes that were nearly impossible to look away from. He was wearing a dark blue suit and an open-collar white shirt, and she knew the disrespect was intentional. Where Lane came from? One only ever wore black and a full tie to anything that resembled a funeral. What he had on now was more for lunch at the club.

It was a screaming f-you to his father's memory.

Indeed, his tribe had a lot of rules. And didn't that make the fact that he loved her loud and proud a testament to how much he valued her over the elitist way he'd grown up.

Lizzie was well aware that people in town thought he was just with "the gardener."

As if there were something wrong with getting your hands dirty for a living.

Fortunately, she didn't care what they thought any more than he did.

Putting her hands on his shoulders, she looked up into that blue stare she loved so much. "We're going to get through this. We're going to shove that urn where the sun don't shine and afterward, we'll visit Miss Aurora at the hospital and hope for some good news, 'kay? That is our plan."

His lids closed briefly. "I love you so much."

"We can do this. I'm right by your side."

Lane wrapped his arms around her and held her tightly to his body. Everything about him, from the way he fit against her, to the scent of his aftershave, to the tickle of his still-damp hair on her cheek, grounded her.

"Let's go," she said as she took his hand.

Walking down to the kitchen and then proceeding out to the front of the house together, she managed to discreetly take a piece of Wrigley's out of her purse and pop the gum in her mouth. What a relief. The mint taste not only cured her dry mouth, but it seemed to settle her stomach a bit.

When she and Lane stepped out of Easterly's broad front door, she paused to appreciate the landscape down the hill to the river. The green descent to the shimmering stripe of water was the kind of thing you saw on the cover of a coffee-table book about how beautiful America was.

Annnnnd then there was the "car."

The Bradfords had a Phantom Drophead, and not an old one, either. Then again, how could they not have at least one Rolls-Royce while living in a place like Easterly? Today the top was up, and as Lane went ahead and opened the passenger side for her, Lizzie looked inside at the mother and daughter pair who were in the backseat.

Suicide doors were good like that, providing a completely unobstructed view.

Gin was dressed in peach and she lifted a graceful hand with a huge diamond on it in greeting. Amelia was in skinny jeans and a red and black silk top that, yup, was Chanel, going by its double-C buttons—and the girl didn't seem to notice anything, her attention riveted on the iPhone in her hands.

Lizzie almost didn't accept the palm Lane held out for her, because she was used to getting in and out of such non-dangerous, non-moving, non-threatening things as—gasp!—cars, by herself. But she knew the gesture was both reflexive and yet important to him, a way for him to show her that he was thinking about her and taking care of her.

As she settled in and clicked her seat belt, she glanced back at Gin.

"Isn't Richard coming?"

"Why would he?"

Back before the two of them had made their peace, Gin's quick retort would have been a jab at Lizzie designed to make sure she knew her place as a staff member. Now, it was a total dismissal of the woman's husband—and though it was sad to consider such a thing an improvement, Lizzie had learned well before she had come into the lives of the Bradfords that she had to take good news where she could find it.

Amelia glanced up. "I'm glad he's not here. He's not family."

Lizzie cleared her throat. "So . . . ah, what's on your phone?"

The sixteen-year-old swung the screen around. "Dymonds. It's like Candy Crush, but better. Everyone plays it."

"Oh. Cool."

As the girl refocused, Lizzie turned back to the windshield and felt as though she were eighty years old. Make that a hundred and eight.

Lane slid behind the wheel, and Gin spoke up. "This is just us at the cemetery, right?"

"And Max."

"He's coming?"

"Maybe." Lane pushed a button to start the car and put them in gear. "I hope so."

"I don't understand why we can't just empty that urn on the side of the road. Preferably in a ditch or over a dead skunk."

"That argument is not without merit," Lane muttered as he reached out and squeezed Lizzie's hand. "And I'm taking the staff road out. I don't want the reporters down at the front gates to see us."

"Vultures."

Lizzie had to agree. The news crews had set up camp around the main entrance to the estate days ago, their trucks and equipment crowding River Road and nearly eclipsing the great stone pillars of the Bradford estate.

Harpies. All of them. Just waiting to take pictures through car windows that they would curate to fit their headlines, regardless of the actual context around the snapshot: If Lane looked down to adjust the air control on the car's console, that head tilt and expression could be paired with *Bradfords Lose Everything!*; a hand raised to scratch a nose would suddenly represent *Lane Baldwine Cracking Under Pressure!*; the twitch of a mouth and shift of a gaze sideways would be used to punctuate *Unrepentant in Bankruptcy!*

To think there had been a time when she had trusted the press. Hah. There was nothing like being on the inside of a scandal to learn just exactly how much of the news cycle was engineered to get viewers, clicks, and comments. As opposed to report the facts.

Walter Cronkite turned in for Ryan Seacrest.

The trouble was, the Bradford fall from grace was clickbait, bigtime. People just loved to see the rich tumble from their lofty heights.

It was better than any success story.

SEVEN

Cave Dale Cemetery was the only place in Charlemont that a Bradford would ever be buried—and even then, they were not put into the ground like commoners but rather locked in a marble temple that, as Lane's grandfather had always said, was only a vestal virgin and an animal sacrifice away from securing the fortunes of Rome.

As Lane drove down the outside of the cemetery's wrought-iron, Addams Family fencing, he looked through the bars to the countless grave markers, religious statuary, and family crypts that hodgepodge'd around the rolling grass, specimen trees, and pools. How the hell was he going to find where his ancestors were kept? Once you were inside all those acres, in that maze of winding lanes, everything looked the same.

But first, an immediate problem.

As he rounded the corner to the entrance, there were reporters . . . everywhere. With cameras. And news crews.

Damn it, he should have known—

"Are those . . . more news trucks?" Lizzie said as she sat forward in her seat.

Sure as bourbon burned the gut, there was yet another encampment of paparazzi around the great stone-and-iron pillars of the cemetery—and with the Phantom Drophead being about as inconspicuous as a Macy's Thanksgiving Day float in May, there was a flurry of activity at its approach, cameras flashing even though at eleven a.m. there was plenty of light.

Great. So he had two choices. Pump the brakes and give them a fishbowl into the car.

Or he could just plow through the bastards.

Not really much to deliberate, was there.

"Duck your heads," Lane barked as he hit the gas.

The Rolls-Royce surged forward and he wrenched the wheel, piloting that heavy bank-vault front grille with its Spirit of Ecstasy on a path directly into the throng that was blocking the way in.

"You're going to hurt someone!" Lizzie yelled as she braced herself.

"Mow them down!" his sister called out from the back.

Meanwhile, the men and women with the cameras just kept snapping away, ignoring the whole $E=mc^2$ thing.

Gripping the steering wheel, he hollered, "Get the fuck back!"

As security guards came rushing out of the guardhouse, he did indeed strike someone, the guy with the Nikon bouncing off the hood, while somebody else kicked at the bumper and all kinds of people cursed and threatened to sue.

Lane just kept barreling through, until the Rolls was on the cemetery's property.

In the rearview, he checked to see if anyone was bleeding or down on the pavement—or if the security guards were coming after him with guns drawn or something: Nope, although it was going to be a long while before Lane forgot the sight of one of those paparazzi smiling even though he was in the choke hold of one of the guards.

Clearly, the harpy had gotten what he'd been after.

As another of the guards started waving and coming after the car, Lane slowed to a stop but kept his window up.

"We'll hold 'em in place, Mr. Bradford," the man said through the glass. "Y'all just keep on going down to the left. Follow the signs for Fairlawn Lane. You're right there, 'bout halfway down. We gotchu ready at your place."

"Thank you." Lane cursed under his breath. "And I'm sorry about all those reporters."

"Y'all don't worry now, just go on, though. We can't calm them down until you're out of sight."

"How should I leave when we're through?"

"Follow any of the lanes down the hill. It will hook into the back road and take you to where the rear entrance is by the outbuildings."

"Great, thank you."

"Y'all take care, now," the man said with a little bow.

Lane drove on quite a distance before he was confident they were out of telephoto lens reach. "Okay," he said. "The coast is clear now."

The women uncurled themselves, and as he took Lizzie's hand again, he checked on Gin and Amelia in the rearview.

The girl's eyes were shining with excitement. "Oh, my God, that was so cool! That, like, happens to Kardashians."

Lane shook his head. "I'm not sure that's a standard anyone should want to be measured by."

"No, I'm serious, I've seen it on TV."

"I thought Hotchkiss taught you important stuff." Lane frowned as they came up to an intersection. "Like calculus, history—"

He hit the brakes and tried to remember. Left or right? Down the hill? Or over to—was it Fairlawn?

A tinny little horn *meep-meep*'d behind them. And as God was his witness, Lane was so ready to flip the glove box open, grab the nine that was in there, and start shooting—

"Samuel T.?" he said as he did a double take in the rearview.

Hitting the window button, he stuck his head out and was so glad to see the other guy in that vintage Jag. "That really you?"

Like there could be another classic maroon sports car in this grave-yard with a model-worthy Southern gentleman farmer/attorney behind the wheel?

"You lost there, boy?" Samuel T. drawled as he lifted his Ray-Bans. "Need an escort?"

"I do indeed. Lead on, wayward son."

As Samuel T. lowered those dark lenses back into place and headed forward, Gin muttered, "Who invited him?"

Lane shrugged and followed the leader, sticking close to the convertible. "I mentioned it yesterday."

"Next time, perhaps discretion would be appropriate."

"He is my lawyer," Lane said with a smile.

Gin calling for discretion? Huh, he thought. Maybe this all was some kind of a bizarre dream, and he would wake up with the company still okay, Edward out of jail, Miss Aurora back in her kitchen, and Easterly staffed up and ready for a Memorial Day party to beat all others.

He'd keep his happiness with Lizzie, of course.

And . . . yes, he'd still have his father in the trunk.

In ashes.

*A*s Gin sat in the backseat of the Phantom, she couldn't decide whether to shut down or start throwing the f-bomb around like it was confetti.

In the end, she went with the former for two reasons: One, screaming and yelling required more energy than she had, and besides, that former act of hers was getting old; and two, she was concerned about what would come out of her mouth. And not as in the cussing.

There were things Amelia did not know. Things Samuel T. did not know. And Gin could not guarantee that her current bad temper would not make revelations that were best left behind a figurative iron curtain.

What the hell was he here for, anyway.

And while she was at the bitching, she found it sublimely annoying that Samuel T. knew where the Bradford crypt was. Then again, the man never forgot anything that was said or shown to him. He was like a goddamn elephant.

Which was also incredibly irritating.

Many turns and straightaways later, Samuel T. led them to their destination like a bloodhound after a scent, and Lane pulled the Rolls-Royce over to the side behind the Jag. As her brother put them in park, all around doors were opened, but Gin stayed where she was.

Her initial burst of anger had shifted to another emotion. One so much more destructive, as far as she was concerned.

Rubbing her suddenly sweaty palms on her skirt, she discovered that her heart was pounding, and she felt dizzy even though there was plenty of air-conditioning left inside the car. And then for some reason, the burns on the insides of her thighs, from when Richard had forced them open, became almost unbearably painful.

Memories of the unpleasantness that had occurred with him were not what weighed on her mind, however.

Instead, she heard Samuel T.'s voice in her head.

I think Richard hits you. I think those bruises came from him, and that you're wearing scarves to cover them up. . . .

She and Samuel T. had met in secret only a few nights before, at the Presbyterian Theological Seminary, in the beautiful darkness of its main gardens. He had called her to come see him there, and even after all their ups and downs, she had never expected what he had said to her.

You can call me. Anytime. I know you and I haven't made sense. We're bad for each other in all the ways that count, but you can call me. Day or night. No matter where you are, I'll come for you. I won't ask for any explanations. I won't yell at you or berate you. I won't judge you—and if you insist, I won't tell Lane or anybody else.

Samuel T. had been dead serious, no evidence of his jocular nature or his usual sexual teasing evident. He had been . . . sad. Protective and sad.

Looking through the car window, she focused on Amelia.

The girl had walked forward onto the bright green grass, her red and black blouse billowing in the hot breeze, her dark hair whisking off over her shoulder. Ahead of her, looming surely as the burden of their bloodline's legacy did, the great Bradford crypt rose from the earth, a marble monument to the family's greatness, with twenty-foot-tall carved statues on all four corners, a great pediment over the entrance marked with a gold-leafed crest, and iron gates that were every bit as intricate and strong as the ones at the entrance of the cemetery itself.

Amelia stopped at the five steps that led up to the aged brass doors, which remained closed even as those iron bars had been opened for the family.

As the young girl tilted her head back as if to regard the crest overhead, the sun glinting in her hair drew out the same copper highlights that were in Samuel T.'s.

Like father, like daughter—

Gin's door was opened for her and she jumped, putting a palm to her mouth just in case her heart decided to make a run for it up her throat.

As a hand extended into the car for her, she mumbled, "Thank you, Lane."

Accepting the help, she pulled herself up and out—

"Not Lane."

At the low words, she jerked to attention, her eyes flipping up to meet Samuel T.'s. She needn't have worried about encountering his stare, however.

He was looking down and a little to the left . . . at the marks on her forearm that were exposed by the three-quarter sleeves on her silk dress. As his face darkened to violence, she removed herself from his hold, tucked her clutch into her elbow, and smiled.

"Samuel T. What a surprise. I haven't seen you in forever."

All of that was supposed to come out smooth and steady. Instead, her voice was reedy and insubstantial, and her body began shaking for no apparent reason. She wasn't cold, for heaven's sake.

You're better than this. Your family's glorious past is not worth a man hitting you in the present just because you're afraid you won't be anything without the money. You're priceless, Gin, no matter what's in your bank account.

Stop it, she told herself.

Smiling even more broadly, she expected him to say something and waited for him to play along with the social pleasantries.

As usual, he took his own path.

Samuel T. simply bowed in a gallant fashion, and left her to follow—or not.

EIGHT

*L*ane had always thought that the family crypt looked sinister, with all its dark eaves and the twisted iron designs over the opaque windows and the ivy choking out the aged white marble. And somehow, the prospect of his father being interred there made all of those Vincent Price prejudices take on an even more dire cast. But where else was he going to put the man? If he disrespected the dead, he was worried Daddy Dearest was going to haunt him for the rest of his life.

As if William wasn't going to do that anyway.

With the urn held like a football in the crook of his arm, Lane walked across the grass, the broad leafy branches of sycamores and beech trees filtering the bright sunshine, creating a ripple effect underfoot that would have been cheerful in other circumstances. As promised, cemetery staff had unlocked the deadbolts and muscled open the great sets of bars, leaving the brass double doors undefended and ready to be put to use. Instead of handles or knobs, there were a pair of heavy brass rings, and as he went up the low steps and reached for the one on the right, he was reminded of the time he had come here as a boy with his grandfather.

Just as Mother's father had done back then, he rotated the ring on its base, the mechanism clanking in a way that echoed in the interior. Hinges as big as his forearms creaked as he pulled the great weight open, and the rush of cool, dry air smelled of autumn leaves and a century's worth of dust.

The interior was a forty-by-forty-foot perfect square topped by a dome of translucent glass panels that let in more than enough light with which to read the plaques on the walls. In the center, two marble sarcophagi were aligned side by side, the first Elijah Bradford and his beloved Constance Tulane Bradford lying in prominent view, surrounded by the lineage they had created. And in spite of how eternal their repose appeared to be, he understood that this crypt was actually their second burial place. The pair evidently had been dug up and relocated from somewhere on Easterly's property when this awe-inspiring monument had been constructed in the mid-1800s.

As the footfalls of the others shuffled in, he looked around at the markers that were mounted in orderly rows on the walls, the block lettering on the old brass plaques detailing who had been put into what space at what time. And yes, a vacancy had been prepared for William Baldwine: Across the way, there was a single opening in the lineup of compartments, one that had been revealed by the removal of a square of the marble veneer.

Going over, Lane placed the urn into the darkness and was impressed by how precisely it fit within the confines of the hole, the lid having only an inch to spare.

Stepping back, he frowned, the enormity of the death dawning on him for the first time. Ever since he had come back to Charlemont, it had been one crisis after another, his attention drawn from emergency to emergency. That chaos, coupled with the fact that he had never felt close to his father—and in fact had disliked and mistrusted the man—had made William's passing almost a footnote.

Now, the reality that he would never again see the man or smell that trademark tobacco scent or hear that commanding stride in Easterly's corridors, or anywhere else, struck him as . . . not sad, no. Because he honestly did not mourn the loss as one would somebody they loved and cared about.

It was more surreal. Unfathomable. Unbelievable.

That somebody with that big an effect on the world, albeit a negative one, could be gone in the blink of an eye—

Heavy footfall on the marble steps outside the entrance made him turn around, and before he recognized the tall figure cutting a black shadow in the sunlight, his brain tricked him into thinking that it was his father, back from the dead.

His brother Maxwell's deep voice cleared up any confusion. "I'm late again, huh."

That lazy drawl suggested the guy didn't care if he'd offended anyone, but that was Max's way. He excelled at convincing himself and everyone around him that he didn't give a shit about anything.

And a lot of times, Lane supposed, it was true. Still, he had showed up, hadn't he.

"I just put Father's urn in," Lane remarked as he nodded at the compartment.

"He doesn't deserve to be here. He's not part of this family."

Naturally, Max was not in a suit, but rather wearing a biker jacket and jeans. With his beard, and the tattoos on his neck, he appeared to be exactly the rebel he in fact was, a man tied to no one and nowhere.

And for no apparent reason, Lane remembered something Edward had said when he'd been making that confessional to the police at the Red & Black: *They're going to try to tell you I had an accomplice, but I didn't. I worked alone.*

Lane narrowed his eyes on his brother.

"What?" Max demanded.

In the periphery, Gin glanced across sharply, and that was a perfect reminder that they were hardly alone—and especially with Amelia around, this was no place to bring up touchy subjects like, *Hey, did you team up with Edward to murder our pops?*

"Will you help me put that in place?" Lane said as he pointed to the marble slab that was in the corner.

"Trying to be sure he stays where he's supposed to?"

"Can you blame me?"

"Not in the slightest. I only came to make certain the bastard was ashed."

The two of them went over and bent at the knees around the three-by-three-foot section of marble. Lane had only asked Max to help with the stone as a way of covering up the awkward moment, but it turned out he needed the extra pair of hands. The white veneer was attached to steel backing that weighed a bloody ton, and both of them grunted as they got the thing up off the floor.

Shuffling back to where the urn was sitting rather unceremoniously in its hole—sort of like a soup can on a shelf, actually—they hefted the square up and fitted the thing into place.

Stepping away, Lane wondered if it just sat like that . . . ? Or did it need to be bolted in?

"Is it going to fall out?" Max said.

"I don't know. I mean, it's heavy as hell. I didn't see a latch on the back or anything, did you?"

"I wasn't really looking." Max glanced around. "Are they all just sitting in there like that? 'Cuz one good earthquake and those urns are going to go flying—and this place is gonna need a Dustbuster and a half."

Lane laughed first. And then Gin joined in. When Amelia, Lizzie, and Samuel T. followed suit, it was pretty clear they all needed a release of tension as they stood around the sarcophagi.

"So this is it?" Gin murmured as everyone quieted down again.

"So surreal." Lane put his arm around Lizzie and drew her in close. "Like some kind of dream."

"Not a nightmare, though." Max shook his head. "Not for me, at least."

"Nor I," Gin agreed. "Are you going to get him a plaque?"

"I don't know." Lane shrugged. "I don't really want to."

"Let's leave it." Max crossed his arms over his chest. "He's already getting more than he deserves. I would have scattered his ashes in the cornfield before we laid the manure—"

As another figure came into the tomb's open doorway, Lane noticed the intrusion first—and instantly recognized who it was.

Chantal.

His curse brought everyone else to attention.

"Did you think I wouldn't find out?" she demanded.

In the back of his mind, Lane heard Glenn Close in *Fatal Attraction:* "I'm not going to be *ignored*, Dan."

Who in the good God had told her about this? he wondered.

As Chantal came inside, her perfume was an assault on the sinuses, a fake bouquet that made him want to sneeze. And her brightly colored blouse and white jeans were utterly out of place.

"Well?" she said. "I have a right to be here, too, Lane."

When she put her hand on her belly, he rolled his eyes. "Let's not play this game, shall we. You're not any more of a mourner than we are."

"I'm not? Says who. I loved your father—"

Lane looked over at Samuel T. "Would you be so kind as to escort my sister and her daughter out of here?"

"Of course." The lawyer turned to Gin. "Let's go."

"As his attorney, wouldn't you prefer to stay?" Gin said dryly. "And you only have a two-seater. What are you going to do with the both of us?"

"I'll take Amelia on my bike." Max put his hand on his niece's shoulder. "I got another helmet. Come on. Let's give the grown-ups some privacy. You want ice cream on the way home?"

"I'm sixteen, not six." Amelia tilted up her chin exactly the way her mother did. "And I want Graeter's double chocolate chip. In a cone. With sprinkles."

"Whatever you like." As Max came up to Chantal, he dropped his voice—but not by much. "You either get out of my way or I'm going to push you back until you fall on your ass."

"Your father always said you were an animal."

"And you've been a gold-digging bitch since birth. So there's that."

Chantal was so flabbergasted at the insult, she tripped out of his path. Then again, anyone who had ever met Max knew better than to take him on, and Lane's soon-to-be ex-wife was no dummy.

"Come on, Gin," Samuel T. said as he took her elbow.

Lane stared at his sister and tried to will her to be reasonable and leave. The last thing they needed was her going wild card here.

For once in your life, he thought at her, just back the hell off. *Please.*

As Gin felt Samuel T.'s hold on her elbow tighten, she smiled across at her brother Lane's biggest mistake: Chantal Baldwine was second tier, all the way. The only thing that was first place on her?

Social ambition.

"Gin," Samuel T. prompted. "Shall we?"

For a moment, Gin enjoyed the tension that sprang up in the

crypt, each one of them wondering what in the hell she was going to do next. Except she wasn't going to bicker with Chantal.

No, she was better than that.

"But of course, Samuel," she said sweetly.

She could practically feel the easing in his and Lane's bodies, and that was exactly what she was after.

And she behaved herself alllllllll the way to the exit.

Almost.

When she came up to the other woman, Gin leaned in and quickly put her hand on Chantal's stomach. Before Chantal could jump back, Gin spoke fast and low. *"I curse this child."*

"What? What did you say?"

"You heard me." Gin smiled again. "And when you lose this baby, I want you to think of me."

"What!"

"Bye for now."

Gin sauntered out of the tomb and waited at the bottom of the steps for Samuel T. to catch up. Behind her, Chantal had started to yell and Gin rolled her eyes as he paused to try to do damage control.

Ah, lovely. The discord in her wake was so lovely. Chantal was crying now, and trying to get to Gin, but Samuel T. wouldn't let her.

Meanwhile, Gin was outside in the sun, feeling the warmth on her cheeks and sternum.

After quite some time, Samuel T. emerged and took Gin's elbow again. "Come on, witch doctor. We're over here."

Ordinarily, Gin would have been inclined to pick an argument with him just to keep the drama going, but she remained quiet and content as he escorted her across the grass to the Jaguar. After opening the door for her, he handed her down into the seat—and when she glanced up to thank him reflexively, she was struck by those looks of his.

He was unbearably handsome, it was true. But that wasn't her attraction to him. The sizzle was a result of his arrogance coupled with his rank independence and total disregard for her sense of superiority. She had always wanted to win against him. Have him submit to her and do what she wanted. Force him to be the purebred dog who heeled to her command.

But Samuel T. wasn't like that. Never had been, never would be.

And that was why she loved him.

"You don't have to say it," he murmured as he closed her door.

Gin's eyes tracked every move he made as he went around the long hood and got behind the wheel. After he put his Ray-Bans on, he looked across at her through those dark aviators and her heart leapt.

"What don't I have to say?" Her voice was so husky, it was nearly inaudible, and for a moment, he just stared at her.

I want you, she thought. I just want to feel you in me again.

It seemed as though it had been forever since they'd been together. In reality? It was only the matter of a week or two, maybe less. She couldn't recall.

Wipe Richard's stain off of me, she thought to herself. Fuck him right out of me.

As if he could read her mind, Samuel T. reached across and took her hand in a warm, strong grip. As his thumb made circles on the inside of her wrist, she felt the touch throughout her body.

"Samuel . . ." she whispered.

With a slow shift, he turned her palm over and then lifted it, as if he were going to brush her knuckles with his lips.

Instead, he held her hand up so that her engagement ring and wedding band were facing her. "I was going to say that, of course, I was going to take us out through the back gates. The last thing we need is to be seen together by the press."

Samuel T. dropped his hold and started the engine. And as he drove them away, he was so calm and in control that they might as well have been in a modern automatic, instead of a classic manual.

Goddamn it, she thought. How dare he be so composed.

The lanes they followed were winding, the views of ponds and weeping willows, stands of specimen trees and beds of ivy, lending precisely the kind of peacefulness that one would wish to find in a final resting place.

None of this reached her as she seethed. But Samuel T. couldn't know that. She didn't want him to see inside of her any more than he already did.

"Aren't you impressed with me," she asked tightly.

"Always."

"And now he decides to be charming. After he turns me down."

"I didn't turn you down."

"You didn't? Hmm . . . if you in fact kissed me back there and I've forgotten about it already, I'd say you're losing your touch."

"Tell me why I'm supposed to be impressed with you?"

She smiled at the change of subject, taking it as a small victory, but she noted a change in the quality of their banter, and saw in it a loss of something she had once held dear. The back and forth was very much their currency of relating, but gone was the sexual edge and the roiling erotic anger. As recently as a week before, this would have escalated into name-calling and a revisit of all past slights and indiscretions . . . until they fell into a bed and consumed each other.

Now? She got the sense they were both skating over the real issues, moving across the frozen surface of their past . . . and the bitter-cold reality of her present.

"What am I impressed with, Gin?"

"That I didn't mention, not even once, that hideous blouse Chantal was wearing. See? I am turning over a new leaf."

"You told her to miscarry her baby. I think on the scale of insults that is far worse."

"I don't get points for honesty? Come now, you've always told me how much you hate when I lie—and I do want her to lose that monstrosity."

"I didn't know you cared that much about the sanctity of your brother's marriage vows."

"Oh, that doesn't concern me in the slightest. I'm just looking to reduce the number of claims to the estate."

"There's my girl."

"Not that there's much to it—and isn't that the true tragedy."

Samuel T. pumped the brakes as they descended a hill and took a turn toward a series of outbuildings. On the far side of them, a concrete wall was broken up by a section of chain-link fence that was wide open.

As they passed through the gate, a couple of uniformed groundsmen who were smoking over in the shade perked up and gawked at the car.

"Remind me not to mess with you," Samuel T. murmured.

"Too late for that."

"Yes," he said grimly. "I believe that is true. So where's your husband, Virginia Elizabeth."

"Don't call me that. You know I despise that name." Gin shrugged. "And Richard is at work. Or in hell. It doesn't matter to me."

"How are things between you?" The inquiry was casual. The tone was not.

Gin stiffened in the old leather seat and thought about what had happened in her dressing room. "The same. He leaves me alone, I leave him alone."

"You want to get a drink?"

"Yes, please."

NINE

Chantal treated the doorway of the crypt like it was a Shakespearean theater stage, her arms flying left and right, her weight playing contrapposto to the swings, her hair cascading around her shoulders, a blond ocean in a tempest.

"—treat me like that! I mean, how could you simply stand there as your brother insults me and your sister assaults me!"

Lane watched the show from a distance, easing back against the corner of Elijah's sarcophagus and just letting things roll. He wasn't going to tolerate the emoting forever, but he was operating on the belief that the woman would eventually lose this burst of energy, given that it was eighty-five outside and she wasn't in the shade as long as she stayed where she was.

In fact, he was far more concerned with Lizzie, but he should have known better than to think she'd get involved: She was across the way, one hip against the flank of Constance's marble tomb, her left eyebrow cocked like she was considering what kind of Rotten Tomatoes score to give the performance.

And as for Gin's comment that had started it all?

Well, that could have been worse, couldn't it. Which, considering what had actually come out of his sister's mouth, was a true testament to Gin's history of outrageous behavior.

"Well?" Chantal finally demanded. "What do you have to say for yourself?"

"I thought my divorce petition was pretty self-explanatory."

"This is not a joke."

"I'm not so sure about that."

"You've tried to keep me out of everything. I wasn't there for your father's will reading, you didn't tell me about this—"

"You were left nothing in the will. And you are not a member of this family—"

She grabbed her stomach. "*This* is a member of the family. This is the next Bradford—"

"No," Lane snapped, "*that* is the next Baldwine. Theoretically."

Chantal wheeled around on Lizzie. "You need to leave. This is between him and me."

Before Lizzie could respond, Lane cut in: "She can stay—or go, but it will be on her terms, not yours."

"You always did have a preference for the help."

Lane smiled coldly. "Watch yourself, Chantal. You went down that road once before and it didn't end well for you."

"Oh, yes, your 'momma.' I forgot—tell me, have you replaced Miss Aurora in the kitchen yet? Or are you going to wait until she dies."

Lizzie shook her head. "I think I will leave, actually."

"And I'm done here, as well." Lane straightened. "This is going nowhere—"

"You can't shut me out of your life, Lane! This gives me rights." Again, she put her hands on her lower belly. "This is the next generation of your family! What you couldn't give me."

As Lane went up to the woman, he tried to keep his temper under control. "You aborted my child, in case you forgot. Which I have not."

Chantal's face went red. "You gave me no choice!"

"And I don't even know if it was mine."

"How *dare* you."

"After what you did with my father? Really?"

As she raised her hand to slap him, he caught her wrist and held it firmly. "I'm walking out of here right now, and if you know what's good for you, you will let me go. Without. One. More. Goddamn. Word."

Lizzie ducked her head and hustled by Chantal, striding for the steps and the Rolls parked down below. The way she stared at the ground scared him. She had made it clear that his drama was not attractive or enticing in the slightest: She loved him in spite of his family, not because of his money and his position and the emotional upset that seemed to be cresting in every corner of his fricking life.

"Lizzie," he called out.

"Will you pay attention to me!" Chantal demanded. "I matter! I am important!"

With a sudden surge, Chantal jumped at him, throwing fists, kicking him, screaming and tossing her head until her hair was in his face, in his mouth. Grabbing on to her, he tried to hold her at bay, but also keep her from falling and hurting herself in those high heels.

"Chantal, will you stop—"

And that was when the flashbulb went off.

From over behind a beech tree trunk, a camera captured the altercation as fast as its shutter could blink open and closed.

"Oh, for fuck's sake, seriously—"

"Lane! Stop, Lane!"

At first, he wasn't sure who was trying to get his attention. But then he realized it was Lizzie, and he did his best to talk over Chantal. "I know, I saw the camera. Go get in the car—"

"Lane! The blood!"

"What?"

As he froze, Chantal curled up a dainty fist with her free hand and served it like a Louisville Slugger, catching him right on the jaw. The impact caused his teeth to clap together, but she wasn't done with him. Ripping her wrist free, a second shot came flying at him and nailed him in the nose, the pain like a bomb burst in the middle of his face.

Oddly, the only thing that went through his mind was those combat classes she'd taken at that health club she was a member of.

Guess they'd done more for her than just burn calories.

"Lane! The blood!"

Yes, he was bleeding and he stepped back from Chantal, bringing up his hands to his face. Meanwhile, Lizzie was right on it, coming to his defense and holding the other woman back.

"Chantal, you're bleeding! You've got to stop this! The baby!"

And that was when the cops showed up.

Yup, that was definitely a police vehicle with its lights going, coming to a halt right behind the Rolls-Royce.

Like a streaker about to get chased off the fifty-yard line, the photographer bolted from behind the tree, the man running like hell across the field of gravestones. But Lane didn't care about that.

What had Lizzie just said? What about the baby?

As Sutton got out of the front of the state-police vehicle, she wasn't sure what she was looking at. Yes, that was the Bradford family crypt, with its iron gating open and both brass doors wide. And yes, that was Lane Baldwine, with his Lizzie—and Chantal Baldwine, whom he was in the process of divorcing.

But the rest of it didn't make any sense.

Lane had blood running down his face and staining the shirt under his suit jacket. Worse, however, was the bright red rush on the inside of Chantal's white jeans.

Had someone been stabbed . . . or shot? Or . . .

Even though Sutton wasn't sure how to help, she rushed up the steps—and the police officer came with her.

"Chantal," Lizzie was saying, "calm down, you're bleeding!"

Whether it was the state policeman, the squad car, or the fact that there were now two more people involved, Chantal fell back into Lizzie's arms and went lax as if she had either given up . . . or fainted.

Lane stared at the stain on the jeans. "Oh, dear Lord . . ."

"What's going on here?" The state policeman who had driven Sutton over from Sanford Airport had been at the end of his shift, but now, he was clearly back on duty. "Do we need an ambulance?"

"Yes," Lizzie said urgently as she helped Chantal lie on the marble landing.

Chantal widened her thighs, looked at the brilliant red stain, and let out a scream that flushed birds from a magnolia tree. "My baby!"

Lane ripped off his jacket and put it across the woman's legs. "Call nine-one-one!"

As the policeman raced back to the squad car, Sutton crouched down. "What can I do?"

"How did you know we needed help?" Lane asked.

"Chantal," Lizzie said to the woman, "just take some deep breaths. You need to stay calm—if you want to help your baby, you have to stay calm. . . ."

Chantal's frantic eyes were the kind of thing you never forgot. "What's happening to me? What's wrong?"

Sutton glanced at Lane and tried to remember—oh, right. "I came in from the airport. I needed a ride over here to make it on time."

"In a state-police car?"

Chantal let out a groan and then stiffened. "My baby!"

"Here." Sutton took off her loose over-shirt. "Your nose is bleeding badly."

As she held the folds out to Lane, he seemed momentarily confused. But then he took what she offered and put it to the lower half of his face.

"T-t-take me inside," Chantal stammered. "There are photographers all around here—I don't want this on the Internet!"

Lane leaned down closer. Through the muffling of the shirt, he said, "Chantal, we don't know what's going on here, so maybe we shouldn't move you—"

"This is embarrassing! I'm bleeding!"

Sutton could only shake her head. "I've got her feet."

Together, the three of them picked the woman up, carried her into the crypt, and laid her down again. Then Sutton went and closed the great brass doors.

"Is the ambulance coming?" Chantal's panic echoed inside the interior. "When is it going to be here? What is happening to me?"

Sutton took a step back and wondered if she should leave. But no, she couldn't do that. Instead, she cracked the doors and stared outside, praying for the ambulance to come—and it seemed like they were in there forever with the dead, with what possibly was another death happening in stages.

In reality, probably no more than ten minutes passed before distant sirens announced that the medics were somewhere in the twisted lanes of the cemetery.

"I see them!" she said. "They're here!"

The state policeman went forward and waved the boxy vehicle over and then Sutton stepped aside as a gurney and equipment were carried up the stairs by a woman and a man in blue uniforms.

"That's my husband," Chantal said as soon as the EMTs entered. "Lane Baldwine is my husband and I'm eleven weeks' pregnant."

"Sir," one of the medics said to Lane, "can you please help me get some basic information down while my partner examines your wife?"

Without thinking about it, Sutton went over to Lizzie and whispered, "Let's step out, shall we?"

"Yes," Lizzie said roughly. "I think that would be best."

As they came out on the front step and went down to the lawn, Sutton blinked in the sunlight. She still wasn't sure why she had come. Didn't like to consider why she couldn't seem to stay away. Really wanted just about everything here to be different.

"Your timing couldn't have been better," Lizzie murmured.

"It's a little uncanny. And I know I shouldn't intrude . . . I mean, this is not my family. But I—"

"Oh, God—"

Lizzie wobbled on her feet, threw out an arm, and Sutton caught her just as she seemed about to fall down. "Are you okay?"

"I'm going to be sick."

Sutton glanced about and couldn't see any paparazzi, but who the hell knew. "Come over here."

Drawing Lizzie around the corner of the tomb, Sutton held the woman's hair back as Lizzie crouched and dry-heaved.

For some reason, tears came to Sutton's eyes.

Oh, who was she lying to. She knew exactly why.

Edward should have been here. And in her convoluted thinking, she had come as his proxy.

Yes, because that made sense. It wasn't like they were together or anything. Then again, she supposed that when someone was in your heart to the degree Edward was in hers, it was as if you carried them with you wherever you were. And he should have been here for them all.

"Shh . . ." Sutton murmured as she rubbed Lizzie's back. "It's all right. . . ."

When the heaving relented, Lizzie collapsed on the ground, sitting against the tomb. "Oh, that's cool. That's good."

With a curse, the woman let her head fall back. Her flushed cheeks were cherry red, but her mouth was a slash of white. And then she dropped a bomb.

"I think I'm pregnant," she said in a thin voice.

TEN

No, I'm *not* going in the ambulance with her." As Lane shut that idea down, he didn't care that the medics looked shocked. "We're separated. She is *not* my wife and that is *not* my child."

But he was going to go to the hospital. For one, he wanted to find out whether or not Chantal had in fact lost a baby. For another, they were taking her down to University Hospital, where Miss Aurora was, and he'd intended to visit his momma, anyway.

First, though, he had to talk to Lizzie.

As the medics got Chantal up off the cold marble floor and started strapping her onto the gurney, he left them to their job and went out. Lizzie and Sutton were down at the car, the Phantom's suicide door wide open, Lizzie sitting in the front passenger seat.

Descending the short steps, he crossed over the lawn. "I'm so sorry about that."

Lizzie didn't meet his eyes. "Oh, not to worry."

Glancing at Sutton, he nodded at the other woman. "Listen, we're going to head down to the hospital—"

"Actually, that stomach flu is really making me sick." Lizzie lifted her head. "Sutton, do you suppose your friend over there with the badge would be willing to drive me back to Easterly? If not, I can catch an Uber—"

"I'll take you home." Lane kneeled down and took Lizzie's hand. "Dear Lord, you're freezing cold."

"I'm just under the weather." Lizzie stared up at Sutton. "And if I can just get a ride home—"

"We'll take you, of course."

Lane frowned. "No, I'll—"

Lizzie cut him off with a shake of her head. "It's fine. Honestly. You don't have to worry about me. But I don't want to give this to Miss Aurora, and I know you're going to see her."

Well . . . shit. "I won't stay long."

"Take as much time as you like. I just want to lie down."

As Sutton went over to talk to the officer, Lane moved his face into Lizzie's stare. "Chantal's crazy—she's totally delusional, and the only reason I'm going is because of the estate situation now that my father's died—"

"I know. It's fine."

"Mr. Baldwine?" one of the medics said. "We're about ready to leave now if you want to follow in your car."

Lizzie stood up and Lane had to move back to give her space. As she smiled at him, he told himself the expression reached her eyes. "I'm going straight home and taking a nap. By the time you get done, I'll be back on my feet and ready to go."

"I love you."

"I know. Me, too."

She patted his arm and then turned away toward Sutton, and he hated her slow, careful steps—hated even more that it was clear she didn't want him to escort her to the police vehicle.

This whole thing was his fucking fault.

And the mere appearance that he might be picking Chantal's crisis over Lizzie needing him sucked.

He waited as Lizzie slid into the front passenger seat of the marked car, and he waved until he couldn't see the brake lights through the gravestones anymore. Then, cursing to himself, he got in the Rolls-Royce and followed the ambulance out of the cemetery. He wasn't looking forward to tangling with all the reporters at the front gates again, but what else could he do? If he took a different route, he ran the risk of getting separated from Chantal as she was checked in.

And he was right. There were still plenty of reporters on the outside of the gates, and another round of flashbulbs went off as he pulled through in the Phantom. But he was not going to cover his face or duck. Screw that.

Once they were on the road proper, the ambulance hit its sirens and lights, and they sped along, taking a short route into downtown that avoided the highway.

For the entire trip, the only thing he kept thinking . . . was that it was a damn shame he couldn't kill his father all over again.

The University Hospital's complex took up multiple city blocks, the various steel and glass skyscrapers linked by pediwalks that extended over the network of streets and alleys around them. On the sides of the buildings, the titles of the services were preceded by the names of families who had given donations in support of their missions: the Bradford Stroke Center, the Smythe Cancer Center, the Boone Rehabilitation Center, the Sutton Emergency Department.

The ambulance went around to a series of Authorized Vehicles

Only bays, and Lane parked the Rolls in the lot off to the side while the medics backed into position. Getting out, he put his hands in his pockets and strode across the hot asphalt to a set of electronic doors. As soon as he walked into the waiting area, people stared at him because they recognized his face.

This happened a lot. And not just in Charlemont.

Thanks to his previous playboy lifestyle, he'd been in the press even before all the current bankruptcy problems had hit. Now? After his father's death and Edward's arrest and Chantal's bullshit domestic-violence accusations, he might as well have had a neon sign around his neck that read YES, I AM WHO YOU THINK I AM.

"May I help you?" the receptionist asked as she fixated on him.

"I'm here for Chantal Baldwine. She's being admitted right now— she came in by ambulance?"

The woman nodded. "Someone will come to get you as soon as I can. They can, I mean—ah, may I get you anything?"

Like she was the hostess at a cocktail party? "No. Thank you."

As her eyes followed every move he made, Lane went across the waiting area and took a load off in a plastic chair in the far corner, away from the TV and the vending machines. God, he hoped this didn't take forever—

"Mr. Baldwine?" somebody said from a door marked AUTHORIZED PERSONNEL ONLY. "Your wife is—"

"Thank you." Lane got to his feet and strode over. Dropping his voice, he muttered, "And she's not my wife."

The nurse blinked. "My apologies. I thought she said—"

"Where is she? And forgive me for being rude."

"Oh, I understand, sir." The nurse stepped back so he could pass by—while sparing him a glance that suggested she didn't understand at all. "This is a difficult time."

You have no idea, he thought.

Lane was led past a nursing station and various glass-enclosed treatment areas. Chantal was down on the left, and as he walked in, she threw out her hand and looked at him with wild, scared eyes.

"Darling, the baby . . ."

The two nurses who were hooking up IVs and monitoring equipment to her froze and glanced over at him. And as they struggled to refocus on their job, he wanted to scream at Chantal to cut the shit—but he wasn't going any more public than they already were with this.

Sitting down in a vacant chair, he stared into Chantal's carefully made-up eyes. Her mascara wasn't smudging in spite of the tears, and he wondered if she'd planned that for the confrontation—or whether she kept things waterproof just in case she had to bust out the crying.

Still, she really didn't look well. Gone were her fancy casual clothes, the pale blue hospital johnny she'd changed into too loose for her small frame, the swell of her belly more obvious now, even through the thin blankets that covered her.

And she was very pale; underneath her spray tan, her skin was the color of a tissue.

"The attending will be in here directly, Mr. and—ah, Mrs. Baldwine." The nurse who'd brought him in focused on Chantal. "Is there anything we can do to make you more comfortable?"

"What's going to happen next?" Chantal stammered. "What about my baby . . ."

"The blood tests will take about a half hour, and I'll let the attending talk to you about next steps—but I imagine we'll do an ultrasound."

"Am I losing the baby?"

"We're going to do everything we can to help you, Mrs. Baldwine."

And then they were alone, the glass door shut, the drapes drawn.

"You are so cruel," Chantal sniffled. "You are so mean to me."

Lane sat forward and scrubbed his face. The urge to remind her of every awful thing she had ever done, not just to him but to Easterly's staff and every waiter and waitress that had ever been within a Cosmopolitan's order range of her, was nearly irresistible. But if she kicked him out, he was never going to know what was really going on.

She had lied before about pregnancies.

"Let's just get through this," he said through gritted teeth.

"And afterward . . ." She swallowed hard. "Perhaps we can have a future together . . . a true future, without interference from third parties."

Is that what you call fucking my father, he thought. Interference?

And as far as he was concerned, the only future they had was signing the divorce papers that were going to terminate the mistake he'd made when he'd married her.

"Lane, we don't have to end our marriage."

Keep your mouth shut, old boy, he told himself. Just shut the hell up.

Chantal started to say something else, but then her voice was strangled by a moan. And suddenly, she jerked one of her legs up. "Get the doctor! Get the doctor!"

As Samuel T. followed Gin into the elevator of his penthouse's high-rise, he was consciously aware of everything about the woman: The way her hair gleamed in the illumination falling from the inset lights above them. The smell of her perfume and that hand lotion she always used whenever she washed up. The perfect fall of her peach silk dress and the glimmer of gold at her ears and across her throat.

She wasn't wearing a scarf today and he stared at her neck.

The bruises had faded already—or at least they appeared to have faded. There were fresh ones on that wrist of hers, however.

The subtle *bing!* that announced they had reached the top floor brought his attention to the button panel; as the doors opened, he retracted his key out of the slot that allowed you to get all the way up.

"I don't know how you do it," Gin said as she walked forward onto his thick carpeting.

"Do what?"

While the elevator closed itself back up and disappeared, he watched her body move across the wide-open living space to the bank of floor-to-ceiling windows that looked out over the Ohio River toward Indiana's farmland. She was such a stunner, those legs so long and smooth, her ankles tiny, her high-heeled shoes dainty. Her hips were likewise an erotic swell, her waist the kind of thing he knew damn well he could span with his hands, her shoulders the perfect break for that hair of hers.

Amidst the modernist, monochromatic decor, she was everything vibrant and sensual.

She glanced back at him. "Have that thing open right up into your space."

What the . . . ? Oh, the elevator.

Samuel T. shrugged and went across to the bar. "I think of this as a hotel room that I happen to own. It's not my space."

"Someone could come up here."

"Not without this, they couldn't." He flashed her the key and then disappeared the thing into an inner jacket pocket. "What's your noon tipple?"

"You've forgotten?" She sauntered over and sat down on one of the pale gray leather sofas. "I'm hurt."

"Wasn't sure if you'd taken a new preference."

"I haven't."

Unlike the farm, which was filled with personal effects, family antiques, and things that mattered to him, this two-thousand-square-foot anonymous enclave was nothing but a party venue, an existentially vacant place to crash after he'd been out all night downtown.

What it did possess, in spades, however, was every top-shelf liquor there was on the market.

Opening up a wine cooler the size of a Sub-Zero refrigerator, he took out a bottle of Krug Private Cuvée and then he snagged the LB Crème de Cassis from the room-temperature lineup on the shelves. The cassis went into the flute first, after which he peeled off the foil from the Krug, twisted the cork until a controlled *pop!* was released, and filled the rest of the way to the lip with the bubbly.

He chose some Bradford Family Reserve for himself.

He and his people didn't drink anything but Bradford.

Crossing the distance between them, he handed her glass to her and waited as she held it up to the light, inspecting the color.

"Perfect."

"You are a spoiled brat, you know that."

"Tell me more. I'm in the mood for revelations, and I know that you lawyers love hearing yourselves talk."

Samuel T. sat on the other end of the sofa and crossed his legs at the knee. He couldn't take his eyes off of her and knew . . . *knew* . . . that he was the addict who had once again resolved to quit—yet was weakening by the second. Her with her haute couture clothes on and her taunting airs was his crack pipe and his needle, his rolling papers and his rolled-up hundred-dollar bill.

Her naked and on top of him?

That was his undiluted narcotic.

God, when he'd found out she was marrying Richard Pford—and then when she'd actually gone and done it? He'd been so angry, he'd vowed to fuck a woman in every place he and Gin had ever been together.

It had been, and was going to continue to be, a veritable travelogue of orgasms, the kind of thing that would keep him busy for six months or a year.

And he still intended to complete that itinerary with plenty of volunteers. But somehow, seeing her in that cemetery had chipped a hole in his facade of strength and intention to remain at a distance.

Yes, because grave markers and statues of saints and crosses were just so sexy.

Then again, Gin could have been anywhere, wearing anything, and she would have rocked his world. And the trouble with his plan for revenge? For his idea of working out his aggression with other women? No female had ever come close to Gin for him.

It was like treating a filet mignon withdrawal with Burger King.

"Where's your husband?" he heard himself demand.

"You already asked me that." She took another sip, her lips lingering on the knife edge of the flute. "And I told you, he's working. Are you going to offer to be my protector against him again? Volunteer to put yourself in harm's way to keep me safe?"

Tough, taunting words. But there was pain in her eyes, even as she tried to hide it.

God, he wanted to kill that sonofabitch.

"Well?" she prompted.

As Gin cocked an eyebrow the way she used to, and spoke the kind of words in the sort of tone she always had, he knew damn well they were both reminiscing on how they had been with each other. All that was gone now, though: She lacked the energy and he no longer had the inclination to get into one of their old dogfights.

"I will always come if you call." He threw back his bourbon and surged to his feet. Back at the bar, he poured himself a second. That was more like a second and a third together. "You know that."

"You could just bring the bottle with you," she drawled. "More efficient."

"I'm still drunk from last night."

"Who were you with."

"Nobody." Which was not exactly a lie. Prentiss/Peabody/Whomever hadn't mattered to him. "And you?"

"Richard was traveling. He came back this morning."

As Samuel T. walked back across to the sofa, he didn't return to where he had been. Instead, he went over to stand in front of her . . . and then slowly knelt down.

Gin tilted her head and regarded him with a heavy-lidded stare. "You look good like this, Samuel T. On your knees in front of me."

He swallowed nearly half the bourbon in his rocks glass before putting what was left aside. Then he slipped his hands around the backs of her calves and stroked his way up under the hem of her dress.

"I thought we weren't going to do this anymore," she said in a husky voice.

"Me, too."

"I told my husband I was going to remain faithful."

"Then you lied to him."

"Yes, I believe I did."

With a graceful arch, she loosened her body for him, her legs parting so that he could move his hips in between them. Her eyes were to die for, that blue stare so deep, he was instantly lost. And as her lips parted, he knew what was going to happen next:

He was going to kiss her, and he wasn't going to come up for air until he finished inside of her.

"I'm giving you a chance to stop this," he said in a guttural voice.

"When?"

"Right now. Tell me to get off you."

"Is that what you want me to say?"

"No."

"Good." She held her Kir Royale off to the side. "Because I don't want you to stop."

She made no move to meet him halfway, so he had to bend down to her mouth . . . and that subtle defiance made him nuts—and drove him wild. She was so contrary and always out of reach, the hunter in him ever in pursuit of her, even as he held her in his arms. And that was the difference. All other women begged him to stay. Gin? Challenged him to keep up.

And oh, God, her lips were just as he remembered, and exactly how he never forgot, soft and yet unyielding. He kissed her so deep and so long that he had to break things off to get in a draw of air.

"Why do you always taste like my bourbon when you kiss me?" she whispered.

"Because we're usually drunk and I have impeccable taste."

"Ah. That explains everything." When he went to kiss her again, she held him off by touching his chest. "Why did you bring me here?"

He curled his hips into her so she could feel his erection. "I would think that is self-evident."

"We could have gone to the farm."

"It was farther away."

"We could have gone to Easterly."

"Not private enough."

"My family's estate has more doors than most hotels." She smiled. "Why not your office? We've had a lot of fun there and I know you always keep alcohol in the lower drawer of your desk."

"Not the Krug, I don't, and you can't stomach cheap champagne. Besides, my secretary is getting a little tired of having to turn her radio up so she drowns out your moans."

Gin laughed. "She is so prudish."

"Something you've never had to worry about."

"So why this place, Samuel T., hmm?"

In lieu of answering, he dipped down and brushed the side of her throat with his lips. Moving his hands farther up under her skirt, he brushed the tops of her thigh highs—and then kept going until—

"You're not wearing panties," he growled.

"Of course not. It's eighty-five degrees out there and humid as the inside of a shower."

Samuel T. became unhinged then, his control snapping, his greed for her overtaking everything. With sure fingers, he unbuckled his monogrammed belt and unzipped his slacks—and Gin was clearly as impatient as he was. Moving herself down on the sofa, she brought them together at the very moment he angled his erection forward.

They both shuddered, and then he started moving.

As Gin lowered her lids, and somehow managed to hold the flute steady over his pale rug, she said, "I think I know why it's here"—she gasped—"and in this room."

Through gritted teeth, he asked why. Or maybe what his own name was. Who knew? She was always the best, always the tightest around him, always the sweetest and the slickest.

"My husband's office building . . . is right over there." She looked out to the view and indicated with the glass—while he was pumping into her sex. "In fact . . . his office . . . faces this building. . . ."

She began panting, just as he was, and she was so right.

He had brought her here so he could fuck her on this sofa . . . and look over her bobbing head while doing so at that sonofabitch Pford's office windows that were but one block down and over, at the top of the Pford Building.

"I don't know what you're talking about," he grunted.

To keep her from speculating further, Samuel T. reached between their bodies and thumbed at the apex of her sex.

As she orgasmed, her Kir Royale spilled all over the place. And wasn't that totally satisfying.

ELEVEN

The ultrasound machine was portable, a mini-Zamboni with a monitor that was rolled in by an orderly and operated by a tech. In order to accommodate it, Lane had to get out of the chair he was in, and while the exam was being conducted, he stayed to one side and averted his stare. One thing he could say for certain? Chantal was bleeding badly. From time to time, as her hospital gown was rearranged, he caught horrific glances out of the corner of his eye of what was going on underneath her, the padding soaked through.

Clearly in pain, Chantal flinched as they squirted her slightly rounded belly with clear gel and got some kind of transducer going on her. And the tech stopped periodically, tapping a little rolling ball on a keyboard to take pictures that, at least to Lane's eyes, looked to be nothing but gray and black smudges.

"The attending will be in in a moment," the tech said as she wiped the gel off with a paper towel.

"Where's the baby?" Chantal's head thrashed back and forth on the thin pillow. "Where's my baby?"

"The attending will be right in."

As the tech was leaving, she spared him a quick glance, and he was surprised at the compassion on her face.

Maybe Chantal hadn't been lying. At least not about the pregnancy.

"This hurts," Chantal groaned. "The cramping . . ."

Lane sat back down in his chair because he wanted to afford her some dignity, and as she sawed her legs like that, he kept catching sight of the blood.

"Lane . . . it hurts."

Her face was pale, her lips white, and she kept gripping her midsection like someone was trying to saw her in half. Gone was any calculation. Hostility. Poor-little-rich-girl drama.

"*Lane* . . ."

He lasted another minute and a half, and then he burst up, yanked back the curtain, and opened the glass door. Sticking his head out into the corridor, he flagged a nurse down.

"Hey," he said, "can she get some pain medication? She's really hurting?"

"Mr. Baldwine, the attending is coming right away. I promise you. You're next to be seen by her."

"Okay. Thanks."

Ducking back in, he went over to the chair, sat down again . . . and when Chantal threw out her hand, he took it because he didn't know what else to do. "The doctor's coming. Right away."

"I'm losing the baby," she said with tears in her eyes. "I didn't hear the heartbeat. Did you? The machine was silent. When I went last week, you could hear the . . ."

As she began to weep, he didn't know what to do. Then again, in

the two-plus years they'd known each other, he wasn't sure they'd ever shared a real, honest moment together. And it did not get more real than this.

"Am I going to die?" she said.

Where the hell was that fucking doctor? "No, no, you're not."

"Promise me? That I won't die and the baby is okay?"

The fear in her eyes and her voice stripped her bare to him, revealing her as more than an adversary—and for some reason, he thought about when he'd seen her for the first time at that garden party. He'd only gone because there were going to be drinks and he'd always felt like less of an alcoholic with a bourbon in his hand at two in the afternoon if he were around a bunch of other people doing the same.

The sun shining on her blond hair had been what had gotten his attention.

And he would never have guessed then that they would end up here, in these circumstances.

"You're not going to die."

In the silence, she just kept staring at him as her body contorted this way and that. Who knew if she had ever loved him—or loved his father. Maybe it was all a gold-digging scheme gone bad, and yes, she had done a horrendous thing ending her previous pregnancy. But as her pain continued to ramp up, the suffering she was in took precedence over her past misdeeds.

Lane reached out and brushed a tear from her blotchy cheek. Now her makeup was melting, black smudges forming under her eyes.

"I'm really sorry," he said roughly.

Chantal looked away and shuddered. "This is my fault."

The glass door of the treatment bay opened, and a young woman dressed in scrubs and a white coat came in. "Hi, you all. How are we doing?"

Dumb question, he thought. How do you think?

Lane dropped Chantal's hand and rubbed his palms on his thighs. "She's in pain—can you help her?"

"What about my baby?" Chantal begged. "Where is my baby?"

The attending went over to the bedside and put her hand on Chantal's shoulder. "I'm so sorry, but—"

"Nooooo . . ." Chantal shook her head on the thin pillow. "No, no, *no* . . ."

"—we didn't find a heartbeat. I'm afraid you've lost the pregnancy."

Chantal exploded with tears, and the doctor said some more things about follow-up appointments, and Lane tried to keep track of everything.

Okay, good, there was going to be paperwork with notes on what needed to be done next.

After the doctor left, Lane took out his phone. When he'd moved up to Manhattan—or fled Charlemont, was more like it—he hadn't erased any of his Kentucky contacts.

When he found what he was looking for, he triggered a call.

A female answered tersely on the third ring. "Well, this is a surprise, Lane."

He took a deep breath. Chantal's best friend hated him, and he wasn't fond of her, either. But that was hardly important. "Listen, I need you to come down to the ER at University Hospital. . . ."

After Lizzie got back to Easterly, she ended up in Chantal's old bathroom again—but this time, she meant to go there as opposed to her just taking advantage of the nearest loo.

As she started to go through the cabinets, drawers, and shelves, she couldn't believe what she was looking for. Then again, she hadn't

been about to ask a state policeman in his squad car to pull in to a Rite Aid and hang out while she bought herself a pregnancy test.

Especially not with Sutton Smythe in the backseat.

"Jeez, talk about well-stocked," she muttered as she found enough Q-tips to clean the ears of an entire junior high school. "Zombie apocalypse comes and we're going to be stinking beautiful."

There were backup bars of fancy soap and pots of facial creams with French labels and bags of cotton balls. Under the sinks, she found lineups of shampoos and conditioners, and hair dryers and curling wands and straighteners. Behind the mirrors, there were prescription pills and laxatives and astringents.

She had assumed her best chance of finding something like a Clearblue or a First Response or whatever the damn things were called would be in here. Certainly, the woman had recently wondered whether or not she could be pregnant.

But no. Nada.

"Crap."

As Lizzie shut the double doors under the basin on the left, she decided she needed to woman up, get in her truck, and go out herself.

Pivoting away, she headed for the exit—and decided to check the tall closet by the shower on a whim.

Holy terrycloth, she thought as she got a gander of the stacks of towels. "Of course. More than you'd have in an NFL locker room, except in shades of pink—oh, bingo."

In a wicker basket by the folded washcloths, she found what she was looking for, along with a bunch of UTI tests and Monistat boxes.

She wasn't taking the damn thing in this bathroom, however.

Tucking the Clearblue box in the folds of her black dress, she hustled down to her and Lane's room and closed herself in. Her first inclination was to tell Lane what she was doing, but what if she was wrong and this was just the flu? Or stress? She would not only feel like a fool, she would regret getting him worked up over nothing.

Besides, she had no clue whether he'd be excited or if this would be more bad news on top of everything else that was going on: They had never talked about kids, either the having or the wanting.

Hell, she wasn't even sure how she felt about being pregnant— well, not that she wouldn't have the baby if she were—

"Okaaaaay," she said out loud. "Let's just get off the plank, shall we."

Marching herself into her own bath, she read the directions, broke out one of the two tests, and peeled the thing of its wrapper. After doing the duty on the toilet—and managing to not pee on her hand, which, as far as she was concerned, meant she was a genius— she held the end of the stick down and laid the test on the counter between the two sinks.

Her heart pounded against her ribs like it was scared of being alone in there in the dark.

Checking her watch, she tried not to stand over the thing. Passed a little time folding a damp towel. Flushed a stink bug down the loo.

Oddly, the sight of her toothbrush standing up next to Lane's in a sterling-silver cup caught her eye and held it. His was red. Hers was green. Both were Oral-B. Over a little farther, her hairbrush was next to his shaver, and his can of shaving cream was by her bar of Clinique facial soap. A hand towel they had both used was wadded up and left where it had been thrown by whoever had taken it off the rack.

It was all so good to see, even though it was a little messy: The daily-existence chaos was evidence that their lives were enmeshed.

Bracing herself, Lizzie glanced at the test.

When she saw the plus sign, she started to smile. Oh, my God. *OhmyGod.*

Mother, she thought. She was going to be—

Abruptly, she remembered Chantal standing in front of the Bradford family crypt, blood down the inside of her legs. It seemed like a bizarre twist of fate that she should be finding out she was pregnant while the other woman might well be losing her child.

What was Lane going to think about this?

Putting her hands to her face, Lizzie looked at herself in the mirror and that happy smile faded.

Shit, what was she going to say to him?

TWELVE

s Samuel T. pulled the Jaguar around to Easterly's front entrance, Gin looked up at her family's great house. There had to be two hundred glossy black shutters on the thing, and those clapboards that covered all four sides? If you laid them end to end, she was willing to bet it would lead you across the Big Five Bridge over into Indiana—and possibly all the way north to Chicago.

"Well?" Samuel T. murmured as he hit the brakes.

"But of course. I am home."

She spoke absently because her mind was on other things. Especially as she shifted her stare to the second floor, to Amelia's bedroom.

"I am going to be out of town for a few days," she heard herself say.

"Are you? A little trip planned with the husband?"

"No."

"Shopping, let me guess."

She opened her door and got out. A burning headache, right between her eyes, made it difficult to focus on him. "Amelia needs to go back to Hotchkiss. She has to finish her exams."

"Ah, yes, your daughter." Samuel T. frowned. "She came in for the funeral, then."

"Yes." In fact, it had been more complicated than that. Amelia had lied and said she'd been kicked out, just so she could return home. "But she's moving back."

"For the summer."

"For the rest of high school."

Samuel T. recoiled and then glared out over the long hood of the Jag. "Did Pford refuse to pay?"

"I'm sorry?"

"Did that cheap sonofabitch say he wouldn't cover her costs?" When Gin didn't reply, he looked over at her. "And before you try and deny just how bad your money situation is, I'll remind you that I've seen your brother's financial disclosures as part of the divorce I'm handling for him. I know exactly what's going on."

"Richard didn't say no." Then again, she hadn't bothered asking. "Amelia wants to be home. She wants . . . to be with her family."

"She going to Charlemont Country Day in the fall, then?"

"Of course."

He nodded sharply as if that were the only proper choice. "Good. Amelia's a good kid. She looks a lot like you."

"I'm hoping she doesn't follow in my footsteps."

"Me, too." Samuel T. waved a dismissive hand. "Sorry, that came out badly."

And yet I do not disagree, Gin thought.

"She wants to go to New York City. To work in fashion."

"She needs a real college degree first. Then she can mess around doing artistic bullshit—assuming you and your husband can afford to feed, board, and clothe her while she's working as an intern at *Vogue*. But that's none of my business."

Gin rested her fingertips lightly on the top of the door. Then dug them into the slot into which the window had been retracted.

"What is it, Gin?"

Looking down at the seat she had vacated, she thought of the many times she had ridden side by side with him in this sports car. Usually it had been in the dark, not the daytime, and nearly always it had been on the way to, or on the way back from, one of their trysts. Or fights.

Then again, those two things had usually gone hand in hand with them.

"I meant what I said." Samuel T.'s voice grew remote and his eyes shifted away to the view down the hill to the river. "You can call me anytime. I will always come help you."

It took her a minute to realize he was talking about the Richard Pford situation. And she had an instinct to falsely reassure him that everything was okay.

Maybe because it was hard to admit that, once again, she had made a bad decision.

One of so many.

"I have to go," she said roughly.

"So go. You're the one hanging on to my car."

Gin had to pull her fingers out of the door, and the tips hummed from having been jammed into the mechanicals of that window.

For a moment, she had a notion that she would tip her chin up, quip some sort of witty rejoinder, and flounce off, confident in the knowledge that he would be measuring her ass and wishing he had his hands on it as she walked away.

She could not manage the show, however.

As she stepped back, Samuel T. put the convertible in gear. "Take care of yourself, Gin."

"Always."

He muttered something that was drowned out by the flare of the engine, and then he was gone down the hill, the sweet smell of gas and oil lingering in the still air.

Standing in the golden rays of the low sun, she waited for the two little red lights to disappear. Then she turned and looked up to Amelia's windows again.

As if the girl had witnessed the departure, one of the sashes went up and their daughter put her head out. "I'm all packed. Not that I had much. Can we go now?"

Gin took a second to memorize what the girl looked like, leaning out, that brunette hair flashing hints of auburn in the sunlight, her red and black blouse loose and flowing.

Mothers were supposed to be kind and nurturing. Whether they were stay-at-homes or full-time professionals . . . whether they were mavens of an organic lifestyle or proponents of Oreos and soda . . . whether they were strict or lax, vax or no vax, rich or poor . . . mothers were supposed to be the ones that kids felt safest around. They were the kissers of boo-boos, the cheerleaders of accomplishment, the dispensers of Tylenol and tissues.

Mostly, behind all the labels that were applied to them, good mothers were just supposed to be good human beings.

"What's wrong now?" Amelia said.

The exhaustion in the kid's voice had been well-earned by Gin's failure on pretty much all accounts: Amelia had been raised by a series of baby nurses and nannies, and then as soon as she was a freshman in high school, she had been shipped off to Hotchkiss like a piece of furniture that had to be re-upholstered before it could be put back in the parlor.

The girl's decision to come home permanently had been the first pivot point in her life that Gin had been involved in. And Gin had decided to drive her back to that prep school not just because the family's private planes were grounded, but because it was time for her to learn about who her daughter was.

What better way than fourteen hours in a car?

"Hello?" Amelia prompted.

"I'm sorry. I'll just gather a few things and we'll go right away." Best to leave before Richard got home from work. "Lane has the Rolls-Royce, but there's a Mercedes we can take."

"Good. I'd rather not be on campus in the Phantom. Too showy."

"Says the girl who's wearing Chanel." Gin smiled so that she didn't seem censorious. "You have quite a sense of style, you know that?"

"I get it from you and Grandmother. That's what everyone says."

For some reason, Gin couldn't process that. It was too painful. "You should probably say good-bye to her."

"She doesn't even know who I am."

"All right."

"So come on. The sooner I leave, the sooner I can come home."

Amelia ducked back in and shut the window.

And still Gin stayed where she was, the afternoon sun falling on her shoulders as if God Himself were laying His hands upon her in support.

Yes, she decided. It was time to tell them both the truth.

Amelia and Samuel T. had every right to know about each other, and it was more than appropriate for Gin to finally own up to her sin of omission.

And parts of it were going to be okay. The girl was most certainly going to gain a father. Samuel T. would absolutely do right by her, now and into the future.

But Gin would lose the man she loved forever.

Wasn't that what you did for your children, though? Sacrifice your happiness for theirs? Then again, was it really a sacrifice when she had created the problem?

It more like a well-earned punishment.

One thing was certain. Samuel T. was never, ever going to forgive her—and for the first time in her selfish life, she acknowledged that nor should he.

*T*he intensive-care unit was on the other side of the hospital campus, blocks away from the emergency room, but Lane didn't mind the walk through the various buildings. As he went along, following signs and consulting visitor desks along the way, he composed himself in the vain hope that Miss Aurora would be conscious and thus in a position to try to read his expression, his mood, his stress level.

As he crossed over Broad Street on yet another pediwalk, he looked down at the roofs and hoods of the traffic that was thickening as the workday ground to an end. Soon enough, spaghetti junction, that knot of intersecting highways by the Big Five Bridge, was going to be congested to the point of stop-and-go delays.

It wasn't anything like Manhattan had. Or L.A. But it was enough to annoy the locals.

Him, too, as it were. God, it was amazing how quickly the standards of Charlemont had seeped back into him. Here, if you were stuck at rush hour for ten minutes, it was a tiresome insult to your dinner plans. Up in New York City? You had to pack an overnight bag and a sandwich if you wanted to try to use the Long Island Expressway to go five miles at four twenty in the afternoon.

Craziness.

As he entered what he hoped was his last building, he stopped by the visitor desk and waited for the pleasant-looking older woman to glance up at him.

No-go. She was absorbed in her *People* magazine crossword puzzle.

"Ma'am?" he said. "I'm looking for the ICU?"

Without bothering to shift her eyes away from the little squares she was filling in, she muttered, "Down to the right, take the first set of elevators up four floors. There you go."

"Thank you."

Lane followed the directions, and as soon as he came to the elevators, he knew where he was by the atrium down below. The problem had been where he'd started from. As long as he parked in the garage off Sanford Street, he could find his way to Miss Aurora's room no problem.

When the elevator's doors opened, he caught a ride up with a man in a wheelchair, a woman in a hospital johnny who smelled as though she had been out for a smoke, and a couple who were holding hands and looking very nervous. The smoker and the couple got off before he did. He didn't know where the wheelchair guy was headed.

As Lane stepped out onto the unit, his stomach contracted like a fist. Following protocol, he checked in with the nursing station, and it was a relief to be nodded at and sent down the hall.

This meant his momma was still alive.

Like Chantal's emergency bay, the ICU rooms had glass walls and interior drapes that could be pulled for privacy. Unlike in the ER, there were dry-erase boards next to the entrances of the rooms, with the patient's name and the shift nurse and attending who were responsible.

Lane stopped when he got to the one that said *Aurora Toms*.

Actually, it read *rora Toms* because of a smudge.

He picked up the black pen that was on top of the board, uncapped it, and added the *Au*. When that just looked messy, he wiped out the whole thing with his fingertips and carefully re-did it so it was proper.

Miss Aurora Toms

Her surname was because she'd been one of Tom's twelve kids.

When Lane opened the glass door, a seal broke and a little hiss of air was released. Inside, there was a lot of beeping and very bright lights and so much medical equipment, it was as if she were in an operating room.

His momma seemed so tiny in the bed, her body shrinking as the tumors in her grew bigger and stronger—and his first thought, as he went over to her, was that she would hate the way her hair looked. Her short weave was messy, the bob's ends all this way and that, and he did what he could to straighten it.

His next thought was that she was never coming home.

She was going to die here, in this bed.

How could she not?

She looked so ill: Her eyes were closed, but he could tell they had sunk back into her skull, and her cheeks were so hollow, it was as if the bones were going to break through the flesh. There were count-less wires going under the top of the johnny she had on—and a port, too, pumping who knew what into some kind of vein or another. There were more tubes going into her arm. And still others, under the sheets.

You never realized how much the human body did on its own until you had to try and re-create its functions via external means.

He glanced around for a chair and found one all the way over in the corner, a non-priority afterthought for a patient whose continued existence was so iffy, visitors were not what people were worried about.

Bringing the thing around, he sat down and took her hand.

"Hello, Momma," he said as he rubbed his thumb back and forth.

He couldn't decide whether she felt warm or cool, and for some reason, the fact that his mind wouldn't vote one way or the other made him so frustrated, he wanted to scream.

"Momma, what can I do for you? Do you need me to . . ."

Lane thought about that Mercedes he'd gotten her just this past winter. She had been riding around in an old POS without four-wheel drive—the same car that she had had for, like, a decade, which she had stubbornly refused to replace—and an ice storm had struck, one that had been so bad, it had made the news all the way up north. As soon as he'd seen the reports, he'd called the local dealership, chosen an E350 4MATIC in U of C red, and had the sedan delivered.

Oh, how she'd bitched about it to him. Had maintained the thing was too expensive and flashy. Had insisted she was going to return it.

Except then she'd taken the car that Sunday to Charlemont Baptist and proudly parked it in the lot, telling people her boy had gotten it for her so she'd be safe.

Miss Aurora had never thanked him for the gift, at least not verbally—and that was her way. The special love she had always had for him had been in her eyes, though. And so, too, in her secret delight.

"Is there anything left undone?" he whispered as he stared into that face he knew so well. "Can you talk to me? Tell me what you need me to do before you go?"

On some level, he knew he should probably be focusing on all kinds of positive things, like how she was surely going to come out of this, and return to Easterly, and go back to ordering him and everyone else around. But he had of late become a fan of reality over optimism, and in his heart, he was well aware that this was the end—

As his phone started to ring, he reached into his inner chest pocket and silenced it.

"I just want to do right by you. Make sure everything is as you wish."

Miss Aurora had never taken a husband or had children of her own, but there were so many family members of hers in town, her brothers and sisters all married with kids for the most part—and then there was her extended network of cousins, friends, and the whole congregation at Charlemont Baptist. He wanted to be certain they all had a chance to say a proper good-bye—

"Lane?"

Jerking up, he wrenched around. "Tanesha. Hey. Hi."

He got to his feet and embraced the woman in the white coat and the stethoscope. Tanesha Nyce, daughter of Charlemont Baptist's Reverend Nyce, was in her late twenties and just completing her residency—and she had been an incredible source of comfort ever since Miss Aurora had been admitted.

As they pulled back, Tanesha smiled. "I'm glad you're here. She's listening to everything you say, you know."

Clearing his throat, he tried to look casual as he went over and sat on the chair again. The truth was, he felt wobbly on his pins and didn't want to fall over.

Because he couldn't not ask. And Tanesha wasn't going to speak anything but the truth.

It was not that Miss Aurora's doctors had withheld anything from him, it was just . . . it was time to find out how long they had— and somehow, hearing that no-doubt grim news from Tanesha seemed more palatable.

"So how are we doing?" he said.

Dimly, he was aware that he was rubbing his thighs, and he deliberately stopped his incessant palms.

"Well, let's see." Tanesha went across and smiled down at Miss Aurora. "How are we today, ma'am? It's Reverend Nyce's daughter, Tanesha. I'm just stopping by to say hello as I get off shift."

Her tone was light and casual, but her eyes behind her glasses were the absolute opposite as they scanned all the screens around the bed. And as she studied the numbers and patterns and graphs, Lane focused on her. Was she the reason Maxwell had finally come back to town?

Or had Max returned to help Edward kill their father?

Tanesha and Maxwell had always lit up a room whenever they were together, but the pastor's daughter and the Bradford family's rebel had never taken their attraction any further than sparks—at least as far as Lane knew.

Then again, as Reverend Nyce's daughter, would you really want to bring *that* home?

"How is she?" Lane repeated.

Tanesha patted Miss Aurora's hand. "I'll be back first thing tomorrow. You take care, Miss Toms, and get yourself some rest."

When Tanesha nodded at the door, Lane got up and followed her out—and noted that the doctor waited until things were fully shut before she spoke.

In a hushed voice, Tanesha said, "I'm sure her physicians have been updating you."

"I don't remember much of what they've said, to be honest. I'm sorry—it's just been . . . a blur. Plus I trust you more."

Tanesha stared at him as if assessing how much he could take. "May I be blunt?"

"Yes, and I'll thank you for it."

"You might want to hold the gratitude until I'm finished." Tanesha made a circle around on her right side, just under her ribs. "As you probably know, the tumor in the pancreas is quite large, highly abnormal, and has not responded to her current treatment. The metastasis in the liver is the same, and they have found further tumors in the superior mesenteric vessels. But even more problematic is this sickle-cell crisis. The chemotherapy kicked it off, and it hit her so hard and so fast—and is continuing to cause problems with her spleen and other major organs. There's just a lot of bad things going on for her right now, and as her healthcare proxy, I think you're going to have some decisions to make in the next day or so."

"Decisions?" As she nodded, he looked through the glass door at his momma. "What kind of decisions? Like to try a different chemotherapy or . . . ?"

"As in, when it's time to withdraw life support."

"Jesus." He rubbed his head. "I mean, I thought you all were trying to bring her out of this."

"Her doctors are. And I've followed her case every step of the way." A kind hand was placed on his forearm. "But if you want me to be truly honest, I think it's time to gather the family, Lane. And be efficient about it."

"I'm not ready. I can't . . . I'm not ready for this."

"I'm so sorry. I truly am. She is a very special person, who is loved by so many. My heart is breaking."

"Mine, too." He cleared his throat. "I'm not ready to lose her."

Back to the house, he thought. He needed to head back, get Miss Aurora's old-fashioned, handwritten address book, and start calling people.

This was the last thing he could do for his momma while she was alive and he'd be damned if he was going to let her down.

THIRTEEN

As Lane stepped out of the building the ICU was in, he was so distracted that he forgot he had left the Phantom all the way across the complex in the emergency department's parking lot. It wasn't until he had hunt-and-pecked for a good ten minutes in the Sanford Street surface lot that he realized, *Shit.*

Heading down the sidewalk in the heat, he tried to remember on what side he'd left the Rolls—

A shrill honk spun him around—and he jumped back onto the curb just as a Volvo screeched to a halt.

Oh, right, he thought. Green meant go for oncoming traffic.

Something he might have noted if he'd been paying attention at all.

When the coast was clear, he tried it again with the whole off-the-curb-and-cross thing, and resolved to focus better. Yeah . . . nope. All he could think of was Lizzie, and he ducked his hand into his jacket for his cell phone. When he got the thing out, he frowned at the missed call and voicemail notification on the screen. It was from a number he didn't recognize, one with an out-of-state area code.

After he tried Lizzie and she didn't pick up, he left her a message that he was coming home. And then he hit back whoever it had been. . . .

"Hello?"

The voice that answered was female, and accented with all kinds of South, and Lane realized he should have just listened to the damn message first. Then again, at least that particular space-shot move didn't leave him almost eating the grille of a Swedish tank.

"I believe you called my number and left a message?" He didn't give his name. If this was a wrong number, there was no reason to ID himself. "About a half hour ago?"

"Oh, thank you, Mr. Baldwine. Thank you for callin' me back. And I don't want to bother you none, but you did tell me t' call you if I needed help."

"I'm sorry, who is this?"

"Shelby Landis. At the Red and Black, if you remember?"

Lane stopped again, his hand tightening on his phone. "Yes, I remember you. But of course. Is everything okay out there?"

There was a pause. "I really need to talk to you. Somewhere private. It's about Edward."

"Okay," he said slowly. "I'm happy to come see you, but can you give me an idea what this is about?"

"I gotta show you something. Now."

"All right, I'll come to you. Are you at the farm?"

"Yessir. I'll be mucking stalls at Barn B for the next hour."

"I'm downtown and it's going to take me some time. Don't leave until I get there."

"I live over the barn. I ain't goin' nowhere."

Lane set off at a jog, even though the late-afternoon sun was scorching and the humidity was just short of a rain forest. By the time he got to the Phantom, he had sweated out his shirt—even though he'd removed his jacket a hundred yards into his run—and he cranked the AC as soon as he turned on the ignition.

The ride out to the Red & Black took almost forty-five minutes thanks to a gas tanker having jackknifed on the Patterson Parkway and then three tractors on the rural roads clogging things up. Finally, he was able to take a right between the two stone columns and start up the hill toward the matching red and black barns.

On either side of the winding drive, five-rail fences that were painted brown intersected rolling fields, the grass of which was, according to popular belief, tinted blue thanks to the limestone content in the soil. Beautiful thoroughbreds in browns and blacks lifted elegant heads in inquiry as he passed them by, a couple of the horses taking such an interest in him that they galloped along with the Rolls-Royce, manes flowing, tails pricked high.

At the top of the rise, the asphalt turned to pea-stone gravel and he slowed, not wanting to kick up rocks. There were a number of barns and outbuildings, as well as the caretaker's cottage, and everything had a gracious air of well-tended age to it, a reminder that Kentucky horse racing was a fierce, but old-fashioned and gentlemanly, pursuit.

Or at least it had been in Lane's grandfather's time. And the Bradford family was known for valuing and upholding the traditions of the past.

Lane parked in front of the middle of the three barns, and as he got out, he smelled freshly cut grass and wet paint. Sure enough, as he approached the open bay, he caught sight of a mower churning in the pasture closest to him and there was a caution tape around the jams he walked through, a fresh coat of red glistening on the trim.

Inside, the air was cool and he had to blink as his eyes adjusted. Several of the mares, whose heads were outside of their stalls, whinnied at his arrival, and that got the attention of the others until a chorus line of peaked ears and nodding muzzles and stamping hooves announced his presence.

"Shelby?" he called out, as he walked down the broad aisle.

He knew better than to try to pet anyone without a proper introduction—and the wisdom of this became evident as he came up to an enormous black horse who was the only one in the collection of maybe thirty with the upper portion of his door closed. And what do you know, the bastard flashed his teeth through the bars, and not in a hi-how-ya way.

More in like a hi-how-'bout-I-eat-your-head fashion.

And what do you know, the fact that the great beast had his forehead bandaged seemed appropriate. Made you kind of wonder what the other horse looked like after that bar fight.

"I thank you for comin'."

Lane turned around and thought, Ah, right. The little blond stable hand with the fresh face and the old eyes, who had stood off in the corner of the cottage as Edward had made his confession to the police. She had seemed remote then. Now, her eyes were direct—

The horse with the bad attitude kicked his stall so hard, Lane jumped and had to check that he hadn't been caught by a hoof that had come through the door.

"Neb, don'tcha be rude." The woman, who couldn't have been more than five feet tall in her barn boots, shot a glare big as a cannonball at the stallion. "Come away from him, Mr. Baldwine. He's cranky."

"Cranky? He's like Hannibal Lecter with hooves."

"Do ya mind comin' up to the apartment?"

"Not at all. Long as he doesn't come up the stairs with us."

Lane followed her into a tack room and then ascended in her wake a set of steps to the second floor—where the temperature was three hundred degrees hotter.

"I'm over here." The woman opened a door and stood to the side. "This is where I stay."

As he went in, he noted that she didn't call the place her home. Then again, it was little more than a storage room with a galley kitchen, the open space cooled by a window unit that hummed in the key of B flat. The sofa and chair didn't match and the two area rugs had nothing in common with each other—or those ragtag pieces of furniture. But it was neat and it was clean, and this woman with her blue jeans and her T-shirt had the same kind of quiet, hard-won dignity that Gary McAdams did.

"So what about my brother?" Lane asked.

"Can I get you some sweet tea?"

As Lane nodded, he was embarrassed that he hadn't allowed her to make the offer to him before he got down to business. After all, Southern hospitality wasn't owned by the rich.

"Yes, please. It's hot out."

The glasses were mismatched, too, one blue and opaque, the other a frosted orange with writing on it. But the tea was this side of heaven, as cool as the ice cubes that floated in it, as sweet as a breeze on the back of a hot neck.

"This is wonderful," he said as he waited to see if she would sit down. When she did, he followed suit in the chair across from her. "I'ma need a refill."

"I went to see your brother at the jail last night."

Thank God she was finally talking. "You did—how? Wait, Ramsey?"

"Yessir. Your brother . . ."

He waited for her to continue. And waited.

What, Lane wanted to scream. *My brother . . . what!*

"I don't think he killed your pappy, sir."

Through a sudden roar in his skull, Lane struggled to keep his voice calm. "What makes you say that?"

"See, Edward lied to the police. He hurt his ankle right in front of me."

"I'm not following, I'm sorry?"

"Remember when he told the police that he'd hurt his ankle down by the river when he was movin' the . . . ah, the remains? He said that he had to call the doctor 'cuz he hurt hisself then—but that wasn't what happened. I called Dr. Qalbi because Edward fell downstairs here in the barn before the murder. I was there, and I had to help him back to the cottage."

Lane took a sip from the glass just to give himself something to do. "But couldn't he have hurt the ankle again? Down by the river that night?"

"But he was walking just fine when I read about the death in the paper. And again, I know when that doctor came out because I was the one who phoned him. Edward hurt himself after the killing."

As Lane's mind raced, he blinked. A couple of times. "I, ah, so, this is a surprise."

Was Edward lying to protect someone? Or was Shelby's timeline off?

"There's another thing that don't make no sense," the woman interjected. "That truck Edward said he took to Easterly and put the body into? The winch was broke—the one he told them he used to get your all's pappy up onto the bed, it's broke."

Lane got to his feet and paced around, ending up in the cold blast coming from the AC unit. He thought back to everything that Edward had said to Detective Merrimack and the other policemen . . .

and also the evidence the CMPD had on him, namely, that he had destroyed the footage from the cameras on Easterly's garage side from that night. If only there was—

He pivoted back to his hostess. "Shelby, are there security cameras here on the property?"

"Yessir. And I asked Moe how to work them. There's a computer in the downstairs office that runs it all, and that was the next thing I was gonna tell you."

"Did the police ask to see anything? Any footage, I mean, from here."

"Not that I know of."

What the hell, Lane thought. Then again, the CMPD was short-staffed and they had a confession along with evidence of Edward's having tampered with the security monitoring files. Why would they need to go any further?

"Can you take me to the office?"

Ten minutes later, he was seated at a beat-up pine desk in a room that was about the size of a shoe box. The laptop was new, though, and the camera system was easily navigated, the six zones offering images of the entrance gates, each of the three barns, both front and back, and the two other exits on the farm. There was nothing on the caretaker's cottage; then again, the value of the enterprise was in the horse flesh, not anything inside that little house.

"He didn't leave the premises," Shelby said as she leaned back against the rough wall. "I checked the footage. The night that the newspapers say that your pappy was . . . he died? Edward dint leave this farm. There ain't no camera on the cottage, but that truck he says he used? It was parked behind this barn all night. And no one came in or left in any other kinda vehicle."

Lane sat back in the chair. "Well . . . shit."

Shelby cleared her throat. "No offense, Mr. Baldwine, but I don't care for cussing."

*I*t took almost two hours to go through all the files thoroughly, and in the end, Lane agreed with Shelby's assessment. That truck with the winch that was evidently broken had stayed put behind Barn B all night long. And there were no comings or goings of any other cars or trucks. No one even walked around the property.

What was he missing, though? He wanted to get all excited, but the cottage wasn't on a camera feed. Edward could have . . . oh, hell, he didn't know.

"Thank you," Lane said as he took out the USB drive that he'd saved all the files on.

"Your brother ain't no murderer." Shelby shook her head. "I don't know what happened between him and your all's pappy, but he didn't kill that man."

"I hope you're right." Lane got to his feet and cracked his neck. "Regardless, I'm going to take this to the right place and we're going to get to the bottom of it."

"He's a good man, your brother."

Lane had an urge to hug the young woman, and he gave into it, wrapping his arms around her quick. "I'm going to take care of this."

"Your brother gave me a job when I dint have anywhere to go. I owe him—even though he'll not be appreciatin' how I'm paying him back like this. But I gotta do what's right."

"Amen to that."

On the way back to Easterly, Lane tried Lizzie's cell phone again. Twice. When he got voicemail both times, he cursed and would have texted her something, but he was driving and decided a car wreck was not going to help any one of the nightmares he was stuck in.

He was about a mile away from home, heading along River Road in the direction of Charlemont's downtown, when the shore made a turn and he could look up at his family's estate on its hill. In the gloaming, the great white house was bathed in the last of daylight, as if it were being illuminated for a movie shoot.

Quite an impression, even to the jaded, and it was clear why one of his ancestors, he wasn't sure which, had decided to take that famous pen-and-ink drawing of Easterly and slap it on the front of every bottle of No. 15.

The best of the best. No compromises, no exceptions.

Would they even have a bourbon company after all this?

Instead of tangling with the press who were at the main gates, Lane took an early left onto the service and staff road that ran up the back of the estate's acreage. As he passed by the greenhouses where Lizzie and Greta cultivated plant material for the gardens and the terraces, he pictured his woman in and among the ivy sprouts and the flowers and the nascent shrubs, happily doing the job she loved. And then there were the fields that would be planted with corn and other crops soon. She loved being out on a tractor or a mower in the fresh air.

His outdoor tom girl. Whom his momma had approved of.

As a hot spear of pain shafted his heart, he focused on the lineup of 1950s-era houses that were cookie-cutter close in style and now, following the dismissal of the staff, all abandoned—except for Gary McAdams's cottage and then the one his brother was staying in.

As Max's motorcycle was gone, it was clear he wasn't around, and hopefully, the reckless bastard wasn't getting arrested.

One Baldwine behind bars was more than sufficient.

Easterly's service and delivery area was concentrated in the broad gravel courtyard in the back of the house, a sprawling vacant expanse which was bracketed on one side by the ten-car garage and the other by the business center. Lane parked the Phantom undercover in its slot and then walked over to the lineup of cars sitting grille-first against the converted stables. Miss Aurora's red Mercedes was showing a fine covering of dust and pollen that had been pockmarked by raindrops, and Lizzie's truck had a bed full of mulch. Gone were the Lexuses and the Audis of the senior executives who had worked on site with his father—and good riddance.

Lane pivoted and looked at the back kitchen door. Then he glanced up to the security camera mounted under the eaves.

What if Edward hadn't done it, but was covering for someone else?

Then there was only one other person it could be. And unfortunately, that suspect wasn't much more reassuring, on a family scale, than the one who was currently putting his feet up in jail.

Taking out his phone, Lane bit the bullet.

And called Detective Merrimack.

As the phone started to ring through the connection, Lane had to wonder if he was going to get one of his brothers out of prison . . . just so he could put the other one in it.

FOURTEEN

The best thing about doing eighty on a motorcycle was the blur in your peripheral vision. Everything took on a comforting haze, the landscape becoming only stripes of color: gray for the pavement, green for the shoulders of the road, velvet purple and blue for the twilighting sky overhead. And then there was also the heaven of the physical demands of controlling the bike. Leaning into the curves of the farm road, crossing the yellow line to get a better pull around tight corners, curling over the tank like it was an extension of your body . . . you could almost believe you'd left your demons behind.

You could almost believe that you found peace.

Maxwell Baldwine knew by the gathering darkness that it had to be about eight thirty, but he didn't care about the time. He was going to stay out all night. Find a bar, find a woman or two, get drunk, and wake up somewhere he didn't recognize.

In the three years since he'd been gone from Kentucky, he had seen more of the country than he had learned about at that fancy private school he and his brothers and sister had gone to in town. More even than from his four years at Yale. On his travels, he had been through the high and dry of Colorado, the low and humid of Louisiana, the flat and monotonous of Kansas, the salted humidity of California, and the drenching gray of Washington State.

He couldn't say he had found a home anywhere in his explorations. But that didn't mean he had one here in Charlemont.

Easterly was precisely that which he had been, and was still, trying to get rid of. And as he had traveled, with no goals or itinerary, he had been hoping that with each mile on the road, with every rootless week spent somewhere new and different, through all the odd jobs and strange people he'd done and met, he could somehow shed his ties to that mansion and all the people under its roof.

And yes, in his bid for personal peace, he had been prepared to let his relationships with his siblings go, leaving Edward, Lane, and Gin as collateral damage in the war to reclaim himself.

Or maybe it was more like to find himself in the first place.

In the end, however, he had been forced to recognize that everywhere he went, there he was—and the reality was that he could no more change what he had learned before he had left than he could alter his own flesh.

Destiny was a bitch with a bad sense of humor—

The sudden sound of a siren behind him was harmonized by a pair of screeching tires that he heard even over the din of his bike.

With a curse, he straightened and looked behind himself.

The Ogden County cop car was jumping out from behind a stand of trees, its joe-blow suspension causing it to lurch like a drunk as the officer at the wheel punched the accelerator.

"Motherfucker."

Max doubled down on his tuck and cranked his grip on the accelerator, sending the Harley to light-speed. The fact that the sunset's glow was draining from the sky helped as most cars and trucks were going to have their headlights on—so he was likely to see them.

Hopefully see them.

Like all adrenaline junkies, he entered a strange zone of calmness as he pushed the bike to the very edge of its function and structural integrity. The air rushing at him streaked his hair back flat as the helmet that he might have put on had he been required to by law, and the vibration veining its way through his tight palms into the locks of his forearms was like the rush of a drug. Soon, his crouch became not just desirable but necessary, the force of the speed he was going sufficient to peel him off the motorcycle if he tried to sit up.

Faster, and faster still, until the world became a video game with no consequences, the cop and the reality of him getting caught and losing his license, if not more, disappearing, left in his wake.

He wasn't scared of being apprehended. He didn't care if he crashed.

Nothing mattered at all.

The old rural road twisted and curved, dodging thick trees that had been preserved not out of a respect for their arboreal splendor, but because it was cheaper and easier to run the road around them. Farm pastures with buffalo in them and cropland that would have soybeans and corn on it soon provided the straightaways. And then there were more hairpins. And another straight section.

Max duck-checked under his arm. Well, well, it appeared that he had the Jeff Gordon of local cops on his ass, the guy right on his tail and closing in—

As Max refocused in front, he cursed, cranked the brake and leaned hard to the left.

It was either that or he mounted the back end of a horse trailer that was going about four miles an hour.

The bike heaved in the direction he asked it to go in and he went nearly parallel with the pavement, the tires just barely hanging on to purchase.

At the very moment, a car came around the corner in the opposite lane.

Horns. Tires. An indelible vision of the two people in the front seat of the Honda screaming as they braced themselves for impact.

In that moment, Max's life did not pass in front of his eyes. He didn't think of anyone or God or himself, even.

It was only emptiness, just like his soul.

And yet his body reacted instinctually, his heavy shoulders yanking the bike out of a free fall, his thick thighs grabbing on to the sides of the engine, every molecule in him staying in the saddle. If he fell off? He was going to end up with scrambled eggs for brains and maybe only half his arms and legs still attached.

Except, even as he confronted death and dismemberment, even as the motorcycle inched by the front bumper of the sedan and popped back in front of the truck and trailer, he felt nothing within himself. He was a void with a heartbeat, and shouldn't he find that depressing?

Max screeched around another turn and glanced over his shoulder. The cop had gone off the road, the squad car embedded in the brambles at the shoulder. No one was hurt, the truck rolling to a stop, the Honda pulling over, the policeman getting out . . . the near-miss and almost-awful slowing everyone but him down.

As the last of the light left the sky, Max roared off into the night.

Regrets stung his eyes with tears . . . but he blamed his wet cheeks on the wind.

*B*ack at Easterly, Lane was in the front parlor pouring some Family Reserve into a rocks glass. "Are you sure I can't tempt you?"

When his invited guest didn't answer, he looked across the formal room. Homicide Detective Merrimack from the Charlemont Metro Police Department was over on an antique silk sofa, his lanky body bent toward a laptop that had been put on the coffee table. During the course of the murder investigation, Lane had learned to dislike the guy, not because the detective was evil, but more because of his annoying habit of smiling like a kid who had just put the cat in a mud puddle and was attempting to reassure Mom and Dad that there were no problems, none whatsoever, to report.

"Well?" Lane said as he sat down in a bergère chair. "I mean, clearly my brother was at the Red and Black all night. So he couldn't have done it."

More waiting as the detective moved a finger over the mouse pad like he was reversing the footage.

After Lane had called, the detective had come right over, even though it was dinnertime. Or past it, actually. And Merrimack was dressed in what was clearly his standard work uniform of a white polo with the CMPD crest on the chest, dark slacks, and a loose windbreaker. With his military haircut, his dark skin, and his black eyes, he looked like the by-the-book operator he acted as, and Lane decided that that smile thing was a technique the guy had maybe been trained to do in a course entitled "How to Put Suspects at Ease."

Lane focused hard on that face, as if he could read what was going through the man's head as those eyes bounced around the screen. When that didn't work, Lane distracted himself by thinking about the dynamics in his family. Max was the only person who hated their father as much as, or maybe more than, Edward did. Yes, Edward's motive might have been a little more clear, but his personality had never been violent or explosive: Edward was more a tactician—and then there was the reality that he lacked the physical strength and coordination to move his own body around, much less anyone else's.

Max, on the other hand? Fights at Charlemont Country Day, in college, afterward. It was as if their father's temper had skipped all of the other kids and focused on Max exclusively. And Max truly didn't care about offending people, which if you extrapolated, could be generalized into something sociopathic.

Like the kind of distemper that could make somebody kill their own father.

"Well?" Lane prompted again.

Merrimack took his damn time before sitting back and looking up, and—yup, oh, there it was, that condescending smile.

"I'm not sure what you think you're seeing here, Mr. Baldwine."

Lane resisted the urge to speak slowly, as if the guy was a moron. "No one took the truck. Left the property. Drove off."

"And you take this to mean what?"

Are you fricking kidding me, Lane thought. "That my brother Edward could not have killed our father."

Merrimack steepled his fingertips and rested an elbow on a tasseled throw pillow. "The cottage is not covered by a camera."

"The exits to the property all are. And what about the truck?"

"There are a number of trucks."

"Including the one you impounded. As evidence," Lane snapped.

"Again, I'm not clear on what you think this proves, in light of everything else."

"My brother is a cripple. You think he snuck out under cover of darkness and jogged all the way here from Ogden County?"

"Look"—the detective motioned to the laptop—"I'm happy to take this downtown to the station and add it to the file. But this case is closed as far as we're concerned. We've already sent it to the D.A.—with your brother's confession."

Lane jabbed a finger at the computer. "My brother didn't leave the farm and those recordings prove it."

"I'm not convinced the footage goes that far." Merrimack popped the USB drive out of its slot. "But I'll take this to the D.A."

"Oh, come on, did we not look at the same thing?"

"What I saw was that nothing unusual happened within the sight of six cameras on a farm that's a thousand acres in size. The Red and Black has seven trucks of the same year, make, and model, with the same paint jobs, with winches on the back—and from the camera angle shown here, you can't tell the license plates of those three parked at the barn." The detective held up his palm as Lane tried to cut him off. "And before you tell me there are only three exits, I'll caution you that I've walked the property and identified at least a dozen cut throughs, lanes, and trails that will take you out to the county roads. You think your brother doesn't know all of them? Couldn't have taken one of the trucks from an outbuilding? He tried to get away with the murder by erasing the footage at Easterly. You're going to tell me that he didn't think about how he could leave the farm without being seen?"

"Edward said that it wasn't premeditated. That he came here just to talk to my father—if that were true, why didn't he simply leave the farm through one of the main gates? He had nothing to hide."

"And you believe that?"

"It's what that footage shows!"

"I'm talking about the premeditated part. You mean to tell me you haven't considered, even for a second, that that whole lack-of-malice-aforethought argument might not just be a smart guy trying to get the charge down so that he doesn't get the death penalty? Do you really know what your brother had in mind that night?"

"He didn't come with a weapon."

"He cut off that finger. With a knife."

"My father wasn't stabbed."

"My point is that who's to say your brother didn't sneak off the farm with a knife, in a truck with a winch, with the intent to kill the man—only to find that Mother Nature helped with his plan first."

"Edward couldn't kill someone the size of my father with just a knife."

"Most murderers do not have good plans, Mr. Baldwine. That's why we catch them." Merrimack got to his feet and smiled. "I'll turn this over to the D.A. But if I were you, I wouldn't plan on welcoming your brother home anytime soon. I've worked a lot of cases in the last decade, and they don't get much more solid than this one. I can understand your wanting to save the man, but that's just where things stand. I'll let myself out."

As the detective headed back for Easterly's front door, Lane wanted to scream.

Instead, he finished the bourbon in his glass . . . and poured himself some more.

FIFTEEN

*L*izzie woke up in the dark, and she was not alone. Strong arms were coming around her and she recognized instantly Lane's scent and warmth.

"What time is it?" she asked as she lifted her head. "Oh, wow. Dark. Like, really dark."

"I've been debating whether or not to let you keep sleeping." He stroked her waist. "I decided you might want dinner."

As she turned and faced him, a shimmy of unease tripped her heart up. "When did you get home—"

"I'm really sorry."

"About being so late? Oh, listen, I was asleep—"

"About what Chantal said to the medics. I made it clear to everyone down at the hospital that we were separated, also."

"It's all right."

"Not really."

Lizzie had to agree on that one, but what the hell was Lane going to say or do to change the situation? Chantal was on the periphery of their lives until the divorce was final, and it felt like the equivalent of a hammer over a bare toe: You could only hope the damn thing wasn't going to fall, and if it did, that it missed.

You couldn't take a deep breath, that was for sure.

"Are you okay?" Lane asked as he brushed some hair out of her face.

"Oh, absolutely. Sure. I mean, there's just a lot going on, and I really needed to sleep. Did, ah . . . did Chantal lose the baby?"

"Yes. She was actually pregnant."

Lizzie's stomach rolled. "Is she okay? I know that's a stupid question, considering everything, but I don't care who you are, that's a lot to go through."

"I'm not sure. I called her best friend and had her come down so Chantal wasn't alone. It was . . . horrible. I don't want to get too graphic here, but, God, I've never seen so much blood. And she was in a lot of pain. There's some follow-up stuff that has to happen. I guess they need to make sure she passed it all?"

As the bedroom went on a spin, Lizzie tried to keep calm. "I'm really sorry for her. No one deserves that."

"Yeah, there's no love lost between Chantal and me, as you know. But she was suffering."

There was a long pause, and Lizzie told herself not to jump into it. "Have you, ah . . . do you think about children? Of your own?"

Crap, had that really come out of her mouth?

Lane's headshake was immediate. "No. Absolutely not." Then he seemed to catch himself. "But you know, with you? That's a different story, of course. I mean, sometime in the future? I might be open to it if it was important to you, sure."

Wow, there was a ringing endorsement of the prospect.

"What about you?" he prompted.

"I can't say as I've given it much thought." Then again, she hadn't had to. Until now. "I've always been too busy working."

"Well, after the example my father set? I had decided no kids, for me."

"And yet you married Chantal because of it."

He shrugged. "I had to. I wasn't not going to live up to my responsibilities—and you know, I had certainly used protection with her. She swore it was mine, though, and sometimes things fail. I will never know the truth—and in quiet moments? And I hate to admit this? I'm . . . not glad, no . . . but I'm relieved that I don't have a child with her. Anyway, enough about Chantal and the past. I'm only about you and me and the future—and if, someday, you want to have kids, we can talk about it then."

"Well, that's good to know." Lizzie fixated on her nails, inspecting the tips. "Yup, very good."

God, her heart was pounding in her chest. And not in a happy way.

"So you'll never believe where I went after I left the hospital," he said.

The change of subject was good. Yessir—*ohdearGodwhatwasshegoingtodo*? "Um, Disneyland?"

"No." He smiled. "The Red and Black."

With the efficiency she had always valued in him, Lane shared what Shelby Landis, a stable hand out at the farm, had told and showed him. Then he talked about his meeting with Detective Merrimack. Lizzie followed most of the update, which was a miracle considering the banging and crashing in her head. Part of her wanted to just blurt out that she was pregnant, but like he didn't have enough going on already?

Take another test, she decided. In a day or two. Make sure before she jumped the gun.

Snapping back to attention, she caught up with the story. Wait, what was this about Edward? "Holy crap, this is huge."

"Not according to the police." Lane shook his head. "As far as Merrimack's concerned, they have their resolution to the case. The bus has left the station, as the saying goes."

Lizzie opened her mouth to comment—but then remembered something. *Shit, the test was still out on the counter in the bathroom.*

With a quick surge, she brushed his lips, rolled over him, and got off the bed. "Will you excuse me? Nature calls, you know."

He nodded and eased onto his other side as she hurried across the carpet. "I mean, what if Edward didn't do it? So who's he covering for?"

"Right?" she threw over her shoulder.

In the dim bathroom, she made sure that she kept her back to the open doorway as she scooped up the pregnancy test, the wrapper, and the open box.

"Did you see Miss Aurora while you were down there?" she asked to distract him.

"Yes. It's not good."

Lizzie froze with the positive stick in her hand. After closing her eyes briefly, she snapped back into action and went around the corner to the wastepaper basket. Picking up some Kleenexes and an empty bottle of her Pantene conditioner, she put the Clearblue stuff in the bottom and covered it up.

"So what does that mean exactly?" she said as she went across and opened the linen closet.

"It's time to bring the family in."

Lizzie stashed the box with the unused test underneath the towels. One advantage of having no maid service and doing the cleaning herself? She didn't have to worry about anyone else finding what she'd thrown out.

As she closed the door, she put her hand on her belly. The reality of miscarriages loomed, that image of Chantal on the steps of that crypt, looking down at herself in horror, the kind of thing that made nausea rise.

"Are you okay in there? Still feeling sick?"

"No, I'm much better." She ducked into the little private room and flushed the toilet for show. "Just waking up."

Back out in the bedroom, she went over and lay down beside him. "I'm so sad for you about Miss Aurora. I'm really sorry."

He put his arm around her and pulled her even closer. "It's killing me, to be honest. Seeing her there so damned helpless? It's as if she's already died."

"I'd like to go with you next time."

"Tomorrow. I'm going tomorrow—oh, shit, I have to meet with the board in the morning. Jeff and I are giving them an update. John Lenghe's cash infusion from that poker game has helped, but we need another way out of the crunch."

"What can I do to help? Short of winning Powerball."

"This is what I need." Turning to face her, he kissed her mouth. "And this . . ." Moving lower, he brushed his lips over her collarbone. "And this . . ."

Lizzie felt her body uncoil from its tension, but she knew that it was only temporary. As he loosened the side tie on her dress, she wanted him, needed him, was hungry for their connection. This time together wasn't going to change anything, however.

Fortunately, in the moment, that didn't matter to her.

Lane moved on top of her, and then their clothes were gone, nothing but skin and love between them.

Just as he was about to enter her, Lane pulled back. "Shoot, let me get a condom."

"It's okay—" As a look of shock hit his face, she shook her head. "Just, you know, pull out. I trust you."

"I'll be careful," he whispered against her lips.

Lane entered her with a roll of his hips, and she closed her eyes and arched into the pleasure. It was all she wanted to feel. Nothing else was welcome.

Lane was the only thing that mattered.

SIXTEEN

*P*ounding on the bedroom door woke Lane up and he jumped out of bed, twisting his ankle as he landed badly.

"Lane?" Lizzie asked in the dark.

"I've got it."

Buck naked and not giving a damn, he marched over, and opened things a crack. When he saw who it was, he cursed. "Richard, what the hell are you doing—"

His sister's husband pointed down the hall, in the direction of Gin's suite. "Where is she!"

Lane glared at the guy. "Will you lower your voice—my mother is asleep next door."

"As if she is ever awake."

"Excuse me—"

"Where is your sister? Is she out picking up men at the club—or maybe it's the street now—"

Lane shut the door on the man's face, grabbed a pair of boxers from the bureau, and yanked them on so hard, he nearly wedgie'd himself.

"Try not to kill him," Lizzie muttered as he headed back for the idiot.

"I make no promises."

Ripping the door back open, he nearly got his forehead knocked on as Richard warmed up for another round of pounding.

"My sister," Lane hissed as he stepped out and closed things up behind himself, "has taken Amelia back to Hotchkiss for her finals."

"You're lying."

"I beg your pardon?" Lane resisted the urge to grab the man by the throat and shove him off balance just on principle. "Look, I can assure you, when it comes to Gin and you, I do not have a dog in this fight. But if you insist on disparaging my sister's character, that is going to change quick."

"Don't threaten me, Baldwine. Your family needs me."

"How do you figure that?"

As Richard's thin face stretched into an ugly grin, Lane decided, based on the flush and the fact that it was after midnight, that the guy had been drinking.

"I could sink the Bradford Bourbon Company like that." The man snapped his fingers right in front of Lane's nose. "I'm your distributor. If I want, I can stop your product from reaching all retail outlets. If I choose to, I can block you from the shelves, from restaurants, from bars. Do you think the BBC has enough cash on hand to last through a couple of months of bad sales? I'm very sure it doesn't. From what I understand, you can't even afford to buy corn to make mash."

Okaaaaay, douchebag, Lane thought.

"We're going to be just fine," Lane bit out. "Do what you want for whatever convoluted reason you wish. But I guarantee you, we will handle it—now go the hell to bed or get out of my house. Either way, shut your mouth in front of my mother's door and stop disparaging your wife."

"This family is going under." Richard waved his arms all around, indicating the long hallway. "All of this? It's going away. You can't save any of it, Lane. You're nothing but a playboy slut, just like your sister—"

Annnnnnnnnd it was lights-out time.

Lane wasn't aware of snapping, but the next thing he knew, he had his hands around Richard's neck and was squeezing so hard, his arms were shaking. And Richard tried to fight off the attack, his fingers clawing at the hold on his throat, his body whipping back and forth like a fish on the line, but he couldn't break free.

"Cutting off," Lane gritted as Richard stumbled back. "You want to talk about cutting off? How's this for cutting off?"

As the other man tripped over his own feet, and his mouth gaped open, Lane followed Richard down as he fell in slow motion to the corridor's carpet—and still Lane cranked his hold tighter and tighter. Everything got channeled into the effort, to the point where, in the back of his mind, he had some thought he was going to murder the man—

"Lane!" Lizzie came rushing out of their bedroom. "Lane! What are you doing—"

"Go back in the room, Lizzie—go back in there and—"

"You're going to kill him!"

It was hard to disagree, especially as he'd come to the same conclusion. But he didn't stop.

Lizzie grabbed on to one of his arms and started to try to pull him off—and then, from down at the end of the hall, Jeff broke out of his own suite of rooms and came hightailing over.

"What the hell is going on!" the guy barked.

Lane wanted to scream at them to just leave him alone with his brother-in-law a little longer—at this rate, he was only going to need about five minutes. Just three hundred seconds, max.

Jeff had other ideas. He joined the fight to pry things free—and Lane kept the choke hold going for as long as he could. His woman was just as strong as his old roommate was, though, and the pair of them succeeded in getting him off of Richard, a bulldog no longer able to keep his jaws locked on the stick he'd claimed as his own.

As Lane went flying back and slammed into the wall, Richard rolled over and coughed into the carpet. His suit jacket had split open in the back—amazing, considering how baggy the thing was on him—and one pant leg was halfway up his pasty white calf.

Jeff got between them, splaying his arms wide as if he expected Lane to charge again. "Come on, buddy. What the hell are you doing here?"

Lizzie, meanwhile, went over to Richard. "Are you okay?"

Pford was coughing and dragging in air, a man who had nearly drowned on dry land. And when he could, he lifted his head. "I'm . . . going . . . to . . . ruin this family." His voice was harsh, his breathing ragged. "I'm going to make you all pay. Every one of you. All of you!"

Lurching to his feet, he stumbled down the corridor, bouncing off the wall, crashing into one of the decorative tables, tripping over his own wingtips again.

Lane put his head in his hands and let himself slide until his butt hit the carpeting. "You can back off of me now."

"You sure about that?" But Jeff stepped away. "And can I just say, you people in Kentucky—never a dull moment."

Glancing up at his old roommate, Lane noted the dark circles under the guy's brown eyes and the smudged black hair and the—

"You're still working?" Lane mumbled while he nodded at the

button-down and business slacks Jeff was wearing. "Or did you pass out in your work clothes?"

"I think it's important to remain professional at all times." Jeff took a load off in the hall, too. "And also I passed out reading spreadsheets."

"Again," Lane tacked on.

"Again."

After a minute, Lizzie sat down with them, her baggy T-shirt and set of boxers from his own closet—and he loved that. "So, boys, what are we waiting for?"

As if on cue, Richard stormed back out of his room and came at them like a freight train.

"Oh," she muttered, "this."

The man had a suitcase in one hand and that busted-up jacket in his other. "I'm leaving, but I'm coming back for my things. You can tell your sister when, and if, she gets home that I want the ring returned or I won't annul her. Don't worry, I won't ask for any money— I'm going to take it out of your fucking hides at the BBC."

Jeff spoke up. "What the hell are you talking about?"

"Wait and see, CEO. Just wait and see—oh, and this *is* personal. It's not business."

Richard lanked off, his long strides taking him quickly to the grand staircase. Seconds later, the front door was slammed shut so hard, they heard it all the way up on the second floor.

"He can't actually hurt us," Lane asked. "Can he?"

Jeff shrugged. "If he acts within the law, not really. But if he doesn't? The cash-flow analysis I just ran is as tight as we can get. He might be able to sink us."

"Even with John Lenghe's help?"

By some stroke of amazing luck, John Lenghe, who owned about half of all the corn and wheat crops in America, had offered the BBC financing while they rode out the cash crunch.

In spite of the fact that he'd lost a fifty-million-dollar-plus poker pot to Lane just last week.

Lenghe was the father Lane wished he'd had.

"Yeah, even with his help." Jeff peeled one of his eyes wide and looked to the left like he had an eyelash problem. "I was going to tell you this before the board meeting tomorrow. It's even worse than I thought it was. Your father's off-balance-sheet financing is all coming due. The bank debt is piling up left and right and there's no end in sight. Pretty soon, those creditors are going to start dialing their legal departments and when that happens? Paying for production essentials like corn and rye is going to be the least of our problems. We're going to be dealing with summary judgments for millions of dollars and bankruptcy."

As Lane considered the embezzlement, he had to admit his father had been crafty about transferring assets into his control. If the man had just written himself a bunch of checks from BBC accounts, it would have been clear that he was stealing from the company. Instead, he'd identified other businesses and endeavors around the world and put himself in an ownership position in those entities, using both BBC funds transferred into something call WWB Holdings as well as bank loans that had the BBC as collateral. When those other companies failed—or didn't even exist—as John Lenghe had disclosed? The banks still wanted to get their loans paid off and had the legal right to come knocking on the BBC's door for all that interest and principal.

Lane shook his head. "My father's ability to pick bad investments was unparalleled."

"He was not business savvy, for sure." Jeff got to his feet and stretched, his back cracking. "If you don't mind, I'm going to take a shower and go to bed so I can get up and take a shower and go back down to headquarters."

"As chair of the board, I'll be doing the same."

"Listen, it could be worse. We could not have paid off all the trustees with the money I gave you so that they'd vote the way we need them to. Best two and a half million I ever spent, getting those country-club idiots off my back so I can save your company. Second move was firing all those senior vice presidents. If three times are a charm, my next decision is going to be epic."

Lizzie glanced at the guy. "Let's hope it's not wasted choosing between two conditioners in your shower. You don't want to blow that kind of firepower on Pantene versus L'Oréal."

Jeff regarded her for a moment. "I really like you, you know that." He looked at Lane. "You don't deserve her, just to be clear."

"As if I am not fully aware of this."

As the Bradford Bourbon Company's new CEO got up and ambled off down the hall, Lane took Lizzie's hand and searched for the right words. "I want to say something."

"Okay." When he didn't go any further, she gave him a squeeze. "And that would be?"

"I wish I knew what it was. That's my problem. I want to reassure you everything's going to be okay, and it's like . . . if I could only find the precise combination of words, they will defuse the bomb, you know? Put the pin back in this grenade. But that's just crap, isn't it."

"I'm not leaving you."

"You sure about that?"

"Yes, I am."

"Thank you." He let himself fall back so he was lying on the runner and looking up at the crown molding on the ceiling's edges. "You know, I've never done this before."

"Tried to turn around a company?"

"Laid here." He lifted his head and smiled at her. "Also never saved a company. But at least I have Jeff's help on that one."

Lizzie stretched out beside him and the two of them stayed like that for the longest time, like two gingerbread men on a cookie sheet, arms and legs out straight, feet lolling to the sides, shoulders and hips flat.

"I guess we should go back to bed," he murmured as he listened to the house creak. "I mean, it's pretty stupid to be just lying out here in the hall on the carpet. Especially considering we have that nice, far more socially acceptable bed, oh, about twenty feet away. Although granted, we would have to open a door to get to it, and that will require a lot of energy."

"Or we could just screw it and stay here. Who's going to care?"

"I love you." As she laughed a little, he sensed the tension between them because of its current absence. "I'm glad you're here with me."

"So you know what this is like?"

"The seventh ring of Hell?" When she laughed again, he twisted to the side and kissed her. "Wait, I know. You're going to tell me this is like being on a beach. Without the sand. The ocean. The sun . . . okay, so this is not like being at Wianno."

"This is having meatloaf for breakfast."

Lane popped his brows. "Wow, and I thought my Cape Cod metaphor was a left fielder."

"We're accomplishing the same thing as being in bed, right? I mean our stomachs don't recognize the difference between having meatloaf at seven in the morning or seven at night."

"I think my brother Max would argue that depends on how much tequila you've had the evening before, but I'm kind of splitting hairs here."

"You get my point, though. We're off our feet, relaxed and pretty comfortable. Does it really matter that we're out in the hall? I mean, who's coming with a clipboard and a list to check off that we're not in our room? Ohhhh, you get a demerit because—"

"Have I mentioned how much I love you lately?"

"I'm not sure. How about you tell me again—"

When the muffled sound of a ringing phone cut her off, Lizzie went quiet.

"Shit, that's my cell." Lane jumped to his feet. "Miss Aurora."

*T*wenty minutes later, Lane squinted and leaned into the Rolls-Royce's windshield as he pulled in to the White Snake's parking lot.

Most of the vehicles in the bar's spots were trucks, but there were a couple of motorcycles, and as he parked the Phantom between two Fords, he saw Max's Harley right in front. Opening his door, Lane was about to get out when the bar's entrance was thrown wide and three big-and-burly's pulled a Richard Pford and stumbled onto the walkway. They noticed the Rolls immediately and started talking among themselves—like they were of half a mind to try to steal it.

Lane reached across to the glove compartment and took out the handgun kept in there.

When he stood up from behind the wheel, he tucked the weapon into the small of his back. Then he locked the Phantom, its Spirit of Ecstasy disappearing into the hood.

"That your car?" one of the three-hundred pounders asked him.

"Just an Uber."

"What?"

As he brushed past them, they were sweating so much alcohol out of their pores, he nearly got a contact high. And fortunately for them, they let him go on about his business.

Inside, the White Snake was your standard-issue beer-bucket dive, the redneck hangout sporting Coors and Bud neon signs on its rough wood walls, and seventies-era carriage-house chairs around tables that looked like they had been rescued from the bottom of a bog. Given that it was two a.m., there were only fifteen people in the place, but they were hardies who had been drinking since happy hour at five—in other words, they appeared to be only two functioning brain cells away from a coma.

Unfortunately for the clientele's livers, the bartender, who was like a bearded Jabba the Hutt, was still throwing the hooch behind a beat-up stretch of countertop, his meaty hands refreshing those pitchers with pulls of golden-bodied, white-froth-topped domestics.

Yup, this was definitely a fuck-craft-beers establishment. And as the piped-in music registered, Lane thought of *The Blues Brothers* movie, where the woman in the honky-tonk bar says of its music, "We got both kinds. We got Country and Western."

Looking through the dim, smoke-filled air, it was clear that the no-smoking laws were being ignored—either that, or someone had spontaneously combusted thanks to the hot wings.

Where the hell was he, Lane thought. That SOB was—

In the back corner, an argument exploded between two men, the pair of them standing up and knocking their chairs over, a woman leaping out of the way—and yet somehow being quick thinking enough to take the beer pitcher with her.

But at least it wasn't Max: Neither of them had a beard.

Lane walked through the place, trying to be discreet. Except no one paid him any mind, and he didn't find his brother.

Heading back over to the bartender, he had to wait as a couple of Coors were drained from the tap and handed off to a pair of women who stared at Lane like they were hoping to be chosen for a school kickball team.

He ignored them and nodded at Jabba. "I'm here for my brother."

"Do I look like I know you or your kin?"

"He's tall, bearded, tattooed?" Yeah, like that cut through the other candidates. "And he rides a Harley."

Annnnd that was going to help, too. Although in Lane's defense, it was two o'clock in the goddamn morning, and he wasn't thinking much more clearly than anyone else in the joint.

"Check in the back if you don't see 'im." The bartender nodded his head to the side. "Go past the bathrooms and down that hall."

"Thank you."

Lane walked all the way to the rear and proceeded past the women's room, which had a broken sign, and the men's room, which had a broken door, to a barely lit storage area so choked with crap, it could have been on episode of *Hoarders*.

He was about to take his brother's name and give it an f-bomb workout when he heard the moan.

From behind the stacks of extra chairs and tables.

Following the sound, Lane looked around the barrier of cheap wood and chipped varnish—

—and got a gander at his brother braced like Leonardo da Vinci's Vitruvian man, arms out and feet spread, with a woman on her knees in front of him.

"Christ, Max, what are you doing?"

His brother snapped his lolling head up. "Oh, hey, Lane."

Like they'd unexpectedly met in the middle of a shopping mall or something.

The blond just continued working on things, her halter top and blue jeans covering at least some of what would have gotten her arrested—although this lewd sex act in a public place could well have led to handcuffs, clothes or no clothes.

Please let him not have paid for this, Lane thought.

"Come on," he muttered as he turned away, "let's go."

"I won't be long."

"What the hell, Max!" Lane went back around to the far side of the tables and chairs—because there was no way he was having a conversation with the guy while watching all that. "You called me to come get you."

"I'm drunk."

"No shit—"

A man with a handlebar mustache, arms like an ape, and faded military tattoos came tooling into the storage area like he'd been told someone had said something bad about his momma in this land of discarded junk.

"Reggie! Where you at, Reggie!"

Oh, dear God, please let that blond's name be Agnes. Colleen. Callahan—anything but Reggie.

"I know you back here, girl." The guy stopped short as he noticed Lane. "Hey, you seen a blond—"

Reggie came out from behind the tables and chairs, making like she hadn't just been doing anything even remotely blow-ish or job'y. "Baby, I was just—"

Naturally, Max emerged zipping up his fly.

Holy. Jealous. Former. Marine.

Reggie's BF, or whoever he was to her, went for Max like the dumbass was an intruder in a private home, but Max was ready for it. As fists flew, big bodies slammed into things, toppling stacks of furniture, knocking over empty kegs and crates of glasses, crushing debris on the floor.

Lane had to admit that the two of them were far better at the fighting than he and Richard had been. These guys were professionals, not amateurs, and Reggie—just like the woman who had deftly saved a pitcher out in the bar proper—knew exactly where to stand so she avoided the churning men. She even took a cell phone out of her back pocket, turned the camera on herself, and checked her lipstick.

I don't have time for this, Lane thought.

Just as the boyfriend slammed Max back into a door, Lane took the gun out of his waistband and went across to the altercation.

Placing the muzzle at the boyfriend's temple, he said, "Let him go. Right now."

And didn't that put everything on a freeze frame.

"I got this," Max slurred. "I'm winning this—"

"Shut the hell up." Lane focused on the Marine. "I'll get him out of here and you won't have to worry about him ever coming back. *Ever.* In return, you let us walk."

"And if I don't?"

"Then I'll blow your head off. Trust me, after the week I've had, it will be the least dramatic thing I've had to deal with."

SEVENTEEN

"I'm telling you, I had him."

As Lane punched the Phantom's accelerator and sped him and his idiot brother the hell away from the White Snake's den of ridiculousness, he didn't bother replying to that. Then again, there wasn't much to argue with in the passenger seat. Next to him, Max was slumped against his door, with the only thing keeping him upright being the belt that cut across his chest.

"I'm serious, Lane. . . ."

The words drifted off into an exhale that was part curse, part snore. And so help him God, Lane was ready to open that door and let the bastard fall out onto the side of the damn road. He was so sick of cleaning other people's messes up—and more than that, there was important shit going on, all kinds of things that were a helluva lot more critical than a drunken bar fight.

Plus, hello, in the last two nights, he'd taken a gun out twice and gotten into a physical altercation himself. He did not like the trend. He wasn't Maxwell, goddamn it.

"How'm I get the bike?" Max asked.

"We'll go back tomorrow. See if it's still here."

"Don't tell Edward 'bout this, 'kay?"

As if they were still kids, and this was another of Max's stunts.

"Edward is not going to care," Lane snapped. "He's too busy rotting in jail to worry about you as a grown-ass man getting into a fight in a frickin' bar because some woman you don't know and don't care about is giving you head."

"Okay, let's not blow this out of proportion." Max looked over. "Blow—get it?"

"What the *hell* are you doing, Max? Seriously, how old are you—"

"Like you haven't been in similar situations—"

"Not anymore. I grew the hell up."

As they stopped talking over each other, Lane came up to a three-way stoplight and put his left blinker on. In front of them was a housing development of million-dollar homes, the new colonials and brick Georgian-like houses clustered around man-made ponds with fountains that were under-lit. The property had previously been one of the grand old farms, back when Charlemont hadn't had suburbs.

If he hit the gas and plowed through the intersection, he and Max and the Rolls would end up in a lake.

Maybe it would sober Max up.

Tempting.

In the end, though, when the light turned green, he made the turn onto the four-laner that had been the city's main thoroughfare before the highway system had come along. There were no other cars out, and soon enough, he came up to the first of the strip malls of little shops and restaurants. Then there was a larger Kroger parking lot and a bank and a library branch.

"When are you leaving town?" Lane demanded as he came up to another red light.

"Trying to get rid of me so soon?"

"I just figured you'd be going." Lane glanced over. "You never stay put."

"Well, I can't stay here."

"Oh, yeah? You want to tell me why?" When there was only silence, Lane smiled grimly. "So I learned something today."

"What was that?" Max pushed himself upright like he was hoping the greater verticality would help clear his beer-brain. "Hopefully it was useful information."

"It appears that Edward couldn't have killed Father." Lane looked over again. "He didn't do it."

Max seemed to keep things cool, that bearded face not changing its expression, those eyes staying focused on the road ahead. "How you figure that? And he confessed, didn't he—"

As the light turned green, Lane wrenched the wheel and shot the Rolls into the parking lot of a BBQ place. Then he hit the brakes hard enough to jerk the seat belts and threw the engine into park.

"What the hell, Lane! You want to get us killed—"

Lane spun around. "Be honest with me."

Those pale gray eyes narrowed. But did not meet his own. "About what."

"Edward and Father and the murder. You were there, weren't you. You were part of it." As Max refused to answer, Lane wanted to grab the guy and shake him. "I know you and Edward met before Father was killed. A couple of days before, someone saw the two of you on the far side of the Ohio. You must have planned things then—or was Edward trying to talk you out of it?"

Max's big body shifted in the seat and he pulled at the seat belt. "I got to go—"

"You can't let Edward take the fall for this." Lane snagged the guy's arm, because he was worried Max was going to bolt. "Edward shouldn't have to clean up this mess—it's not like when we were kids. This is not a beating he's volunteering to take for you when you more than deserve one. It's life in prison, Max. If you did it, you need to man up."

"Can we just go back," the guy muttered as he fumbled with the belt's release.

"Why—so you can pull a runner in the middle of the night again? You're a coward. I don't know how you live with yourself—"

"Says the man who's spent a decade distinguishing himself by who he's been fucking. I can read headlines, you realize. Yale taught me that much."

Lane opened his mouth to hit that jab back as hard as he could, but then he stopped. "You know, for the first time, I feel like I'm really seeing you for who you are. And it's nothing I respect."

He popped the locks on the doors. "Go. I'm done with you—but know this. I'm going to get Edward out of jail, whether he wants me to or not—and even if it means you're in that fucking cell as his re-placement."

Max released his seat belt and gripped the door handle.

But instead of opening things up and falling out face-first onto the pavement, he just sat there.

After an eternity, he whispered, "I can't keep going like this."

"Damn right you can't." Lane banged the dashboard with his fist. "Come on, Max. Just tell me the truth. We can handle anything. We can get you a good attorney, and we can fight it—"

Max put his head in his hands and began to weep.

At first, Lane was so stunned, he just stared across the leather seats at his brother. He had never seen Max break down like this, the sobs wracking the man's strong body, the misery so manifest, he contorted in on himself as if he were struck by blows.

Lane reached over and gripped Max's shoulder. "It's okay—"

The words came fast, pushed out by great emotion: "Edward didn't kill his father . . . oh, God, he didn't kill him. . . ."

"I know." Lane's voice got rough. "I know, Max. I know he didn't do it."

Max threw his head back and wiped his face with his broad palms. "He didn't kill. . . ."

"It's okay, Max. Just tell me what happened."

The silence that followed was so long, if Lane hadn't seen his brother's chest pumping up and down, he might have thought the guy had passed out with his eyes open.

Just when Lane couldn't stand it any longer, Max repeated, "Edward didn't kill his father."

"I know he didn't." For godsakes, they were going around in circles here. "I know it wasn't Edward—"

Max let out a hollow laugh. "You don't understand. He didn't kill *his* father . . . he killed *ours*."

After Max heard the words come out of his mouth, he closed his eyes and tried to reconnect with his buzz. Floaty, spacey, and not-giving-a-fuck had been much better than what he was feeling now—and damn it, he was so sick and fucking tired of swimming in this cesspool of sadness and grief he'd been thrown into three years ago.

"I'm sorry," Lane said in a falsely reasonable tone. "What did you say?"

"Edward didn't kill his father."

"You shouldn't—Max, you shouldn't throw around something like that."

"It's the truth." He turned his head and looked at his handsome-as-sin brother. "You and I and Gin are William Baldwine's children. Edward is not."

"How did you—I don't understand." Lane's expression vacillated between shock and oh-hell-no. "No, Mother is—she's only ever been with him."

"No, she hasn't."

"Max, I need you to get serious—"

"Right before I left Charlemont, I came home late at night. Gin was out somewhere. You were in Virginia. Edward was traveling on business. Amelia was sleeping over at a friend's house." He pictured the scene like it was yesterday. "I snuck in the back because I was high and looking for food, and I was really fucking quiet in the kitchen. I mean, if I'd woken Miss Aurora up? She'd have killed me."

He made a pair of fists and dug his knuckles into his watering eyes. "So, yeah, I creeped around and when I was done eating, I went out front to the main staircase because my room's right at the top of it."

Lane nodded. "And the staff stairs go directly over Miss Aurora's bed."

"I'd have been busted." Max took a deep breath. "I heard their voices as I came up to the second floor. They were down the hall out-side of Mother's room—she was yelling at him for having been out with another woman. And then Father . . ."

"What?"

Max cursed. "He said she had no right to comment. That they both knew Edward wasn't his—that he'd known it all along, and if she didn't shut up about what he was doing, he was going to tell Ed-ward."

"Oh, my God." Lane closed his lids. "Oh . . . shit."

"She got really quiet. And then she started crying. He just turned away really fast and disappeared into his own suite. I didn't know then whether he'd seen me or not—and I've always been afraid of him. So I ran out of the house and slept by the pool. I kept expecting him to come find me and . . . I don't know, he was capable of anything, right? But the next morning, he went to work like nothing had happened. I sat in the pool house for a long time, thinking about him at his desk, ordering people around in the business center. I couldn't stay. Not knowing what I did. Leaving was the only way—so I packed up what I could stuff into a duffel bag and took one of the Mercedes. I drove over the river into Indiana, and I didn't know where I was going—eventually I sold the car for, like, twenty grand in St. Louis and lived off the money. I just wanted to get as far away as I could from this family."

"Does Edward know?" Lane blurted as if he were speaking to himself.

"That's why I came back. I decided I had to tell him. I mean, the guilt. All that shit he did for us when we were kids? He was protecting us from someone who was all but a stranger to him. I couldn't deal with it anymore—so I called him and we met that day. But when I was sitting across from him, I lost my nerve. He looked so bad, so . . . worn out. And the limping and the scars—it was so much worse than I had seen in the papers."

"So you knew about the kidnapping."

"Who doesn't—it was all over the news."

"Edward thinks Father set it all up." Lane rubbed his face. "If what you overheard is true . . . maybe that's why Father wanted him dead."

"And why Father was so hard on him for all those years. It wasn't his son, but he had to pretend like the kid was—meanwhile, Edward was a living, breathing fuck you to him, every day, year after year."

"Edward doesn't know, then?"

Max shrugged. "If he does, it isn't from me. And you're right, I am a coward. I just . . . I couldn't do it. So after he and I talked about absolutely nothing, we went our separate ways, and I kept on moving through town. But then Father died . . . so I came back to Easterly. For reasons I'm still not real clear on."

Lane's eyes were direct. "You gotta be honest with me. Were you involved in the murder?"

Max met that stare right on. "No, I wasn't. I saw the report on the local news when the body was found. That's as close as I am to it, and I will swear to this on anything you want me to."

"Maybe Edward did do it after all."

"I don't know."

Lane turned back to the windshield and got very still in his seat. "I'm sorry I accused you."

"Don't be. I don't care—and I can see why you'd think it was me."

After a long moment, Lane murmured, "So who is Edward's father?"

"I don't know. And I don't know how to ask something like that of Mother."

"Edward has a right to know."

"Does it really matter anymore? Besides, trust me, recasting an entire family is not a party. It's like . . . everything you know to be true is suddenly wrong. It makes your head go bad. I mean, are any of us related? Father only talked about Edward not being his, but what about the rest of us?"

"I can't believe this."

The pair of them sat there, side by side in the Rolls, for so long that Lane cut the engine and put down the windows . . . and eventually, the dawn's glow appeared behind the BBQ joint. And still they stayed put. It wasn't until the first of the commuters began to hit the road into town that his brother restarted the engine and they headed off to Easterly in silence.

From time to time, over the intervening three years since Max had heard what he had, he had wondered how he would feel if he came clean. If he told . . . anyone . . . in his family what he knew. He had imagined there would be relief—but also even more guilt, because in unburdening himself, he would be infecting others with the ugly truth.

To his surprise, he felt nothing.

Maybe it was the booze.

As he and his brother traveled down River Road, they followed the curves of the Ohio's shoreline, and he wondered exactly where Edward had taken their father out and dumped him into the water, still alive but incapacitated. Where had the deed been done? How had Edward chosen the spot? Had he been worried about being caught?

"Are you going to tell Edward?" Max said as Easterly's hill came into view.

Behind the house, the sun was rising, peach and pink rays flowing around the mansion's grand contours as if the Bradford family's great house had to be deferred to.

"I think you should." Lane glanced over. "And I'll go with you when you do."

"No," Max said. "I'm leaving. And before you tell me I can't—"

"I'm not going to stop you." Lane shook his head. "I'll remind you, though, that Edward is still our brother. He's still our family. Mother is the connection—actually, Mother has always been the thing, hasn't she. She's the Bradford."

"I don't care about either one of them." Max crossed his arms over his chest. "I wish you well, but Charlemont and Easterly—and this whole family—are a waste of my time. And they're a waste of yours. You need to take that good woman you got and put all this shit in the rearview." He looked over the river to Indiana, to the wide-open highway, to more of a future far, far away from the name Bradford. "Trust me, it's a better life out there. Way better."

EIGHTEEN

*L*ater that morning, Lizzie pried the keys to a riding mower out of Gary McAdams's extremely disapproving and reluctant hands and went to town on the front lawn.

Indeed, the prospect of making neat, clipped lanes all over the acres of grass that ran from Easterly's grand entrance all the way down the mountain to the gates on River Road made her OCD side tingle with happiness—and no, she did not care that it was "hotter'n blazes out," as the head groundsman had put it.

Unfortunately, her enthusiasm proved less enduring than the heat.

Some lemonade, she thought as Easterly came into view once again on the ascent. She'd get something cool, and after a little hydration, she'd be ready to go back at it.

Parking the mower under a dark-leafed magnolia, she had to smile as she dismounted and went right in the front door with grass clippings stuck all over the sweat on her bare legs. Previously, there had been a limited number of ways staff had been allowed to enter the mansion. Two doors. That was it—and both of them were in the back of the house. If that had meant someone like herself or Greta had had to walk all the way around, in the heat, because they had been pulling weeds in the ivy beds or the urns out front? Too bad.

At least she didn't have to worry about that inconvenience anymore.

Although, that being said, she did take her work shoes off and leave them just inside on a mat—and not because some English butler like the one who had quit was going to give her a hard time. Nope, it was again because she was it for housekeeping.

As she moved through the cool interior, her skin goosebump'd all over. The house had had central air added only about ten years ago, and the HVAC upgrade was certainly appreciated on a day like today—although she also knew she was going to come to regret this respite. As relieving as it was to get a break from the heat, going back outside was going to be a bitch.

But she'd been worried she was about to pass out.

Passing by the formal parlors, with all their grandeur, she opened the wide door by the dining room and entered the staff portion of things—and it was as if she were in a different house. Gone were the oil paintings and the silk wallpaper, the drapes and the Orientals. Now the walls were painted a crisp clean white and the only adornment on the floorboards was a coat of varnish well-scuffed by footfalls.

The controller's office was on the left and she put her head in. "Hey there."

Greta von Schlieber looked up from the desk. In front of her, the open laptop and piles of papers were everything Lizzie would have hated to deal with. The German, however, found great peace in making order out of bookkeeping chaos—and after Rosalinda Freeland's untimely suicide, and the subsequent firings of almost all the staff, there was much to do in the land of paper clips and staples, documents and forms.

"Guten Morgen," the woman said as she took off her pink reading glasses and replaced them with a pair of tortoiseshell distance lenses. "How are we doing?"

With the accent, *"we"* came out with a *"v"* and there was an *"-ink"* at the end of *"doing"*—and the familiar soundings of both made Lizzie want to tell her decade-long friend what was going on about her possible pregnancy. But no. If Lane didn't know, nobody else was going to.

"It's hot out there."

"Ja. I finish processing these dismissals, I go and trim hedges around the pool house. Then I deadhead the pots."

"After Lane's done with the board meeting, I'm meeting him down at the hospital to see Miss Aurora."

"I heard that the calls have been made to family? I have been speaking to the former staff to make sure they get the unemployment and one of her nieces told me. I go after I am finished with work."

"It's really sad."

She hadn't seen Lane for more than two seconds before he'd left for the trustee meeting—because apparently getting Max home in the middle of the night had been a thing. But Lane had told her there was something he wanted to talk to her about, and she wondered what it was. He had certainly seemed distracted and unhappy, although that was, sadly, nothing new—

A *bing-bong* sounded out high on the ceiling, and Lizzie looked up over her shoulder. "Someone's at the back door. I'll get it."

As she hurried into the kitchen, she averted her eyes as she passed by the door to Miss Aurora's suite of rooms. God, the prospect of cleaning out Lane's momma's things from that space—or having the woman's family come and do that—seemed both surreal and inevitable.

When she opened the back screen door, there was a young guy in a blue uniform and a hat. Behind him, in the courtyard, a van with the name of a local delivery company was parked and running.

"I got something for a Mr. Richard Pford here?" the guy said. "Can you sign for it?"

"Yes, sure." Lizzie took the manila envelope and then scribbled her name on a clipboard. "Thank you."

"Thanks, ma'am."

She was closing things up when she remembered that technically Gin's husband had moved out, and she tried to flag the van down as it pulled away, but the vehicle didn't stop.

Fine, she'd leave it on his bed for whenever he came to pick up his things. Besides, knowing Gin's love life, it was likely that the two would reconcile after Lane's sister got back from dropping Amelia off up north. Gin had a way of getting what she wanted, and she had wanted to be married to Pford.

Although how she could stand being anywhere near that nasty piece of work was a mystery.

Then again . . . money.

The lemonade was every bit as refreshing as Lizzie had thought it would be, and the idea of going back out to the mower was as unappealing as it had first seemed like a great idea. No matter, however. It was time to get showered and changed and meet Lane down at the hospital. Besides, she'd gotten the left half of the lawn done. Maybe at the end of the day, she could finish the other side.

As Lizzie didn't have time to drive the John Deere all the way back to the grounds-keeping outbuildings, she settled for running it around to the rear courtyard and leaving it in the shade by the garages. Then she forced herself to take a handful of pretzels up with her to the second floor, dropped the envelope just inside Pford's room, and got herself showered and dressed in khakis and a fresh polo.

She was once again down in the kitchen and texting Lane for his ETA at the hospital when she was struck by an impulse. Going over to Miss Aurora's door, she hesitated.

Her first instinct was to knock, and how crazy was that. It wasn't like there was anyone in there.

Opening things up, her heart ached at the memory of when she had come in and found the woman on the floor by her bed, unresponsive.

As with Miss Aurora's workspaces outside, everything was in its place, not just tidy but vacuumed and dusted as well, and although the furnishings were modest, you couldn't help but want to have good posture and your hands tucked into each other as you stood inside the space. There were two BarcaLoungers against a bay of windows, a TV across the way, and a galley kitchen with a sink, a little stove, and a refrigerator. Naturally, there were no dishes left out in the drainer, and a hand towel had been precisely folded and hung on the oven door's handle.

Boy, it felt all wrong to be in here without an invitation.

Moving quickly, she went over by Miss Aurora's chair, to the shelves that ran up to the ceiling. There were over a hundred pictures in frames old and new on them, the photographs ranging from elementary school snaps to college graduations, from smiling summer-camp candids to serious-faced lineups around Christmas trees and at church altars. Many of them featured basketball and football players in mid-jump or mid-tackle, and a couple even had players in NFL and NBA uniforms, the subjects ranging from Miss Aurora's brothers and sisters, and their children, to Lane, Gin, Max, and Edward.

Lizzie had come in with the thought of taking a couple and bringing them to the hospital, so if Miss Aurora had a moment of consciousness, she could see the faces of some of her most beloved people. But now, confronting all of the pictures, Lizzie became overwhelmed.

Reaching out, she took a picture of Lane off the third shelf up. He had been twelve or thirteen at the time and grinning cheekily into the camera. The hints of his adult good looks were all over his face, his features already showing a proclivity to that strong jaw, his eyes flashing with his flirtatious nature.

If Lizzie was carrying a son, he would be just like this at the same age.

Suddenly obsessed, she began searching for more photos of Lane, and she found at least a dozen or so. She followed them chronologically, watching him grow up . . . until she got to the last one, when he'd graduated from U.Va. Now, he was in a cap and gown, and had Wayfarers on, his handsome assurance making him look like something out of *St. Elmo's Fire*, even though that had been well before his time. And he had his arm around—oh, that was Jeff Stern.

Funny, where life took people.

Reaching out, she took the large frame from its careful placement and brought it in for a closer look.

As she stood there, staring at the image of the two best friends in the sun, the sky over their heads so blue, the grass under their feet so green, she realized she was looking at Lane's face and trying to read what his reaction would be to her pregnancy news. Which was nuts.

Leaning in to put the frame back, she—

Frowned and stopped.

There was something tucked in behind the photograph. A plastic bag?

Lizzie went back there with her hand before she thought about the invasion of privacy . . . and what she took out didn't make a lot of sense.

It was a large, gallon-sized freezer bag, inside of which was a chef's knife.

Putting the picture of Lane and Jeff aside, she examined the contents. There wasn't anything notable on the blade or the black handle, no stains, chips or abrasions. Nor were there any identifiers, like a special nameplate or whatever.

Lizzie eyed the rest of the photographs. After a moment, she put the knife back and replaced the picture exactly where it had been. Then she left to go downtown.

And resolved to mind her own business.

"*W*hat do you mean he won't see me?"

As Lane spoke, he leaned into the county jail's registration desk. Like that was going to do any good. And what do you know, the female officer who had taken his name and typed a bunch of stuff into her computer just shook her head.

"I'm sorry." She pointed to the monitor in front of her. "The request was denied by the detained."

"Is Deputy Ramsey around?" He hated bothering the guy unless he had to. But this was serious. "Can I speak with him?"

"Deputy Ramsey has taken his unit in for hostage training all day today. Would you like me to leave him a message?"

"No, thanks." He knocked the counter with his knuckles. "I'll call him myself later."

As he headed for the double doors, he was pissed, but until Ramsey was free, he wasn't going to make any headway seeing Edward.

Damn it.

Then again, he'd had more emotion than agenda as he'd stopped by here on his way to the hospital. It probably wouldn't have gone well. For godsakes, what could he say?

How could he say it?

Passing by the people who were cooling their jets in plastic chairs, he let himself out of the reception area and joined the march along the courthouse's promenade of corridors. Instead of waiting for an elevator, he took the polished granite stairs in the center of the building's seven-story atrium down to street level and exited onto the sidewalk.

He ended up going to the hospital on foot. It wasn't far and he had the time because the board meeting had gotten out early.

But he didn't go to see Miss Aurora first. At the visitors' center, he asked for, and got, another room number.

Which turned out to be in the same building, though.

Going up to the third floor, he got off at a general inpatient unit and checked in at the nursing station. Then he went down a long hall, passing by carts of cleared meals, rolling bags of laundry, and pieces of medical equipment.

When he got to room 328, he knocked.

"Hello?" came a female voice.

"It's Lane. May I come in?"

"Hold on."

There was some rustling, and then Chantal said in a stronger tone, "Please. Thank you."

So polite. And as he entered, he kept his eyes averted because he knew she wasn't going to want him to look at her too much. Chantal had always preferred only to be seen when her makeup and her hair were done and her clothes were properly matched to the situation.

A quick glance confirmed that she was in a hospital johnny and fresh-faced.

Or rather, without foundation, blush, lipstick, eyeliner, and mascara.

In fact, she was anything but "fresh" looking. Her skin was sallow, her mouth a flat line, her eyes bloodshot and badly bagged.

"You are kind to come by," she said as she unfolded and refolded the top edge of her blankets.

"I wanted to see if you were okay."

"I have a nice view, don't you think?"

As she indicated the bank of windows, he obligingly went over and checked out the skyscrapers, the river, and the green farmland of Indiana.

"They're going to have to operate on me," she murmured.

He changed his focus so that he saw her reflection in the glass. She was examining her manicure.

"What do they have to do?"

"A D and C. Apparently, I haven't . . . passed everything."

He closed his eyes briefly. "Is your mother coming?"

"She's on a plane now. She arrives in about an hour."

"Good. She will take fine care of you."

"She always does."

Turning around, he put his hands in the pockets of his slacks. "Do you need anything?"

"Have you seen today's paper?"

"No." He thought of those pictures of them that had been taken at the cemetery. "But I can guess what's being reported."

"I've been asked to comment."

"My phone's been ringing, but I haven't been picking up." He had other things to worry about. "I don't have anything to say."

"Neither do I."

His brows lifted of their own accord. "Really."

Chantal nodded as she inspected her thumbnail. "I'm going back to Virginia. After all of this. I'll be at Briarwood for the foreseeable future."

Her parents' estate, he thought.

She cleared her throat. "So, yes, Samuel T. can send anything he needs to there. You know, pertaining to the divorce."

"What about your lawyer here in town?"

"Just send the papers home. I'll sign whatever. I don't . . . I don't really care anymore."

Now he stared hard at her. It was difficult to know whether or not this subdued version of the woman could be believed. Or whether it would last. He had come here out of a sense of obligation—and maybe a little because he had wanted to know how her mood was.

He had certainly not expected this.

"I'm not going to fight you," she tacked on.

"Okay."

"I'm done with that."

"All right."

After a moment, he cleared his throat. "Well, I'm going to go see Miss Aurora now. Let me know if you need anything?"

"How is she?"

"She's fine."

"Oh, I'm glad. I know she means a lot to you."

"Okay, then. Take care of yourself."

"You, too."

He nodded once and headed for the exit, stepping around the foot of her bed. He was almost to the door when Chantal's voice stopped him.

"I'm sorry."

Lane looked over his shoulder. She was staring across the shallow space at him, her face serious.

In the silence that followed, he supposed he could have asked her exactly what she was apologizing for, and maybe he would gotten some particulars. But they both knew what had been said and done on each of their parts, particularly hers.

He thought again about that party they'd met at. He could have taken any one of a number of women home that night. And he could have chosen not to follow up with Chantal afterward. Looking back on it, he couldn't remember why he had called her again, why he had met her out for dinner a couple of days later, why, following that, he had agreed to escort her to a gala for some ballet or opera or whatever it had been.

Was destiny just an accident, he wondered, the intersecting paths of people's lives nothing more than marbles spilled on a floor, the contacts random and purposeless? Or was there a higher plan?

He knew what his momma would have said to that. Knew also what Miss Aurora would have wanted him to say right now.

"I am sorry, too," he whispered.

And it was a surprise for him to find . . . that he meant that.

After Chantal nodded once, Lane lifted his hand as a good-bye and then he turned and did not look back again. As he made his way back down the corridor to the elevators, he had the strangest feeling he was never going to see her again.

And that, like so many other outcomes currently unveiling themselves, had once seemed an impossibility.

NINETEEN

As Lane came up to Miss Aurora's ICU room, there was a crowd of people milling around outside in the hall, and he approached two of Miss Aurora's nephews as he waved to everyone else. The men were in their twenties, and one was a wide receiver for the Indiana Colts with the other a center for the Miami Heat. Both of their faces were showing all kinds of heartbreak.

"D'Shawne." Lane clapped hands with one and then the other. "Qwentin. How y'all doing?"

"Thanks for calling us, man." D'Shawne glanced at his brother. "We don't know how to handle this."

"Have you been in to see her?"

"Yessir," Qwentin replied. "Just been. Our sisters are coming at the end of the day."

"Mom said we need to be talking about the funeral?" D'Shawne ran his hand down his face. "I mean . . . is it really time?"

"Yes, I think so." Lane glanced at the closed door with its privacy drapery. "I've spoken with Reverend Nyce. He said the church is ours and he'll get the word out to the congregation."

"She's on the prayer list already." Qwentin shook his head. "I can't believe this. She was just calling me last weekend. Telling me what I needed to work on over the off-season."

Lane clapped a hand on the man's neck. "She was always so proud of you. Both of you. She used to brag on you so hard. And she always said you were her favorites."

Next thing Lane knew, he was locked in one bear hug and then another. And then the two men walked off.

"Are you telling everyone that they're her favorite?"

At the sound of Lizzie's voice, he turned around and smiled. "When did you get here?"

As he held out his arms, Lizzie came forward and embraced him. "Just now. I didn't want to interrupt. How was the board meeting?"

"Good enough." He brushed her hair back from her face. "I'm glad to see you, and yes, I'm telling everybody they're her favorites."

"How is she? Have you been inside yet?"

"No, not yet." Lane checked his watch. "Let's see if we can head in—"

A nurse came rushing out and searched through the crowd. "Mr. Baldwine! She's coming around—she's asking for someone? I think it's you!"

Lane could only blink. "I'm sorry, what—"

"Miss Toms is coming around! I'm calling for the attending right now."

Lane glanced at Lizzie as people started talking loudly, and then after a quick conversation with the family, it was decided he should go in because he was both the healthcare proxy and the executor of Miss Aurora's estate.

And he couldn't handle it without Lizzie so he took her in through the glass door with him.

Over at the side of the bed, Lane skidded to a halt.

"Miss Aurora?" He took the still, cool hand. "Miss Aurora?"

For a moment, he thought it was a cruel joke. But then he saw her mouth move. Leaning down, her mumbling was low but insistent, a stream of words coming out of his momma's lips.

Lane tried to interpret the syllables. "What are you saying? What do you need?" He glanced up at Lizzie. "Can you hear this?"

Lizzie came around to the other side. "Miss Aurora?"

More with the mumbling, and Lane couldn't decide whether he wanted the medical staff to arrive—or give him a little more time. If this was the last thing his momma ever said, he didn't want an interruption before he could figure out what it was.

Suddenly, Lizzie straightened. "Edward? You want to know where Edward is?"

At that moment, Miss Aurora's eyes popped open. "Where is Edward. I need Edward. . . ."

She didn't appear to be focused on anything, her pupils dilated and unfixed.

"Edward! I need Edward!"

The onset of the agitation was like a train gathering speed, her arms starting to move and then her legs, some inner engine of panic animating her body.

"Edward!"

As the attending came in with other staff members, Lane backed up so that the white coats and nurses could gather around the bed.

He didn't want to admit it, but it killed him that, of all the people his momma wanted to see . . . it was his older brother, not him. And how petty was that.

The important thing was that she was conscious.

"What's going on?" he demanded of the staff as Lizzie came over next to him. "Is she . . . going to be okay?"

Come on, though. Did he think she'd just slept off the damn cancer?

The same nurse who had rung the bell came over. "I'm going to have to ask you to step out. I'm so sorry, but we need space to work."

"What's going on? I'm not leaving until you tell me."

"It's probably the morphine. At these levels, it can cause hallucinations. One of the attendings will give you an update in a little bit, okay?"

"Come on," Lizzie said. "We'll just stay right outside."

Lane allowed himself to be drawn back out into the corridor. And then he started pacing up and back, up and back. As time passed, and the family dispersed into chairs in the hall, he kept his head down and his eyes on the linoleum. He didn't trust himself to meet even Lizzie's kind and worried stare.

Why the hell did she want to talk to Edward?

"Lane."

"Hm?" He stopped in front of Lizzie and shook himself. "I'm sorry, what?"

"There's something I need to tell you," Lizzie whispered as she stared at the glass door.

She spoke fast, but very quietly, and when she was done, all he could do was stare at her.

Then, with a shaking hand, Lane took out his cell phone and made a call that was, as far as he could tell, his only option.

*T*he timing for meals in jail was based on a shift rotation of preparers and servers, and one of the things Edward had

had to get used to was having breakfast at six a.m., lunch at eleven, and dinner at four in the afternoon.

So when his cell door released at what certainly seemed like late afternoon, he hauled himself up from his bunk in preparation for his shuffle down to the cafeteria with the others. But it was not mealtime, as it turned out.

The guard who opened things up was the same one who had come just before lunch to tell him that his brother wanted to see him.

"You got another visitor."

"I told you, if it's Lane Baldwine, I am going to regretfully decline."

"It's not him."

Edward waited for the name. "And it is . . . ?"

"It's a woman."

"Okay, that's a no, too." He sat back down on his bunk. "I don't want to see Shelby Landis, either."

"Well, here's the thing. I got a call from my supervisor? And he says I have to bring you down. Or I'm going to have to explain to him how I messed this up. And if I mess this up, my supervisor is going to give me bad shifts for the rest of this month—"

"That's not legal, you know. A hostile working environment is not just about harassment—"

"—and I got a new girl, and I need my weekends. So I'm sorry, you're going to have to come with me."

"Who is your supervisor?" Even though Edward knew.

"Deputy Ramsey."

"Of course." Edward closed his eyes. "Look, this is really unnecessary—"

"Come on, I have to have you out of here and into the meeting room in five minutes. He's calling to make sure you get down there."

"And let me guess, you're prepared to throw me over your shoulder and carry me out of here if you have to."

"Yup." At least the guy had the grace to seem honestly chagrined. "I'm sorry, but I gotta do what my supervisor tells me to."

As Edward stood back up, he was thinking about two things: one, that whole line parents gave their kids, the old "If so and so told you to jump off a bridge, would you do it?"; and two, that he might owe Deputy Ramsey his life, but even that debt was getting stretched thin with all this visiting bullshit.

Why couldn't they just sentence him now and move him out of state?

Except there was no stopping this train, evidently. So he and Ramsey's fricking subordinate with the new girl and the need-my-weekends problem left the block and followed the same path Edward had been led through the other night.

When he was let into the interrogation room, he sat down in the same seat as he had before.

It had to be Shelby giving things another shot. She and Ramsey were best friends, weren't they. Who else, other than her, would the guy take things this far for?

But never again, Edward thought.

This time, he'd play real hardball with the young woman. He was due a phone call or two a week—and if she insisted on shirking her duties out at the farm, just so she could drive all the way into town to bug him about absolutely nothing? That was grounds for dismissal—

He knew by the smell of the perfume.

As the interrogation room door opened, he closed his eyes and took a deep breath. *Must de Cartier.*

And then came the delicate clipping sound of expensive high-heeled shoes.

Which was harmonized by a low, very well-modulated female voice: "Thank you."

The guard stammered something—a not unusual response of the male sex when they were addressed by Sutton Smythe. And then the door was re-shut and locked.

By the sounds of those stilettos and the shifting of clothes, Edward knew she had taken a seat opposite him.

"You aren't going to look at me," Sutton said softly.

His heart thundered and he could feel the heat in his face. And the only reason he popped his lids was because he refused to appear to be as weak as he felt.

Sometimes pride was a poor man's only sword and shield.

Oh . . . dear God.

Red Armani suit. Cream blouse. Brunette hair in a chignon. Nails painted the same red as the suit. Pearls at the throat, face tinted with just enough makeup to give her a little color. And yet none of those details really registered.

He was too busy being knocked on his ass even as he stayed in his bolted-to-the-floor chair.

Oh, God, she was still wearing his earrings, the ruby ones he'd bought her from Van Cleef & Arpels. And as he focused on them, her fingertips went to one lobe.

"I've come from work," she said. As if that explained something. "I just decided to stop by."

All he could think about was the fact that she wore what he had given her even when she didn't know she was going to see him.

Edward cleared his throat. "How are you? Growing into your new role as CEO?"

"Really." Her eyes narrowed. "We're going to make social chitchat?"

"You've just started to run a multi-billion-dollar corporation. That is hardly chitchat."

"And you've been arrested for murder."

"I guess we're both in for some life changes. I'm certain yours come with a better salary and food."

"Damn you, Edward."

As he fell silent, he tried to ignore the sheen in her eyes.

After a moment, he said, "I'm sorry."

"For what? Blowing me off right before you came in here? Or killing your father."

"Sutton, you don't need this"—he motioned around the interrogation room—"in your life. I knew I was going to end up here. What did you expect me to do?"

She leaned in. "I expected you not to take my choice away from me. Which is what grown-ups do with other grown-ups."

"You're the new head of the Sutton Distillery Corporation, a company that your beloved father spent his entire life helming. What you do and who you relate with matters—now more than ever, and you know that—"

"Stop it," she bit out. "Stop trying to cover up that you're a coward."

"Did you come here just to argue that point with me? Because I don't believe that agenda is going to get either of us anywhere."

"No, I'm here because your brother asked me to see you—and because Lane was smart enough to know that unless Ramsey was involved, you would shut me out, too."

Edward crossed his arms over his chest. "Lane needs to leave well enough alone."

"Miss Aurora is asking for you. At the hospital."

Now Edward was the one narrowing his eyes. "She's awake? Last I heard she was not doing at all well."

"She is evidently saying your name, over and over again."

"I'm surprised it isn't Lane's."

"I believe so is he." There was a pause. "Can you think of any reason she would feel the need to speak to you right before she died?"

Abruptly, Edward found it hard to breathe. He kept that to himself, however.

Making sure his face showed nothing, he slowly shook his head. "No. Not at all."

TWENTY

As Sutton sat across from Edward, she was torn. She wanted to keep confronting him about their relationship—or, hell, whatever it was they had between them—but there was a larger, more important imperative. When Lane had called her from the hospital, it was obvious he was shaken up, and as he had spoken to her with great, shocking candor, it had become readily apparent why he was upset.

And of course she had volunteered to try to get in front of Edward.

She didn't think she was going to have the magical effect on the man that his brother seemed to think she would, however. Edward Baldwine had always gone his own way, and she would be a fool to think she was the one person who could get through to him.

But she had to try.

"None whatsoever?" she prompted him. "You can think of no reason your name would be on Miss Aurora's lips."

"Maybe she's worried about Lane and wants me to help. I don't know. Ask her."

"Are you aware that there are security cameras out at the Red and Black?"

"Why are we talking about my farm? I thought this was about Miss Aurora."

"Cameras." She pointed high in the air. "Up under the roofs of the barns?"

"You know, I think it's time for me to go—"

"Sit down," she snapped as he began to get to his feet.

Edward's brows lifted. And something about her resolve must have shown in her face because he slowly sank back down into the metal chair.

Good move on his part—she had been prepared to tackle him if she had to.

"You didn't leave the farm on the night of the murder," she announced. "And don't deny it. There's nothing on the cameras to show you or anyone else did—and if you'd used the truck you said you'd taken, there would have been footage of you driving off in it."

"Do my brother a favor, would you? And tell him to stop with the theories."

"Lizzie found a knife in Miss Aurora's quarters this morning."

"She's a chef. They're known to use—"

"In a plastic bag. Behind a picture of Lane."

Edward planted his hands on the tabletop and pushed himself up. "I'm leaving. Have a nice life, Sutton—and I mean that."

Sutton let him limp over to the door and start knocking. When no one came, he called out, "Guard."

"They're not going to answer," she said without turning around.

"Why."

"Because I told them not to."

He knocked louder. "Guard!"

"Talk to me about the knife, Edward. You know something. You're protecting someone. And I get all that—it's in your nature. But here's the thing. Lane's not going to quit until you walk out of here a free man, and neither am I."

"What the hell is wrong with you people!" He wheeled around and came back over. "You've got lives to live! Companies to run— why the fuck do either of you care—"

She jumped up and met him face-to-face. "Because we love you! And when someone you love is doing something wrong, you want to stop them!"

Edward's fury darkened his eyes to almost black and the veins stood out in his neck. "You're not even a member of my family—you don't count. Mind your own damn business!"

Oh, no, you don't, Sutton thought. I'm not going to be diverted into some kind of a tit-for-tat argument.

"Did Miss Aurora kill William Baldwine?"

As she put the blunt question out there, she kept her voice level and calm. At the end of the day, this was the information she had come to get, and she was nothing if she wasn't capable of focusing. It was one of her best skills.

"Of course not," Edward said as he started to pace around, his bad leg dragging. "How the hell can you even suggest something like that."

"What about the knife, then?"

"I don't know. Why are you asking me about it?"

"You don't think if that blade is turned in to the police that it won't have your father's blood on it?"

That got him to stop. And it was a long while before Edward

spoke again. "I'm getting really sick and fucking tired of telling people to leave this alone."

"So stop trying."

"Miss Aurora is dying. Let her go in peace, Sutton."

"Don't you think she wants that, too? Why else would a woman who's in an ICU become panicked and call your name? You don't think that maybe her guilty conscience is the only thing keeping her alive?"

Come on, Sutton thought at him. *Talk to me. . . .*

But she knew better than to give voice to that. Edward was liable to shut up and never speak again.

"Miss Aurora loves you like a son," she insisted. "You are so precious to her. She isn't going to be able to pass if she knows you're lying to protect her."

Edward said something under his breath.

"What was that?" Sutton asked.

"It's not her I'm worried about."

*A*s Edward heard the words leave his mouth, he wanted to snatch them out of thin air and shove them back down his own throat.

"What did you say?" Sutton repeated.

He had had everything so perfectly arranged. All the players separated into channels of action and communication that didn't cross. No ends to tie up. No questions to be asked.

But like actual murderers, he'd missed one little detail. Although he'd been careful to make sure the police found his trail when he'd erased the security footage from Easterly's cameras, he'd forgotten that the Red & Black's monitoring was going to be a problem.

Shit.

What else had he missed? And what if Miss Aurora survived?

Limping back over to the chair, he sat down and steepled his fingers. "Sutton . . ."

She shook her head. "No. You're not going to be able to charm your way out of this. I'm really pissed off at you, independent of all this. So that tone of voice is going to get you nowhere."

He almost smiled. She knew him all too well: If anger didn't work, try cajoling. If cajoling didn't, a distraction.

Naturally, kissing her came to mind, but he knew better than to attempt that when she was in this kind of mood. She was liable to knock his damn block off.

"Well?" she prompted. "What do you have to say for yourself?"

"Not much. Considering you've cut me off."

"Because you were going to try to feed me some line." Sutton shook her head at him. "Just so you know, Lane's going to the police. As we speak. He's heading home to Easterly to get the knife and he's turning it in. And you know what he's going to do next?"

"I don't care."

"He's going to the press. He's going to tell them everything—"

"He'll be lying, then." Why the hell didn't his voice sound stronger there? "He'll make himself look like a damn idiot."

"—to put pressure on the district attorney. Oh, and before he left the hospital?" When Edward looked way, she came across and loomed over him. "He told Miss Aurora you'd put yourself in jail."

Edward closed his eyes.

And still Sutton continued. "And you want to know what her response was?"

"No."

"She started to cry . . . and said she'd done it and that you were protecting her. So yeah, that about brings us up to date." Sutton went over to the door and knocked once. "Guard?"

The door opened immediately, and Sutton paused between the

jambs. "My guess is you'll be out of here in two days. Three days tops. And if you want an opportunity to prove to me that you're not the coward I think you are, you'll come find me, and you'll apologize for ever sending me away."

"What then," he said bitterly. "Happily ever after? I didn't fancy you as a romantic."

"Oh, no, I was thinking straight-up raw sex. Until I can't walk right, either. Bye, Edward."

As the deputy who'd brought him down here coughed, Edward just about passed out from a combination of sexual arousal and did-she-just-say-that'itis. Meanwhile, Sutton left with her head up, her shoulders back, and that French perfume of hers in her wake.

Man, that woman knew how to make an exit.

Just his luck.

And as for the Miss Aurora stuff? All he could do was pray that everyone stopped talking nonsense and that the police stayed resolved in their current conclusions.

Because Lane was not going to be able to deal with the idea that his momma was a murderer.

That was going to kill him.

TWENTY-ONE

*S*amuel T. had not expected to leave his office so early. He
had planned to work until ten or eleven at night and then
stumble down the two blocks to his penthouse and crash there. After
a week or so of being in court during business hours, he had a back-
log of billing to catch up on, and then there was the other more pressing, but less acknowledged, reality that he was thinking about Gin
non-stop.

And that meant he needed distraction.

As usual, though, the woman surprised him and changed his direction: Call him she did. Needed him, she maintained.

Great, now she had him talking like Yoda.

It was just after six as he turned in to his farm's drive and proceeded down the allée of trees that had been planted by his great-

grandfather. With the Jag's top down, he could let his head fall back and look at the sky through the bright green leaves, the arboreal flags waving in celebration of warm weather's permanent arrival.

What the hell had Pford done now, he wondered. And was he going to need a gun.

As he pulled up in front of his farmhouse, his first thought was that the Mercedes Gin had used to take her daughter back to school was in ridden-hard-and-put-up-wet condition. Dead bugs riddled its front grille and windshield, and road dust smudged the hood and the quarter panels behind its wheels in aerodynamic patterns.

Had she driven all the way through? He wasn't exactly sure where Hotchkiss was located—as a Southern boy, those New England prep schools all seemed the same to him—but he was fairly sure Connecticut was over a thousand miles away.

You could make that round trip in a day and a half. If you never stopped.

Taking off his Ray-Bans, he left them on the dash and got out with his great-uncle's old briefcase in one hand and the stainless-steel coffee mug he had brought with him into work.

Insomnia. What else could you do other than caffeinate its effects away during the daylight hours?

Walking over the gravel, he passed under a great maple and then mounted the five steps of the wraparound porch that looked out over the rear acreage.

He stopped when he saw Gin curled up on the padded sofa that faced the pond. Dear Lord, she was in the same clothes she had been wearing when he had dropped her off at Easterly, after they had . . . done what they had back at his penthouse. What the hell had happened?

As if sensing his presence, she stirred, except her exhaustion was clearly too much to fight: With a sigh that sounded anything but relaxed, she fell back into her sleep.

Samuel T. was quiet as he approached her, setting his briefcase and mug down by the screen doors and continuing on into the farmhouse. He had some silly notion of putting a blanket over her, but it was eighty out, and in another few minutes, the setting sun was going to lick under the porch roof and bathe her in even more warmth.

In the kitchen, he found a lineup of notes from his estate manager covering everything from what to feed himself for dinner to phone calls she'd answered for him to a confirmation that the roof guys were coming next Tuesday. The mail stack was over in the corner, and he glanced through it. Also checked out a big hand-addressed manila envelope that he didn't bother opening.

He wanted a shower. He wanted to offer Gin a bed.

He wanted to know why she had called him to meet her out here after she'd driven for so many hours straight. Especially given that her voice hadn't sounded right when he'd spoken to her.

Loosening his bow tie, Samuel T. slid the red and gold strip of silk from under his collar and then ditched his suit jacket. He also took off his shoes and his socks. Then he grabbed two rocks glasses, filled them with ice, and tucked a bottle of her Family Reserve under his arm.

Heading out on the porch, he sat down in the wicker chair next to her and started to pour.

As if she caught the scent of her family's product, she opened her eyes and jerked upright. "Oh . . . you're here."

"And you're back in Charlemont." He extended a drink to her and tried to act like he wasn't alarmed. "Where is that school, anyway? Connecticut? I didn't think you could make it up and back in a day and a half."

"It's eight hundred miles and change. You can do it if you don't sleep and don't eat."

"Not the safest of driving paradigms."

"I was fine."

"Why the rush?"

Gin stared down into her bourbon and moved the ice cubes around in their bath of liquor with her fingertip. "I wanted to come see you."

"Your devotion is a surprise."

"I need to talk to you, Samuel."

Samuel T. frowned and eased back in the chair, the weave creaking as it accepted the shift in his body weight. "What about?"

As a lawyer who worked trials, he was used to reading into the vagaries of an expression and extrapolating what an eyebrow twitch meant, or how the corner of the mouth could reveal a lie . . . or a truth. When it came to Gin, however, his skills were disarmed because of his own emotions.

And he was seriously concerned. If she stayed with Pford, he had a feeling she was going to not only regret it, but be in danger. And although it was going to kill him to sit on the sidelines while she got hurt, Gin Baldwine was well known for making choices that took her into chaos, instead of away from it.

She sat up and rearranged that peach dress. The color usually looked fantastic on her—then again, what didn't? But she was as worn out as that Mercedes parked out front looked, her skin too pale, the tight line of her lips suggesting she was upset and trying to hide it.

"This is hard for me." She closed her eyes. "Oh, God, Samuel, please don't hate me."

"Well, I've tried that in the past and I've never made it stick."

"This is different."

"Look, if you want an annulment, I can help you and I'm not going to judge—I told you that before." He thought of her coming forward and telling him that she loved him with a desperation he hadn't respected because he'd assumed it was just one more game. "And I'm not volunteering to replace him, if you're just looking for a bank account. But if you want more than that? We'll see—"

"This is not about Richard."

He frowned. "Okay."

Gin went still. To the point where she barely seemed to breathe. And then he noticed the tears that were silently falling from her eyes.

Samuel T. sat forward. "Gin, what's going on?"

As she sniffled and rubbed at her nose, he eased to the side and took out the handkerchief he always kept in his back pocket. "Here."

"Thank you." She put the bourbon aside and mopped up. "I don't know how to begin."

"*A dark and stormy night* always worked for Snoopy."

"This is not funny."

"Clearly."

She took a shuddering breath. "Do you remember . . . way back when I was in school and I took some time off? I was pregnant then, as you know."

"Yes."

"And I had Amelia."

"Yes."

"Do you remember about nine months before I had her where I was?"

"With your professor," he said dryly. "You were sure to tell me. With no small amount of pride, I might add."

"Amelia was born in May. Do you remember?"

"Gin, will you just come out and tell me whatever it is—"

"She was born in May." Her eyes lifted to his. "And nine months before, do you remember where I was? It was September."

He threw up his free hand. "Why are you going in circles here? I don't have any clue what you were doing way back then—"

"Fine," she said sharply. "Do you recall where *you* were that September?"

"Oh, of course, 'cuz I can remember fifteen years ago—"

"Sixteen. Sixteen years ago."

As an alarm started to go off way down at the base of his skull, the ringing sound drowned out his thoughts—but not his memories. Sixteen years ago. September. It had been right before they'd gone back to school . . .

. . . and they had met up in Bora Bora.

They had fought. And had sex. And gotten drunk. And had sex. And been sunburned. And had sex.

Samuel T. swallowed even though his mouth went dry. "What are you saying."

Even though he knew. He suddenly *knew.*

"Please don't hate me," she said roughly. "I was young and scared. I didn't know what to do—"

Samuel T. got to his feet so fast, bourbon spilled all over his hand. "Say it." He raised his voice. "Say it!"

"Amelia is yours. She's your daughter."

He grabbed for the collar of his shirt, even though it was already open. And then the anger came, hard and fast.

"You fucking *bitch.*"

As soon as Lane heard back from Sutton, he returned to Easterly, leaving Lizzie with Miss Aurora and the doctors. He parked the Rolls in the rear by the garage, and then he entered the mansion through the kitchen—or tried to.

When he went to open the door behind the screen, it was locked.

So strange. For all his life, Easterly had always been accessible. Then again, there had been plenty of people inside the house, no matter the hour. Now? With Jeff at work, and his mother upstairs with a nurse in the middle of a twelve-hour shift? Doors had to be bolted.

Fortunately, there was a house key on the Phantom's ring.

The hinges on the screen creaked as he propped the thing open with his hip, and then he was opening the solid door and taking a deep inhale of the specific scent of Miss Aurora's kitchen: lemons and Danish and astringent.

His momma had cooked and cleaned in the space for so long, he imagined it would always smell like this. Or at least he hoped it would.

He went directly to her quarters, and had to stop as he walked in. The sight of that pair of BarcaLoungers was like a punch to the chest. It seemed like two seconds ago that he'd arrived here from Manhattan and she had cooked him his favorite soul food. And by all that was holy, he would have killed to sit just one more time side by side with her, their feet up, their plates on matching tray tables that folded away when they were through, the TV chattering off in the corner.

But that was no more, he thought sadly.

Snapping into action, it was easy enough to find the picture of him and Jeff from their U.Va. graduation, and the knife was exactly as Lizzie had described it: clean and in a plastic bag.

Dimly, he was aware of his heart starting to pound.

Miss Aurora, what did you do? he wondered.

Closing her door behind himself, he went over to the Wüsthof butcher-block holder by the stove.

Yes, it was the one that was missing.

Turning the blade in its bag over and over in his hands, he looked out the windows that faced the garage and the courtyard.

Miss Aurora's red Mercedes was parked grille in to the business center, exactly where it had been since he had arrived home. And it was on an impulse that made him sick to his stomach that he put the knife down, went back into Miss Aurora's suite, and got her car keys.

Before he headed outside once again, he found a pair of nitrile gloves under the sink and snapped them on.

It seemed appropriate that there was a rumble of distant thunder as he walked across to Miss Aurora's car, and he glanced up. Storm clouds were gathering over Indiana and about to follow the normal track of weather that would bring them to Charlemont.

Unlocking the sedan's doors, he opened up the entire vehicle, got out his phone, and shined the flash into floorboards, around the seats, over the armrest. Nothing seemed out of place, but this was just a delay tactic to get his shit together. When he'd gone through everything in the car proper, he retracted himself and hit the trunk release.

Before he looked in there, he walked around the exterior of the car, looking for dents and scratches. Then he checked out the wheels. No mud or anything in the tread or the rims.

It was like the car had been detailed.

Bracing himself, he went to the back and slowly opened the trunk's lid. He wasn't sure what he expected to find . . . maybe a tangle of leaves or sticks, bloodstains, twine that had tight knots in it. Fragments of his father's clothes.

There was nothing.

The sound of tires coming over the pea-stone drive brought his head around. The unmarked police car was gray with darkened windows and he checked his watch. Not bad.

Detective Merrimack got out, and for once, he didn't bother with that smile thing. "What are you doing?"

"Looking at the car."

"That's possible evidence in a murder investigation."

"I've got gloves on."

Merrimack came over and started shutting the doors, his hand covered with a bandanna he had taken out of the pocket of his windbreaker.

"When can you get forensics out here?" Lane said.

"They're on the way." Merrimack looked up to the security cameras mounted on the business center. "Where's the knife?"

"In the kitchen." Lane snapped off his gloves. "Come on in."

"I'll take those car keys—which you've touched."

"Sorry." Even though he wasn't. "Here."

As they went inside, Merrimack wrapped the keys up in the bandanna and disappeared them into his windbreaker.

"Did you handle the knife?" the detective asked.

"I didn't take it out of the bag, no."

Over at the counter, Merrimack inspected the blade without picking it up. "Can you show me where it was found?"

"In her private quarters. This way."

When Lane came up to the door, he glanced over his shoulder. "I've already opened and closed this."

"Of course you have."

Inside, he pointed to the picture he'd taken down and the hole it left in the lineup. "There. Lizzie found it there."

"Earlier today, right?" Merrimack went over and leaned in. "That's when she found it?"

"Yes."

"And why was she in here? What was your fiancée doing in Miss Aurora's quarters?"

Merrimack started to walk around, his hands clasped behind his back as he inspected everything. And yeah, Lane wanted to shove the guy out of Miss Aurora's private place. She would have hated this stranger with his suspicious eyes and his judgmental airs in here.

"I told you. She wanted to bring some photographs down to the hospital."

"For a woman who is in a coma?"

Lane narrowed his eyes. "She came around enough to talk today.

Lizzie thought it would be nice for her to see some of the people who love her."

"From what I understand, she's very ill."

"You want to tell me what you're getting at here?"

Merrimack poked his head into Miss Aurora's bedroom. "I just think it's a little curious, s'all."

"What is." So help him God, but Lane wanted to get one of Miss Aurora's iron skillets and forehand the guy in the head with it. "What's curious?"

Merrimack took his sweet damn time in answering. And then dodged the question entirely. "I heard from down at the jail that your brother Edward declined to see you this morning."

"So."

The detective wandered over to the BarcaLoungers and seemed to look out the bay window to the courtyard. "Are you aware that he was recently paid a visit by one of the staff psychiatrists?"

"No." When there was another pause, Lane put himself in the detective's way as he straightened. "I'm really bored of this."

"Your brother tried to slice his wrist open with a homemade prison knife a couple of nights ago." As Lane felt himself go numb, he was aware of Merrimack focusing on him with the intensity of a searchlight. "You didn't know this?"

"No."

"You sure about that?"

Edward had tried to commit suicide? Lane thought.

"I understand that your family is very close to Deputy Ramsey," Merrimack continued. "That in the past, you've called on him to help you all out. For instance, I know you asked if he was available this morning when you were trying to see Edward. It's nice that you have found such a source of support in him."

"Ramsey never told me about Edward."

"Of course he didn't."

"He didn't tell me! You want to call Ramsey and get his side of it? Because I will guarantee you that he'll say the same thing. He didn't call me."

"I've already spoken to him."

"Then why the hell are we talking about this?"

Merrimack dropped his voice. "You don't think it's even slightly suspicious that your brother tries to commit suicide, you have ties in the very department that oversees the jail, and within no more than a day or two, you start hitting me up with theories that he didn't commit murder—and then try to provide me with some proof? Like cameras that show nothing, a knife in a bag, a car you yourself have just gone through."

"I'm not faking anything here. My brother didn't kill his—my father."

"But, wait, it gets better—to top it off, the person that you're wanting me to believe did do it is a woman who is about to die. Pretty effective way of getting your brother out of jail. And you can't put someone who is dead on trial or in prison, can you."

Lane considered getting into it with the guy, but then decided it was better to show, not tell, wasn't it.

"Your forensics people are going to find what they do."

"They will. And you should be aware that tampering with evidence is a very serious crime, Mr. Baldwine."

"I didn't touch a damn thing."

"You were just poking around a car you told me I should find evidence in, remember?"

"Why are you so determined to blame Edward? Let me guess, you don't like rich people, and you've put me and my whole family into that category."

The detective pointedly glanced around. "We're not exactly in a double wide here, are we."

"Your job is to find the truth."

Merrimack walked out of the open doorway of Miss Aurora's quarters. "You don't need to remind me of my duties."

"I'm not so sure about that."

As Lane exited as well, the detective took a spool of police tape out of his windbreaker. "Do not go in here for any reason. Or the car. And if you find that you can't abide by those rules, I'll make it really easy for you and turn this whole house and all of its grounds into a crime scene. Now why don't you head back to that hospital while we work. If Miss Aurora comes around again, I'm going to want to speak to her."

For a moment, Lane wanted to protest being dismissed from his own goddamn property. But then he just nodded and walked away.

Arguing with Merrimack was going to get him nowhere.

Other than more pissed off than he was already.

TWENTY-TWO

Eight hundred miles.

Well, eight hundred and twenty-seven, according to what the Mercedes's trip computer had read.

As Gin felt the heat of Samuel T.'s anger, she decided it had been stupid to think she could get herself ready for his reaction. Even driving through the night, with nothing but endless role-playing and hypotheticals to keep her awake, had not prepared her for the reality of his fury.

"Are you even kidding me," he demanded.

She didn't try to respond. He was pacing now, his bare feet slapping against the floorboards of the porch, his hands on his hips, his head down as if he were trying to control himself and losing the battle.

Eventually, he stopped in front of her. "How do you know it's mine."

"Amelia," she corrected sharply, "is definitely yours. There is no question."

"You told me you were on the pill."

"I was. But I had that sinus infection. I was on penicillin during the vacation. It caused the pill to fail. I didn't know, Samuel T. I did not know."

He went back to the pacing, and the distance he covered grew longer and longer, until he was traversing the entire length of the porch.

"I was a child, Samuel."

"So you're saying this is my fault. Because I was two years older than you?" He shook his head. "Why the hell did you make the story up about your professor? Why did you lie?"

"Because the weekend we got home, you hooked up with that girl, Cynthia."

"What?"

"Don't play dumb." She felt her own anger rise. "You know exactly what I'm talking about. We got into that fight on the plane on the way home. And to pay me back, you took Cynthia to Aspen the next week. You picked her because you knew she would tell me."

He pushed his hand through the air as if he were erasing everything. "I don't remember any of that—"

"Bullshit! You know what you did! So yes"—she sat up and then got to her feet, too—"I made up that story about my professor."

"You got him fired!"

"He was fired because he was sleeping with three of his students!"

"But you lied about him and you didn't care! You never fucking care! You use people, you don't give a good goddamn about how their lives are affected by your—"

"Really! What about you? You're just as bad. I had to comfort

Cynthia after she got back and you refused to answer her calls. You do that, you sleep with women knowing damn well you don't give a shit about them, and then you leave them out to hang because God forbid if someone doesn't like you. And meanwhile, you're on to the next. Don't pretend that's not how you operate."

She must have hit a nerve of truth because Samuel T. didn't immediately come back at her with anything.

His quiet didn't last, however: "You are the most self-centered person I have ever met. You're spoiled and you're entitled and you should have aborted that poor child when you had the chance—"

Her palm went flying before she was aware of wanting to hit him, and the smack of the impact was so loud her ears rang.

Then she jabbed her finger right in his face. "Amelia is *not* a mistake. She is a smart young woman who's had a really shitty mother and no father to speak of. Hate me all you want, but don't you *ever* suggest she is a waste."

"No father, huh. And whose fucking fault is that? You want to poor-me that girl on the basis that she didn't know her dad, but *you* did that, Gin. That is all your fault!"

"And how would that have worked for you? You think you would have been a stand-up guy and been there when she was up in the middle of the night? You think you would have stopped getting your degree and moved in to Easterly to change diapers? That you would have manned up back then and given her what she needed? You excelled at two things in college, drinking and fucking. The fact that you got into law school at all was only because your father begged them to take you—"

"Wait, wait, wait, are you saying you are mother of the year? As far as I understand it, you had a baby nurse for the first six months and then nanny after nanny after nanny. Exactly what did you do for her? Did you even change a diaper yourself? Hey, answer me this.

When you ran out of wipes, did you put her in the back of your father's Rolls-Royce and drive her into the 'burbs to Target? Did you,
Gin? And when you got there, did you put her in a cart and push her
around in your Chanel dress and your Prada heels? No? I didn't fucking think so."

In the back of her mind, Gin was very aware that they could just
keep going back and forth all night with this no-you're-shittier-than-
I-am, no-you-are, no-YOU-are. But at the end of the day, this was
about Amelia.

"You win," she heard herself say. "I was a horribly negligent
mother who cared more about her life than her child's. I ignored
Amelia and I was relieved when she went off to prep school because
all we did was fight. I have been . . . unforgivably selfish. There is no
way I can make up for those years, and I will have to live with that
reality for the rest of my life. Amelia is who she is in spite of me, not
because of any good example I've set."

Samuel T. seemed taken aback at the candor and she took advantage of his surprise. "I decided after my father died that enough was
enough. She's coming back home because she told me that was what
she wanted to do, and I've helped her figure out how to make it happen. I don't have any clue how to be a good mother, but goddamn it,
I'm going to give it a shot—and part of my change is coming clean
with both of you. I would like her to know who you are and spend
time with you—and I'm hoping you will agree, because it is the best
thing for her."

Wrapping her arms around herself, she looked toward the storm
clouds that had gathered on the horizon.

As silence reigned between them, she knew that she had been
right about one thing: Samuel T. was never going to forgive her. She
could tell by the way he was staring at her, as if she were a stranger
he didn't want to be anywhere around. She had earned this animus,

however, and was going to have to live with it as a consequence of her failures.

What she was truly terrified of, though? How Amelia was going to react. They had talked all the way to New England about nothing, and everything, and Gin had come to truly appreciate the girl. If Amelia shut her out now? It would be like losing her just when Gin was getting to know her.

But she had earned that, as well.

"She is up north finishing her exams," Gin said. "Then she's coming home. She's going to ship her things and fly back."

As she spoke in short sentences, Gin prayed that Samuel T. would agree to meet with the girl. Get to know her. Maybe . . . after a while . . . learn to love her.

After so many years of demanding things of the man, it was the only thing she would ever beg for from him. And his answer was life and death to her.

*S*amuel T. was ready to keep arguing. He was so fucking beyond ready to keep throwing shit at Gin, to continue marching down the road of their previous mutual indiscretions, to spiral directly into the full force of their conflicts.

It was so much easier than dealing with the reality that he had a child.

He had a child, a daughter, on the face of the planet earth. And not only that, he had had her with Gin.

Gin had given birth to their child.

Gin . . . and he . . . had had a baby. Together.

And she had cheated him out of sixteen years of knowing his own flesh and blood.

As a renewed blast of white-hot anger hit, Samuel T. opened his mouth to point out another transgression of hers—but something about the way she was staring across at him made him stop: Standing before him, she had become a perfectly self-contained unit, her arms wrapped around herself, her body unmoving, her expression remote and calm. It was as if she had unplugged from the socket of their electricity, and somehow, this drained him as well.

Dimly, he thought of what he knew of Amelia.

Not much. The girl hadn't been a big topic of conversation for Gin, and he had certainly never felt compelled to ask her how her child by another man was doing. Amelia had been smart enough to get into Hotchkiss, though. That was one thing.

From out of nowhere, an image of the girl in that crypt at the cemetery came to him. She had been looking up at the lineup of plaques, reading the names of her ancestors, her head tilted to one side, her long, thick brown hair down way past her shoulder blades.

As a vague feeling of panic threatened to overwhelm him, Samuel T. went right for the bottle of bourbon, finishing what was in his glass on the way. He poured himself a second serving only because his fine breeding prevented him from guzzling the stuff directly from the open neck.

If he'd had any medical training, he would have run himself an IV of Family Reserve.

With the booze burning its way to his gut, he opened his mouth again. What stopped him from lobbing more insults this time was what Gin had called him out on. Preston/Peabody/Prentiss had indeed been phoning him and texting him, using excuses as original as inviting him out to meet her and her friends, asking him to a birthday party, wondering if he'd lost her number.

Well, actually, those were just the texts. He hadn't bothered listening to the voicemails.

Although he might finally learn her name if he did that.

Off in the distance, thunder rolled across the sky, and he thought absently that he was wrong. There would be no light from the setting sun on the porch tonight. Storm clouds had roiled up over in Indiana, the purple and dark-gray big boys promising a rough couple of hours.

"I want you to go," he heard himself say.

"All right."

"I will never forgive you for this."

"I know. And I do not blame you."

He thought about the last sixteen years of his life. Yes, he had gotten himself a fancy law degree and started a practice here in Charlemont that was thriving. He had also slept with how many women? Not a clue. More than a hundred? More than . . . God, he didn't want to think about it. And how many nights out had he had, stumbling, laughing, drunk and stupid with other adult frat boys like himself?

Where exactly would he have fit a child into all that?

Not the point, he reminded himself.

His choice had been taken away from him.

As Gin stared at him, he knew she was waiting to hear whether or not he would see Amelia—and his first instinct was to walk back into his house and slam the door without giving her an answer, just to hurt her.

"I want a paternity test," he said as the first drops of rain began to fall.

"You can't take my word for it? I'd rather spare her the unpleasantness. And she might feel as though you're obligated thereafter."

"I *am* obligated—or I will be if I am her father. I'm going to have to pay for things."

"I'm not looking for money," Gin bit out. "Do you think this is a fundraiser for her college or something?"

He shot a glare across at her. "You don't get to pull any kind of holier-than-thou card with this. And there should be a test so that she knows she's safe investing in any kind of relationship with me. Think about it. How would you feel if this news got dropped in your life all of a sudden. Wouldn't you want to know for certain?"

As Gin got silent, he shook his head. "Has she never asked about me—" He caught himself. "Her father, before?"

"It hasn't really come up, no."

For some reason, he thought of those daddy/daughter dances they did at the club and at Charlemont Country Day. Had anyone taken Amelia? Or had she had to sit those events out while the rest of her friends went with their fathers?

Had she been sick as a child? Bullied? When she had woken up in that huge white house during thunderstorms, had she imagined her father coming for her and saving her, like some white knight—

"Who is she dating?"

"I'm sorry?" Gin said.

"Who. Is. She. Dating." He punctuated that with a hard pull off the rim of his glass. "Does she have a boyfriend."

"No." Gin cleared her throat. "There was a guy she liked at the beginning of the year, but I guess it didn't work out. She told me while we were on the Pennsylvania Turnpike."

Okay, he was so relieved that some dumbass teenage boy with all those hormones and bright ideas wasn't hitting on his little—

"I want the test." He looked back over. "I want it so that I know I'm safe to feel for the kid. I don't trust you, and after this, I never will. I'll meet with her as soon as she gets back."

He thought about telling Gin it had to be without her presence, but that wasn't going to help the situation.

"Good." Gin lowered her voice. "That's good. Thank you—"

"I'm not doing this for you." He turned his back on her and headed for the door into his kitchen. "I'm not doing anything for you, ever again."

*I*n spite of the fact that Merrimack had all but ordered Lane off the premises, he was not about to leave his family estate as the CSI vehicles showed up by the garages. Yet neither could he just hang out on the sidelines, a pedestrian bystander on his own damned property.

He ended up in the business center, in his father's office—from which, every half hour or so, he would head down to the other end of the facility so he could look out of the shallow window in the supply room at what they were doing to Miss Aurora's car.

Unfortunately, he couldn't see much. The CMPD had put up a bright blue awning so that the rain that had started to fall wouldn't disturb their investigation, and the thing had a side flap that the wind had to kick aside in order for him to get any visuals.

Merrimack was everywhere, though, going back and forth between the kitchen's screen door and the car and the trucks. He didn't seem to notice that there was a storm blowing things around, and in other circumstances, Lane would have respected the guy's tenacious focus on the job at hand.

But he kind of hated the man.

With a curse, Lane turned away and walked back through the dim corridor. The business center had been ostensibly designed and decorated as a testament to the power and prestige of the Bradford Bourbon Company—but in reality, it was more like William Baldwine's tribute to himself, the maroon and gold carpeting and the heavy velvet drapes and the company seals creating a cultivated environment of power.

Especially the reception area.

Behind the vacant desk, which had not been occupied since Lane and Jeff had thrown all of senior management out, there were flags of both the Commonwealth of Kentucky and the United States—as if you were entering the damn White House. And to that point, the space itself was even circular like the Oval Office, the carpet bearing the ornate Bradford family crest on it in the center.

The CEO's office had an anteroom where William's German shepherd of an executive assistant had enjoyed control over access to him. And beyond . . . was a space that Lane still had a hard time walking into.

For one, it continued to smell like his father's cigarettes and cigars, the lingering tobacco aroma making it seem like a humidor with a throne and a desk inside. Then there were the pictures in the shelves behind the command center. Whereas Miss Aurora's photographs were all of other people, William's were always of himself with prominent folks like presidents, movie stars, socialites, and politicians.

Staring at the images, Lane picked out his father in each one. The expression on that distinguished face was always the same, no matter the age or context, whether it was black tie or on a golf course, at the opera or the theater, in the White House or on one of Easterly's terraces: cold, narrowed eyes, and a smile that was, actually, not dissimilar to Merrimack's.

A professional's mask.

Then again, William had had to hide who he really was. He had come from a lesser Southern family and had set his sights on Lane's mother as the first of many conquests. As for why she had married him? There was supposition that Little V.E. had taken a shine to him because he was so handsome, but clearly she had soon learned to regret her romantic notions.

Lane did look a little like the man.

Actually . . . quite a bit.

Refocusing on the desk, he went back around to the piles of folders he had taken out of the file cabinets in the business center's back storage room. He'd reviewed most of the deals struck by the BBC under William's reign, and found nothing out of the ordinary for a bourbon company.

Nothing owned by WWB Holdings, either.

And none of the businesses John Lenghe had detailed from memory.

Lane sat down in his father's leather chair and swiveled things around. Underneath the shelves, which ran only halfway up the wall, there were a series of locked cabinets, and it didn't take a genius to surmise that a man who was operating outside the scope of the law and who was not computer savvy would probably keep details of his deals right behind where he sat every day . . . in an office that, when he was away for so much as a trip to the loo, was guarded by that executive assistant of his . . . in a facility that, when he left for the night, was not just locked, but secured by an alarm system to rival the Smithsonian's.

Lane had already tried the brass knobs before and found the handmade doors locked.

He was done with that.

Reaching across the desk, he picked up an ashtray that was as big as a dinner plate and as heavy as a nautical anchor.

This was going to feel *great.*

He stood up, pushed the chair out of the way, and hefted the weight up over his shoulder. Then he swung the thing like it was a baseball bat, crashing it into one of the double-door'd lower compartments.

It was an inconvenient testament to the makers that he had to strike a number of times before the heavy-duty mahogany splintered and cracked. Phase two was all about the bare hands, his fingers clawing into the panels and snapping them off their hinges.

When he was done with the first of four sets, there was wood everywhere and he was panting, but, God, it was satisfying.

And hey, what do you know.

Files.

His knees popped as he got down on his haunches and transferred bundles of papers up onto the wide lowest shelf. There were so many that, to accommodate the load, he shoved pictures of his father out of the way—and yup, that also felt good.

And then, in a moment of hey-wait-let's-not-confuse-things, he had the forethought to take all the documents he'd gotten out of the "official" records storage and move them off the desk to the conference table across the room. That way, he would know what had come out of where.

Before he sat down and started to work his way through the new batch of files, he ran back to check on Merrimack again. He had told the detective he was leaving, but then had disappeared into the house—only to enter the business center through one of its French doors on the garden side.

He didn't want Merrimack to come looking for him in here and find all of this.

For godsakes, Jeff was already worried the Feds weren't going to buy the diversification story that had been "leaked" to the press. And with Lane's luck, that homicide detective had a lucrative side job handling embezzlement charges for the U.S. Government.

Hey, stranger things had happened.

Like every fucking day since he had come back to Charlemont.

Staring out of the tinted window at the CSI guys, he saw a whole lot of nothing-much, just people in uniforms and latex gloves walking around in the rain, coming and going out—

Oh, check it. They were removing things from the house in plastic bags with seals on them.

He thought of that knife.

Shit. If Miss Aurora had sacrificed one of her beloved knives, it would only have been for a very specific reason. Those blades were her pride and joy, the tools of her trade, the kind of thing that no one ever used but her.

A chef's knives were private. Hell, even the sous chefs who came in for events brought their own rolls of blades.

No, she had used that Wüsthof for something important.

She had kept it for a good cause.

And she had placed it behind his picture to send a message.

He would never have thought her capable of something so violent. But one thing had always been true about her.

She loved him more than anyone else. Theirs had been a special connection.

And he feared that a mother's love could turn murderous, under certain circumstances.

"Miss Aurora," he whispered, "what did you do?"

TWENTY-THREE

*W*hen Gin returned to Easterly, she was so sleep deprived and emotionally wasted that she missed the staff road because of her daze—and then lacked the energy to turn the Mercedes around and head back. At the estate's main entrance, flashbulbs went off as she had to pause for the wrought-iron gates to open, but at least the storms had caused a good half of the news trucks to leave.

As she went up the hill, the mansion's imposing facade was spotlit by a lick of lightning, the brilliant, jagged flashing making her think of the start of a horror movie.

She parked the sedan right in front and left the keys in it.

Then she waited.

For the butler to come out and retrieve her with an umbrella and a free hand to take her things in.

It was quite some time before she remembered there was no more staff. No one poised for her to give a command to draw a hot bath. Nobody to unpack for her and summon her a light salad and a bottle of Chardonnay.

Getting out, she gathered her Louis Vuitton duffel and her quilted Chanel bag and lugged them up the steps through the rain—and then realized there was no one to take the car around to the garages. No man in a chauffeur's uniform to wash and detail it after its long trip, or check its tire pressures and refill its tank.

Whatever, she thought as she muscled the mansion's heavy front door open. The thing had been rained on before. It would survive.

As she stepped in out of the storm, the air in the house was cool and still, and all was quiet. Which was eerie. Easterly had never been a silent house, what with the crowd of people who had lived and worked under its roof—

"You're back."

She slowly turned her head. Richard Pford was sitting on the silk sofa in the receiving parlor on the left, his legs crossed at the knees, his fingers bridged up, his elbows tucked into his sides.

"Not now, Richard." She dropped her duffel and couldn't believe she had to close the door behind herself. "I'm tired."

"Isn't it more, *I've got a headache?*"

"As if that matters with you."

Another flicker of lightning permeated the windows, turning Richard's face into something sinister.

"Where were you."

"Taking Amelia back to school."

"I thought she usually flies."

"Not this time."

"No?" He sat forward. "Too expensive? So you decided you would drive her. What a good mother you are."

Gin moved her eyes toward the stairs without shifting her face away from him. Was there anyone else in the house? Where were Lane and Lizzie?

"You haven't been answering my calls, Virginia."

"I was driving."

"All the way through the night? You didn't rest even once?"

"No, I wanted to get home."

"Back to me, of course." He put his thin hand over his heart. "I'm touched."

Richard surged to his feet and picked up something from the low table in front of him. An envelope. A large manila envelope, the kind you'd put through the mail.

Gin took a step back. "I'm going to go up and have a shower."

"Oh, I can imagine you're ready for one." He smiled as he came closer. "I want you to do me a favor first, though."

She glanced down the hall, hoping to see someone coming out of the door into the staff part of the house.

If she screamed, would her mother's nurse hear it? Maybe.

But probably not, she decided as thunder answered the lightning's call.

Richard didn't stop until he was a foot away from her, and he made a show of opening the flap on the envelope. "I really need you to see these. Tell me, did your brother Lane mention that I've moved out?"

Gin narrowed her eyes. "No. Have you?"

"Yes, I don't think this marriage is working out for me. I left last night and came back today after work to gather my belongings."

"Where is your car, then?"

"Just under the magnolia tree. I was going to bring my things down, but then I decided to wait for you."

With a steady pull, he took out some floppy eight-by-ten sheets of—photographs; they were glossy photographs.

Of her and Samuel T. in the Jag at the cemetery: He was holding her hand and they were staring into each other's eyes—just before he had turned things around to show her her own engagement ring. And then they were driving off. There were others, too, from when they had come out of his penthouse's building after they had made love.

But the most frame-able, of course, was the one from when Samuel T. had helped her back into the Jag. She had gripped the man's black tie and pulled him down to her mouth.

"Do you know what else these came with?" Richard said with a voice that vibrated with growing menace. "An invitation by a reporter to comment on them. They're being printed in tomorrow's *Charlemont Courier Journal*—what kind of fool are you trying to make of me!"

She ducked just before he hit her, and then she spun around and lunged for the front door. As thunder roared across the sky, she tried to yank the vast weight open, but Richard caught her by the hair and pulled her back.

"You whore! You fucked him, didn't you! And then you ran away with him! You didn't take your goddamn daughter to school—you went—"

Gin pivoted around, her hair long enough to let her turn. Richard's face was twisted in rage, and she had some thought that this was it. He was going to kill her right here, her blood spilling over the black and white marble floor, her brother or maybe Lane's fiancée the one to find her body.

Thank God she had hocked the diamond out of that engagement ring and put those gold bars in a safety-deposit box for Amelia.

And thank God she had told the jeweler and the bank manager that if she died, it was Richard's fault.

And lastly, thank God she had come clean with Samuel T. At least Amelia would still have one parent.

Oh, and while she was making her final list? Fuck you, Richard.

Without being conscious of moving, she grabbed on to his forearms . . . and drove her knee up right between Pford's legs, nailing him so hard, she felt the impact all the way through her own pelvis.

As he jacked in half and released her in favor of his manhood, she kicked off her heels so she could run properly and bolted for the door again. This time, as she cranked on the handle, a gust from the storm hit the front of the house and blew things wide open.

With rain and wind in her face, she raced for the Mercedes, skidding around its trunk, her bare feet getting torn up by the loose stones of the drive. And then she was in behind the wheel, slamming the driver's door shut, locking everything. Her hands skipped and fluttered around the ignition button—

Boom, boom, boom!

Richard was pounding on the driver's-side window, beating the glass with his fist—

"Leave me alone!" she screamed.

The Mercedes came alive with a subtle shiver and she threw it into reverse and punched the accelerator, the weight of the car lurching in Richard's direction, knocking him down. She didn't even look to see if she was going to hit him: As soon as the drive down the mountain was in front of her, she jerked the gearshift down and floored the gas.

In the rearview, she had a brief impression of him jumping to his feet, his arms banging on the trunk before he was again thrown off to the side.

Gin kept the car on the lane, even as gravity increased her speed and buckets of water lashed the windshield. Holding on with both hands, she didn't dare turn on the wipers because she was afraid to loosen either grip for even a second.

At the base of the hill, she hit the brakes, the car skidding on the slick pavement as she came up to the gates. She was of half a mind just to ram them open, but she was worried the Mercedes wouldn't drive afterward—

With a glance in the rearview, she prayed she wasn't going to see any headlights.

Yet she feared Richard was going to—

Just as the gates were almost open enough, a twin set of beams made the turn at the top and started down for her at a dead run.

*S*amuel T.'s farmhouse had a kitchen that overlooked the same meadow that the back porch did, and he watched the storm come in through the picture window over the sink. Or, rather, he and his bottle of Family Reserve did. And as the ice cubes melted from his glass, he didn't bother replacing them; he just continued on with the warm heat of the bourbon, neat.

As he stood there, his eyes tracking the rolling clouds and patterns of downfalls, his mind was a superhighway of random thoughts, fears, and regrets. He didn't let any hope in. Too dangerous—

When his cell phone rang in the pocket of his discarded jacket, he didn't answer it. He did not want to talk to anyone about anything.

God, the lightning was so beautiful, forking through the angry, aubergine sky, the sheets of rain falling as curtains from cloud to land, the thunder stomping through the air, an invisible giant.

Racking his brain, he tried to remember any time that he had ever seen Amelia: He had one vague memory from right after she was born. He'd come home to Charlemont and there had been an event at the Bradfords'—something that he had only attended because he'd wanted to eyeball the Scandal of Easterly.

Gin Baldwine, home from school, with her professor's baby.

He'd had to engineer an excuse to go up to Lane's room and then had "gotten lost."

Gin hadn't been home. The baby nurse had been uniformed, pleasant, and very protective.

Amelia had looked . . . like a baby. She had been swaddled in a pink blanket and there had been a mobile of plush toys over her head. Yes, he thought . . . a mobile with a white moon, three yellow stars, and a sky-blue cow with a milkmaid's pink and lace dress on.

It seemed totally inappropriate that he remembered more about that fucking mobile than he did about his own child.

Or . . . *maybe* his child, was more like it.

And as he tried vainly to recall Amelia's infant face, or whether she had hair, or what color her eyes had been, the enormity of what Gin had cheated him of became truly apparent: A father's first moment with his child had been stolen from him. She had denied him that breathtaking, awe-inspiring, heart-wrenching meeting where he held an infant to his chest and vowed to care for her for all of his life.

Samuel felt a tickle on his face, and when he went to brush it away, he was surprised to find a tear on his fingertip.

Of course, Gin had also robbed his parents of their first bondings with their grandchild. Ever since Samuel T.'s brother had died, he had been the only son left in the family. And he knew that his mother and father were quietly waiting and hoping that he would settle down and give them another generation to carry forth the Lodge name.

There had been so much pain for the two of them, proof positive that wealth might insulate you from worrying about whether your house was paid for, but it didn't do shit against destiny: They knew all too well that nothing was permanent, no life guaranteed. So heirs mattered, not just for the dissemination of material things, but as recipients of love and tradition.

They had never talked aloud of any of this, however.

Sometimes, though, unspoken hopes were the hardest to bear.

And so Gin had denied them of their proper first meeting with their grandchild.

Assuming Amelia really was his.

As a gust of wind shouldered against the farmhouse, the swinging bed on the porch got pushed back on its tethers, and some of the wicker furniture shifted over the floorboards as if it were considering taking refuge inside the house.

With a curse, he turned away from the view . . . only to stall out.

There wasn't even anything to clean up in the kitchen, everything put away from breakfast, the dishwasher emptied, the counters tidied of the detritus of life.

Considering the chaos in his skull, he felt in desperate need of something that required his attention, a task that he could exert his intelligence over and improve, on his terms, in his way, at his choice and doing.

His mail and his phone seemed the two most logical avenues for this goal, and he went over to where he had dumped his navy blue suit jacket. Fishing out his cell phone, he accessed his voicemail. There were three messages, two from unknown numbers and the other from an attorney here in town who was suing one of Samuel T.'s clients.

He started with that one, which had come in just now, because why not. And as he listened to the guy make demands, he held the phone in place at his ear with his shoulder and began flipping through the household bills that had come in.

Deleting the message, he thought, Okaaaaay, maybe he'd tackle another situation first.

He triggered the next message down because he liked to do things in order, and as he put the phone back into position, he picked up the big flat envelope.

But the sound of a woman's voice on the recording stopped him.

"Hi, Sam. It's Prescott calling. I, ah, I've left you some messages. I haven't heard back about this coming weekend? Are you going to join me or . . . or is the fact that I haven't gotten anything from you the answer? Anyway . . . I'm just up in New York for today and to-morrow on a shoot. Then I'm back in Charlemont. It's no biggie, ei-ther way. But, yes, I'd love to know what your plans are. Thanks, bye."

Taking the phone from his ear, he hovered over the *delete* button.

He ended up skipping that and called forth the final message. It had come in about an hour before, when he'd been heading home with the top down and hadn't heard the ringing.

As the message started with nothing but static, he flipped the envelope open—and what was inside confused him.

What the . . . hell? Photographs?

". . . Hello, Lodge," came a muffled male voice. "I just want to say fuck you. I'm going to kill her first and then I'm coming after you. You fucking . . ."

The message continued on as Samuel T. flipped through what turned out to be close-ups of Gin and him from the cemetery and then later as they left his building together after they'd had sex on his sofa at the penthouse.

Meanwhile, on the message, Richard Pford's cadence grew stron-ger in volume and urgency, the man working himself up into a lather that was going to hurt someone. Badly.

The final thing in the envelope was a single sheet of paper with a reporter's name and number on it, and a statement that a quote would be appreciated before everything ran the following morning.

Samuel T. cut off the message and didn't delete it. Calling up Gin's phone number, he waited through the rings until voicemail kicked in. Then he called her again. And a third time.

He lasted a split second after that.

With curses leaving his lips, he raced through the house to get one of his handguns out of the study.

As the storm raged across the land, he ran back to the kitchen, grabbed the keys to his Range Rover, and punched open the door to the garage, triggering the opener—

Only to stop.

Heart pounding, body flooded with adrenaline, he became trapped on a precipice he wasn't sure he wanted to be on anymore: Gin's drama was a sinkhole for him. It always had been. She was the siren who called him into tumultuous seas, the beacon that he followed toward chaos, the fire off in the distance that he couldn't resist, even as it threatened to burn down his house.

He thought of Amelia.

The lie.

The losses he had suffered with his daughter.

As the garage door finished its ascent, the hot, wet breath of the storm barged into the bays.

He imagined himself crouched over the steering wheel, the Range Rover's engine powering forward, visibility poor, his destination unclear. She had been headed back to Easterly—or at least he assumed she had been. He wasn't sure where she was.

Maybe Richard was waiting for her there.

And Easterly always had people around. So she wouldn't be alone.

Samuel T. watched the storm from this different vantage point a little longer. Then he turned away from the torrential rain and damaging winds . . . and went back in his house.

The door shut on its own behind him.

TWENTY-FOUR

*G*in could barely see River Road in front of her as she shot down the Ohio's shoreline, the fury of the storm muscling the car around so that she constantly had to realign left and right to stay on the pavement. As she breaknecked along, she passed a number of cars that had pulled over to the side, their blinkers flashing as they waited the worst of it out.

Richard was right behind her.

No matter how fast she went into the curves or how much she tried to pull away on the straight sections, he was sticking with her. Closing in.

As she kept going through the gallons of water falling from the sky and the flashing lightning and pounding thunder, part of her was in the car, hands locked on the wheel, body braced, foot pressed hard on the accelerator. Yet even more of her was floating above the speeding Mercedes, watching everything from a position somewhere above her right shoulder.

It was, she supposed, as it would be if she died in a crash, her spirit lingering over the chaos of the corporeal world as the car fireballed into oblivion.

Funny, she was familiar with this splitting experience. She had it whenever Richard was on her sexually, and there had been times before he had come along that she had done this: Whenever she got too wild, too drunk, too out of control, the disassociation could take over.

It could also happen if she were scared.

The first incidence had been when she was a child. Her father had come after her and her brother Lane, for some reason. She could remember the man marching down the hallway outside of the bedrooms, his face in a rage, a strap in his hand, his voice like the thunder in this storm.

She had run as fast as her feet could take her. Run, run, run, and then she'd hid—she had known that was the only thing to do to save herself.

She had known because Lane had told her so: *Run, Gin, run, and hide.*

Hide, Gin, so he can't find you—go into a closet or under the bed. . . .

She had been three and a half? Maybe four?

She had chosen the bed in her room to take cover under, and she could still recall exactly what it smelled like under there, the dusty rug and the sweet floor polish. She had been shaking and breathing hard, and tears had come out of her eyes, but she had not cried out loud.

Lane had gotten beaten but good. She had heard everything from his room next door.

She hadn't even been sure what he had done. And she didn't think Lane had known, either—no, wait, he had refused to tell their father where Maxwell was. And she had gotten caught up in it all when she had seen Lane run by and had chased after him, thinking at first it was a chance to play.

Yes, that was how it had gone down.

And she could still recall that sound of the strap on her brother. He had cried out over and over again . . . and the beating hadn't stopped until he had told William that Max was in the basement, in the wine cellar.

Those heavy footfalls had then come down the hall and paused in front of the open door to Gin's room. How her heart had pounded. She could have sworn he'd hear it. And yet her father had continued on—and she had stayed put.

Eventually, she had had to go to the bathroom.

She had remained there, however, until she had peed herself. Some five hours later.

She had told no one about that part; she had been too ashamed to admit that she had soiled the carpet under the bed.

When they had done her suite of rooms over when she had turned thirteen, she could still remember the decorator frowning at the stain when the old bed had been taken away.

That was why she liked her rooms to be white: In a convoluted way, it proved to everyone and everybody that she hadn't been weak and lost control of her bladder.

Craziness.

And so was this, she thought as she tried to draw herself back down into herself.

Checking the rearview again, Richard was so close to the Mercedes's bumper that she could clearly visualize him over his own steering wheel, his face full of rage, his mouth open like he was screaming at her.

As fear spiked and she decided he was truly mad, she had a strange realization. Richard, and his particular brand of unpleasantness, with its threat of violence never far from the surface, was what she had grown up around. In this way, he was like her father, a simmering explosion about to find a target.

Yes, she thought. She had chosen him for a number of reasons.

Not all of them money.

Had her father known this? Had William been aware of Richard's proclivities? Probably not. And even if he had been, it was doubtful that her father would have cared whether or not the torture continued. After all, when William had tried to force her into marrying Richard right before he had died, it had been all about the business imperative: William had assumed that with Richard "in" the family, Pford Distributors would offer better terms to the BBC.

So she hadn't been taken into account except as a lever to be pulled.

In fact, William had known what was coming with all those bad deals and bad loans, and he'd clearly planned to cut some of the financial shortfalls off at the pass by selling her to Richard. And of course, she had refused. Only to then volunteer for exactly what he'd demanded of her when it had become clear she was going to lose her lifestyle.

Her father's daughter, indeed—

Richard rammed the rear end of the Mercedes, the bump hard enough to kick Gin's head back against the rest. As she screamed, she fought to keep control and stay on the road—

He did it again. Just before a tight turn that would take them over a thin bridge which spanned one of the Ohio's larger feeding streams.

"Stop!" she yelled at him. "Leave me alone!"

But he was a nightmare of her own making, a Grim Reaper she had let into her life because she had been too scared, too lazy, and too spoiled to go forward without the money and the prominence she had grown up with.

He was her own damn fault, the culmination of her sins and her weaknesses, the reckoning she had never thought would come for every snotty thing she had ever done.

He was going to run her off the road, and he had a gun in that car of his—he had told her just a week ago that he kept it under the front seat because he had to drive around at night in that Bentley of his.

Richard was going to shoot her and maybe himself and that was how all this was going to end.

How *she* was going to end—

Thump!

As he rammed her car one last time, the Mercedes began to lose traction, and that was when everything slowed down. She steered hard away from the river to counter the drift, and the car corrected for a moment. But then the hood ornament over-swung to the marshes and the trees on the right.

The guardrail popped the front two wheels off the ground and she had a brief moment of weightlessness . . . and then the slam on the far side clapped her teeth together and made her head ring—oh, she wasn't wearing a seat belt. She'd hit the ceiling.

There was no time to think. Airbags exploded in her face, powder going everywhere as she was punched in the chest.

And the ride didn't end there.

Her foot hit the accelerator again after she landed, giving that powerful engine a huge boost that propelled her further off the road and into the marshes. Trees hit the front of the car, scratched down the side, clawed at the undercarriage.

As the airbags had already begun to deflate, she caught sight of the huge swamp maple directly in her path—and there was no stopping any of it, no changing her course, no altering the inevitable crash.

Rather like destiny.

The impact was like an explosion, and her forehead hit the wind-shield. Then the rebound threw her back into her seat, and she ping-ponged in between the steering wheel and the headrest.

Until she finally fell back against the seat.

Dizzy, confused, and in pain, she heard a subtle hiss in front of her from the engine and tried to focus, but her vision wasn't working right—

Bright light. Very bright light.

Had she died and this was the afterlife that people talked about?

Except no, she had stayed in her body. Hadn't she? She thought she had—

Click. Click. Clickclickclick.

She lolled her head toward the sound. And then jumped back from her door.

Richard was trying to open things, trying to get at her, pulling and yanking at the handle, getting nowhere because of the locking mechanism.

As something blurred her eyes, she pushed her hands across her face and prayed that the sunroof hadn't broken—and thus provided him with another way at her. But it wasn't rain. It was blood.

"Let me in!" Richard screamed as he pounded on the glass with his fists. "You let me in, Virginia!"

Lightning flashed and the rain fell, plastering his dark hair to his head, his face like a Halloween mask, slick and pale and horrible.

"Let me in, Virginia!"

Bam! Bam! Bam—

Scrambling across the seat, she put her back to the other door and tucked her knees up to her chest. As she linked her arms around herself and shivered, blood dripping down onto her dress, she thought it was just like being under that bed. Waiting to see if her father would come after her or stick to beating her brothers.

Bang, bang, bang—

As the sound changed, it was because Richard was hitting the window with something else. Something metal . . . the butt of a gun—

The safety glass spidered first—and then broke free in a chunk that fell where she had been sitting behind the wheel.

Richard put his head through the hole, his eyes and smile all Jack Nicholson from *The Shining*. "No more running, Virginia . . . now be a good girl, and open this door."

TWENTY-FIVE

s Richard ordered her to let him in, something made a connection in Gin's brain. Unhinging her right arm, she patted at the glove compartment without taking her eyes off Richard. The latch evaded her fingers—and when she did find it, she fumbled with pushing it.

"You don't want to make me madder, Virginia."

Rain was running down Richard's face, but he didn't seem to notice, and as lightning flashed again, she glanced up through the closed sunroof.

"Looking for God?" he said. "I'm going to help you meet Him, Virginia—"

"That's not my name," she choked out.

"What was that? Not your name? Should I call you 'whore,' then? Is that what Lodge calls you when he's fucking you?"

Finally, the glove compartment fell open, and she shoved her hand in, pain registering in her knuckles as she clawed through its contents, praying that—

As her hand locked on the butt of a nine millimeter, she closed her eyes and tried to remember what her brother Edward had taught her about how to shoot. Where was the safety? How did she disengage it?

Oh, God, if there were no bullets, she was a dead woman.

She was probably dead, anyway.

"I'm so sorry, Richard," she said quickly to distract him. "I didn't mean it, I was wrong. I'm sorry, I was wrong—"

As Richard frowned, she sat forward and reached out to him with her free hand. "Please forgive me, please don't leave me—"

Lightning flashed, illuminating the inside of the Mercedes, and she knew the instant he saw what she was doing with her other hand. Just as she flicked the gun's safety off and started to swing the muzzle up and around, he shifted back and double-palmed his own weapon, pointing it through the hole in the glass.

"Don't call me Virginia!" she shouted at the top of her lungs as they both pulled the triggers.

Loud popping, multiple shots, the ringing sound of at least one bullet hitting metal. And as Gin kept shooting, she closed her eyes and twisted toward the dash, trying to get her major organs out of the way. Ears hurting, eyes stinging, something wrong with her leg, she just kept that forefinger down on that fucking trigger, the autoloader doing what it was supposed to do until there was nothing left in the clip.

And still she kept her arm up and that grip hard, even though she was shaking so badly that the back of her skull was repeatedly banging into something.

What was that sound?

There was some kind of rhythmic—

It was her. She was panting. And there was still a hiss, coming out of the front of the car. And rain, softer rain now, pattering on the hood, the roof, the windshield, like cats with quiet paws.

Staring sightlessly ahead, every time she blinked, she saw Richard's face. And then her father's. And then Richard's . . . until the two men became as one, an amalgam of each other—

"Gin."

At the sound of the disembodied voice, she jerked to attention and once again looked up through the sunroof's transparent cover.

"Put down the gun, Gin," it said.

Opening her mouth, she gave voice to her confusion: "God?"

As Samuel T. lay on top of Pford in the mud about six feet past the Mercedes's driver's-side door, he thought, Well, he'd been called a lot of things in his life. Never God, though.

He'd also never saved someone from being riddled with bullets on a flying tackle, either.

So it was a night for firsts.

"Stay down, motherfucker," he bit out.

While he spoke into Richard Pford's ear, he kept his voice low, but just to make sure he got his point across, he palmed the back of the man's skull and shoved the bastard's face into the marsh.

Although maybe that was more on principle than to ensure comprehension.

"I have your gun," he said to the man roughly. "If you move, I will shoot you—and I've killed deer bigger than you. Gutted them, too—and I have no problem revisiting that skill. Nod if you understand me."

When the nod came, Samuel T. spoke more loudly. "Gin, I need you to put down the gun, okay? You're safe. Do you hear me? Gin. Say something."

There was a long, long period of silence. And he prayed that it wasn't because she was reloading and about to stick the gun out of that broken window and fill him full of lead.

Or because she was dead from a bad-luck lead slug to the head.

"Samuel T. . . . ?"

He closed his eyes. His name sounded like it had been spoken by an eighty-year-old, the syllables weak and wobbly. But he didn't care. She was still alive.

"Yes, it's me. And I've got Richard."

Shit, he wished he still had a tie on. He'd feel better if he could secure the other man's hands with something.

"Why are . . . you here?" she said from inside the car.

Samuel T. cursed, having wondered that himself—all the way down River Road until he'd seen the two sets of brakes lights off in the marsh.

"Because I can't not be," he muttered. "With you, I can't *not* be here, goddamn it."

He gave Richard another shove for good measure and then slowly lifted himself up and off. Before he stood up fully, he said to Gin, "I'm going to approach the car, okay. At the window. If you've ever wanted to put a bullet in me, now is your chance."

Samuel T. was keeping things light because he was afraid if he didn't, he was going to break down. He still couldn't believe what he'd come up on after he'd parked on the road and run into the trees: Richard rearing back and pointing a gun into the car, the promise of death in his eyes and his stance . . . and his weapon.

Without thinking, Samuel T. had rushed forward and jumped the guy, taking him out of range just as bullets went flying inside and out. The pair of them had landed hard, and he could still feel the wet flapping of their clothes in his face as they had fought for control over the gun.

Samuel T. had won that one.

And now he needed to control the other weapon.

Slowly, he straightened up. He had taken Richard to the ground on a forward trajectory, so he was in front and just off to the side—and that meant, through the spidered windshield, he could see Gin inside the car.

She remained in shooting position on the passenger side, the muzzle pointed in the direction of the driver's window, but the gun was not stable because she was trembling so badly. He had a feeling her finger was still on the trigger and the fact that no bullets were coming out suggested the clip was empty. Except he wasn't prepared to bet his life on that.

"Gin." He spoke sharply now. "Put the weapon on the dash so I can see it. I can't help you until I'm sure I'm safe."

He had no fucking idea how he was talking so slowly and reason-ably, but some outside force was governing him, controlling his movements, his voice.

Thank God.

"Gin. Put the gun on the—"

From out of nowhere, a car came crashing into the swamp, and as the headlights pierced the Mercedes's rear window, they cast a hard illumination on Gin's bloody face, startling her so that she turned the gun in that direction.

Samuel T. ducked, and as he recognized the car, he called out, "Stay in the car, Lane! Stay in the car!"

Gin was pulling the trigger again—her eyes wide with terror, her mouth opened in a silent scream—and still nothing was coming out of the muzzle. But was that luck or running on empty?

"Turn off the engine!" he yelled to her brother. "Kill the lights!"

Samuel T. prayed, *prayed*, that his old friend heard him, and Lane must have, because everything went dark and quiet again.

Of course, now Samuel T. was blinded, and with the storm clouds still so thick, it might as well have been pitch black out.

To settle his concern about what the fuck Richard was up to, he threw a foot out, stomped on the guy's shoulders, and then put his weight on them.

As his vision gradually returned, and Lane didn't get out of his vehicle, Samuel T. refocused on Gin.

"Sweetheart," he said, "put the gun on the dash. That's just Lane. I called him when I couldn't get ahold of you."

"What," she said. Or at least, he thought that was what she said.

"I called Lane when I couldn't get ahold of you. Please put the gun on the dash where I can see it."

For shit's sake, he had meant to stay out of this. And that resolve had lasted about . . . two minutes. After he had called Gin one more time and gotten voicemail, he'd dialed Lane, who had gone looking for her in the house while they were on the phone—only to find Easterly's front door wide open in a storm and the photographs of Samuel T. and Gin scattered all over the wet marble.

Samuel T. hadn't waited any longer than that.

"I'm coming closer, sweetheart."

He really wanted her to put that gun away, but he had a feeling they were going to be at this standoff for quite a while—and there were now three cars off the road, lead slugs littering this marshy stretch of trees and undergrowth, and at least one, most likely two, injured people.

The last thing he wanted was the cops showing up.

Moving into position at the busted glass of the window, he put his face into the hole that Richard had either punched or blasted through. And in response, Gin swung that muzzle right around and pointed it at him. Her eyes were positively insane, blood dripping down her forehead and face, her body shaking so hard her teeth were clapping together.

Everything stopped. Time, thought . . . the universe itself.

At this range, if she hit him, she was going to blow the back of his skull off.

"Samuel T.?" she gritted out. "Is that really you?"

He was careful not to nod too fast, and he kept the gun he'd taken off Richard down at his thigh. "Yes, honey. It's me."

She blinked.

Then she started to breathe harder and harder. Until she began to sob.

"I'm so sorry about Amelia. I'msosorryaboutAmelia. I'msosorry—"

As that gun lowered, Samuel T. took a chance and dove through the broken glass, forcing his hands out until he grabbed the weapon and took it from her.

And then she was in his arms, albeit awkwardly as he hung half in and out of the car window.

"It's okay," he said as he went numb all over his body. "It's all right . . ."

TWENTY-SIX

*A*s soon as Lane saw Samuel T. lean in through the driver's-side window, he leapt out of his own car and raced for the Mercedes. Dear Lord, Gin had hit a tree, and Richard was facedown on the ground and—

He couldn't really hear what Samuel T. and Gin were saying to each other, but she had to be alive or her voice wouldn't be coming out of there.

So he focused on Richard.

The man wasn't moving much on the ground, but he was breathing.

There was a click, and then Samuel T. backed out of the window and opened Gin's door. Wait . . . there was a gun in each of his hands?

Lane snapped into action. "What the hell happened—Gin! You're seriously hurt!"

As Samuel T. helped her across the seat and out of the car, it was clear she was in trouble. There was blood all over his sister, and she couldn't stand on her own.

"Where have you been shot?" Lane asked roughly. "What the hell happened?"

Gin stuttered a whole lot of words that Lane couldn't understand. But then Samuel T. filled things in—

The man didn't have the chance to get the full story out.

Lane cut him off by rolling Pford over in the muck and dragging him to his feet. Slamming him against the car, Lane put his face into the other man's.

"Did you shoot at my sister? Did you fucking *shoot* at my sister!"

"Okay, okay." Samuel T. grabbed Lane's shoulder and jerked him back. "Enough. We've got a cleanup problem to deal with right now—because I know we want to handle this privately. Don't you agree, Richard."

Pford didn't seem injured. There was no blood on him—except on one of his hands—and other than him weaving like he was in a stiff wind, he was clearly going to be fine.

But Lane could fix that.

"Can I borrow your gun," he demanded of his attorney. "The one with a bullet left in it?"

"Back off, Lane," Samuel T. barked, "and let me take care of this."

Lane shook his head. Yet he had to follow his attorney's very sage advice. After all, there were other, far more sane ways of ensuring his sister's safety and freedom.

"Work your magic, counselor," he said gruffly.

Samuel T. put himself between Gin and Richard.

"You two are getting an annulment." Samuel T. looked at her. "I will file the papers tomorrow on your behalf." He looked at Pford.

"You will grant this without contest. There will be no financial obligations for you. You're free, and so is she, provided you do not retaliate in any way, and that includes behind the scenes with the BBC. Do you agree?"

There was a pause as Pford didn't respond.

Lane was about to start yelling, when Samuel T. took a gun and put it underneath Pford's chin. "Do. You. Agree."

As the man's eyes popped, Richard nodded as if his life depended on it.

"I can't hear you."

"Yes," Pford stammered.

"Good." Samuel T. didn't lower the weapon. "And I'm throwing a private order of protection in there for good measure. You get within one hundred feet of her, and her brother and I are coming after you. You won't know when or where or how, but he and I will make things extremely mortal for you. Do you understand? This is not something to test, trust me."

When Pford nodded again, Samuel T. eased back and disappeared the weapon.

"Go," Lane said to the sonofabitch. "I don't want to see you on the property again. I'll have your things returned to you—"

"I'm keeping the ring," Gin interjected. "I get to keep the ring."

As Samuel T. seemed to wince, Lane got up in Pford's space again. "The ring is hers. No conversation. You got it?"

"Yes," Richard said.

"You keep this to yourself and stay away from her, and there will be no problems for anybody. It will be like nothing ever happened."

"Yes."

"Now get the *fuck* out of here."

As Richard walked off toward the Bentley, Lane watched him until Pford was in his car and back on the road proper, driving away. Then he turned around. Samuel T. had an arm around Gin, and she was up against him, but they both had run out of gas, their shell-shocked expressions the kind of thing that was going to take a while to dissipate.

Shit, his sister's wounds needed to be dealt with.

Lane took out his phone. "We can't take her to a hospital. And she can't go up to the house, the police are there."

Samuel T. blinked. "Why?"

"Long story." He went into his contacts and hit *send* on a local number. "I want you to put her in your SUV and take her where I tell you to—hey, hi, how're you—what? I sound weird, huh? Well, there's a reason for that. Listen, I need you to do a favor for me. . . ."

*M*ax waited in his cottage on staff row for the worst of the storm to pass and then he carried his saddlebags out to his Harley. The rain was still falling, but not nearly as bad, and what the fuck did he care? He had ridden wet loads of times, and it had never killed him: He had his waterproof chaps to put on, and his leather jacket was impervious to all kinds of weather.

Strapping the bags to either side of the seat, he was glad that no one had messed with his bike when he'd had to leave it outside that bar. As he'd Uber'd it back to the beer joint at four in the afternoon, he'd had no clue what he was going to do if the thing was jacked up or just plain gone.

Lucked out again, though. He'd come home on the Harley just fine and packed up his things—only to get waylaid by the storm.

Forced to chill out, he'd passed some of the time in the shower because he didn't know when he'd have a chance to get his next one, and then he'd eaten everything that had been in the refrigerator and the cupboards—also on the theory that he didn't know when and where his next meal was coming from, either.

Now, as he measured the sky, he figured he'd head west, because according to radar, the storms were moving east and there was nothing behind them. If he could make it to St. Louis, that would be great. He could bunk down somewhere cheap and decide what he felt like doing from there—

Straightening, he frowned and looked to the staff road. A fully blacked-out SUV was coming up the rise at quite a clip, and the Range Rover slowed as it approached him.

When the thing turned in and stopped behind his bike, he put his hands up and went into full-blown no-way. "Hey! I'm leaving—"

Samuel Theodore Lodge got out, and the guy did not look right. Wait, was that blood all over his clothes? "No, you're not going anywhere."

"Look, man, I don't have time for whatever this is—"

The passenger side opened, and as Max saw what got out, he forgot about his bike and his shit and his travel plans for a moment. "What the fuck, Gin."

His sister was covered in blood, limping and in a ruined, stained silk dress that had probably been peach at one point. Now it was a Pollock painting.

"We need to go inside," Samuel T. said as he put an arm around the woman and helped her toward the open door. "She needs a doctor."

"So why isn't she going to a goddamn hospital?"

They didn't answer him. They just went into the cottage—as, next door, Gary McAdams came out of the identical unit, got in his four-by-four truck, and went roaring off down the staff road.

"What the hell is going on here?" Max asked absolutely nobody.

He glanced over at his cottage's open door, and thought . . . whatever, he didn't have to stay. All he needed were his wallet and his keys, and both were just sitting on the counter in the galley kitchen. There was nothing under that roof that was his, and no reason for him to stay a moment longer, even if his sister looked like she'd been in a car accident.

He had never wanted to come to Charlemont, and now that Lane knew the secret, Max had basically done his job: Someone else in the family was aware of the truth, and hell, Lane was getting a reputation for being pretty fricking reasonable. So no doubt, the guy would find the right time and the right words . . . and get Max off the hook.

It was fine to go.

Really. It was absolutely fine.

With a curse, Max marched into the little house and headed directly past where his sister was collapsed on the couch with Samuel T. bent over and pressing a dish towel to her head.

He got his keys and his wallet. Oh, right, his jacket and chaps. Where were they?

"You're leaving," Samuel T. snapped. "Seriously. You're going now?"

"Looks like you're taking care of everything. Besides, I've got somewhere I have to be."

"Your sister was almost killed just now."

"Well, she's still breathing, isn't she."

Before Samuel T. and he really got into it, Max went farther in to the little kitchen and picked his jacket and chaps up from the back of a chair—

"I could lose my medical license for this."

At the sound of a female voice he knew all too well, Max had to close his eyes. Maybe he'd just imagined it. Yeah, that had to be it. Surely, the one woman he had not wanted to see wasn't—

He pivoted around.

Well, hell. Tanesha Nyce, the preacher's daughter, was standing in the open doorway, her white coat and hospital scrubs doing absolutely nothing to disguise her perfect body, her makeup-free face and simple haircut just as he remembered them, her beauty still as arresting as it always had been.

"Oh . . . hi, Maxwell," she said as she noticed him, too.

But then she was all business, focusing on Gin. "What the hell happened to you?"

Keep on going, Max told himself. You just keep right on working your plan—which is to get as far away from Easterly and these people as you can get.

Nothing good was going to come if he stayed.

Nothing.

TWENTY-SEVEN

*G*in looked over to the door of the staff cottage as Tanesha Nyce arrived—and even through Gin's haze, she could tell the doctor was not happy. And that bad mood got even worse as the other woman looked at Gin.

"Here," Samuel T. said. "Hold this."

For a second, Gin wasn't clear on whom he was speaking to. But then he lifted her arm and put her hand on the towel he was pressing against her forehead.

"Thank you," she whispered.

As he backed off so the doctor could come over and inspect things, Gin followed him with her eyes. After a little pacing, he settled across the way, leaning against the wall and crossing his arms—and then saying something to her brother Max.

Samuel T.'s shirt was ruined, blood and mud staining what had been bright white Egyptian cotton.

Even though he had plenty of other monogrammed button-downs in his closet, she felt an absurd need to pay for the dry cleaning—even though given the extent of the mess, that wasn't going to help much. Maybe she would just order him a new one. Did he still get them from Turnbull & Asser? No reason to think he'd changed.

Tanesha knelt down in front of her, put a red box with a red and white cross on it on the floor, and laid her hands lightly on Gin's knees. "May I take a look at your head?"

"Thank you."

Gin lowered the dish towel slowly. She had a feeling she was going to be moving that way for a while. "It doesn't hurt."

"I'm glad." The doctor leaned in and tilted Gin's chin left and right. "Okay, let's check your pupils first."

Tanesha took a penlight out of her pocket and flashed it in one eye and then the other. "Good. How many fingers am I holding up?"

Ordering herself to focus, Gin murmured, "Two."

"Follow my finger, but keep your head in place, okay? Good." Tanesha sat back on her heels, opened the box, and took out supplies. "You've got a nice little laceration over your brow—but I think I can close it with butterfly bandages. Have you had a tetanus shot lately?"

"Yes, six months ago. I tripped outside and needed to get some stitches in the bottom of my foot."

And to think she'd felt like that was a big deal.

"Good. I'm glad you're up to date." Tanesha drew blue gloves on and smiled in a way that suggested Everything Was Going to Be Okay. "After this, we're going to check your leg, all right?"

"Is it hurt?"

Tanesha stilled. "Yes, Gin. It is."

"Oh, I don't feel anything."

There was a sadness in the doctor's face as she set to work cleaning the wound with medicated pads, and to help ignore that, Gin passed the time looking at the two men in the barren little room: Samuel T. was still up against the wall, although he was watching Tanesha carefully, as if he were prepared to help even though he was a lawyer, not a physician; and Max was over in the shallow kitchen area, a leather jacket hanging on his arm as if he were leaving at any moment.

He was also watching the good doctor. No doubt for a different reason.

What was it about her generation in the family that bred relationships that went nowhere? She and Samuel T., Edward and that Sutton Smythe . . . Max and Tanesha. Lizzie and Lane appeared to be getting it together, but that was either because they were the exception that proved the rule . . .

Or destined to fail terribly.

"All right, how about your leg?"

"Do you think I've been shot?" Gin extended one foot, and when Tanesha shook her head, she offered the other. "I'm not . . ."

Well, this was interesting. There appeared to be a deep stripe running up the front of her shin. As if she had been branded.

"Oh, God," Tanesha said tightly. After a moment, she moved back and just stared at the wound. "As a mandatory reporter, I'm in a difficult spot here."

"I'm sorry," Gin offered. "I'm sure it will be fine."

Tanesha rubbed her eyes with the back of her forearm, keeping her gloved hands out of the way. "Okay, let's just see what we have here."

The woman refocused, and gently moved Gin's leg left and right—and then she was feeling her way around with careful fingertips. Gin didn't really care what was going on down there, but it seemed rude not to participate in some way—so she sat forward.

"That should probably hurt, shouldn't it," she said.

"I think you've got some shock going on." Tanesha took more supplies out of her box. "The good news is that I don't see any evidence that there's a bullet embedded anywhere—it looks like one got very close to you, however. You were very lucky."

What was the polite response to something like that, Gin wondered. She was quite sure that Emily Post had never covered anything under the heading of "Gunshot Wounds: Aftercare."

She went with the bog standard: "Thank you, kindly."

After her leg was bandaged up, Tanesha looked over at Samuel T. "Where is the other party?" When the man just shook his head, she frowned. "Is he or she dead? Because I might be willing to fudge this one wound here, but if there's a homicide involved in all this, I will not be a party to any of it."

"The other individual is very much alive and well," Samuel T. said. "And they are getting an annulment."

Tanesha took a deep breath. "Let me ask you something. Dr. Qalbi and his father are your all's personal physicians, why didn't you—"

Samuel T. cut in. "We called you because the father is retiring, and the son is in Scotland visiting the other side of his family. He's out of the country for two weeks."

"Fair enough." Tanesha glanced across at Max. "Could you please bring me a trash bag?"

As he obligingly ducked down under the kitchen sink, the doctor turned back to Gin. "I'm going to need to check you in a day. And I want you on antibiotics. I'll write you a prescription for a broad spectrum—are you allergic to anything?"

"No, thank you."

"Good."

Max brought the trash bag over and fluffed it out, holding the thing open for Tanesha as she put all the used gauze and wipes in there. When the doctor was finished picking up, he closed the bag and tied it; then walked the medical debris out the back of the little house.

"I want you to get this filled tonight." Tanesha wrote quickly on a pad. "And take one before bed. I don't think you'll need anything more than Motrin or Tylenol for pain. If you have blurred vision, nausea, or vomiting, let me know. You may have a concussion, but it's not like I can tell by an X-ray or a scan. Who's filling this for her?"

Samuel T. cleared his throat. "I will. Should she be in bed?"

"Yes, I want you to take it easy," Tanesha said to Gin. "Definitely."

"Thank you."

Tanesha gave her a hug. "You're welcome—and I'll see you late tomorrow. I'll stop by on the way home from the hospital."

As Max came back in, Tanesha stood up. "Walk me out, Samuel T., if you don't mind."

"Yes, ma'am."

Tanesha hesitated. And then glanced over at Max. "It was, ah, nice to see you, Maxwell. Although I'm sorry for the circumstances."

"Yeah." He gave her a little bow. "Me, too."

Samuel T. and the doctor left, and Gin eased back into the stiff cushions. As an awkward silence cropped up between her and Max, she was reminded that she and her brother had never had much in common—and clearly, all of the drama she had been through hadn't changed that: He shifted his weight from one black boot to another. Put his jacket on. Played with his keys.

Looked anywhere but at her.

Ordinarily, she would have poked at him just to pass the time: Made fun of that hideous bushy beard he'd grown. Questioned the why of all those tattoos. Demanded to know, not that she cared, when exactly he was leaving: now . . . or how 'bout now?

She closed her eyes.

After a moment, she heard him move around. And then he said, "Here."

Opening her lids, she frowned at the paper towel he was holding out to her. "I'm sorry?"

"You're crying."

"Am I?" She took what he offered only so he didn't have to keep his arm out like that. "Thank you."

Except then she just closed her eyes again. And slowly wadded the thing up into a fist.

It was odd to cry and not feel anything. But that was far better than the alternative.

Wasn't it?

As Lizzie eased her truck off River Road and bumped her way over to the clutch of vehicles that were in the marsh and among the trees, her first thought was: The Rolls-Royce, really? Lane had seriously taken that beast four-wheeling into this swamp?

Then again, when you got a call that your sister was in trouble, you didn't stop to get choosy with car keys—and when you found her waaaay off the road? That was where you went with whatever vehicle you were in.

Fortunately, Lizzie's truck was all-wheel drive. So thanks to that and well-treaded tires, she had no problem pulling around and— okay, wow. Just . . . *wow.*

One of the Bradford family's Mercedes was embedded in a tree, with a busted-out window on the driver's side and a half-spidered windshield in front. The good news? Gary McAdams was on it. With his far larger and even better-equipped Ford, he was backing right up to that rear bumper, Lane waving him forward inch by inch.

As Lizzie got out, she made sure her headlights were off, even though she wasn't sure what she thought about no one going to the police with all this. Lane had called her a couple of times, updating her, and finally she'd just had to leave the hospital. Besides, Miss Aurora was no longer even remotely conscious, and so there was nothing really to do until, or if, that changed.

And this situation in the marsh was the sort where another pair of hands was going to help.

Another set of chains, probably, too.

Lane spoke up over the growl of the truck's engine. "You're there."

Gary put things in park, and as he got out, Lizzie went up to Lane and shared a kiss with him. "What the hell happened here?"

"A whole lot of batshit nuts."

"Clearly." She glanced at the groundsman. "Hey, I've got extra chains, if you need 'em."

The man repositioned his John Deere cap on his head. "Might. Gonna have to get the big 'un out, too." As he nodded at the Rolls, he started dragging pounds and pounds of steel links out of his bed. "That's the one I'm worried 'bout. 'Cuz we gonna need to keep 'er pretty."

As Gary turned around, he had to have almost forty pounds in one hand, and he handled the load like it weighed nothing. Lane and Lizzie both helped him find the hooks under the Benz's rear bumper and then they were all working together to get the hooks locked in. After that, it was a case of Gary getting into his truck and slowly . . . carefully . . . gently . . . inching the Mercedes off of the tree and through the muddy, sloppy ground.

When the S550 was free and clear, Gary leaned out of his window. "I'm takin' 'er back to the shop. Then we're gonna chop 'er and sell 'er for parts, bury what's left on the mountain. We cain't be turnin' 'er in. Bullet holes, everywhere."

"Good plan." Lane put his hand on the man's forearm. "Thank you."

"Just doin' m' job." Gary looked at Lizzie. "You got the Rolls, then?"

"Yup, I got it."

"That's m' girl."

Funny how the approval from him about getting a half-million-dollar car out of a swamp meant so much to her.

As Gary eased down the tracks that had been made and then inched onto the road, Lane put his arm around her and kissed her on the forehead. "Let's just go home in your truck for now, 'kay? We need to see what happened with Gin, and—"

"Nay, we shall leave no man nor motorcar behind." She nodded at the Rolls. "First, let me try to drive that out, though. We might get lucky."

"Oh, that's okay. I've got it."

As he broke away, she tugged him back around. "Lane. I'd prefer not to have to chain that thing. We've got one shot to make it out of this mess"—she indicated the mucky ground—"and only one shot. That car has to weigh at least six, maybe seven thousand pounds. It's been sitting there how long? An hour? If you put it in reverse and hit the gas? You're going to dig a hole to China and I'm going to have to trash the back half to pull it out."

Lane opened his mouth. Shut it. Frowned.

"I know," she pointed out reasonably, "that the guy in you doesn't want to be upstaged by a female, but who are you going to trust? A city boy like yourself—or a farm woman who's been getting heavy machinery out of the mud since she was twelve? And please remember, the longer we're out here, the better the chance we have of getting caught."

Lane jacked up his pants. "I'm a real man," he said in a deep drawl. "Man enough to step aside when the situation warrants it."

She gave him a big hug. "I'm so proud of you."

Heading over to the Rolls, she tried to kick off at least half the mud on her shoes, and then she got behind the wheel. The automobile started up softly, and she put the gearshift in reverse. Testing the accelerator, she gave it a little gas. A little more.

It was like a hundred-mile-long train, a huge monolith that barely moved. But that was because she was taking things slow: In increments of millimeters, with the gentlest of coaching, she got some traction and some trajectory. And a little more. And a little more . . .

All was going well—until she hit an obstacle and couldn't make any more progress. It could have been a root. A stump.

Jeez, with the way things were going tonight, a dead body.

She added some more juice. And more.

Nothing. And she was on the very edge of the wheels beginning to dig.

Easy on the gas, she told herself. And then redouble it. And easy off. And more with the gas . . .

With careful control, she started to rock the Rolls—

Okay, that was funny.

Rock, the Rolls, rock, the Rolls—

And then, just as she felt that she was on top of whatever it was, she gunned it—and up and over she went.

"You got it!" Lane yelled.

"Not yet," she murmured.

Please, she thought. Let's have the front go just as well.

As she repeated the careful process, Lane watched her, the glow from the running lights illuminating the smile on his face: Unlike most guys, who might have gotten shirty, he was clearly impressed—and when she finally got the front of the Phantom over the hump, and coaxed the massive convertible up onto the pavement, he was clapping as he came over.

Annnnnnnd that was when the cops showed up.

TWENTY-EIGHT

*A*s Samuel T. came up Easterly's hill for a second time, he was staging another intervention with himself. Which, he supposed, was a bit like a lawyer representing himself in court— you know, that whole fool-for-a-client thing. But he wasn't going to anyone else with this, and besides, he sure as hell knew both sides to the argument by heart.

Parking in the front of the mansion, he grabbed the little white Rite Aid bag and went in the front door. Across the black and white marble floor. Up the stairs to the second floor.

He didn't knock at Gin's door. Just walked right in, and as he saw her lying down over on the bed, he frowned.

"No shower?" he said as he closed things up.

When she didn't respond, he got scared. Again. But no, she was still alive. She was still breathing.

But he couldn't believe this nasty-neat of a woman was lying on her white duvet in that dirty dress. Clearly, all rules were off, however.

Leaving the bag with the prescription in it on her bedside table, he went into the bathroom and filled up a monogrammed glass with water. Back by where she was curled up, he got the bottle out, popped the lid, and made sure that the description of the pills matched what was inside.

Then he sat down on the very edge of the mattress.

She didn't move.

And you know, it seemed especially apt to conclude his intervention right here, at the basis of his addiction. Somehow, in spite of his best intentions, he had managed to fall for her once again: When she had looked up at him, through tears and her own blood, and said she was sorry about Amelia? He had been, stupidly, ready to forgive her for even the worst betrayal anyone could ever do to him. In that moment, as their eyes had met and she apologized . . . it was as if she had wiped the slate clean between them.

Taking her into his arms at that point had been a reunion, even though he had seen her only thirty minutes before.

But then?

Oh, Gin, he thought. Then you showed up again, didn't you.

I get to keep the ring.

Even after she had nearly been killed, and nearly killed someone else, and in spite of how badly she might have been injured . . . Gin Baldwine had still showed a finesse and a focus for the bottom line. The financial bottom line.

As if he needed a reminder of her capacity for calculation.

And the thing was, after all these years, and all of the backs and the forths, if he couldn't make a break with her now—after the Amelia revelation? When would it happen? What else could she do to him?

He didn't want to find out.

Getting to his feet, he stared down at her for a little longer. Then he quietly left, shutting the door behind him. Before he departed from the house, he tried to find someone—and when he failed, he considered knocking on her mother's door and asking the nurse in there to do double time. But that felt like an invasion of the family's privacy.

In the end, he went out to his Range Rover and texted Lizzie and Lane that somebody needed to make sure that Gin took that pill. With food—as the bottle's label had mandated.

That was not his job, however.

As he drove back down to the main gates, he called a number out of his *recents* log and waited. When he got voicemail, he cleared his throat.

"Hey," he said as he hit his brakes. "I'm sorry for my delay in response."

The gates opened slowly, and as he passed through, flashbulbs went off but did not penetrate the SUV's darkened windows.

"So, yes, Prescott. I will go to that party with you this weekend. I'll be there, and I'm looking forward to it."

"What happened here, folks?"

As the officer got out of his squad car by the Rolls-Royce, Lane lifted his forearm to shield his eyes from the flashing lights.

"I went off the road," he called up to where they were on the road. "It's my fault."

With a quick glance behind, he prayed that all that illumination wasn't picking up on the bullets, shell casings, ruined tree—*shit.*

"During the storm, then?" the officer said as Lizzie got out of the Phantom's driver's-side door.

"Hi, Officer." She stepped in and shook his hand. "My boyfriend—"

"Fiancé," Lane corrected from the marsh.

As the officer laughed, Lizzie continued in a calm way, "My fiancé got stuck driving in the storm—"

"—and I was blown off the road," Lane finished.

"So I had to come with my truck to help him out."

"But she managed to get my car free by herself."

"Without using my chains."

"No chains were used," he echoed.

Shit, he should go up there, but he was frozen, all deer-in-the-headlights.

Glancing over his shoulder again, he tried to see what the officer could see: Lots of tire tracks, mud, a couple of saplings that had been bent over, Lizzie's truck off to the side. Was the guy going to pick up the fresh scars on that trunk?

"What about the truck?" the officer asked. "Do you need a tow for it?"

"Nope," Lizzie said. "She's a four-by-four, with good treads. I'll be fine."

"Well." The officer looked around. "Bad storm, huh."

Lane waited for the other shoe to drop. What the hell were they going to do if—

"You want me to wait while you get the truck free?" the officer asked.

"Sure," Lizzie answered. "But would you mind moving your car this way? You're kind of in my best path out."

As she spoke, she moved her arms in a manner that . . . yup, if the uniform followed her direction, he would get those headlights pointed out of the marsh, not into it.

Lane could have kissed her. And made a mental note to do that as soon as he could.

"No problem."

As Lizzie came back down into the weeds, she whispered, "Go up there. Occupy him."

"I love you."

"I am *not* happy about this."

Lane traded places with her and kibitzed with the officer as she slowly backed her old Toyota through the trees and maneuvered it up onto the road.

As she pulled in next to the cop, she smiled. "Not bad for a country girl, huh."

"Only a country girl could do that," the cop said with respect. "But, listen, you mind if I take a look at your license, registration, and proof of insurance? Both of you?"

"Right here, Officer." She leaned across the seat and popped open the glove box. "Here's the last two. License is in my wallet, which is here in my jeans."

"Thank you, ma'am." The man took a penlight out of his front shirt pocket and beamed it on the documents. And when Lizzie passed him her license, he did the same. "Everything looks great. But your headlights are off."

"Oh!" She took the documents and laminated card back. "Sorry. They are. You going to give me a ticket for breaking the law?"

He smiled. "If I catch you without them on at night again, I sure am."

"Thanks, Officer," she said. When there was a pause, she glanced between them both. "Ah, so, Lane, I guess I'll see you back at the house?"

"You sure will," Lane murmured.

As Lizzie headed off down River Road, the officer turned to Lane. "Before you go."

"Yup, I've got my license and registration, too." He took his wallet out of his back pocket. "Here's this. The rest is in my car, hold on."

While the man checked out that part, Lane went over to the passenger side of the Rolls and got the other stuff. After the cop looked it all over, he returned everything.

And promptly dropped the act.

"So you want to tell me what really happened here?" The young man nodded into the marsh. "That tree looks like it was hit pretty hard. By a car."

"We haven't been drinking. The storm was bad."

"I believe you about the drinking. You're not slurring your words, and her ability to get that truck out of here like that is a sobriety test if I've ever seen one. But your car's in perfect shape. So's the front of her truck. What happened to that tree, Mr. Baldwine."

Lane took a deep breath. What he wanted to say was this was none of the police's business. He had handled things privately, and that was all anybody needed to know. The trouble was, that was the 1950s talking, back in the era when the privilege of wealth and status put his family above the law.

"Mr. Baldwine," the cop said. "I think you knew my father, Ed Heinz. He worked up at Easterly on the grounds crew until he died four years ago. And my brother, Rob, is one of the painters you all use on the regular."

"Oh, sure. I knew Mr. Heinz. Yup. He used to plant and tend all the fields on the flats."

"You went to his funeral."

"I sure did. You want to know why?"

"We were surprised, to be honest."

"He helped my brother get—well, actually, it was a Rolls-Royce, too, as a matter of fact—out of the cornfield once. Max drove my father's new car in there. This was, like, back in the mid-nineties. I never forgot how nice he was. We ruined his corn. Well, part of it. And he still helped us."

The officer started to laugh. "I remember him telling us all about that. Oh, he used to tell that story a lot."

"And there were others, I'm sure."

"Never a dull moment at Easterly."

"Not as long as Max was around, for sure."

There was a long pause. And then Lane looked at the officer.

"My sister married Richard Pford the other day."

"Oh, yeah, sure. I read about it in the paper—my wife and I were saying that there should be some big wedding up on the hill. That going to happen?"

"No." Lane shook his head. "Richard beat her tonight. Chased her out into the storm. She took off in one of the family cars and he followed her in his own. He ran my sister off the road and her Mercedes is what hit the tree. If you want, I can take you to the car."

"Do you want to press charges? Where is Mr. Pford? I'll arrest him right now."

Lane shook his head. "She just wants to be done with it. The marriage was a mistake. Anyway, I'll be honest with you. When I got out here, I was not gentle with the guy, if you know what I mean—and he's agreed to an annulment. Look, my sister is okay. Or, she will be. But if she goes to the hospital or we get him arrested, the press is going to have a field day, and frankly, my family's had more than its fair share of coverage lately. She's already ashamed and embarrassed, and he's out of her life now. We'd rather just let this lay."

The officer nodded and reached into his chest pocket. "It's a private affair."

Lane exhaled. "It is private. Yes."

"Here's my card. Call me if she or you have a change of mind."

"Thank you"—he glanced at the card—"Charles."

"Charlie. Charlie Heinz."

"I'm happy to pay to replace the tree?"

"This isn't private land. It's part of the city park system. It'll take care of itself."

"I really appreciate your understanding where I'm coming from."

"Mr. Baldwine, 'round here, we take care of our own. Don't you worry, no will know about this—not unless you want them to."

They shook hands, and then the officer got back in his car and drove away. Left on his own, Lane looked back at the swamp.

And was very glad for the interconnected nature of Charlemont.

TWENTY-NINE

As Lizzie pulled her truck in to its spot by Easterly's business center, she stared over at the blue tent that had been erected over Miss Aurora's car. That detective and the CSI folks seemed to have moved onto the property for the duration, and she wondered what they were finding—and whether some police radio of theirs would broadcast what that cop had come upon down at the marsh just now.

Gunshots. Busted car. Towing. Not that the officer had seemed to recognize any of it.

Dear Lord, how was this her life?

When she got out, that detective, Merrimack, smiled across at her. "Quite a storm, huh."

"Yes, it was."

"And it looks like you went through some mud." He pointed to her tires. "Have some trouble on the road?"

"I was coming back from the hospital during the worst of it. There was flash flooding."

"That can happen." More with the smile. "I'll bet you're glad to be home safe."

She glanced at the crime-scene vans. "How much longer will you be here?"

"Trying to get rid of us?"

Yes. "Not at all. Do you want anything to eat or drink?"

"Well, aren't you kind." Merrimack looked over his shoulder at the two men who were crawling all around Miss Aurora's car. "I think my guys are fine and we're just finishing up. Oh, by the way, there are two more of us working in Miss Toms's private quarters. I wouldn't want you to be surprised."

"Thank you." She cleared her throat. "Well, I'll just head in. It's been a long day."

"You do look tired, if you don't mind me saying. And I want to thank you for your statement earlier. Very helpful."

As she gave him a wave and headed for the back door into the kitchen, he said, "Miss King?"

"Yes?"

"Lot of mud on your shoes there." Smile. "You might want to wipe them extra good on the mat before you go inside. Or maybe take them off altogether."

"Oh, yes. You're right. Thank you."

With her heart pounding, she went to the screen door and let herself into the mansion, without taking his advice. And as soon as she was out of his view, she sagged—

"'Scuse me, ma'am."

Jumping back to attention, she put her hand over her heart. "Oh!"

"Sorry. Didn't mean to startle you." The man was dressed in a casual uniform and had paper bags full of things in both his hands. "We're finished in there. We're going to ask that no one enter that space, though."

With a lean to the side, Lizzie looked around him and saw a woman dressed in the same way putting a seal on Miss Aurora's door. "Of course. No one will go in there."

After they left, she went over and sat down on a stool at the island in front of the stove. About ten minutes later, headlights flared in the windows as the vehicles began to leave, and then there was another panning of illumination as if someone was pulling in.

Lane entered the kitchen. And closed the door slowly behind himself. "Hey."

"Hi."

"Would you like some dinner—"

"I'm going to go over to Indiana for tonight," she said quickly.

"Oh, okay, sure. I'll just grab some of my things and—"

"Alone." As he frowned, she said, "Someone has to stay with Gin. She can't be alone right now."

"Lizzie." He shook his head. "Please don't go."

"It's just for the night."

"Is it?"

She nodded. "I need some rest. And I have to check my property, especially after the storm. You have to stay here."

"But my mother's nurse—"

"Needs to be with your mom."

"Lizzie."

She closed her eyes and shuddered. "You have to let me go right now. This has been a lot, tonight. I'm not . . . I just need to sleep in my own bed and wake up in my little house on my farm. Have a cup of coffee by myself. Take the four-wheeler around the fields and look for downed limbs. I need . . . to be normal, for a minute."

Or, in other words: not involved in any murder investigations or shoot-outs down by the river or lying to cops. Oh, and also, if she could have no one bleeding or hurt or dead, that'd be great, thanks.

Lane opened his mouth to speak, but he didn't get a chance to.

Jeff came striding in from the front of the house, his suit still on, a metal briefcase in his hand. "Well, good news."

"What's that," Lane inquired in a dead voice.

"We're getting sued by two banks."

As Lane let himself fall back against the wall, Lizzie had to ask, "How is that good news?"

"If it were three," the man said, "they could force us into bankruptcy. So, yay for us. What's for dinner, kids? I can't remember the last time I ate."

THIRTY

Hours later, Lane woke up in a dark room in a strange—no, wait. He wasn't on a bed. He was lying on the sofa—in Easterly's front parlor.

Turning his head, he found that he was eye to eye with a bottle of Family Reserve that—oh, yup, right, he'd taken down to the a-quarter-left level. Next to it was his rocks glass, which was empty. His shoes were off, his head was against a decorative throw with tassels that had dropped into one of his ears, and his body was at weird angles.

As he tried to figure out what had disturbed his blackout, he had some vague thought that he'd had a bad dream.

Pity that the return to consciousness was a case of out of the fire and into the frying pan.

Wait, wasn't that . . . frying pan first, then fire?

"Who the hell cares."

Sitting up, his head spun and he looked around—

Across the way, at the base of the elegant room, one of the French doors was wide open, and the night breeze, lovely and mild, had come in—so maybe it had been the scent that had roused him?

Getting to his feet, he walked over and leaned out. There was not enough wind to have blown it open, and he looked down at the high-gloss floorboards. Things were still damp out there and debris from the trees littered the terrace—so if someone had come in, surely they would have left prints?

He turned on a lamp. Nothing marred the floor.

Stepping onto the flagstones, he glanced around—

Someone was walking right next to the house.

Over there. A figure in white . . . a woman . . . was drifting down the stone steps into the garden proper.

Lane jogged over. "Excuse me? Hello?"

She stopped. And then turned to face him.

"Mother?" he said with shock. "Mother, what are you doing out here?"

As he stopped before her, his heart rate regulated to something close to a normal rhythm, but he remained concerned. After all, didn't people with dementia take to wandering? Was this the drugs or a worsening of her mental decline?

Or both?

"Oh, hello, Edward." She smiled at him pleasantly. "It is such a lovely evening, isn't it? I thought I should like to take the air."

His mother's accent was more House of Windsor than South of the Mason–Dixon, her consonants arched sure as a lifted brow, her haughty vowels drawn out with the expectation that what she had to say, and who she was, guaranteed people would wait for her to finish her sentences.

"Mother, I think we should go inside."

Her eyes drifted around the flowers and the blooming trees, and in the shadows, her face was closer to what it had been when she had been young, its fine bones and perfectly balanced features the result of what in the old days people would have called "good breeding."

"Mother?"

"No, I think we shall walk. Edward, darling, do give me your arm."

Lane thought of his father's visitation. She had mistaken him for his brother then, too.

He glanced back up to the house. Where was the nurse?

"Edward?"

"But of course, Mother dear." He offered her the crook of his elbow. "We will make one pass, and then I am afraid I must insist we return inside."

"That is very good of you. To worry over me."

"I love you."

"I love you, too, Edward, darling."

Together, they traversed the brick walkway, passing into the statuary portion of the garden. His mother paused at each stone figure, as if she was recalling old acquaintances of which she were fond, and then she stopped at the koi pond to regard the silver and orange and spotted fish. Overhead, the moon was coming and going under a sluggish cloud cover, the illumination that milky kind one found so often during the warm months.

"My husband is dead."

Lane glanced at her. "Yes, Mother, he is."

"He died recently."

"Yes, he did." Lane frowned. "Do you miss him?"

"No, I'm afraid I do not."

There was a long period of silence. And then Lane just had to go there. "Mother, I need to know something."

"What would that be, darling?"

"Your husband is dead. Is . . . my father dead?"

She went utterly still.

And then she pivoted toward Easterly and stared up at its majestic expanse, a strange light coming into her eyes.

"We do not speak of these things, Edward."

"Is my father dead, Mother. Please tell me, I need to know for my own peace of mind."

It took her the longest time to answer, and even then, her words were a mere whisper. "No, darling. Your father has not died."

"Mother, I need to know who he is. Will you please tell me? With your husband dead, no one will get hurt."

He fell silent to allow her the room to speak. And when she just looked at their home, he worried that her mind had gone on an idle from which it would not return.

"Mother? You can tell me."

A ghost of a smile tinted her lips. "I was in love. When I was younger . . . I was in love with your father. I saw him quite often, although we were never introduced. There were proper expectations for me, and I was not going to go outside of them."

Lane could only imagine how strict things had been back then. The manner in which debutantes and eligible young bachelors were required to meet and interact had been very prescribed, and if you made a misstep? Your reputation was ruined.

The fifties surviving into the eighties.

"I would watch him from afar, though. Oh, how I would watch him. I was quite shy, and again, one didn't want to be troublesome to the family. But there was something about him. He was different. And he never, ever stepped out of bounds. In fact, I often wondered why he never noticed me." There was a period of silence. "And then William came around. He was not exactly what one would expect my father to allow. But William could be so very charming, and he managed to persuade Father that he was a fine businessman—and we needed one. After all, there was no succession for the company as I was an only child, and Father didn't want the BBC to fall into the hands of the other side of the family after he was gone. So William came to work for Bradford Bourbon, and I was expected to marry him."

The sadness in her voice was something he had never heard before, and indeed, did not associate with her. All his memories of his mother were of a beautiful, ornate bird, sparkling with gems in colorful gowns, drifting around Easterly, smiling and chirping. Always happy. Always serene.

He wondered exactly when she had started in with the self-medicating.

"My husband and I were engaged for six months. It took that long to have Dior hand-make my wedding gown—and also a parure of diamonds and pearls had been ordered from Van Cleef, and that, too, took time. There were photo shoots, as well, and planning the wedding. Mother did all of that for me. I was expected to turn up and be pleasant in the dress, and smile for the cameras. William ignored me for the most part, and that was just fine. He was . . . unsettling to me, and that initial instinct proved . . ."

Correct, Lane added grimly in his head.

"I can remember the night it finally happened. When I actually stood face-to-face with your father. I had to come forward to him and introduce myself. He was shocked, but I could tell that he had seen me all along, and he was far from indifferent to me. In spite of the upcoming marriage festivities, I continued to pursue him because I knew I was running out of time. Once I was married, William was never going to allow me out of his sight, and I would never get a chance to . . ."

"You fell pregnant," Lane whispered.

"It was just something that happened." She took a deep breath. "I do not regret it. And I do not regret you. The time that I had with your father was the happiest in my life, and it has sustained me through many a dark time."

"William found out, didn't he."

"Yes, he did. I was already two months into it when we were married, and he was furious. He felt as though there had been a bait and switch, a virtuous wife promised and a whore delivered. He told me that frequently throughout the years. He never denied you, though, because he was worried that the subsequent children, which he insisted on having, would not be seen as his. We had sex four times. Once on our wedding night. And then for each of your siblings. I was, as they say, tragically fertile—but he also insisted that I track my cycle and not lie about it. He didn't want to be with me any more than I wanted to be with him, but the succession of the company depended upon plenty of heirs and we delivered on that."

"Did you continue to see my father?"

"I saw him, yes. But after the wedding, I no longer . . . saw him."

"Did he know you were pregnant?"

"Yes. He understood the situation, however. He has always been most respectful. It is his way."

"You still love him, don't you."

"I will always love him." She looked over at him. "And you must know, my son, that you do not have to be with someone to love them. Love survives all things, time, marriages, deaths. It is more what makes us immortal than even the children we leave in our wake to our graves. It is the way God touches us, as our love for others is a reflection of His love for us. He grants us this reflection of His glory even though we are sinners, and so it is."

"Where is my father now?"

"Right here." She touched her sternum. "He is alive in my heart and will be forever."

"Wait, I thought you said he hadn't died?"

At that moment, someone came rushing out of the house. The nurse, all frantic. "Miss Bradford! Miss Bradford—"

Damn it, he needed more time. But as the woman in the white uniform rounded the corner and saw them, his mother's expression became confounded, that precious window of lucidity starting to close.

"Mother," he said urgently, "who was he? Who was my father?"

Little V.E. turned away from the house and refocused on the koi pond, her former clarity gone—and he worried it was never going to return.

"I'm so sorry, Mr. Baldwine," the nurse said as she came up and took Little V.E.'s thin arm. "I fell asleep. It's unforgivable. Please, please don't fire me—"

"It's okay," he said. "She's fine. But let's be more careful in the future."

"I will be. I swear."

As the nurse led his mother away, Lane stayed by the pond. It was hard not to see in Little V.E. a life wasted, all the best of every opportunity squandered at the foot of a family legacy she had been born into but never volunteered for.

A gilded cage, indeed.

God, he wished his Lizzie was home. Even though Gin, his mother, and Jeff were under Easterly's great roof, the place felt totally empty without her.

THIRTY-ONE

The following morning, Lane got in his Porsche and headed out to the Old Site. The Bradford Bourbon Company's headquarters might have been downtown, but its heart and soul were about thirty miles to the south and east, on a vast stretch of acreage on which his family had been making, storing, and selling its product for well over a century. It took him a good forty-five minutes to reach the tourist destination: The first ten miles were quick enough on the highway, but from then on, it was a series of smaller and smaller roads to get to the campus.

Funny, he always knew he was getting close when he started to see the six- and seven-story-tall rackhouses, where barrels and barrels of aging bourbon weathered climate changes undefended against Mother Nature's whims. But that was the process. In those barn'y, rack-filled spaces, the seasons of warm, hot, cool, and cold, repeated over and over again, caused the nascent alcohol to penetrate and be expelled from the charred white oak of the barrel, the flavor of the bourbon coming alive over the passage of days, months, years.

After all, bourbon was a product, but it was also a labor of love. As one alcohol-producing maven once said, *I don't worry about my vodka supply. I can turn a spigot and give the market plenty of vodka. Bourbon, on the other hand, takes time. So much damned time . . .*

Turning off onto what was little more than a chicken path, Lane went three miles farther and then took a left on a more properly finished road, beside which was a sign with an arrow indicating that the Old Site was up ahead. As always, the Bradford Bourbon Company signage was discreet, nothing but an ink drawing of Easterly and the BBC name—and likewise, the landscape was well-tended, but not overdone. After about another mile and a half, a massive parking lot unfurled itself, next to which was a modern-style visitors' center that housed a conference hall for events and a small museum.

Even though it was early in the day, there were already people puttering around, groups of retirees, mostly. But on the holiday weekends, especially in the fall, there would be tour buses parked in all the far corners and the spaces for cars entirely full. The Old Site also hosted plenty of weddings, reunions, bourbon groups, Kentucky tourists, and all sorts of foreigners looking to experience an old American tradition.

In fact, the Bradford Bourbon Company's Old Site was the oldest continually operating business location in not just the Commonwealth, but this part of the nation.

Bypassing the visitors' center, he continued on to an Authorized Personnel Only road that took him to the main office where the master distiller, Edwin MacAllan, worked. Parking the Porsche under a tree, Lane got out and tried to focus.

He'd called Lizzie. Twice.

And gotten a text in return that she was going out to check the property and would phone him later.

Lane gave her space, but, man, it killed him—and reminded him that, among all the things vying for his attention, she was the anchor of the life he wanted to live. If he lost her? Nothing else mattered.

Walking along a little path, he tried to distract himself from the angst by looking over the familiar environs. All of the buildings, from where the stills were, to the storage facilities, to the packaging and distribution units and the half dozen original cabins, had windows and doors painted in red and wooden siding painted black. Paved walkways linked everything together, and tours were given on the hour, visitors guided by experts through every step of the bourbon making, aging, and bottling process, culminating in an opportunity for patrons to bottle some of their own.

With the carefully cultivated experience and pervasive vibe of early Americana, there was a Disneyland feel to it all, but in a good way: Everything was clean, orientated to families, and magical, what with the flower boxes that would soon be planted with petunias and geraniums, and the rolling lawns connecting the fifty or so buildings, and the cheerful uniformed guides, workers, and administrative staff who walked around and always took personal ownership of both the product produced on site and the property.

The master distiller's office was in a modernized cabin, and as Lane walked into the rustic reception area, a nice-looking woman glanced up from the desk.

"Hey, Lane."

"Beth, how's our boy?"

"Mack's as good as he can be given the situation. He's in there with Jeff. I'm just printing out more Excel spreadsheets and then I'm joining you guys."

"Good, thanks."

Mack and Lane had known each other for nearly all their lives, as

Mack was the son of the BBC's previous master distiller. In turn, Beth Lewis was someone the man had hired to fill an office support vacancy—but evidently, it had turned out to be an eHarmony solution as well as one from Monster.com.

Love had a way of coming into people's lives at the right time.

Okay, his heart hurt just thinking that.

As he entered the office, he was momentarily struck by all the labels on the walls. Instead of wallpaper, it had been the tradition of the company's master distillers to paste labels of their era of products around them—and some went back a hundred years or more. Lane had heard that when it came time to pump some money and attention into modernizing this building, the preservation of this tradition had nearly given the architects, contractors, and designers a heart attack.

Across the way, Mack and Jeff glanced up from the conference table. And both looked like they wanted to be on a beach in Cabo.

With a beer.

Or a fruit punch made with rum.

Basically, anything other than bourbon, in a place anywhere other than Kentucky.

"How we doing?" Lane asked.

Jeff sat back. "Bad. Just bad. If one more bank comes in? We're in Chapter Eleven. We don't have the cash flow to cover these debts, no matter how I crunch it. I mean, I keep looking for a solution, but there isn't one. We need a massive cash injection from somewhere."

Lane clapped palms with Mack and sat down as Beth came in and passed around columns of numbers.

As all four of them focused on the financials, and Jeff started talking in technical terms about money, Lane tried to keep track of things—and just completely failed. He was waiting for Merrimack to call, praying Lizzie would talk to him soon, and wondering what in the hell to do about Edward—

"So what do you say, Lane?"

"Huh?" Looking up, he found the three of them staring at him. "I'm sorry?"

Mack sat back and crossed his arms over his thick chest. "I've got something that could save us. If you want to come meet her."

"Her?"

Mack glanced at Beth. Looked back. "Yeah, come on."

The four of them got up together and proceeded through the reception area. Out in the warm sunshine, Mack led them over to a modern building that had no windows and an air-locked door. Taking out his pass card, he swiped the thing and waited as the seal disengaged itself.

Before they went in, the guy stared into Lane's eyes. "Just so you know, this is going to kill me."

Oh, God, Lane thought. He'd never seen Mack look so grim.

And heaven knew they had been through all kinds of things together, from their shared high school days at Charlemont Country Day, to the later years in college all the way to when Mack had been earning his stripes here at the Old Site under his father and Lane had just been loafing around, doing nothing with his degree.

They both loved U of C basketball, good bourbon, bad jokes, and the Commonwealth of Kentucky—and were essentially positive guys.

At least until recently.

Mack glanced at Beth again, who seemed likewise subdued, and then he held the door wide so that one by one they could file into the laboratory's anteroom. All around, white suits hung on pegs, and there were boxes of blue booties to slip on your footwear. Goggles, masks, and hairnets were also organized on shelves and on hooks.

The BBC's master distiller ignored all that and walked right through the glass door and into the lab space beyond. There, stainless-steel counters, bright lights, and microscopes made the place seem like an IVF lab or maybe part of the Centers for Disease Control.

"She's over here."

Mack stopped by a relatively innocuous glass container with a slip of tinfoil across its top and a fat belly full of a dark, thick liquid that had a frothy, cream-colored head.

"Meet my new strain. Or, shall I say, our new strain."

Lane popped his eyes. "You're kidding me. I didn't even know you were working on a new yeast?"

"I wasn't sure I'd find anything worth talking about. But it turns out, I did."

The rules and method that governed bourbon making were very clear: The whiskey had to be made in the United States and the mash had to be a minimum of fifty-one percent corn, with the balance being from rye, wheat, and/or malted barley. After the mash was ready and at the right pH, yeast was added and fermentation occurred, and that fermented mash had to then be distilled to a given alcoholic percentage in the stills. The resulting "white dog" was placed in new, charred, American oak barrels for aging, a process whereby the caramelized sugars in the charred wood colored and flavored the alcohol. After maturing, the bourbon was filtered and balanced with water and finally bottled at at least eighty proof.

What affected the taste was, essentially, three things: the composition of the mash, the length of the aging . . . and the yeast.

Yeast strains were the top secret for bourbon makers, and for a company like the BBC, they were not just patented, they were kept under lock and key, the mother strain carefully tended to, DNA'd, and checked every year to make sure there were no contaminations.

If the yeast changed, the taste changed and your product could be lost forever.

The strain used for Family Reserve, for example, had been brought over from Scotland to Pennsylvania during the early days of the Bradford family. And there hadn't been a new one since about fifty years after that.

"Right before Dad died," Mack said, "I had started working on this. You know, traveling throughout the South, getting soil, nut, and fruit samples. And this one . . . she just started talking to me. I've analyzed her thoroughly and compared her DNA to everybody else's. It's proprietary, and more than that, it's going to make a hell of a bourbon."

As Beth came up to the man, he put his arm around her and kissed her.

Lane shook his head. "This is downright historic—"

"Yeah, in, like, ten years," Jeff cut in. "I don't mean to be a downer here, but we need to generate cash now. Even if this results in the best bourbon on the planet, it's still going to have to be aged before we can distribute it."

"That's my point." Mack focused on the beaker. "We can sell this yeast strain today. Any other bourbon maker—or whiskey maker, outside of the United States—would kill for this, and not only because it's going to make a great liquor. They'd pay a premium for it just to get it out of our hands."

Jeff's affect changed on a dime. "No fucking kidding."

"It's got to be worth . . ." Mack shrugged. "Well, you tell me we need about a hundred million to pay off all those banks, right? Something like this—it's practically invaluable. Hell, I'm not even sure how to put a dollar figure on it. But it's at least that much. Or more. Think about it, a proprietary blend, never before on the market, and a competitor who will be diminished by its sale."

"Priceless," Jeff murmured.

Lane focused on Mack. Master distillers were usually much older than Mack's thirty-something years, and for him to not only be his father's son, but to discover something like this? It would make his career, put him in the big leagues—and break his heart if someone else got to claim the bourbon that flowed from his discovery.

"I can't let you do it," Lane said. "No."

"Are you out of your mind?" Jeff barked. "Seriously, Lane. We're in beggars-not-choosers land over here. You've seen the hole we're in. You know what's at stake. A cash infusion on that level is what could save us—assuming we can get the money in time."

In the silence that followed, Lane thought about Sutton Smythe.

The Sutton Distillery Corporation was sitting on a boatload of cash—because, hello, they hadn't had some jackass in the top office stealing money.

She was the CEO. She could make decisions like that, and fast.

And as the BBC's biggest competitor?

Mack extended a finger and tapped the tinfoiled beaker. "If it'll save the company, I'll be a hero of sorts, right? And I'll be saving my job while I'm at it."

As all three of them stared at Lane, he hated the position he was in.

That his father had put him in, he corrected.

"Maybe there's another way," he heard himself say.

Although if that were true, he thought, why was he hearing crickets in his head?

After a moment, he cursed and headed for the door. "Fine. I know who to call."

*A*ll things considered, Max thought as he dismounted from his Harley, it was a surprise that he hadn't had more experience with jails.

Looking up at the Washington County Courthouse, he marveled at the many floors and wondered exactly where the jail was located in the complex. The building had to be an entire block long. And wide.

As he walked up the series of steps and levels, he braced himself to get profiled as a criminal. Beard, black leather, tattoos. He was the poster child for a certain kind of folks who tangled with the legal system, and sure enough, the sheriff's deputies around the metal detector you had to walk through gave him the hairy eyeball.

He put his wallet and its chain in the black basket along with his cell phone and went through the trellis of a sensor. On the far side, he was wanded. Twice.

They seemed disappointed when nothing went off.

"I'm looking for the jail check-in?" he said.

"For prisoners?" the woman asked.

"I want to see one, yes."

Of course you do, her eyes said. "Go up to the third floor. Follow the signs. They'll take you into the next building over."

"Thank you."

Now she seemed surprised. "You're welcome."

Following her directions, he found himself waiting in line at a check-in desk, in front of four people in sheriff's uniforms typing requests into computers.

He would have glanced at his watch. If he'd had one. Instead, he relied on the clock on the wall behind them all to assess the time. At this rate, he wasn't going to be able to leave town until noontime—

"Max?"

He turned at a familiar voice and then shook his head. "Hey, man. How you?"

As he and Deputy Ramsey clapped palms, he kind of wanted to explain the beard and the tats. But whatever, he was an adult. He didn't have to be accountable to anyone.

"You here to see Edward?" the deputy asked.

"I, ah, yes, I guess. Yes."

"He hasn't been much for visitors."

"I'm pulling out. Of town. I wanted to see him before I go, you know."

"Wait over there. Lemme see what I can do."

"Thanks, man."

Max went across the linoleum floor and parked it in a lineup of plastic chairs. But he didn't sit back and relax. None of that happening, nope. He just put his hands on his knees and passed the time checking out the other people milling around. Not a lot of white-collar types.

Yeah, his dad, with all his fine-bred bullshit, wouldn't have liked it in here. Then again, William would have been in the federal system, not this local one. Would that be any classier, however. No.

Too bad the bastard had been killed before the hammer had fallen. . . .

For once, Max didn't fight the onslaught of bad memories, the snapshots of arguments, beatings, disapproval . . . downright hatred . . . filtering through his brain like the worst kind of slideshow. The way he looked at it, though, he was never coming back to Charlemont after this, so it was the last time, in his entire life, his father was going to get any airtime under his skull.

In other cities, in other climates, in other time zones, it was so much easier to leave everything that had hurt behind.

So much easier to pretend things had never happened.

From out of the corner of his eye, he saw a mother-and-son duo come in and get in line. The kid was scrawny and lanky, with the all-cartilage, no-bones body of a typical sixteen-year-old. Mom had the gray skin of a smoker and more tattoos than Max did.

It was hard to tell who was talking back to the other more.

Clearly, a fair fight.

When the kid finally shut the hell up, he turned around, like he was considering a bid for an escape—and that was when he saw Max.

God, Max knew that rebellion so well, those crazy eyes, the cruisin'-for-a-bruisin' routine. He'd done all that. But when your dad beat you with a strap at least once a week, sometimes because you'd done something, and sometimes because he just felt like trying to break you again, you did one of two things. You got quiet or you got crazy.

He'd chosen the latter.

Edward had chosen the former.

Ramsey came out from the back. "He'll see you. C'mon."

As Max got to his feet, that kid looked at him like he was some kind of status to aspire to, and Max understood. If you got swolt and you got ink, if you wore a scowl and had a mean light in your eye, you were defending yourself against not so much the people standing in front of you . . .

. . . as the one you had left behind.

The one with the strap and laugh, who'd enjoyed your pain because it had made him feel stronger.

"Max?"

"Sorry," he said to Ramsey. "I'm here."

He had the vague impression of a number of corridors, and a checkpoint with bars, and then he was down a hall with multiple doors that had caged lightbulbs above them. Two were lit. Three were not. He was led all the way down to the last lit one.

Ramsey opened the door and Max hesitated. There was something about Edward that always made him feel like an ass—and not because, when they were growing up together, he'd frequently, in fact, been an ass.

The thing was, Edward had been their leader, their chief, their king. And Max just the jester with psychotic tendencies.

With all that in mind, he forced himself to walk in with his head up—but he shouldn't have bothered. Edward wasn't watching the door. He was sitting with his hands folded on the table and his eyes on his fingers.

Ramsey said something and closed the door.

"So I understand you're leaving." Edward glanced up. "Where are you headed?"

It was a while before Max could reply. "I don't know. Not here. That's all that matters."

"I can totally understand that."

Max exhaled his tension and went over to the seat opposite his brother. When he tried to pull the stainless-steel chair out, it didn't budge.

"They're bolted to the floor." Edward smiled a little. "I gather that some of my fellow inmates have trouble expressing their emotions. Without throwing things, that is."

"I would fit in here."

"You would."

Max squeezed himself into the spot, his knees and thighs bumping into the bottom of the table. "This thing's bolted down, too."

"Trust no one."

"Isn't that from *The X-Files?*"

"Is it?"

There was a period of silence. "Edward, I need to tell you something before I go."

THIRTY-TWO

*A*nnnnnnd this is why they called it morning sickness, Lizzie thought as she slowed the four-wheeler down and leaned to the side to dry-heave. For, like, the fourth time.

But she was determined to get around her full property.

The good news? At least the fresh air, and the sun on her face, and the scent of the grass and the good earth, were a balm to her soul. And what do you know, the wide open sky and the solitude helped recast the night before, making what had struck her as a grotesque manipulation of the legal system when it had happened seem more like just a brother wanting to protect his sister by keeping her out of the papers.

Plus there was Amelia to think of.

As Lizzie straightened and took a sip of water from her bottle, she looked down at her lower belly. If she had a kid out there in the world? Attached to the Bradford name? The last thing she would want was the family in the news and all over social media—especially with regard to what had gone down in that marsh.

For godsake, Amelia might be coming home for good in a few days, but even if she weren't in Charlemont, everywhere she went, she would be known as the kid whose mother had . . . yadda yadda yadda.

Horrible for a child.

Lizzie hit the gas and continued in a fat loop that stuck to her fence line. And as she bumped along, searching for downed trees, limbs, and fence posts, she thought about Amelia through the years.

The poor girl didn't even know who her father was.

It was never spoken of.

Surmounting the rise that was in the far northern corner of her farm, Lizzie stopped and turned in her seat. Looking down over the land she owned free and clear, that she had bought and paid for on her own, she realized . . . holy crap, she just might have someone to leave all of this to.

Would her child know and love the earth as she did? Want to sink vital hands into the good soil and cultivate from seeds things that fed people and made a house smell and look beautiful? Would he or she be an artist? Perhaps a painter who would find inspiration here . . . or a writer who would ply many the occupied solitary hour at a keyboard in the front living room.

Would her son be married up here on this hill? Would her daughter keep horses in the barn down there?

So many questions. And so many projections.

Not one of which included Easterly or any of the Bradford lineage.

Perhaps her child would go into the business? Learn about bourbon and its history, and become passionate about its careful tending and the honoring of long-standing tradition.

Or . . . dear Lord, what if she ended up with a Gin? She didn't think she could live through that.

Images from the night before came back to her, and then there were others from when Lane and Richard Pford had gone at it in the hall at Easterly. Lane had been so worried about his sister, so protective. And then there was his preoccupation with Edward. His concern over Max. His love for Miss Aurora and even his addled mother.

And on top of that there was that young boy, Damion, his father's illegitimate son by the family's old controller. Lane was even taking care of him, even though he didn't have to, making sure that the boy was treated fairly.

Lane was scared to be a father. But with everything Lizzie knew about him, he was going to be a good family man—because he already was one.

Putting her hand on her stomach, she decided she was going to tell him about the pregnancy. One, because God forbid if she lost the baby, as sometimes happened before the second trimester, she wanted him to at least know what was inside her while it was there and alive. And two, because he deserved what Amelia's father, whoever he was or had been, had been cheated out of.

The Bradford family had a checkered history with fathers and their children.

And she sure as hell was not going to be a part of it.

*E*dward had never particularly gotten along with his brother Max. He had learned, however, not to take this personally. Max did not appear to get along with anybody all that well. So when Ramsey had come to announce that the black sheep of the family was pulling out of Charlemont and wanted to see him right before his exit?

Something told Edward that this was the last time he was going to see the guy.

"What's wrong, Max. What do you think I've got to hear."

Max rubbed his face. Stroked his beard. Looked as if he was going to vomit.

There even seemed to be a sheen of tears across those pale gray eyes, something that was utterly unexpected.

Struck by an impulse he could not deny, Edward reached across and squeezed a huge forearm. "It's okay. Whatever it is, it's all right."

"Edward—" Max's voice cracked. "Edward, I'm so sorry."

Had he found out about the suicide attempt?

Edward sat back and sorely regretted that silly attempt at self-harm. He had meant it only in the abstract. As soon as he had seen his blood flow from his wrist, he had known that he would not take the coward's way out.

A mistake, not to be repeated. But surely, Max wouldn't have heard about that.

Oh, wait, Edward thought.

In lightning succession, he added and subtracted the equations of both of their lives and came to the only sum total that made any sense in light of this emotional overflow—in a man who fought tooth and nail to remain untouched.

"I already know," Edward murmured.

Max sniffed and frowned. "Know what."

"That William wasn't my father. That's what you've come to tell me, isn't that right?" As his brother looked shocked and then nodded, Edward took a deep breath. "Well, shall I say that I had my suspicions. I guess you're saying that it is true?"

"Goddamn, how did you know?"

"He tried to have me killed in the jungle," Edward said dryly.

"Hardly a parental move even by his very low standards. More than that, though . . . he always looked at me differently. He wasn't kind to you three, but there was a special, nasty light in his eye that he reserved for me and me alone. He literally hated the breath in my lungs, the beat of my heart—it went that deep, and it was there from the start. My earliest memory was of him glaring at me."

"I'm glad he's dead."

"So am I."

"I overheard them talking one night. That's how I found out—and also why I left Charlemont when I did. I should have told you, but I didn't know what to do."

"It's okay. It is not your fault or your problem." Edward leaned in. "And a piece of advice, if I may? You're still running from him, I get that. But you may want to reconsider the effort. To escape from a trap that doesn't actually imprison you is not logical."

Max's bleak eyes drifted off. "He's in my head. I can't . . . I have nightmares, you know. Of running through that house. He's behind me and I know what he's going to do when he catches me, and he always catches me. He always . . . caught me."

"He's not on your heels anymore, Max. He just isn't. And hopefully you'll come to believe that someday."

It was a long while before Max looked up again. "You were a really good brother, Edward. You took care of me when I didn't deserve it. Even when I was—you know, fucking up shit and all out of control, you always stood up for me. You always did me right. Thank you."

Edward closed his eyes. "You deserved better than you got. We all did. And we're all crippled—my version just happens to show on the outside."

That was a lie, actually. He was ruined in his head, too. But his brother had enough on his conscience.

And yes, maybe Edward should take his own advice about letting the past go. File that under easier said than done, however.

"I never thought I would say good-bye to you," Max murmured. "Or any of the three of you. But for some reason . . . I had to see you before I leave for good."

"I'm hardly one to criticize you for cutting ties."

"You're the only person, then."

"The others just don't understand." Edward shrugged. "It doesn't matter, though. Just do you, Max. Find your freedom however you can, and live your life as best you're able. We earned that right. Earned it the hard way in that house with him."

Clearing his throat, Edward grunted and stood up. As his body swayed, he had to catch himself on the table.

"Are you going to be okay?" Max said, his eyes worried. "In the big house, things are rough."

"I'll be fine."

As he held his arms open, Max got to his feet and came over. When they embraced, Edward held on only for the briefest of moments, and then he had to step back.

"Did you really kill him?" Max asked.

"But of course I did. Can you blame me?"

Edward limped over to the door, but paused before he banged on it. Without looking back, he said, "One thing, Max. Before you go, I want you to do something for me—and this is a non-negotiable, I'm afraid."

THIRTY-THREE

When Lane finally got a text from Lizzie, telling him that she was coming over to Easterly, he raced back to the mansion from the Old Site and beelined for their bathroom. He wanted to see her all clean-shaven and smelling fresh, an un-wrinkled polo and pressed shorts on, a smile pinned to his face.

In other words, the opposite from how he'd been the night before.

When he'd roped her into lying by omission to the police to cover up a shooting.

Hell, maybe he just should tell her that he'd disclosed everything to the cop after she'd driven off in her truck—and point out that it wasn't his fault that his family name had gotten him off the hook.

Yup, 'cuz that was going to help his case.

In the bathroom, he ditched his clothes into the hamper. They had been clean when he had put them on, but his body had not been, so he wasn't going to re-wear them post-shower.

After he turned off the central air-conditioning, so he didn't get a chill when he got out, he started the water running.

Towel. He needed a towel.

Turning to the tall, thin closet, he opened things up and fished around for—

A box dropped onto the floor, something falling free of it onto his bare foot. Bending down, he picked up . . .

A pregnancy test.

"I actually came to tell you. That's why I'm here."

He straightened and looked to the door. Lizzie was standing in between the jambs, her face sun-kissed as if she had been out in the good air, her blond hair down on her shoulders, her body looking . . . strong. Healthy. Powerful.

He blinked and glanced back at the box.

And then he snagged a bath towel and wrapped it around his hips. "Are you . . . when did you . . . are you . . . okay?"

As a thousand things went through his mind and his heart, it was a miracle he could speak at all.

"It's why I've been sick," she explained. "You know, in the mornings."

He could tell she was holding back and trying to read where he was. And he wanted to respond to her, to reach past his shock and disbelief and find her in the midst of the announcement.

When that failed, he tried to make himself feel something.

Anything.

God . . . pregnant? She was having a baby, his baby?

Lizzie cleared her throat. "I, ah, I just took the test the day before yesterday. It was on a whim. I didn't actually think I was. When it, ah, came back positive, I was shocked, and I thought, you know, I thought I would wait and test it again and see. But—"

"That's why you asked me if I'd ever thought about being a father."

"Yes, I mean, we haven't discussed it before. And now, you know, we really have to."

"Yes," he said. "We should . . . talk about it."

Lane went over and sat on the edge of the tub. *Say something. You fool, say something, she's waiting for you to—*

"I'm keeping it," Lizzie said roughly. "No matter what happens to you and me, I'm keeping this baby."

He recoiled. "What? Of course you are. And—we're getting married."

"Are we? Still?"

Lane stared up at her remote face. "Yes, of course."

Lizzie frowned. "I'm not Chantal. I didn't do this to get you down the aisle, and the last thing I want is a husband who is operating out of responsibility, not love."

With a sudden rush, Lane burst up, crossed the distance between them, and pulled her against him. Closing his eyes, he realized why he hadn't been able to say anything, think anything, feel any sort of emotion.

He was paralyzed by a fear so deep, it went down into his soul.

When Max reached his destination, he left the Harley on the street again, and as he entered an open atrium that went up a number of floors, he looked around for some kind of orientation or—

Welcome desk. Perfect.

He wanted to be welcomed, thank you very much. So he could get this over with.

As he approached the desk, the little old white-haired lady on duty smiled at him. "Welcome to University Hospital. How may I help you?"

He was slightly surprised she was so open with him. Then again, she had cataracts clouding her eyes, so she probably couldn't see him very well.

"I'm looking for the ICU. A friend—a person who's—she's family, really. Aurora Toms? I'm here to visit her."

Because that was what Edward had asked him to do.

"Let me see if I can find her for you." There was some slow, even tapping on a keyboard. "Why, yes, she's up on the fourth floor. We only let family members see patients on that unit, though."

"I'm family. I'm . . . one of her sons, actually."

It felt so strange to claim that. And yet it was right.

"Oh, I'm sorry. That's my misunderstanding, then. Use those elevators, right there. Check in with the nursing station and they will escort you to her room."

"Thank you."

"You're welcome."

Up on the fourth floor, he did as he was told and was directed down and into a room that was like a pre-coffin: Everything was barren, sterile, lifeless—motionless and quiet except for the blips on the monitors. And as he approached the bedside, Miss Aurora seemed so small . . . a shrunken remnant of the powerful woman he recalled, swaddled like a babe in soft white and blue blankets. Her eyes were closed, and her breathing was not right, the inhales a fast jerk, the exhales these long deflations.

Staring down at her, he took a moment to ponder his own end, whatever it looked like—probably violent, he decided—and he also thought about things like God and Heaven and Hell.

When he finally spoke, it was in a rush. "I'm sorry about that time that I switched all your sugar in the canister with salt. And for when I tried to bake that cake made out of cow flops. Also, that whole latex paint in the milk carton thing. And for when I spoiled the eggs in the sun and put them back. And for the lettuce incident. Oh, and the worms."

No reason to get into the specifics of either of those last two.

"I wish you weren't going."

He was surprised when that came out of his mouth—because it was the truth, and also because what the hell did he care? He was also leaving.

"I worry about Lane, you know." He sat on the foot of the bed. "He's stretched pretty thin, and he always went to you to feel better. He really needs you now."

Max looked down at his boots and knew that she would have disapproved of the scratches on them. Actually, she would have disapproved of a lot about him now, but she'd still have loved him. Not as much as she loved Lane, it was true—still, Miss Aurora would have hugged Max and fed him and smiled at him like he was being stupid, but couldn't help it.

"Do you remember when I decided to ladder up the back of the house to the roof? I really thought strapping those two sliding rungers, one to another, was going to work. I can't believe I only broke two of those gas lanterns. Man, Father was pissed. Or how about when I put moonshine in the punch bowl at the Christmas party, and that woman threw up all over the Secretary of State—you know, I would have been great on the Internet if they'd had it back then. Or how 'bout when . . ."

As he let his voice drift, he shook his head. "What the hell am I doing here, talking. This is crazy—"

"She can hear you."

Max stiffened and twisted around. Tanesha was standing just inside the door, looking like a proper doctor in those scrubs, and that white coat, and the stethoscope around her neck. Then again—when you got great grades through high school and college, were accepted into the University of Chicago's medical school, and busted your ass in your residency? Yeah, you looked like a frickin' doctor.

"I knew you'd go into oncology," he said roughly.

Tanesha's brows lifted. "Why?"

"Am I right?"

"Well, yes." She came in farther. "I've lost a lot of people to cancer. I guess that's why I gravitated to it."

"Both grandparents, your uncle, the little cousin who was three, and your second cousin in college."

Tanesha blinked. "That's right. You've got a heck of a memory."

Only for things about you, he thought as he studied her.

"I'm surprised you're still here," she said. "I thought you were leaving yesterday."

"I'm taking off right after this." He glanced at Miss Aurora. "I had to say good-bye."

"She appreciates it, I'm sure." Tanesha went around to the other side and checked the monitors. "But I'll bet you'd prefer he stays, isn't that right, Miss Toms?"

"How's your father?" Max blurted.

Tanesha smiled and shifted her eyes over. "He's the same."

"Still hates me?"

"He never hated you. He just thought you weren't the right match for me."

"Because I'm white, right."

"No, because you're a jackass. Not that my father would put it in those words."

Max had to laugh. "You were always so blunt."

With a shrug, she sat down on the other side of the bed. "It's just the way I am. Take it or leave it."

"Are you seeing anyone?" he asked, even though he had no right to. "You know, after you broke up with that J.Crew model—"

"He was not a model, he was an engineering student—"

"Who looked like he was ordered out of a catalog that sold pleated pants and penny loafers."

"Chad was a very nice guy."

" 'Was,' huh. Not 'is.' "

"I'm not with anybody, not that it's any of your business. Medical school and then residency is a lot to juggle. Besides, my focus is on my patients—"

"Do you miss me sometimes?"

Her eyes shifted away. "No."

"Liar."

"Max, stop. You're leaving anyway, why do you care?"

"It's just that way between you and me—"

"Okay, you can quit that. There is no 'you and me' and there never has been. We have *never* been together."

"That's not true," Max said in a low voice. "And you know it."

The blush that tinted her cheeks told him that, yes, she was re-membering exactly the same thing he was: all of the times the two of them had snuck off and fallen into each other. It had always been when they were back in town on break from college, or afterward, when he had been farting around and she had returned from medical school. Usually it had happened after he had played pickup basketball games with her brothers—a dangerous proposition because if those two guys had ever found out what transpired after Max and Tanesha left separately? They'd have rolled Max out in an alley and left him for dead.

Although that wasn't a racist thing. They'd have done the same to any African-American suitor who was too stupid to settle down and be a proper boyfriend.

You didn't mess with their baby sister.

"I meant in a relationship," she muttered. "We were never in a—"

"Are you settling down in Charlemont?" He motioned around the hospital room. "Going to work here. Buy a house. You know, be a grown-up?"

"My father wants me to stay, but . . . no. Actually, I wouldn't mind even leaving the country. I'll always come back to see family, but there are bigger places to be and see than Charlemont." With a quick smile, she motioned around his face. "When did you grow that beard?"

"Like it?"

"It's . . . interesting. But I think you're more handsome when you can see your face—" She stopped. "Not that I notice these things."

He smiled. "Of course you don't."

"What have you been doing these last three years?"

"So you've been counting down how long it's been since you saw me last?"

"Not in the slightest."

Max felt his body light up on the inside. "You sure about that? You sure you didn't miss me even a little."

"Maxwell Baldwine, you are just not that big a deal in my life."

"Don't make me call you a liar twice today, come on." As he stared at her through low lids, she looked like she wanted to wrap that stethoscope around his neck and cut off his air supply—and how hot was that? "And as for what I was doing? Just driving around. Working odd jobs for petty cash. Seeing the country."

"I was surprised you left without saying good-bye."

"I had to." He shrugged. "If I'd looked into your eyes one last time, I might have had to stay."

She blinked. "Now, why have you got to be like that."

"It's the truth."

They stared at each other for the longest time. And then he whispered, "For what it's worth, which is not much, I know . . . the one constant on the road for me was lying back, every night, and picturing you as I fell asleep. You're kind of like my northern star, you know? You followed me wherever I went—and you're going to continue to do that."

There was a tight silence. And then she said, "You know what I hate most about you?"

"The beard, I know."

"Well, that's my number two, actually." She came over to him and put her hand on his shoulder. Then she brushed his hair back. "I really hate most how you always say exactly the right thing . . . at the wrong time—"

"Lane?"

At the sound of the croaked name, both of them looked at Miss Aurora. Her eyes were open and focused, and shockingly clear.

"I need Lane," the woman said. "My boy . . ."

"Miss Aurora?"

"Miss Toms?"

With quick moves, Max jumped off the bed, and Tanesha scrambled for the nurse's call button—but Miss Aurora wasn't going to wait to start talking.

"I killed William," she said. "I killed that sorry excuse for a husband and a father. I cut his finger off with m' kitchen knife and then I put him in the back of my car and drove him down to the river."

As Max froze, and so did Tanesha, Miss Aurora repeated everything she said, word for word. And then she added, "He got my boy's wife pregnant. That Chantal woman. I couldn't let it go on anymore. So I saw my chance and I took it. That man never belonged in that house, and he never should have been let stay that long. I need one of y'all to tell the police—Edward said he was putting himself in jail for me, and I didn't want that. I don't want that. Get him out and get me my boy before I die."

THIRTY-FOUR

As Lane stood against her, Lizzie was stiff as a board. Of all the ways she had hoped this would go, his total shutdown was not it.

Heading over the Big Five Bridge from Indiana, she had alternated between daydreams: In one, Lane had felt an instant joy that wiped away all of his misgivings and disinterest, and in the other, he experienced nothing but a happy giddiness as they shared a special secret between only them.

Ah, rose-colored glasses.

Yup, there was a reason people enjoyed fantasies. They turned the buffet of life into an à la carte plate with nothing spoiled, slimy, or overcooked on it. It was mac and cheese, the perfect short rib, and fresh corn on the cob, every time. With chocolate cake for dessert. And a glass of ice-cold milk.

God . . . she had never thought she'd feel the need to put a stake in the I'm-keeping-this-baby territory.

When Lane eased back, she braced herself for him to hit her with all kinds of *This will be fine, we'll get through this together, blah blah blah*—in other words, the stated position of a nice guy in a bad spot who was prepared to make the best of things.

Because he happened to love the woman he'd knocked up by mistake.

But that was not going to be enough for her. Not with something like this.

"Look, Lane—"

"What if I hurt it."

The bleak words were such a surprise, she recoiled. And then she was shocked as he held his hands out, his eyes locked on them as if he were trying to read his future actions in them.

In that moment, the true extent of what he'd been through as a child crystallized in Lizzie's mind. She had always known that William Baldwine was a bad man who'd been mean to his children—and if Lane had come from a poor background, her sympathy and understanding, her anticipation of what might be a trigger for him, would have been much more finely tuned.

Somehow, in her mind, the luxury of Easterly and the privilege afforded to him and his siblings had buffered the contours of the abuse.

This moment stripped all that away.

As his terrified eyes lifted to hers, he was practically begging for a life raft out of his past. "What if I'm my father?"

Lizzie grabbed on to his hands. "You're not. Good God, Lane, you're nothing like him. At all. You're going to be a wonderful—"

"What if I ruin our child?"

Now Lizzie was pulling him against her and holding him tight. As she closed her eyes, she was so angry at William Baldwine, she could have kicked his grave.

"You won't, Lane. I know you won't."

"How, though? How do you know that?"

"Because I love you, and I would never love a man who would hurt a child. It's not you, Lane. And if you don't believe me, it's okay. Because time is going to prove me right."

His arms came back around her, and they held each other for so long, her feet began to ache—not that she cared. She was prepared to stay here for however long it took.

"I'm so scared," he said into her hair.

"And the fact that you are is simply one more sign you're not your father." She rubbed his back in slow circles. "It's going to be fine. I just know it. We're going to have this baby, and we're going to love it and each other. And it's going to be all right, I promise."

"I love you."

She closed her eyes and felt a relief—although not because he was so upset. No, she hated that. But this was a very different paradigm than him not wanting to have children. Lane was going to show up for her and the baby because that was the man he was at his core. He had proved it so over and again, with every curveball thrown at him.

"I love you, too," she said. "Always."

Back in the bedroom, a cell phone started to ring, but they both ignored the sound as he straightened and rubbed a hand down his face.

"Okay, so tell me." He took a deep breath. "How do you feel?"

"Sick." She smiled. "But that's normal. I'm supposed to feel that way."

"And how did you find out? I mean . . ."

"Like I said, I piddled on a stick." She held up her forefinger to emphasize the point. "But not on my hand. Source of pride right there. And I waited until I saw the plus sign."

"All alone?"

"Well, it was private."

"I wish I had been there to see it with you." Lane took her hand. "Hold up. I want a do-over."

"What?"

He tugged her across to the tub, where he'd put the box down. "Let's do it all over again. Come on. Let's have the moment. Let's do this."

Lizzie had to laugh. "You're serious?"

"Yes, I want to be there when you find out. To support you—and now that I'm getting over the shock-and-terror part, to, like, cheer. You know, husband stuff."

"Well, I was going to retake the thing today."

"So let's do it right now." He extracted the test and broke it open. "Let's do this together."

As he held the stick out to her, she took a deep breath and realized she was nervous. A lot of pregnancies were lost before women even knew they had conceived. What if she had miscarried the baby?

She had been less sick today. Or was that because she'd only eaten pretzels . . . ?

With her head going into a spiral, she nodded. "Actually, it would be great to have you here."

"And I want to be with you for everything. Ultrasounds, appointments, maternity-clothes shopping, sore feet, cravings. I mean, I want to do all of it."

It was clear what Lane was doing, she thought. He was banking that the likelihood of him not screwing up fatherhood started with him being a supportive partner during the pregnancy—and Lizzie took this as yet another sign that she was right and they had nothing to worry about.

"Let's do this."

In quick order, she did her business on the stick—neat and tidy. She was getting to be a pro at this, she decided.

And then they laid the stick on the counter, and went over to the lip of the tub.

They sat there, and tracked the time on his Audemars Piguet, and held hands.

"I would love to raise our child at least partially at the farm," she said.

"We can move out there."

She looked over at him. "How can you leave all this?"

"Why would I stay?" He squeezed her hand and kissed her mouth. "My family is going to be in Indiana."

Lizzie started to smile. And then she teared up.

As if he understood where she was at, he pulled her into his chest. "You're going to be a wonderful mother. I can't wait for you to know that as well."

And then he checked his watch. "Okay, it's time. Come on, Mom."

They both took a deep breath, got to their feet, and approached the stick like it was either a bomb or a Christmas present.

Leaning in together, Lizzie started to smile—only to glance at Lane: His eyes were so wide, they were liable to pop out of his skull, and he seemed to pale a little.

But then he wheeled around, scooped her up, and started spinning. "We're pregnant. We're going to have a baby. Come on, say it with me! We're pregnant!"

She could tell he was still uneasy, but deep in her heart, she knew this was all going to be okay. He was going to be a terrific dad, and she was going to love being a mom, and they were going to be out on her land together.

As a family.

"We're going to have a baby!" she said loudly.

Lane kissed her once. And then again. And then . . . some more.

As that cell phone kept ringing in the other room, Lane laid her out on the thick fur rug in front of the tub. With sure hands, they undressed each other and then they made love with a kind of wonderment on both sides, a kind of . . . oh, my God, it worked, the whole sex thing *worked*.

They were going to be parents.

And funny, but the prospect offered a completion Lizzie had been unaware of needing.

No matter what happened with Easterly and the BBC and the rest of Lane's family, life was very, very good for the two of them, and with their love for each other and their child, they were going to make sure it stayed that way.

THIRTY-FIVE

As Lane floored the Porsche's accelerator, he had a serious case of existential whiplash going on. No more than twenty minutes ago, he'd been making love with Lizzie and trying to get used to the incredible idea they'd created a human life together . . . and now he was gunning for the hospital, hoping against hope that the time he had taken to share the joy with Lizzie hadn't cheated him out of a good-bye he didn't want to make.

Pulling up in front of the hospital, he put the 911 in neutral and engaged the parking brake. Lizzie and he both got out and they kissed quick as they traded places.

"I'll be up as soon as I park," she said as she got behind the wheel. "I love you."

"I love you, too."

Lane ran through the revolving doors and waved at the receptionist as she looked up at him. "I know where I'm going. Thanks."

He didn't bother waiting for an elevator. He hit the stairwell and
took the concrete steps up two at a time. When he broke out onto the
fourth floor, he jogged down the hallway, passing a couple of groups
of people and nearly running over a pair of kids playing tag where
they shouldn't have been.

At the ICU, he didn't waste time at the nursing station, and they
didn't stop him. They all knew why he was there.

What did slow him up? The fact that there were two policemen
outside of Miss Aurora's room. Along with Max and Tanesha.

"Is she conscious?" Lane said as he came up to the two of them
and nodded to his brother.

"Yes," Tanesha replied as they hugged quickly, "and very lucid.
Her treatment team lowered the morphine dose this morning to try
to cut down on the terrors. I suspect that may be why."

"What the hell is she saying?"

Lane went over to the closed door and reached to open it, but one
of the officers stopped him. "Sir, I'm going to have to ask you to stay
out of there—"

"This could be the last time my momma is conscious, so no. I'm
not cooling my heels in the hall."

Shoving the guy out of the way, he pulled the glass panel wide as
Merrimack looked up from scribbling on a pad.

"Good," the detective said. "I'm glad you're here. She's been asking for you."

Lane stepped in close to the bed. "Momma?"

Miss Aurora turned her head slowly to him. And the smile she
offered him was steeped in relief, as if she had just barely caught a
plane or a train in time. "My boy."

She lifted her hand and motioned for him to sit down with her.
And as he covered her palm with his own, she smiled even more, al-

though she couldn't hold on to the expression. It was clear she was in too much pain.

"Thank you, ma'am," Merrimack said softly. "I 'ppreciate you."

"You do right, young man." She glared at the homicide detective. "I know your parents."

"Yes, ma'am. I'll take care of everything."

"Don't mess it up."

On the one hand, it was a surprise to find Merrimack cowed. On the other? That was Miss Aurora's way.

"I won't, ma'am. Thank you, ma'am."

And then the detective was out of there. From the corner of his eye, Lane caught a quick impression of Merrimack talking to the other officers outside, but he forgot about all that.

"Hi," he said as Miss Aurora refocused on him.

"You came in time." Her voice was already fading, and she closed her eyes and took a deep breath. "Just in time. You got my will?"

"Yes, ma'am."

"You'll make sure that everyone . . ."

"Gets what you want them to have."

"Service . . ."

"At Charlemont Baptist. It's all arranged with Reverend Nyce."

"Good boy." Miss Aurora shuddered. "I'm so tired. I hurt, boy. I'm tired of hurting."

He cleared his voice. "Your Lord is waitin' on you."

"*Our* Lord. He's Our Lord."

They sat there together for a spell. Lane had no idea whether it was a minute or an hour. Then he got worried.

"Miss Aurora? You still with me?"

"Yes, boy."

"I'm having a baby."

That got those eyes back open. "With Lizzie?"

"Yes, ma'am."

"You better marry her, or I will haunt you."

"We're getting married."

"At Charlemont Baptist. So I can watch over the nuptials."

It was on the tip of his tongue to tell her to stay around and see them for herself, but that was cruel. "Nowhere else but there, Miss Aurora."

She took a deep breath and shuddered again. "I was doing so well. And then . . . it just hit me."

"You've come through other sickle-cell crises. You can—"

"Not this one."

There was a period of quiet. "Momma?" he prompted.

"I'm still here, boy."

"You never told me about the rub on your jerk chicken." He suddenly panicked at all the things he'd taken for granted that he could find out from her. It was as if a piece of him were leaving the planet with her. "And what about the beaten biscuits—"

"Recipe box on the shelves. By my chair. Call Patience if you need help. My mother taught us both together."

"I wish you weren't leaving."

"Me, too. But my time is my time." Her eyes opened again. "When you get sad, I want you to remember what I always told you. The Lord giveth, the Lord taketh away. And I had you and my faith, so I was wealthy . . . beyond means."

He found himself blinking hard. And he had to clear his throat before he could speak. "Beyond means."

"It'll be the same for you. Your children are the joy that makes everything else bearable, and you were mine. You have always been mine, even though you were born of another."

"You are my momma. The only one I ever had."

As tears rolled down his face, he felt her squeeze his hand one last time. And then she released her hold so that he was the only one gripping.

Lane stayed there for some time longer, watching her breathe. When the alarms started to ring, he reached over to an *off* button and killed the noise.

Outside the glass door, he saw medical staff gathering, but Tanesha Nyce was standing in front of the way in and shaking her head, protecting him and his momma.

"Momma? You still with me?"

This time, Miss Aurora did not answer him.

*O*ut of respect for the family, Lizzie stayed out of the way, giving the nieces and nephews and sisters and brothers a chance to be closest to the door. There were medical staff hanging around, too, but when Tanesha had explained who Lane was to Miss Aurora, they had backed off after the alarms had been silenced.

Through the glass, Lizzie knew the moment Miss Aurora was gone. Even though Lane had his back to the hall, the death was in the way his shoulders slumped and his head lowered.

He stayed in there a little longer, holding the woman's hand.

Then he got up and opened the door. As soon as he saw the crowd, he said roughly, "She's gone home."

People began to cry and hold each other, seeking comfort and giving it. And everyone went up to Lane, embracing him.

As Lane shared in the grief, his too-shiny, red-rimmed eyes sought and held Lizzie's stare over the heads of the others. He seemed to have aged a hundred years.

When he finally came over, they just held on to each other. And then he straightened.

"If it's a girl, we name her Aurora," he said.

People instantly stilled and grew quiet. Especially as Lizzie nodded. "And if it's a boy, it will be Thomas."

Plans were made, arrangements set, practical matters handled.

And everyone worked together: there was no discord, no jumping in, nothing but a family and a community who had lost one of its most important members helping to honor the woman's memory.

Lizzie had to excuse herself a couple of times, her morning sickness stretching into the afternoon. And each time she came back, she could feel Lane watching her, checking to make sure she was okay.

Then it was finally time to go. No one but Max left.

Lizzie found herself feeling awkward around the man. He was so remote and unfriendly, even in the midst of the loss. Perhaps especially because of it.

"So," Lane said as he stared at the glass.

The medical staff had given everyone plenty of space and Lizzie had certainly appreciated it. Then again, they no doubt had had way too much experience with where everyone was at in this first stage of mourning. Grief, she imagined, was a weekly, if not daily, occurrence on the unit.

"I don't want to leave her," Lane murmured. "I just want to make sure she's okay, you know?"

"There are good people here." Lizzie squeezed his hand. "They will make sure she is treated with dignity."

As if on cue, an African-American man in a suit with a hat in his hands came around from the nursing station. "Mr. Baldwine?"

"Ah, yes?"

"I'm from the Browne and Harris Funeral Home." He offered a business card forward. "I'm Bill Browne's son, Denny. I'm here to take care of her as she prearranged. I'll stay with her all the way from when she leaves this room to when she is transferred into my vehicle. She won't be alone, and she will be afforded the same respect she had in life."

"Oh, thank God."

Taking the card, Lane grabbed the guy and dragged him in for a hard hug, and the man seemed like he was used to that, accepting the embrace and returning it.

"I think I know your brother, Mike?" Lane said as they separated. "Didn't he teach at Charlemont Country Day?"

"Oh, yes. Mike's still there. He's the headmaster now."

"My niece is going to start in the fall as a junior."

"Is she? What's her name?"

"Amelia. Amelia Baldwine."

"I'll tell Mike to look out for her." Denny smiled. "It's a good school. I was class of—"

"My class," Max spoke up. "You were in my class."

Denny frowned. And then seemed surprised. "Max?"

"Yeah, it's me under here." Max stepped forward. "Been a while."

"Yes, yes, it has." They shook hands. "Well, I'm going to start the process at the nursing station, okay? And you call me anytime. If you text me, I'll give you updates as things progress so you're certain she's okay. The date for the funeral is all set, am I correct?"

"Yes, and she's being buried at Kinderhook with her mom and dad." Lane took a deep breath. "Send all the bills to me. I want her estate intact for her nieces and nephews, okay?"

"Her sister came in with her about three months ago and she picked out a coffin. . . ."

When there was a hesitation, Lane frowned. "It's the cheapest one you have, isn't it. She was always so damn frugal."

"Well, I'm sure it—"

"Do you have anything in red? U of C red?"

"As a matter of fact we do. There are a lot of basketball fans in this town, as you know."

"I want her in the most expensive, reddest coffin you've got. I don't care what it costs—and if she's pissed about it, she can come haunt me for the rest of my life. That way, I won't have to miss her as much."

"Yessir." Denny bowed. "You've got it."

"Thank you. Thank you so much."

As Denny went back over to the nursing station, Lane turned to his brother. "So."

Just as Lizzie wondered whether she shouldn't give them some time alone, Max nodded. "Yeah, so I'm going to take off."

"Lot going on here in Charlemont at the moment. You might want to stay around for a little bit longer. Miss Aurora would have wanted you to sing at her service. You've got that voice she loved so much."

Max shrugged. "They have a choir. It'll all be fine without me."

Lane shook his head, but it was obvious that he didn't have the energy to argue with the guy. "Stay in touch. If you can."

"Yeah. Sure."

The two shared an awkward hug, and then Max jacked up his beat-to-crap jeans and stalked off.

"Come on," Lane said sadly as he took one last look into the glass room. "And you need to drive home. I plan on crying like a little girl in the passenger seat so I can get it all out on a oner. That eulogy I'm going to have to deliver is going to kill me, otherwise."

Lizzie fell in step with him. And then she had to bring it up.

"Does this mean Edward is free to come home?"

THIRTY-SIX

*E*dward's first thought? As he sat in the interrogation room that he was beginning to think of as his second home at the jail?

Goddamn it, why in the hell did she have to talk.

As Detective Merrimack sat forward and put his elbows on the table, Edward had to admit, the man's attitude had done a one-eighty. Gone was that patronizing smirk from the investigation. In its place, a calm, relaxed demeanor, backed up by a surprising respect.

"I didn't want her to do this," Edward said into the silence.

From over in the corner, Samuel T. was watching everything closely. The lawyer had insisted on coming down here even though Edward had earlier refused not just the man's help, but that of the county's pro bono defense attorney as well as several high-powered, nationally known lawyers.

"I know you didn't." Merrimack's black eyes were steady, no longer suspicious. "You deleted that security footage to protect her."

"I wasn't going to allow her to go to jail. I didn't care about myself, I still don't. But you've got to understand. My brothers and sister, they went through a lot in that house. And Miss Aurora, she was the one who kept us all going. Lane was especially close to her, and he never would have gotten over it if she had been sent to prison."

"I gather her motive was your father's affair with your brother's wife?"

"Estranged wife. And yes, that's what she told me."

"So you two spoke about the killing."

"Yes, we did. After that finger was found in the dirt, I just had an inkling. I can't tell you exactly why. I called her from the farm and asked her to meet me. No one saw us. She told me what had happened, and I decided what we were going to do about it. She was adamant that we let things lie, but I knew that you all weren't going to be satisfied without a defendant. I put it to her like this—she could either let me go in for her, or she could watch Lane self-destruct knowing that she was dying of cancer behind bars. I told her . . . well, let's just say we both knew that Lane was not going to do well with that. She saw the logic. And so I framed myself."

"You forgot about the security cameras out at the Red and Black."

"I know, right." Edward tapped his temple. "Missed that one."

"It's really hard to get away with murder."

"She was supposed to have thrown away the knife." Edward crossed his arms over his chest. "I'm really pissed at her that she didn't. But it is what it is. So what happens now? I get downgraded to an accessory after the fact and stay in the system for a while? I mean, there's obviously a lot of proof now, right? From what you all got from Miss Aurora's car and quarters?"

"That's right, yes. We found blood and fibers in her trunk, both your father's and her own. It was a struggle for her to muscle the body in and out of there, and she cut herself in the process. We also found a set of shoes with mud that matches samples from the river's edge in her closet. There were as well all kinds of debris stuck to the undercarriage of that vehicle. What we didn't find were any third-party stains anywhere. So we're thinking she acted alone, even though I'm surprised she had the strength to handle that body."

"Oh, I'm not. I've watched her muscle around huge vats of boiling water and sauce all my life. Cancer certainly weakened her, but she was so strong—she also told me he had stiffened up from the stroke after he collapsed? So it wasn't like he was all loose."

"Back to your question about what happens next with you." Merrimack shrugged. "It's up to the district attorney to decide what she wants to do. It could be probation, or they may want to make an example out of you."

"Ah, yes, rich people getting away with stuff."

"It's a fact."

"That why you weren't particularly fond of us, Detective?"

Merrimack smiled for the first time in a natural way. "I don't like murderers. That's who I don't like. But I will say, you cooperated with the investigation all the way—although that was because you wanted to get arrested."

"I had my reasons, it's true."

"I'm prepared to suggest you get heavy probation, no time. It'll be in my report. You definitely broke the law, so that will have to be addressed, but if there was ever a right reason? You had it. Oh, and if you tell anyone I said that, I'll deny it."

The detective got to his feet and extended his hand. "I'll try and spring you as soon as I can."

"Don't worry. Here or out there. It really doesn't matter."

As Edward reached forward, the cuff on his prison uniform got pulled back and Merrimack's eyes went to the wound there.

"I think it does matter," the detective said. "Actually, it matters a lot. You're going to wait here, okay?"

"I'm not going back to the cell?"

"No. When I told you I was going to try and get you sprung fast, I meant it."

*T*hree hours later, Edward was changing back into the street clothes he had been wearing when he'd been arrested after his "confession." And yet as he signed for his wallet and his keys, he told himself they weren't actually going to let him leave.

This whole bail thing, pending a hearing on charges of accessory after the fact, tampering with evidence, and obstruction of justice, was not what he had planned. Then again, he hadn't really budgeted on getting kidnapped in South America, becoming a cripple, falling into alcoholic status, or turning himself into a murderer, either.

Life had a way of surprising people, though.

"Thank you," he said as he accepted his things out of the slot.

Like a lot of the jail complex, the hall he was in was bald of decoration, nothing but an oatmeal-colored chute that took a person from the exit procedure to what he guessed was his brother Lane waiting for him outside that steel door at the far end.

How the guy had managed to pull together a quarter of a million dollars on short notice, he hadn't a clue. Then again, their mother's jewelry collection was worth that in spades. Maybe a bondsman had accepted a necklace or a ring as collateral?

"You're all set, then."

As Ramsey spoke up behind him, Edward wheeled around at the man in surprise. "Good God, Ramsey, for a big man, you move so quietly."

"Years of careful training." The deputy acknowledged the woman behind the Plexiglas with a wave. "And maybe I had a pretty good knack for it to begin with."

The two of them stared at each other.

Edward intended to say something jocular. Instead, his voice grew rough. "I owe you my life. I don't think I've ever said that to you before."

"You did, actually. You were barely conscious at the time, but you did say it."

"Oh. Well, I'll tell you again, then. I owe you my life."

"I'm glad you're out of here."

"I may be going back in. This could be just a reprieve."

"It won't be. I know your judge. She'll do you right, just like the D.A. did. We take care of our own."

"We shall see. No more dead bodies, though. I can promise you that. The cancer is out of the family, and the rest of us can start healing now. Whatever the hell that looks like."

"Good. And you can always call me. Miss Aurora's family is my family."

As the two embraced, Edward had to smile a little. It was like wrapping his arms around an oak tree.

"I'm back to work, then," Ramsey said, his broad, handsome face smiling. "Be good out there."

"I will."

Edward watched the man disappear through the other steel door. And then as the thing shut and clicked into place, it was hard to think of what to do next. Then again, all he had to do was get into a car. That was a purpose, right? And something he could probably handle.

Turning around, he limped down the corridor, his bad leg even worse than usual, all those nights without sleep catching up to him, his stomach growling for food.

Edward had to put his shoulder into the door and push as hard as he could to get it open—

There was a long black Mercedes waiting at the curb in the darkness. With a beautiful brunette woman leaning against the driver's-side door like a boss.

She was wearing blue jeans and a Kentucky University blue sweatshirt.

Edward stepped out and let the jail's door close on its own. "That sweatshirt is an abomination."

"I know. I wore it just for you."

He started to shuffle forward. "I bleed red, you know. University of Charlemont all the way. I can't stand your team."

"Like I said, I know. And I'm still angry at you, so this is my passive-aggressive way of letting you know it."

God, he hated his limp, especially in front of her. But, oh, he could smell her perfume, and he loved the way the security lights on the back corner of the building made her hair gleam.

Edward stopped when he got up close to Sutton. "You bailed me out. You were the one, weren't you."

"Lane called, and I can't say no to your brother. He also told me about everything, including Miss Aurora's passing, and what you did for her. I mean, it's pretty amazing what you were willing to go through for your family—"

"I'm so in love with you," he said in a guttural voice. "Sutton, I love you so goddamn much."

As she blinked quick, like that was the last thing she had expected him to say, but exactly what she had dreamed of, he limped forward a little more and put his scrawny arms around her.

"I can't pretend anymore," he said into her hair. "I don't want to.

There are a million reasons for you to just get in your car and leave me right now, and never, ever look back. There are so many better places for you to be and people for you to be with . . . but I'm selfish. And I'm tired. And to hell with my pride. I love you, and if you'll have me, I'm yours—and if you don't want me—"

Sutton eased back. "Shut up, Baldwine, and kiss me."

Edward took her perfect face in his hands and tilted his head to one side. Pressing his mouth to hers, he kissed her for so long and so deeply that he started to feel the burn of suffocation in his lungs. He didn't care, though. He had waited for a lifetime to admit what he had felt all along, so something as irrelevant as oxygen just wasn't on his radar.

The relief was enormous. And so was the warmth that bloomed between them.

After a long, long time, he separated their mouths. "Dinner?"

"Yes, at my place in town."

"Privacy?"

"We're going to need it."

As his body hardened for her even more, he smiled. "I like the way you think." But then he frowned. "There's just one thing."

"What is that?"

"That sweatshirt has got to go." He shook his head and motioned to the logo. "I mean, I can't look at that. It's making me sick."

"Well, guess what?"

"What?"

She leaned into him. "I'm not wearing anything under it. So yeah, there's that happening right now."

As Edward groaned, she batted him on the butt. "Get in my car, Baldwine. And brace yourself. I'm going through any red light we come up to."

He limped around and opened his door. "Just an FYI, as someone who's recently gotten out of jail, I can tell you the sleeping arrangements and the food are not what a woman of your stature is used to. So you may want to abide the traffic laws."

They got in together and she looked across the seat. "Excellent point."

Getting serious, he brought the back of her hand to his lips and kissed it. "Thank you."

"For bailing you out? You know, I'm not sure you're aware of this, but it's something that's on my bucket list. So we can check that right off."

"No, for waiting for me."

Sutton grew grave, as well. "I was trying not to."

"Do I need to put a hit out on our governor? 'Cuz I will. I'm kind of the jealous sort."

"Dagney is a very nice man. But he always knew where my heart was—and so did I."

Edward smiled. "Good, that means I can be civil to him the next time I see him. As opposed to kicking him in the nuts."

Her eyes searched his face. "I've always been yours, Edward. That's just the way it's been."

As he stared at her, he thought about all the things he'd been through. And all the years ahead of him in a body that wasn't ever going to work quite right. Then he imagined waking up to her every morning.

"I am the luckiest man, I know," he whispered.

After all, money could come and go, as could health and wellness, and destiny was a fickle master, for sure.

But to be loved by the one you loved?

It was the optimism in the midst of crisis; it was the food when you were starving; it was the air when you could not breathe, and the light that led you from the darkness.

All that mattered was in his woman's eyes, and broken though he might have been by any objective measure, Sutton Smythe made him whole.

THIRTY-SEVEN

Three days later, Gin picked Amelia up at the airport. And come to think of it, it was the first time she had ever retrieved anyone from there, having always allowed the chauffeurs to do the deed—plus, she wasn't at all familiar with the commercial arrivals area, having previously done the private jet routine. She followed the signs, though, and kept the Phantom at a slow speed, falling in with the other people providing rides.

Amelia was not at the curb on the first pass, so Gin went around the loop again, and as she did, she thought about the last couple of days. Richard Pford had kept his promise and signed the annulment papers that Samuel T. had drawn up, and the man had let her keep the ring, thank God.

Wouldn't that have been a cause for awkward conversation if he hadn't.

And Samuel T. had agreed to see Amelia immediately, assuming that was what their daughter wanted.

Gin checked the clock on the dash. Three in the afternoon. Samuel T. had said he'd be at his farm by now, having just returned from a trip somewhere out of town. He hadn't volunteered where he had been and Gin hadn't asked—but she had a feeling he had been with a woman: She had called him before the weekend and left a message when he hadn't picked up. It had taken him two days to call her back.

When they had finally spoken, it had seemed a little bizarre that neither of them had talked about what had happened in the marsh with Richard Pford; specifically how, if Samuel T. hadn't shown up right when he had . . . things would have ended very differently.

Still, he had been perfectly pleasant to her, almost professionally so—and she had endeavored to assume the same affect.

As Gin came through the terminal's cover again, Amelia stepped to the curb and waved, although the girl didn't smile.

Actually, Amelia didn't smile very much, did she. And that was something to mourn—something to own as yet another problem Gin was responsible for creating.

There were so many of them.

Over the past couple of nights, when Gin hadn't been sleeping, she had gone through her failures as a mother, one by one. Literally every single missed opportunity had been reviewed, and there had been a breathtaking number of them: Instances when she had chosen to go out and party when Amelia had been sick, or had homework, or been home alone. Missed plays and performances. Times when Amelia had needed advice, guidance, a smile or a hug, and Gin had either not been around or been completely disengaged.

And the longer Gin ruminated on the memories, the more she

recognized that these were regrets she was going to carry with her for the rest of her life.

And in that way, she supposed, she was going to be a little like Edward: Forever changed, although her scars were self-created and she carried them on the inside.

Coming to a stop, she put the Phantom in park and started to get out.

"I got it," Amelia called over the din of other cars and people. "Just pop the trunk."

"I think it's on the handle in the back?"

"Oh, right."

Gin got out anyway and helped Amelia muscle her two rolling suitcases into the boot. Then they got in and Gin eased them away from the curb and over the first of three speed bumps.

"So how was your flight?" Gin asked as she looked around to make sure she could merge back onto the loop.

"Good." Amelia took out her phone and started texting. "I'm glad finals are over with. And I shipped the rest of my stuff home. What happened to your head? Why is it bandaged?"

"It's nothing." Gin cleared her throat. "Listen . . . could you put that down for a sec?"

Amelia lowered the iPhone and glanced over. "What's up? And I already know about Uncle Edward. Is it true he's out of jail? I mean, and Miss Aurora, are you kidding me? It's like something out of *CSI*."

"Actually, this concerns something else. But you and I will talk about all that. There's been a lot going on."

"Too right."

As they got onto the highway, Amelia frowned. "So what is it?"

"I've gotten an annulment from Richard Pford."

"Thank you, God. He was a total douche."

"Yes, I'm afraid my decision making has not been the best at times. I'm trying to make up for it, though."

"Well, you've never picked me up before. For anything. So there's that."

"Ah, yes, it's true. And, ah, I'm really going to try to make a lot of things up to you." Gin glanced over and then refocused on the traffic. "Along those lines . . . so you and I have never really spoken about your father."

Even as Gin made her way into the center lane, she was very aware of the girl going completely still and staring across the seat.

"I want to be very clear here," Gin said into the suddenly thick air. "It was my bad choice not to tell him about you and my bad choice not to tell you about him. I am . . ."

As tears threatened, she cleared her throat. "I will never forgive myself."

"He didn't know about me, either?"

"No."

"So it wasn't . . . that he didn't want me," Amelia said in a small voice.

Gin reached over and squeezed the girl's hand. "No, not at all. I'm the bad person here, I was in the wrong. It was not your fault and it was not his fault. And you don't need permission from me or anybody else to be really angry at me for that."

Amelia took her hand away and put it in her lap. Then she shrugged. "It just kind of was the way it was, you know?"

Gin gripped the steering wheel hard. "I guess my question to you is, would you like to meet him?"

Amelia jerked back around. "Like . . . when? Where?"

"We can do it right now, if you want—"

"Yes. Yes, now. I want to know now."

Gin briefly closed her eyes. "I had a feeling that was the way it was going to be."

"Do I know him?"

"Actually . . ." Gin took a deep breath. "You do."

"*G*etting ready for someone special?"

As Samuel T. checked his bow tie in the glass door of the microwave, he tried to smile in the direction of his estate manager. But his throat was dry, his eyes were wet, and his digestive tract seemed to be on the verge of letting lunch out prematurely.

It was just a question of which end it was going to use.

"She must be someone real special." The woman nodded at the fruit and cheese plate he had made. "I mean, for you to cook for her? Wow."

Okay, so "cook" was maybe taking things a little far. But he had certainly unwrapped the Brie, washed the green and purple grapes, and taken the sleeve of Carr's water crackers out of the box. What the hell did teenage girls eat, anyway?

"We'll see how it goes," he said.

"Well, I appreciate the afternoon off. I've got some shopping to do. 'Bye now—oh, and the dry cleaners called to say they got the stain out of those white pants of yours. You must have had a heck of a weekend."

"It was interesting."

"I'll bet. Have fun. I'll see you tomorrow."

As the woman left through the garage door, Samuel T. reread the text that Gin had sent and rechecked the time it had come through.

Any minute, they would be here.

He re-examined his bow tie in the micro-mirror and then headed out onto the porch. Proceeding down to the end with the stairs, he sat on the steps and stared off across his land to the county road they would be coming in on.

His weekend had been interesting. That was no lie—just not for the reason his estate manager thought it had been. In fact, it had been the first time ever that he'd not had a drink during a rager, and what do you know, that kind of changed the whole experience. As it turned out, his friends were not quite as fun when you were the one sober guy out of twenty. And Prescott had further surprised him by proving to be a far more well-rounded person than he had expected. She was a marathon runner, a classics major—and the reason she had been eyeing his hills as she had after that first night? She was a fox hunter and had been wondering if he might be amenable to her club coming onto his land in the fall for a lease fee.

That wine stain?

A waiter had tripped on the corner of a rug and had dumped a glass of Pinot Noir on Samuel T.'s thigh.

Prescott had wanted them to stay together, but he had gotten them separate rooms—and not just because he didn't feel like having sex with anybody. He had stayed up all night, both nights, trying to remember what his parents had done right with him for all those years. And then he'd reviewed how other folks who had raised halfway-decent human beings had approached things.

He had read articles on the Internet.

Watched episodes of *Full House* and *Home Improvement*—because he wasn't a TV watcher and thus had no idea what contemporary family shows were good to see, and those two had been what was on when he'd been a teenager.

No Facebook back then. Or cell phones. Or Twitter, Insta—

Yeah, those shows were maybe not real relevant as it turned out. But then again, he'd saved them for the four-to-six-a.m. insomnia shift when he'd been brain-dead anyway.

This meeting with Amelia today was happening sooner than he'd thought it would, and he wished he had more time to prepare. Then again, with the way he was feeling at the moment, he could have had another twenty years and would still have felt like he had his head up his—

Out on the county road, a large convertible with a massive grille slowed and then turned in to the allée of trees.

As the Phantom came cruising slowly up the gravel drive, a boil of fine dust kicking up in its wake, Samuel T. fumbled in his suit pocket and popped another Tums in between his molars.

Bad idea. Chalk and dry mouth?

Whatever, too late to fix it, he thought as he got to his feet and went down onto the grass. Overhead, the sun was shining magnificently, the sky was a bright blue, and under his feet, the lawn was green as shamrocks. A light breeze was blowing across the bluegrass, and birds were singing in the trees.

The Phantom stopped halfway around the circle in front of the farmhouse and both doors opened at the same time.

As Amelia got out, she stared at him, her face wary, her eyes narrowed.

Samuel T.'s heart pounded so hard, he was dizzy as he walked toward her. And other than a quick glance at Gin, he didn't take his focus off the girl.

With long strides, Amelia came foward, too, meeting him halfway by herself, Gin seeming to know, for once, that things were not about her.

They stopped with about five feet between them.

"Hi," he said. "I, ah, I'm Samuel Theodore Lodge—"

"I know." Amelia nodded over her shoulder. "She told me—I mean, I know you from around."

They just looked at each other.

"You're tall," the girl said. "Is that where I get this from?"

He glanced down at her long legs. "Yes, probably? And our hair is—"

"The same color."

"Do you like mayonnaise?" he blurted.

"Oh, God—no. No, no, no."

He laughed a little. "My father? He can't stand it, either. His brother was the same. He gave that to me."

"Everyone puts that stuff on everything."

"Unbelievably disgusting."

"Do you—okay, I know this is weird, but do you have trouble with threes?"

"They flip on you, too?"

"All the time! I'm, like, who else deals with this?"

"Phone numbers, right? Receipts? Wait until you start paying for lunches and dinners. It's a pain."

They fell back into silence. After a minute, he gestured over his shoulder. "Do you want to, ah—come in? I mean, I know you've been traveling and all. But maybe I could show you some photographs of your—my family. My side? And, ah, the house has got some hidden rooms that are—I'm babbling here. Do whatever you feel comfortable with. You probably have a ton of friends you're meeting out. I know that's what I did whenever I got home from school."

He braced himself for her to get back in the car and leave him behind, and reminded himself not to take things personally. She was all but a stranger—

"Is this place haunted?"

"Um, actually, yes. I have seen two ghosts. Some people say there are more, but I've only seen two."

"It's beautiful." Her eyes clung to the roofline. Drifted over the farmhouse's face. Lingered on the porch. "I mean, it's so perfect."

Samuel T. had to blink hard. A small part of him would have died in his chest if she had found his legacy a pathetic second fiddle to the grandeur of Easterly.

Amelia cranked around to Gin. "I'm staying. I'll call you later—unless . . . can you bring me back home when we're done?"

Samuel T. sniffed quick and tried to make it look like his allergies were acting up. "Absolutely."

"In your convertible? I think that is the coolest car I have ever seen. It's totally James Bond."

And then she was setting off for his house, her long, wavy hair bouncing in the sunshine.

Samuel T. glanced back at Gin. She looked . . . ruined, her face downcast, her eyes pits of sorrow. He didn't know whether she was mourning her sins, or scared of losing the girl, or . . . terrified that she was going to be in last season's fashions as her family's fortunes declined.

But none of that was his concern.

"I'll drive her back," he said. "And I'll text you if it looks like she's staying for dinner."

He expected Gin to try to draw him into her emotional state. That had always been her specialty before.

Instead, she nodded. "Thank you. Thank you very much."

She got back into the Rolls like an old lady.

He didn't watch her go. Instead, he went around to the porch and smiled as he found Amelia on the bedding platform.

"This is awesome!" the girl said as she swung back and forth.

Samuel T. nodded. "You know, that's my favorite spot, too." He had to smile. "I used to sleep out here when I was your age. Now that I've taken this house over from my parents, I should do that again, huh."

"A person can sleep out here?"

"Mosquito net keeps the bugs off. And it's real quiet. Peaceful."

Amelia looked over the land. After a moment, she asked, "Can I paint this view sometime?"

Samuel T. took in a deep, ragged breath. He had expected to feel curious and nervous.

But it had never dawned on him that he would want to keep her as much as he did: His daughter, his own flesh and blood, was sitting on his porch, doing what he had done when the house had been his father and mother's.

"Anytime you like," he said in a voice that broke. "You can come here and paint that view . . . anytime you like."

THIRTY-EIGHT

━━━◦⊱✿⊰◦━━━

"Okay, so here are our three piles."

Across the CEO's office in the business center, Lizzie started to go Vanna White at the stacks of documents on the conference table, and Lane eased back in his father's throne and put his feet up on William's desk.

It was the end of yet another long day. After a series of even longer ones. But one thing he had learned? With Lizzie at his side, he could get through anything.

"Hit me," he said as he smiled.

With a swivel of the hips and a pass of an elegant arm, she motioned over the left-most collection. "These are losers that are currently causing, or will soon be causing, problems."

It was depressing to recognize that that category had the largest number of folders, and he rubbed his tired eyes. Jeff was right now on a plane back to Charlemont, coming home from having tried to negotiate settlements with seven banks. He'd been successful with two, persuasive with four, and had failed with one. And there were another ten out there that he was going to have to go visit in the next, oh, four to five days.

No pressure.

"Our next group is the not-yet-due group." As Lizzie made a circling motion around those documents, his eyes found his way to her body. To the indent of her waist. The curve of her breast under that—

Lizzie put her face in his line of sight. And the smile she sported was pretty much the sexiest thing he'd ever seen.

"Let's stay focused, shall we?"

"When can I have you?"

"Be a good boy, get through this, and you can have me all over this office—until dinner."

"Can we skip dinner?"

"No." She kicked her hip out. "But you have all night after that, too."

Things had been amazing, a new depth and commitment sprouting, wordless and powerful, between them: They had been spending the early-morning hours wrapped in each other's arms, talking of the future, of the past, taking everything to a new level. They'd even picked a wedding date.

June twenty-first. The longest day of the year. The one with the most sun and least darkness. A fine way, they thought, to start the future together.

It was going to be a very small, informal ceremony at Charlemont Baptist, with no one but immediate family. Her parents were coming down for a week, and Lane was really looking forward to spending time with them. And then they were taking a honeymoon to upstate New York so he could meet her high school friends and visit her old haunts at Cornell. She figured she'd tell her family about the baby then, after things were a little further along.

His people knew because of what he'd said outside of Miss Aurora's ICU room.

They had also spoken of much harder things, like his momma's death, and Max's revelation about Edward, and Lane's worry over the business. And then there were her fears about giving birth and raising a child who was never going to escape the Bradford name.

But whether the subject was light or heavy, sad or joyful, he knew that neither one of them was ever going at something alone again.

"And this is our last pile." She motioned over the shortest stack. "These are the I-don't-knows."

"Greta hates those."

Lizzie nodded. "She absolutely hates them."

Next, one by one, she picked up stapled sheaths of paper that had been laid out in front of the stacks. "Here are Greta's tables. Each of the sets of papers has been assigned a number and is summarized by date, name of company, equity stake, valuation—if she could find one—debt, and lender."

"She is amazing."

"Her husband is making her take some time off for their anniversary and he nearly had to drag her onto the airplane. I think she's going to last forty-eight hours and then she's going to make him fly back from Captiva. She does not want anyone else touching her piles or messing with her system here."

Lane glanced back at the cabinets behind the desk. After he'd broken them all open, he'd found a positive sea of documents that had been randomly thrown in there, forgotten and disorganized.

Greta had more than risen to the occasion. Thank God.

Getting to his feet, Lane crossed over the thick carpeting to the I-don't-knows. "So in the unlikely event there are any assets to recoup, they're in here. Because all the other businesses are known losers or didn't exist."

"Yup, that's where we're at."

He took the spreadsheet that detailed the unknowns. Glancing through the list, he shook his head. "I've never heard of any of these entities before."

"I can help to try to research them further. Greta focused on the most emergent companies and banks. But I'm sure—well, I fear—that there is more bad news coming with the rest of those."

"Yeah, I mean—Tricksey, Inc.? Out of California? What the hell is that?"

"Do we really want to know?"

"Shit." He put the pages of columns down. "And meanwhile, Jeff's needed down at headquarters, but he's stuck in the air. I don't know how we can have him run the company while he's chasing these lawsuits."

"At least he loves it."

"He's really happy, in a sick way. He's an investment banker to his core. He loves negotiations, facing off across tables. He'd so much rather be doing that—than making bourbon."

Lane thought of the new yeast strain Mack had developed. He'd been sitting on that issue, not moving on it, which was maybe a mistake. But some instinct, some conviction deep in the center of his chest, kept coming up with a big fat "no" on selling the patent. It was like giving away the future of the company for pennies on the dollar—because if Mack was right? They had a gold mine on their hands.

Guess at his core, he was the opposite of Jeff, a bourbon maker, not a businessman.

"You know," Lizzie hazarded, "there's a potential solution to Jeff's problem."

"Really? Do tell."

*O*ut at the Red & Black, Edward leaned into the brush broom as he pushed the bristles down Barn B's concrete aisle. As he went along, catching stray hay strands and clumps of dirt kicked free of shod hooves, he swayed to the music that he'd piped in overhead.

Frank Sinatra was croonin' about flyin' to the moon, and Edward was singing along.

From time to time, a muzzle came out and snuffled over his work shirt and his aching shoulders. He always stopped, sang a couple of bars, and then kept going.

And he knew he'd come up to Neb's stall because his big, black, bad-tempered stallion kicked his door hard enough to rattle the whole barn. Then the thoroughbred seemed to smile slyly as he extended his neck, not for a bite, but to use Edward's shirt as a tissue.

A hot blast blew out from those nostrils as the bastard deliberately sneezed all over Edward. After which Neb threw his head up and down, black mane flashing as he made like he was laughing.

"You are a pain in the ass."

The stallion whinnied.

"Yes, they will be back any minute from their ride, and you could go with them on the trail, but you have no manners because you were raised in a barn."

They squared off, glaring at each other, and then the stallion dropped his head. Which was Edward's cue to rub under that chin.

As those big eyes rolled back in happiness, the sound of approaching hooves brought both of their attentions to the open bay at the end of the barn.

Edward felt a smile spread over his face, and he didn't bother hiding it. Across the open field, at quite a clip, Sutton and Shelby came cantering toward home on a pair of mares with strides as long as football fields and the telltale head structure characteristic of Neb's venerable line.

Both of the women reined up at the same time, their horses slowing to a trot and then a walk.

Putting the broom against Neb's stall, Edward limped out toward the setting sun, his bad foot hindering his forward progress but not his mood.

"Looking good, ladies," he said as he emerged out into the golden light. "Have a nice ride?"

"The best." Sutton smiled over at Shelby. "I love that down trail into the valley."

"It's m' favorite, too." Shelby easily quelled her mount's mincing feet. "But I think Miss Red here still has more gas in the tank. I'ma take 'er over to the north pasture?"

"Sounds lovely." Sutton patted her horse's graceful neck. "I'll just walk Stacy out and put her up."

"Yes, ma'am. Tomorrow?"

"Is after work still okay? I have a board meeting that gets out at six. I can be here by quarter of seven?"

"I'll have 'em saddled and ready to go."

While Shelby gave Miss Red her head and the two galloped off across the land, Sutton dismounted and started to walk Stacy in a fat circle. "I have the best time out there. And Shelby is the real deal."

"Daughter of the best horse trainer I've ever met."

"Is it true she's dating Moe's son, Joey? She was kind of talking about him."

"It's puppy love for sure." Edward moved over to a bale of hay and slowly lowered himself down. "I think they're a good match."

"She seems really happy."

"She deserves it. It's been a hard road. It's about time something went her way."

As Sutton smiled at him, the rubies that glinted at her ears made him love her even more than he already did. Here she was in blue jeans and a three-dollar Hanes T-shirt, her face free of makeup, her hair loose all around her shoulders . . . and she still had his earrings in.

They had spent the last few nights at his little caretaker's cottage, making love on the twin bed, waking up wrapped in each other. In the mornings, she'd left to go back to town at six a.m., so she had time to get dressed and have breakfast with her father. And then she returned to the farm around six, and he made them dinner, and they sat in his chair and watched bad TV.

Without a doubt, he could cheerfully see himself spending the rest of his life living these days over and over and over again, Bill Murray without Punxsutawney Phil.

"You look beautiful with that horse."

Sutton smiled at him. "I think you're biased."

"Accurate is more like it—" As he heard some of the horses whinny, he twisted around and saw visitors. "Lane?"

Edward struggled back up to his feet as his brother and Lizzie King came down the aisle. "Hey, how you guys—actually, not the stallion, okay? You want to stay waaaaaay over to the other side with him. That's right."

Edward had to let the two of them come to him, but when they did, he hugged them both. "Sorry to make you do the walking, but I'm not moving too well."

"You're looking good, old man," Lane said. "Hey, Sutton!"

Sutton waved as she continued to walk out Stacy. "Hi, guys! I'm so glad to see you! I'm just cooling down out here. Give me another five minutes."

Lizzie said her hellos and then shook her head at Stacy. "Holy moly, that's a beautiful horse."

"Isn't she lovely? And such a lady, too."

"So," Edward said as he sat back down on the hay bale. "What brings the pair of you out to farmland? If you're looking for a nice cool glass of lemonade, I can take care of that at the cottage."

As Lane settled against the side of the barn, it was impossible not to notice that it was now a man standing there, staring off into the meadow. Gone was the snarky playboy affect. In its place was a calmer, more grounded adult—and then there was Lizzie, the man's true partner, the one who was responsible, more than anything else, for his transformation.

The love of a good woman was the savior of the aimless man.

Edward should know.

The silence continued for so long that Sutton finished cooling down Stacy and brought the mare in for grooming.

The clomping of those shod hooves stopped at the cross ties over in the cleaning bay, and Sutton deftly swapped out the bridle for a halter and secured the thoroughbred's head. Next was the warm-water hose, which the mare nodded at because she was one of the ones who loved it.

And still Lane didn't say anything.

As Lizzie went over to help with the horse, Edward looked at his brother. "Out with it. What's going on."

Lane reached down and picked a piece of hay out of the bale next to him. Putting it between his teeth, he chewed the base so the tip that stuck out in front of him danced.

When the guy finally looked over, his eyes were dead serious. "I need you to come back."

Edward straightened his torso. And then in a slow voice, he said, "You're not talking about Easterly, are you."

"No, I'm not. I want you to come back and be CEO." Lane put up a palm. "Before you shut me down, here's the situation. I'm chair of the board, and I can do that job. Jeff is an incredible numbers guy, but we have some serious debt negotiating to do—and that is eating up all his time. I'm not CEO material. I don't know how to run a company like the BBC. You do. You've spent your whole life getting ready to do it. Hell, you know every nook and cranny of the business, not just ours, but our competitors'. You're the right person for the job, and what's more, I think you need to do it for yourself."

"Oh, I do, huh," Edward murmured.

"It means you won. You got what he didn't want you to have. What he tried to cheat you out of."

No reason to define the "he" in that one.

Edward stiffly moved his body around so he could see Sutton without straining. She had stopped with the hose and was staring over at him, her eyes wide as if she had heard the ask.

"I need some time. I can't give you an answer right now," Edward said. "I've got to talk it over on my home front first."

"We need you." Lane tossed the hay stalk. "It's make-or-break time, and you're the key to the strategy."

*A*fter Lizzie and Lane left, Edward and Sutton went back to the caretaker's cottage. While she poured them lemonade in the cramped little kitchen area, he eased down into their armchair, feeling every ache and pain more than he had since he'd gotten out of jail.

As she handed him his glass, she sat cross-legged on the floor in front of him.

"What do you think?" he said.

She didn't hesitate, but that was her way. "Lane is right. You've spent your whole life getting ready for the job."

"I don't care about the company right now. I mean about you and me."

Sutton stared into her lemonade and he thought of the last time they had shared a glass. It had been when he'd gotten her to leave, right before he'd put himself behind bars.

And now they were here.

"Well, we've always been competitors," she said. "Back before, you know, now."

"If it costs me you, I'm not going to do it."

She looked up at him, stunned. "It's your family company, Edward."

"And you're my life. There's no comparison at all to me. I'm happy to live out here on the farm, being nothing but a house husband. Or staying at your house with you and your father. I'm not . . . looking to fill any holes anymore. Lane is right, I take the job and on some levels, I guess I've 'won.' But William Baldwine wasn't even a relative of mine. He was just an evil piece of work who screwed over everyone who crossed his path. I don't have any scores to settle with him, because I'm at peace now."

Sutton sat up on her knees and kissed him. "I have never loved you more than I do right now."

Slipping a hand around the back of her neck, he smiled. "And you loved me a lot last night."

The faint blush that hit her cheeks was enchanting. But then she got serious and settled back down on the floor.

Her voice became strong and direct. "There are proprietary issues that we will never be able to discuss, and there are strategies we'll develop in direct response to competitive market conditions that could compromise the other person's position. We're two generals, on different sides of the battlefield. Can we live with that?"

"I don't know. More to the point, is it worth finding out?"

They were both silent for a time.

"You know what, Edward?"

"Tell me, my love."

"I think you need to make bourbon." She smiled slowly. "I think you need to go and strap on your business suit again, and come meet me in the marketplace. Let's do this. It's the way we started out, and if there are any two people on the planet who can make this work?"

He started to nod. "It's you and me."

"It's not going to be easy."

"No, it's not." He looked down at his body. "For one thing, I'm still not getting around at top speed, and those days are long."

"You can do a lot from home."

"Actually . . . if I'm at my father's business center instead of downtown, I could always crash at Easterly if I have to. And I could spend the nights with you at your house—after all, the farm runs itself, with Moe and Shelby and Joey. I wouldn't be leaving them in the lurch."

"You come from a long line of bourbon makers," Sutton said. "And so do I. It's in our blood. It's what we do and who we are. Why argue with that?"

Edward sat forward. He wasn't going to be naive about this. Having two people in a couple be in high-powered jobs was hard enough; having two people whose businesses were head-to-head competitors was a whole different level.

It was weird, though.

He had the strangest sense that this was the right path for them. It didn't make a lot of sense, for most people. But for a couple of bourbon makers?

"Okay, I'll do it," he said as he kissed her. "So get ready to bring your A game, girl."

That fire in her eyes lit up, the one that turned him on and made him feel like he was always going to have to chase her a little.

"I never put it down." She nipped at his lower lip. "It's you who has got to get up to speed there, Eddie, my boy."

Edward started to laugh, and then he was pulling her into his lap.

Whereupon lots of A game proceeded to get laid down, to the consummate enjoyment of both parties involved.

THIRTY-NINE

⁂

$\mathscr{A}$s dinnertime came and went at Samuel T.'s farm, he couldn't say that he had enjoyed a meal more in recent memory.

"—and then the professor asked me what *I* thought," Amelia was saying.

"Which was?" Samuel T. asked as he sat back with his glass of bourbon.

The two of them were on the porch, sitting on the same side of the table so they could watch the sun set over off to the right. They had had steaks on his grill and a fluffy salad she had made and baked potatoes. And as they had cooked together, he was so glad she wasn't a fussy eater who wanted tofu and kale and organic whatever—but he would have given all of those to her if she had wanted them.

"Well, I just believe it's a faulty argument, and frankly, it bores me. I mean, if Fitzgerald was merely a social commenter, a kind of Andy Cohen of his day, why are we still talking about his books? Why am I taking an entire course on him and Hemingway? If you want to dismiss him as nothing more than a Jazz Age blogger, well then you sound like Hemingway, circa nineteen forty. Talk to me about his works, not his relationship with alcohol or Zelda. I'm simply not interested in conjecture over a personality that has been dead for nearly eighty years. The work, talk to me about the work."

"Are you thirty-five, or is it me?"

She laughed and pushed her plate away. "People say that to me all the time."

In the last few days, Amelia had come to the house for hours at a clip, the pair of them sharing stories, trading likes and dislikes, getting to know each other. Well, actually . . . that wasn't quite the right description. It had been more like reconnecting with an old friend, which was strange.

And affirming.

God, the pair of them were so alike. Samuel T. had heard parents refer to children as their Mini-Me's, and he had always dismissed it as the pabulum of people who had no proper emotional boundaries with the younger generation.

But this was what they were talking about.

This identical way of approaching the world.

"I'm sorry that you have had to be so old," he said.

It was the first time he had tiptoed into any controversial territory. He didn't want to bash Gin. Nothing good was going to come from that, and it wasn't necessary. Amelia had been through what she had; she was well aware of the failures of her mother.

She had had to live with them.

"It's okay." Amelia shrugged. "I see some of my friends, and they're just so flighty and unfocused. It drives me nuts."

"Sixteen-year-olds probably should be that way, though. Or at least be allowed to be. I don't know. I don't have any experience with them."

"Can I ask you something about my mother?"

Samuel T. cleared his throat. "Yes, anything. And I'll do my best to answer it truthfully."

"Were you in love with her? Was she in love with you? You know, when . . ."

Samuel T. took a deep breath. "Yes, I was. Your mother has been the only woman I've ever met who I can say I was legitimately in love with. But that doesn't mean we're right for each other."

"Why not?"

He took a sip of his bourbon. "Sometimes, the person you have the best chemistry with is not the one you want to try long term with."

Amelia fiddled with her fork, which she had laid in the proper position for someone who had finished with their plate.

"She's *so* different right now."

"In what way?" he asked.

"She doesn't leave the house." Amelia laughed. "And she's vacuuming. I mean, *my* mother is working a Dyson in the parlors. It's so bizarre. She also took me to yoga last night and did it with me. She's helping me get a summer job. We're going shopping for bikinis later this week." The girl looked away to the horizon. "She's never wanted to spend any time with me before."

"I'm really glad she's making the effort."

And he prayed the trend continued. With Gin? It was unlikely. Within days, she was likely to get over her maternal kick and return to her lifestyle. But at least he would be here to pick up the pieces.

Then again, Amelia had been hard-honed to take care of herself, so the girl would no doubt roll with the flow.

Which was so sad, he couldn't stand it.

"So, she gave me this safety-deposit key, right?" Amelia glanced over. "Do not tell her I told you this, 'kay?"

He put up his palm. "I swear."

"Before I left to go back to Hotchkiss . . . she gave me this safety-deposit key and told me I wasn't supposed to use it unless she died. She wouldn't tell me what was in the box." Amelia went back to staring at the fat, low sun that was glowing like a banked fire at the lip of the landscape. "I got Lizzie to take me to the bank today. I had her wait in the car, and I took the key in. I brought my passport with me because I don't have a driver's license, you know. The manager came out of her office. She was so nice, and she helped me sign in and get the box out—but we could barely lift it. I was scared and I made the lady stay in the private little cubicle with me."

"What was in it?" Samuel T. said tightly.

"Gold bars." Amelia looked over. "Like, tons of gold bars."

What the hell did Gin liquidate, Samuel T. wondered.

"There was a letter. I opened it."

When Amelia got quiet, it was as if she regretted taking the story to that particular detail.

"And?" Samuel T. reached over and put what he hoped was a reassuring hand on the girl's forearm. "I won't tell her. I promise."

"In it, she said that if she died, Richard Pford murdered her. And that this was to be my inheritance from her, free and clear." Amelia shook her head again. "The bank manager looked really worried and asked if Mother was okay. I said, yes. That annulment you did for them hasn't been in the paper or anything so the lady didn't know that they'd broken up."

"Did the bank manager tell you when Gin brought it all in?"

"It was newly taken, the box, that is. The only thing the lady said was that Mother had come in with some guy named Ryan Berkley?"

The jeweler, Samuel T. thought. Of course. Gin had sold one of her mother's pieces and put the value in there for Amelia in case the family went totally under.

Not the dumbest thing in the world to do.

"I think your mother is really trying to take care of you," Samuel T. offered. "And if you can, let her. I know there's a lot of history between you, but sometimes people do change."

Amelia nodded, but it was unclear which way she was leaning on that subject.

"So, I got the test results back today," he said.

The girl looked over. "Really? That was fast."

"I have friends in the lab."

"What did they say?" Then Amelia went all Maury Povich: *"Are you the father?"*

He slid the envelope out of his breast pocket. "I haven't opened it. I was waiting for you."

Samuel T. put the thing between them, the fold in the middle straightening itself out as if reaching for a hand to do the flap duty.

They just stared at the sealed envelope.

"I don't want it to say we aren't related," Amelia mumbled.

Funny, just like that, she was a child, her adult-self veneer vaporizing and revealing someone who was scared and lonely and tired of being brave while she was lost.

And what was truly amazing, in that moment?

As Samuel T. noted those downcast eyes and projected into the future the likelihood of Gin being a reliable, steady influence in the girl's life?

He became a father.

Right then and there.

If one established the definition of a parent as an adult who assumed the responsibility for a minor, seeking to provide them with shelter, guidance, and love? Well, what the hell did blood matter, anyway. There had been loads of examples, many in Amelia's own family, of people who didn't step up even though the DNA was there. And then there were those who provided what was needed, always, even though there was no family tree linking them.

Like Miss Aurora with Lane and his brothers and sister.

Love was what made the difference. Not blood.

Samuel T. cleared his throat and put his hand over the envelope. "If you want me to open this, I will."

"Do you want to open it?"

"The results don't matter to me."

Amelia looked up sharply. "How can you say that?"

"You need a father. I want a daughter." God, it was so strange to say that and mean it. "At the end of the day, is it really more complicated than that?"

An old, worn-out look came into the girl's eyes. "You don't want to get saddled with some other guy's kid for the rest of your life."

"This is an opportunity, not an obligation." He tapped the envelope. "And if we don't open this, if we don't know for sure . . . then you will never once wonder whether or not I want to be in your life. You will always know that I am *choosing* you. You will never for a single moment have to worry that you were a mistake that I feel guilty about, or a burden I'm carrying just because one night, sixteen years ago, your mother and I had sex and the birth control failed. I am picking you, Amelia Baldwine, right now—and if you pick me in return, we burn this on the grill over there and neither one of us ever looks back. Deal?"

As the girl sniffled, he eased to the side and took his handkerchief out of his back pocket. She accepted it and dried her eyes.

"Why would you do that for me?" she asked bleakly.

He put his hand on her shoulder. "Why *wouldn't* I, is the question."

There was a long silence, and Samuel T. gave her all the space she needed.

"Okay," she said eventually. "Let's do it. Let's burn it."

They got out of their seats and went around the table at opposite ends, meeting on the other side and going over to the grill together. Picking up a pair of barbecue tongs, he removed a section of the grate and set it aside. Then he fired up the gas and hit the igniter.

Flames gathered and hissed along the burners, and he held out the envelope.

Amelia gripped it, too . . . and they put the corner into the heat.

The paper caught quick and burned fast, and they had to drop it in or risk getting hurt.

As he watched the results of the DNA test disappear, he had never been more at peace with anything in his life.

When it was done, Amelia turned to him. "What do I call you?"

"What do you want to call me?"

"Dad."

"I'm good with that," he said as he pulled her in close and held her tight. "I'm so good with that. . . ."

As Gin drove down the allée of trees to Samuel T.'s farm, her palms were sweating on the wheel of the Phantom and she had a headache.

The last couple of times she had dropped Amelia off here, or picked the girl up, she had felt the same. It was hard, so hard, to look at Samuel T. as if he were a polite stranger.

Oh, who was she kidding.

It was hard to have him look at her that way. But she couldn't blame him. And it was also impossible not to see and appreciate the effect he had on Amelia. The girl was always happy when she was out here, her eyes sparkling, her smile quick to fire, her hands animated.

Gin hit the brakes and put the Rolls in park. When no one came around from the porch, she cut the engine and got out.

Off in the distance, she heard laughter and she debated whether or not it was appropriate to go and find them. It wasn't as if she had anywhere else she needed to be, but sitting on the sidelines and over-hearing them made her feel like she was eavesdropping.

She waited for a while. Texted. Didn't get a response.

Shoring up her courage, she walked across the lawn, looking up at the manor house as she went along. She had spent so many years going in and out of the gracious old house, free to come and go as she pleased. Now those liberties would have been inappropriate.

As she came around the corner, she stopped.

Samuel T. and Amelia were playing badminton on the grass, the pair of them wielding the long-handled, tiny-headed racquets with competence.

Amelia saw her and waved. "Hello, Mother!"

Samuel T. turned around and missed a return, the birdie landing at his feet. "Oh, hey."

"I'm sorry." She pointed over her shoulder. "I was out front. I wasn't sure either of you knew? No worries, though. I can keep wait-ing."

"It's okay." Samuel T. nodded at Amelia. "She was beating the crap out of me."

"You were winning!"

"She lies. What can I say?" Samuel T. indicated the house. "Actu-ally, Gin, I have some paperwork for you about the annulment. Every-thing's filed and set."

"Oh, thank God."

"Come on up, the stuff's in my study. Amelia, we'll be right back?"

"Okay, Dad, I wanted to go do a fish check on the pond anyway. We on for the day after tomorrow?"

"You got it. I'm not seeing *Deadpool II* with anyone else."

Dad. Wow, Gin thought.

As they headed up to the porch, she said, "So I guess you got the DNA results back."

"Yes, we did."

Gin took a deep breath. "Good, I'm glad it's settled."

"Me, too."

Samuel T. went ahead and held the door open for her, and as she passed by him, she could smell his cologne, and it made her heart ache.

His study was the same as it had always been, lined by leather volumes that he'd inherited, the hearth set for fall's far-off chill with hardwood logs, the mellow oxblood leather sofa and chairs making the room seem like it was in England rather than Kentucky. Then again, the Lodges had always done things with old-school class—which was what happened when you had generations and generations of people shepherding assets carefully onto their children.

Samuel T. opened his great-uncle's leather briefcase, and as he riffled through whatever was in there, she studied the lines of his face, the strength of his shoulders, the elegance he wore with unconscious grace.

"Okay, so here is a copy of the court-stamped papers. I put a rush on them. The judge wants to go quail hunting with me on my preserve in South Carolina, so he was happy to oblige."

"Is that how you got the DNA results so quickly, too?"

"No, but the lab tech does want to be set up with my intern. So I made that happen and she stayed a little late for me one night in return."

"You are good at getting things done."

"I do all right." He gave her another set of papers. "Also, because of the high value of the engagement ring, I had Pford execute a title for it, granting the thing to you free and clear. Probably overkill, but that way, you don't have to worry about him bugging you about it later."

"Oh, thank you." She looked the documents over. "This is great."

"I know you really wanted that diamond," he said dryly.

"Well, yes, I'd taken the stone out and replaced it with a fake one. It would have been awkward to give him back a cubic zirconia."

Gin was vaguely aware of Samuel T. going still as he stared at her, but she didn't dwell on it.

Time to go.

"Thank you again," she said, "and I assume you'll be picking up Amelia for the movie. If you'd like me to bring her out here, though, I'm happy to. Just text me."

Gin started to walk out, but Samuel T. took her arm. "What did you say?"

"I'll bring Amelia to you—"

"No, about the ring."

"Oh. I sold the stone. For Amelia. Don't tell anyone this, please— although as my attorney, I don't think you can, can you? Anyway, if I'd had to give the ring back, Richard would have found that out and demanded the money. Which I don't have." She shrugged. "I just decided it was about time I started assuming the care of my daughter— *our* daughter."

She waited a moment for him to respond. When he just looked at her, she gave him a wave and took her leave.

Out on the porch, she called Amelia over, and as the girl came loping up the lawn from the pond, Gin was glad for the way things had ended.

Not between her and Samuel T., of course. But really, how else were things going to go between them?

No, Gin was glad that the girl knew her father and that from now on Amelia was going to have a mother who did her best to show up. At the close of the day, that was not a bad setup, at all.

And she could certainly learn to exist without the love of her life. People did that all the time, in one form or another.

Besides, she needed to pay a penance—and losing Samuel T. was probably the only thing that could come close to be being painful enough.

FORTY

Something woke Lane up out of a deep sleep, his lids flipping open, his body on instant-alert. Without moving, he glanced at the clock on the bedside table. Just after two a.m.

What had disturbed him?

He listened for a minute and heard nothing but Lizzie's even breathing: no sounds of anyone moving around Easterly's second floor, no creaking of doors opening or closing, nothing out in the hall.

There was a temptation to roll over and resume the work of being asleep, but nope. He had to get up and go to the window.

Sonofabitch, he thought as he looked down below.

There was someone in the garden again: In the darkness, in between the fruit trees, a person was crouched and coming at the house. At two in the goddamn morning.

For the love, Lane thought as he pulled on boxer shorts and got his gun from that drawer. Someone was definitely inside the walls and moving around—and he knew it wasn't Gary McAdams this time.

None of the gas lanterns were off in the back of the house, and Lane and Lizzie had been in the pool before bed. Those mechanicals were working just fine now.

"Lane? Where are you going?"

He hid the gun by his thigh. "Somebody's in the garden. It's probably—I don't know, maybe it's Jeff."

Lizzie started to get out of bed.

"No, you stay here."

"Should I call Deputy Ramsey?"

"I don't want to disturb him and his wife. Maybe it's . . . I don't know. But I'll handle it."

Lizzie got up and went to the window as he headed out into the hall. And in a replay of however many nights before, he didn't hear any alarm going off—because he hadn't set the damn thing, *again*—and as he descended the grand stairs, the mansion likewise seemed silent.

When he got down to the foyer, he stopped. Frowned. And went into the parlor, following the scent of fresh air.

The French doors way at the back of the downstairs room were wide open, a lovely night breeze curling into the house, carrying the scents of the sleeping garden.

Check the house? Or check the outside, he wondered.

Would a thief really leave his ingress so obvious?

Shit, he should have told Lizzie to lock herself in.

Lane moved quickly through the downstairs rooms, looking for someone trying to steal silver or portable electronics or . . .

When he got to the rear of the dining room, he slowed . . . and stopped. Through the glass panes, he stared, transfixed, at a scene he could not comprehend.

But instantly understood.

It was his mother, in one of her diaphanous white nightgowns, out once more on the terrace at night, the gas lanterns down the back of the mansion illuminating her ethereal beauty and turning her into an apparition of loveliness.

She was not alone.

A man was coming up the stone steps, a man with broad shoulders and common work clothes, a man who took a cap off his head in deference to her presence.

Gary McAdams.

The two met at the head of the stairs that led out into the flowers and the statues, and, oh, how the groundsman stared at Little V.E.: The love and adoration in his eyes was resplendent in his weathered face, the emotion transforming him into a prince in spite of his commoner's garb.

From behind his back, Gary presented Little V.E. with a single rose, and her smile made her glow. As she accepted it and said something that seemed to make the man blush, Lane was reminded of all the expensive jewels William had given her during birthdays and anniversaries. She had accepted every one, and worn them all, but she had never looked this delighted.

Proof that the love of the giver could elevate the intrinsic value of what was received—and its absence could also render any gift worthless.

Bare feet running into the dining room had Lane glancing over his shoulder.

Lizzie was animated. "Are you seeing this? Are you—"

"Shh. Come here."

As Lizzie rushed over and tucked herself against him, the two of them watched as Gary offered Little V.E. his arm, and then the pair went down the steps and took to the brick paths, walking side by side.

"That is not the first time they've done this," Lizzie whispered.

"No," Lane said. "It is not."

After a moment, Lane steered Lizzie and himself around. Kissing her on the top of the head, he murmured, "Let's give them their privacy. They've earned it."

FORTY-ONE

The next morning dawned beautiful and clear, and as Lane got dressed in his closet, he picked out black: black for the suit, black for the socks, black for the belt and the tie and the shoes. The only things he had on that were white were his button-down shirt and his boxer shorts.

But he made sure to include a red pocket square.

When he stepped out, Lizzie was coming in from the bathroom and she looked rough—and beautiful in her black dress.

"How bad is it today?" he asked.

"Bad. But that's good, remember?"

"I brought you up some ginger ale. And saltines. I made sure I put some in the car, too. As well as three Kroger's bags, a roll of paper towels, a spare toothbrush and toothpaste, some bottled water, and chewing gum—Wrigley's, your favorite."

"I love you so much," she said as she closed her eyes. "How did you get all that done while I was in the shower?"

"Moved fast. Otherwise, you were going to try to do it yourself."

They met by the bed and embraced for a moment.

"You ready for this?" she asked him.

"As I'll ever be."

"I'm with you all the way. Unless I have to throw up. In which case, I'll be back as soon as I can be."

"I love you."

"Me, too."

They kissed and then it was down to the first floor, where Jeff was dressed in black, Amelia was chilling with her phone on the first step of the stairs, and Gin was not yet around.

"Where's your mother?" Lane asked casually as he sat next to the girl.

"Grabbing a smoothie, I think."

Lane leaned in and looked at what was on the phone's screen. "You're going to have to show me how to play that game. What's it called?"

"Dymonds. With a 'y.' Here, gimme your cell."

Lane reached in and took the thing out of his breast pocket. "Password is one, one, one, one."

The girl rolled her eyes. "Uncle Lane, that is not secure."

"Nothing in there to hide."

Amelia started to flip into programs or . . . he didn't know what, and didn't care—

"Wait," he said sharply. "What's that?"

"I'm downloading the app for you."

"Lemme see it."

There, on the app screen, or whatever you wanted to call it, was the title of the game and then the company that made it.

Tricksey, Inc.

"Jeff? Jeff . . . will you look at this?" Lane glanced over at the guy—who had his head buried in his own phone, no doubt analyzing documents on the damn thing. "*Jeff.* Come *here.*"

The guy snapped to attention and walked across, bending down as Lane held the screen up. "What the—what am I looking at?" he asked.

"Tricksey, Incorporated."

Amelia spoke up. "Oh, yeah. That's the developer of Dymonds. They've done a ton of other games. A girl in my dorm is, like, the owner's niece or something, and she said they were just bought out by—"

Lane bolted up at the same time as Jeff evidently did the same math: Without a word, the two of them scrambled down the hall, punched open the door into the staff wing, and nearly mowed Gin over as they beelined for Greta's office.

"Where's the third stack—where's the—"

The German woman looked up from behind her desk. She had lasted even less than forty-eight hours on her vacation and had arrived back at Easterly at seven a.m. And in order to make sure no information was lost, she had carted all of William's business files over from his office and was systematically scanning each and every page into her computer.

"Vhat are ve lookink for?" she inquired.

"The third stack!" Lane dropped to the carpet and started pulling files out. "The I-don't-knows!"

"Here now," she said. "Do not mess things!"

As a string of no doubt highly uncomplimentary German phrases left her lips, she nonetheless got with the program, pointing the way for him and Jeff in the loads of boxes.

Lane found the agreement in the second box he searched. "I got it, I got it. . . ."

Jeff sank down on the floor next to him as Amelia and Gin and Lizzie came in, and at first, words danced in front of Lane's eyes. But then . . .

"Forty-nine percent." Lane looked up at Lizzie, dumbfounded. "Forty-nine percent of the company. William paid a quarter of a million dollars for it three years ago."

Jeff grabbed the document and looked the thing over. "It's in force. This is a live agreement."

Amelia started typing on her phone. And then she said, "Yeah, it's right here in the *New York Times* business section, under 'technology.' They were bought out for . . ."

"What?" Lane said to the girl. "What were they bought out for?"

The girl slowly raised her head and turned her phone around. "One point two billion dollars."

No one moved. Or breathed.

"I'm sorry," Lane interjected. "Did you say billion with a 'b.'"

"Yes, it's all right here."

As Lane fell back on his ass, Jeff started to laugh. "Looks like Mack gets to keep his new yeast strain."

Oh, frothy relief. Oh, wonderful, magical, lottery-winning moment.

Someone started cheering, and then Lizzie was down in his arms, and he was laughing his head off. With an interest like that, in a company valued at that level, it was going to be very easy to finance out of the bank debt. And then the BBC could survive, and thrive.

On the day he had to bury his momma, the unexpected windfall was the one thing that could possibly have lifted Lane's spirits.

And the only thing his father had ever done to help the family.

*T*he Charlemont Baptist Church was located in the West End, and as Lane pulled the Phantom into its parking lot, he put the windows down so everyone in the car could wave at people they knew. The place was packed already, members of the community gathering in their funeral garb to pay their respects. And as he greeted folks and was greeted in return, he reflected on how beautifully everyone was dressed, the gentlemen in suits, the ladies in hats and fascinators, everything black.

Except for pops of U of C red.

Going around to the back, he left the Rolls next to a couple of Mercedes and a Lexus and told Lizzie and the others where to go and sit. Then he joined the other five pallbearers, all of whom were nephews of Miss Aurora's, by the hearse. Denny Browne, the nice man who'd seen Miss Aurora through the hospital and out into his care, had driven the coffin over himself.

"Would you like to see what she's in?" he asked after they shook hands.

"Yes, please."

Denny opened the back of the hearse, and all six pallbearers went *ohhhhhh*. The coffin was a perfect University of Charlemont red with gleaming brass hinges and handles.

"That'll do," Lane said. "That'll do more than just fine."

They kibitzed for a good twenty minutes, and although Lane got hot in the sun, he wasn't going to take his coat off. Nope, he could catch on fire and he'd still keep that jacket on—and going by the way the nephews kept wiping their brows with their handkerchiefs, yet none of them took any layers off, either, clearly everybody was in the same boat.

After all, when Lane went to his royal reward, the last thing he needed was Miss Aurora scolding him at the pearly gates for not being dressed right at her funeral.

About ten minutes before things were supposed to get started, the Reverend Nyce came out of a side exit.

"Are we ready?" the good man said, Bible in hand, flowing red robes making him look like a saint.

"We are." Lane accepted the man's embrace. "I know she's watching us."

"You bet she is." The reverend smiled and greeted each of the nephews by name. "Now, I'm going to ask you to bring her in this door here. Then go up the ramp and you'll be off to the side in the narthex. As I get the congregation settled, I want you to take her to the closed doors that lead into the church proper. I'll give the sign, those doors will open, and I want you to escort her all the way down to the altar. You will be seated on the left in the front row."

"Yessir," Lane said.

"We clear?"

When there was a collective agreement, the reverend took his leave, and Lane lined up with the others at the back of the hearse, three on each side.

Denny said, "She's going to come out headfirst, so, Lane, you're here. Okay, let's bring her out. She's going to be heavy, so be prepared."

As her son, Lane assumed the front right corner, and Denny was correct, he was surprised by how much the coffin weighed. With slow, coordinated movements, the six of them took their grips sequentially as the coffin was pulled out, and then they were moving together, heading for a door held open by one of the men's wives.

Lane just nodded at the woman as he went in. He wanted to say something pleasant, but his heart was pounding and his eyes were itching.

He hadn't expected to get emotional now.

Inside the church, the cool air felt good, and it cleared his mind some, but then he had to focus to get the coffin on the gurney. One of the assistant pastors added a beautiful satin sash, and then another of the wives put an arrangement of red and white roses on the top as well.

And then they were rolling Miss Aurora up the ramp.

It was impossible not to contrast everything around him and inside him with what it had been like to inter his father. Then it had been a chore to execute, something to check off a list, for the sole reason that he didn't want a damn dead person's ashes in the house.

And the whole thing had had all the internal resonance of a trip to the grocery store.

Now, though, as he walked with the other men, head bowed, hand locked on that brass bar like he could bend the metal, he wasn't sure how he was going to keep it together.

Things got even harder as they positioned her at the closed double doors that would open into the sanctuary. Through the stained-glass sections, he could see a thousand people seated in the pews, and there were still more folks standing against the walls, every square inch of the huge space full.

And how beautiful it all was: candles lit, flowers abounding, the altar shimmering with the glow of heaven above.

I'm not ready—oh, shit, I've got to get ready—

Lane tried to take a couple of breaths.

Except then it was go time, the doors opening wide, the music starting to play, the two-hundred-person choir in their red robes starting to sway back and forth behind the altar.

The music was what saved him.

As the first strains of "God Is Keeping Me" began to play, he had to smile. They had thrown out the playbook for Miss Aurora, and he was so glad. She had been a member of the choir here for years herself; the music had always been her favorite part of the service and this was one of her most-loved gospel songs—

Suddenly, something registered. The male voice . . . the male voice that led the choir . . .

Lane nearly tripped halfway down the aisle.

Standing in front of the singers, in a choir robe—with a clean-shaven face and trimmed hair—was Max. And he had his eyes closed, his head tilted back, his mouth open, that microphone held in place, his incredible voice overpowering even all the other big ones around him.

Lane pulled a discreet pass of the eyes with his handkerchief, and then he and his brother met stares across the congregation.

Thumbs-up was given and received by a nod before Max went on to the next verse.

So many faces in the crowd, the sadness in each of them palpable, men and women alike wiping tears away. There were people Miss Aurora had trained in her kitchen—a new generation of chefs—and fellow singers, and cousins and distant cousins, and friends and acquaintances from church and U of C basketball games. There were folks that Lane didn't recognize, and others he thought of as family, and old friends he hadn't seen for years.

As they stopped in front of the altar, Lane took a moment to look at everyone who had gathered on a workday, having taken the time to get dressed and bring even their small children, just to pay their respects.

He was hard-pressed to think that any of them judged her harshly for what she had done to his father. She was a good force in the world who had taken a piece of evil out of it—hell, maybe his father wouldn't have survived that stroke, anyway. But either way, Miss Aurora had watched the abuse, witnessed the reign of terror, lived with the sadness and fear in that house and the family for as long as she could take it.

And then, as was her way, she had done something about it.

Lane thought of his mother and Gary McAdams. Of Edward and

Sutton, now happy. Of himself and Lizzie, and Gin making peace with Amelia and coming forward, finally, with the news of Samuel T.'s parentage.

Indeed, Miss Aurora had reset the family . . . after William had run roughshod over it for a generation's length of time.

So no, Lane decided as he was overwhelmed by the size of the crowd, the depth of the love, the breadth of the mourning. Neither he, nor anyone else, blamed his momma for taking care of her family, any more than they mourned a man who had gotten exactly what he deserved.

You tell me who was the sinner and who was the saint, Lane thought as he went to sit down next to Lizzie. Who was poor . . .

. . . and who died richer beyond measure.

FORTY-TWO

*A*fter the conclusion of the service, Lane and the pallbearers escorted Miss Aurora back out and returned her to
the hearse. Then Lane led a mile-long procession of cars, all with
their lights on, on a winding course of streets to Kinderhook, a cemetery located on the far edge of the west end.

The Toms family was so big that they had their own section of
markers, and Lane parked and got out beside it, searching for Edward and Sutton as Lizzie, Amelia, and Gin disembarked. When he
saw his brother, he waved the man over.

"Beautiful service," Edward said as they hugged.

Sutton nodded. "Just lovely. So moving. Hey, Lizzie, Gin . . . hello,
Amelia."

The sound of a powerful motorcycle coming in got everyone's

attention, and Lane shook his head as Max parked the bike and dismounted. The black jeans were right. And for Max, the button-down shirt was a miracle: It had no holes and was very clean.

"I didn't think you'd come," Lane said as the guy walked over to the group. "And nice haircut."

Max's eyes bounced around some. And then he seemed to force himself to focus. "I don't know, I guess I wanted to come and say good-bye properly."

"I'm glad you're here." Lane clapped him on the shoulder. "It's the right thing to do."

Max said his hellos, and then it was time for them to join the others by the awning that had been set up over the open grave.

While they crossed onto the grass, Lane leaned in to the guy. "So you're staying, huh."

"What?" Max glanced over. "What are you talking about?"

"You never would have come back if you weren't staying. Never. So I'm guessing it took you a couple of days of driving around out there to realize what you found on the road wasn't quite as satisfying as it used to be—because there was a whole lot less to run from back here in Charlemont." Lane motioned around his own face. "Besides, the cleanup makes me wonder if you're trying to catch the eye of a certain oncology doctor who is—hey, she's right over there."

As Lane lifted a palm in greeting to Tanesha, he had to smile. The woman's eyes were glued to Max as if she couldn't believe his transformation.

"Go on, wave to her." Lane elbowed his brother in the side. "Before I pick your arm up and do it for you."

That snapped Max to attention, and bless him, he became the color of a beet as he raised his hand to the woman.

"Attaboy. And that cottage on the row is yours for however long you need it."

"I don't know. Whatever. Yeah, I guess I'll hang around for a little while."

Lane looked the guy right in the eye. "It's good to put down roots, Max. And it's safe here now. Okay? You're safe."

Max shook his head. "How did you know. . . ."

"About your change of heart?" Lane clapped a hand on the back of the man's neck and gave him a shake. "Because I had one myself for the same reason so I know what it looks like. And, listen, you can't beat the love of a good woman, trust me. If Tanesha Nyce will have you, take her and hold on to her for as long as you can. It will turn your life around."

"I don't know what I'm going to do for a job."

"Well, we have this little family business . . . I don't know if you're familiar with it?" Lane put his arm around his brother and they started walking together. "We make bourbon, realllly, reallllllllly good bourbon. . . ."

As they all lined up together with the rest of Miss Aurora's family, everyone took a red rose from a vase on a stand. The Reverend Nyce said some truly beautiful things, the coffin was lowered in, and then everyone filed by and dropped their roses.

Edward and Sutton happened to be ahead of Lane, and Lane frowned.

He was going to have to catch the guy and talk to him before people headed back to Easterly for refreshments.

There was one more piece that needed to fall into place.

*G*in let Amelia go first to drop her rose, and then mother followed daughter and did the same. After that was done, the two of them walked out toward where the long lineup of cars stretched far, far down the lane.

"I'm sad that she's gone," Amelia said.

"Me, too. She was an incredibly special person."

"She used to make me these lemon cookies so that they were warm, you know, for when I came home from school."

"Really?" Gin laughed a little. "We have that in common. She did that for me, too—"

"Dad?"

Gin looked over across the cropped lawn. Sure enough, Samuel T. was down on the narrow road, leaning back against the door of his Jaguar, looking perfectly handsome in his black suit.

As Amelia ran ahead through the gravestones and the statues, Gin let the girl go and resigned herself to heading back to Easterly alone with Lizzie and Lane. But it was okay, she told herself. It was . . . the way things were going to be.

"I didn't know you were there," Amelia was saying to her father as Gin approached. "I would have had you stand with us."

Samuel T. removed his Ray-Bans. "I thought the front row in church—and for this part—was really more for family. Beautiful service, wasn't it? That choir is incredible—and was that Max? What the hell—oh, hey, Gin."

Gin forced a pleasant smile on her face. "Hello. Well, I'll leave you two—unless you'd like me to take her home?"

Samuel T. looked down at the grass. "Actually, ah, Amelia, would you mind giving your mother and me a moment?"

"Sure thing. I wanted to say hi to Uncle Max anyway."

After the girl went off, Gin racked her brain trying to think of what loose ends they had between them. The annulment was done. The paperwork concerning the ring, check. The arrangements for the movie . . .

"So Amelia asked about you and me last evening," Samuel T. murmured.

Gin snapped her head up. "Oh? What did you tell her? And I

won't be mad if it's the truth. I have given up my pride and don't miss it. I'm also getting used to apologizing for things."

"I told her you were the only woman I've ever been in love with."

Gin's heart started to pound. "You . . . did?"

"Yes." His eyes locked on Gin's. "I think it's important to be truthful with her. And that is the truth."

"But . . . I don't understand."

Samuel T. crossed his arms over his chest. Then he shook his head slowly. "No buts. That's it. You're the only woman I've ever been in love with, and let's face it—and since you brought up pride, I will admit that I'm not proud of this—I've been through enough females to know there's never going to be anyone else for me."

Surely Gin couldn't be hearing this right. "I'm sorry—I . . . but what about Amelia?"

"What about her. She has a mother . . . and a father. And I know this is a shocking concept in these modern days, but in some families, moms and dads and kids live together. For extended periods of time. Like, months. Years. Decades . . ." There was a pause. "Until death do they part."

Gin started to shake so badly that she had to put her hands up to her face to stop her teeth from chattering. "What are you saying, Samuel T.? And please, I know I don't deserve this, but please do not be cruel. I can't take it anymore."

Samuel T. straightened off his Jaguar. "I think you and I need to put the past aside. We need to just leave it back in the days of our youth, relegate it to memory, close that door. And starting today, we're fresh. We're new. We're clean and we're in love and we're going to be together, no games, no lies, no bitterness. We start fresh, right here, right now."

As he pointed to the ground, Gin could feel the tears on her cheeks.

"So what do you say, Gin? You ready to be a grown-up with me? Because I'm ready to be one with you."

At that, he held his hand out to her.

And what do you know, she didn't need any time to think about it.

Given that her voice was gone, all she could do was nod—so she nodded as hard and fast as she could. "I love you," she croaked as she put her palm in his. "I love you so much. . . ."

Abruptly, they were hugging each other.

Laying her head on Samuel T.'s shoulder, feeling him stroke her back and whisper in her ear, she looked across the grass.

Amelia was over by that Harley.

And smiling as she stared at her parents.

FORTY-THREE

*A*s Edward got out of Sutton's Mercedes, he looked up at the grounds-keeping building. The structure was at least two stories high, but from the little he recalled of it, it was a huge open space, not a multi-floor'd kind of thing.

"I'll wait right here," Sutton said tensely. "Unless you'd like me to leave you to it?"

"No, it's too far for me to walk to Easterly from here."

"Okay, I love you."

"I love you, too."

And the truth was, he needed to draw some strength from her.

Closing the door, he straightened his black suit and the knot of his tie. And when he walked forward, he hated how noticeable his limp was—but there was no changing that.

Entering the cavernous space, he smelled sweet gas and oil and felt a dense heat, the result of the metal walls and ceiling being uninsulated under the sun's pounding rays. There was at least one air conditioner humming, however, in the back office.

As he went along, he passed by precise lineups of mowers, backhoes, Bobcats, plows. And everything else in the place was likewise where it needed to be: whether it was gas cans or bags of grass seed, blowers or rakes, wheelbarrows or four-wheelers, someone had made sure all was accessible, in good working condition, and properly accessorized.

The office for the head groundskeeper was glassed in, but the panes were so old and dusty, they were at best merely translucent. Someone was in there, however, the outline of a man moving around.

Edward stopped at the closed door. Clearing his throat, he raised a set of knuckles and knocked.

"Yup," came the curt response.

And then the chipped door was opened.

As Gary McAdams looked out, the man froze—a sudden fear widening his eyes.

In that moment, the questions that Edward came to ask were all answered. And yet he felt compelled to say, "Do you know who I am?"

The older man stumbled back and seemed to find the seat of his chair by luck rather than intention. It was a long while before he answered, and when he did, it was just one syllable.

The only one that mattered, though.

"Yessir," Gary said in his thick Southern accent.

Edward sagged and closed his eyes.

"I know that's got t' be a disappointment t' ya," Gary said quietly.

"No," Edward countered as he forced his lids to open. "It's a relief. I've always wished for a father I could be proud of."

With a recoil, Gary seemed confused. "Whatchu talkin' 'bout, I'm a groundskeeper."

Edward shook his head. "You're a good man, that's what I'm talking about."

The groundsman took that cap off, and as Edward studied the man's face, he could see echoes of his own features, and those eyes . . . yup, it was in the eyes. They had the exact same blue eyes.

"I kept m' distance, you know," Gary said. "'Cuz your momma, she's a real lady. She shunt be havin' nothin' to do with the likes of me. But you know, I love her. I always have, and I always will. And just so yer aware, I never ask her for nothing. She gives what love she can to me when she can, and that's more'n enough for me."

"Do you mind if I sit down? My legs don't work very well anymore."

As Gary made like he was going to get up, Edward motioned the man to stay put while he himself took a load off on a trunk. And then they just stared at each other.

"Are you gonna fire me?"

Now Edward was the one jerking back. "God, no. Why would I?"

"Good. I love m' job and I don't want to leave her. I mean, here."

Thinking back to what Lane had told him, Edward smiled a little. "I'm glad you love my mother. She deserves it. She's had a very hard life inside that big beautiful house."

"I know. I was there for it all."

Edward fumbled for his phone and sent out a quick text. "I'd like you to meet someone who's very special to me."

"Your girl? You got yersself a girl, then?"

"Yes, I have."

The sound of Sutton's high heels echoed through the garage, even over the din of the air conditioner, and then she was leaning around into the open doorway.

Both he and Gary rose to their feet, as was proper when a lady was present.

"Sutton, this is my father, Gary McAdams."

Taking his cap off, Gary looked back and forth between the pair of them. "'Scuse me, ma'am, m' hands are dirty."

Sutton smiled and went right in for the hug. "That's okay, I'll greet you this way."

The poor man nearly fell over in a faint. And then Sutton was pulling up a chair to the cluttered old 1950s desk and smiling like she wasn't in Armani and pearls, having just come from a funeral.

"I'm so happy to meet you," she said warmly. "I know Edward was nervous coming here, but I really think this is all going to work out fine. You two just need a moment to get used to the idea."

As Edward looked over at her, he had never loved her more. And then, as he regarded his father's shy expression, he knew that the truth that had finally come out was so much better than the luxurious, ugly lie they had all lived with for so long.

"Yes," Edward echoed. "I know this is all going to be well."

FORTY-FOUR

~~~~~~~~~~~~~~~~~~~~~~~~~~~~~~~~~~~~

*A*s the reception for Miss Aurora continued well into dinnertime, Lane took a moment to go out onto the terrace,
using the French doors off the front parlor that his mother favored as
a nocturnal exit.

The sounds of talk and laughter, and the scents of food and wine,
followed him out, keeping him company as he went across to the
drop-off down the mountain. Stretching out before him, the view of
downtown Charlemont's skyscrapers and the Big Five Bridge was
set off perfectly by the frame of Easterly's verdant woods and the
lazy Ohio's inefficient path to its falls.

Staring out at it all, Lane tried to imagine the first of his ancestors who had stood here on this majestic rise and thought, *Here, I
shall build* here. *I shall live here with my family and hope to prosper.*

As he considered the history of his family, he knew there had been so many blessings that had come to him and his own. Many curses, too. There had been joy and sadness, change and upheaval, births and deaths. And he had never thought about this before, but there had always been in him the erroneous belief that the past had evolved to this preordained present with a plan known to those who had lived it.

He had assumed that all the people who had come before him had somehow known that their choices and decisions, their graft and their focus, would inevitably lead to this grand house, and this grand life of his own.

Bullshit, he thought now as he turned his back on the view and looked up at Easterly.

There was no way that the others in his bloodline hadn't faced similar challenges as he himself had just been through. History was only set because it was reflected upon. When it was being made? You had no clue what the hell you were doing, or where you were going to end up.

You were building a legacy with your forehead pressed right up against its face, hammering and nailing without any perspective, wondering what exactly you were constructing. Would it be strong enough? Would it weather the storms and the earthquakes? Was it big enough for the people who came next? Would they shepherd it . . . or burn it down?

Looking through the windows into the parlor, he smiled.

Max and Tanesha were sitting together on the sofa, their bodies turned to each other, their faces open and curious and excited. Edward and Sutton were over at the punch bowl, talking to Jeff, looking like they were all in agreement over some kind of deeply discussed issue. Amelia was with Gin and Samuel T., the three of them clustered around the girl's phone, pointing at something.

And all around his family there was a crowd of people, sharing stories about Miss Aurora, laughing, crying, talking.

Lizzie came around the terrace. "Hey, there you are!"

"Just out here to enjoy the view. How's the food holding up?"

"We ran out. So three of Miss Aurora's nieces are in there bashing things together. We should have known this many people were going to show up."

He thought about his father's visiting hours. When none of the high-society folks had bothered to come.

"Would you like me to make a food run?" he asked.

"Nope, we've got it."

"Then come here, because I want to kiss you for a while."

"A while, huh."

As she sauntered over, he sat down on the porch wall and settled her on his lap. She fit perfectly and he put his hand on her stomach.

"I wouldn't change a thing," Lane murmured as he watched the people inside.

"You know what, neither would I."

"Other than Miss Aurora being here."

Lizzie stroked his hair back. "I'd like to think she still is."

"Me, too."

At that, Lane lifted his eyes to the sky—and started to smile as someone on the property began to play the banjo. Strains of old-fashioned bluegrass music got his foot tapping, and he held on to his love, and felt the sun on his shoulders.

With a flush of gratitude, he thought about his unborn child . . . and hoped that he or she would grow up and love Kentucky and making bourbon as much as he did.

"You know something," he murmured.

"What's that?"

"God is good." Lane gave his woman a squeeze. "And if this isn't heaven . . . I don't know what is."

Acknowledgments

First and foremost, thank you so much to all the readers who make it possible for me to do what I love for a living. I am also so grateful to so many: Steve Axelrod and Kara Welsh on the publishing side, and then all the folks on Team Waud. None of this would be possible without you! Further, I owe a great debt to the many people in the bourbon industry here who were so helpful and generous with their time, knowledge, and talents. I have learned so much about this proud tradition and its history—and that is but a drop in the bucket compared to the master distillers and bourbon makers I was privileged to speak with as I wrote this series. Finally, thank you to my husband, my mother, and the rest of my dearest family, both those of birth and by adoption, and all my friends. And my WriterAssistant, Naamah!

About the Author

J. R. WARD is the author of more than thirty previous novels, including those in her #1 *New York Times* bestselling series, the Black Dagger Brotherhood. She is also the author of the Black Dagger Legacy series and the Bourbon Kings series. There are more than fifteen million copies of her novels in print worldwide, and they have been published in twenty-six different countries around the world. She lives in the South with her family.

JRWard.com
Facebook.com/jrwardbooks
Twitter: @JRWard1

About the Type

This book was set in a Monotype face called Bell. The Englishman John Bell (1745–1831) was responsible for the original cutting of this design. The vocations of Bell were many—bookseller, printer, publisher, typefounder, and journalist, among others. His types were considerably influenced by the delicacy and beauty of the French copperplate engravers. Monotype Bell might also be classified as a delicate and refined rendering of Scotch Roman.

85674057829369